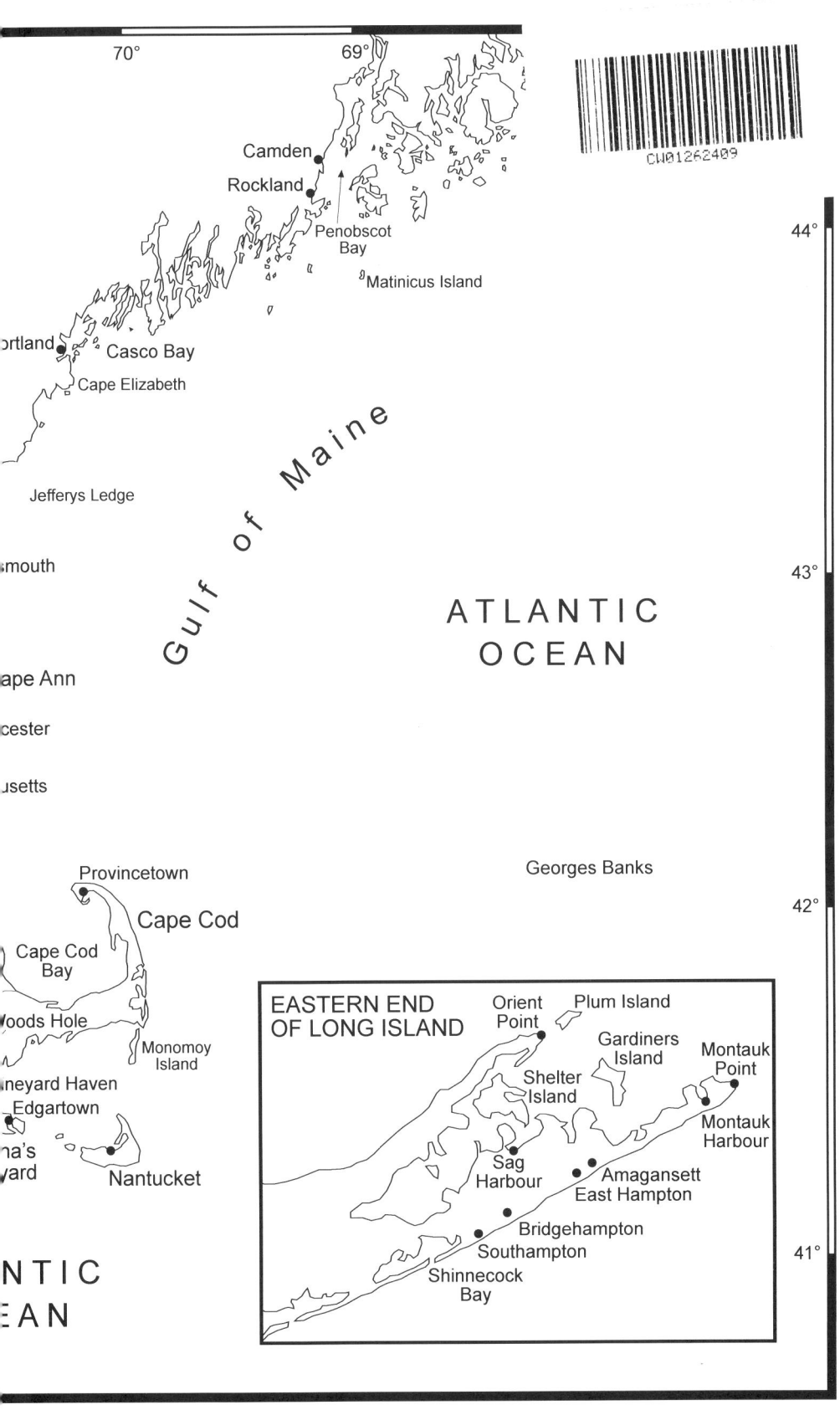

NO MAN'S LAND

SIMON GAUL

NO MAN'S LAND

First published in 2025 by
Simon Gaul, in partnership with Whitefox Publishing

www.wearewhitefox.com

Copyright © Simon Gaul, 2025

EU GPSR Authorised Representative
LOGOS EUROPE, 9 rue Nicolas Poussin, 17000, LA ROCHELLE, France
E-mail: Contact@logoseurope.eu

ISBN 978-1-916797-80-2
Also available as an eBook
ISBN 978-1-916797-81-9

Simon Gaul asserts the moral right to be identified
as the author of this work.

All rights reserved. No part of this publication may be reproduced, stored in a retrieval system or transmitted in any form or by any means, electronic, mechanical, photocopying, recording or otherwise, without prior written permission of the author.

Lyrics from 'The Night They Drove Old Dixie Down' (page 20) written by Robbie Robertson, sung by The Band © Canaan Music (1969)

Excerpt from the poem 'Do Not Go Gentle Into That Good Night' (page 40) by Dylan Thomas (1951)

Lyrics from 'Can't Take My Eyes Off You' (pages 62, 294) written by Bob Crewe and Bob Gaudio, sung by Frankie Valli © Pw Ballads c/o Songs of Universal, Inc., Seasons Four Music Corp. and EMI Longitude Music Co. (1967)

While every effort has been made to trace the owners of copyright material reproduced herein, the author would like to apologise for any omissions and will be pleased to incorporate missing acknowledgements in any future editions.

Designed and typeset by Typo•glyphix
Cover design by Dominic Forbes
Project management by Whitefox Publishing
Printed and bound by CPI Group (UK) Ltd, Croydon CR0 4YY

*For Bill and the Baymen of Long Island.
This one's for you.*

Now I drive my Downeaster Alexa,
More and more miles from shore every year,
Since they told me I can't sell no stripers,
And there's no luck in swordfishing here.

I was a bayman like my father was before me,
Can't make a livin' as a bayman anymore,
There ain't much future for a man who works the sea,
But there ain't no island left for islanders like me.

Billy Joel
'The Downeaster Alexa'

CONTENTS

Author's Note	*viii*
Prologue	*ix*
Part One	1
Part Two	37
Part Three	57
Part Four	93
Part Five	141
Part Six	203
Part Seven	233
Part Eight	267
Part Nine	289
Part Ten	303
Epilogue	317
Coda	329
Afterword	*339*
Acknowledgements	*347*

AUTHOR'S NOTE

No Man's Land is a novel in which fact and fiction blend with conspiracy theories: real people, events and places fuse with the fictional characters. Any resemblance the fictional characters may appear to have to anyone living or dead is coincidental.

PROLOGUE

Sag Harbour, Long Island, New York.
Saturday, 12th December 1992. 10:50.

(This article was first published in *The East Hampton Star* in May 1981. It is one in a series by journalist Peter Duxbury, who documents the lives of those who work the waters of the Atlantic Ocean.)

'It's no fish ye're buyin, it's men's lives'

Sir Walter Scott

IT SHOULD NEVER HAVE HAPPENED. But it did.

Dawn. Monday last. The grey sky was one with the Atlantic Ocean; both were foreboding. It already felt like the day had been set aside for evil. A nor'east wind had angered the ocean's swell. Breaking rollers, mighty rollers, ploughed up the beach at Amagansett as if they were troops eager to wage war. Fork-tailed terns worked offshore, and a flight of cormorants flew where the horizon met the sea. A twenty-five-knot wind ripped the salt-spray off the whitecaps and spat it into a stinging mist. The long undulating expanse of sand dunes – they stretch for thirty-one miles along the Atlantic coast from Shinnecock Bay to Montauk Point – had been scrubbed by the elements. Gone too was the fat stench of seaweed, flotsam and the oily smell of fish.

Amagansett's beach was deserted, save for Jake Dealer, a Bonacker, as the original settlers of the eastern end of Long Island are called. He shared the coarse sand with his haul-seine crew, and a few hardy gulls who cowered in the lee of an immense jawbone of a right whale; sooner or later the scavenging gulls sensed there'd be fish to pirate. Tall and lean at thirty-five, hard chin unshaven, Jake stood apart and stared out beyond the lines of surf. Sweating inside a woollen plaid shirt, he ground his waders deep into the sand. There were fish out there. The barometer had been erratic, and the rapid changes in atmospheric pressure would have renewed the water with oxygen making the fish frisky. All that was missing this morning was sheeting rain.

The Dealers have worked these waters for over 300 years, and Jake could read the conditions. Days such as these were the baymen's sworn enemy. To launch an 18-foot dory through crashing surf and then deploy 500 fathoms of seine net could be treacherous. Afterwards, hauling a net full of fish ashore would be duck soup. So, on that fateful morning Jake and his crew had no alternative but to try. It had been a bleak winter and a wretched twelve months for the Long Island baymen.

Jake had to wait for a 'slatch' – a break in the wave pattern – to launch the dory. His elder brother, Harvey, tried to crack the despondent mood as he pulled on his jack-line gloves and told joke after joke: each one lousy. The crew laughed none the less, for since first light, Jake had had a flinty look in his eye.

Ten generations of observing the Atlantic Ocean coursed through Jake's veins. He had an envied sixth sense, a peculiar gift, one they call hereabouts a Posey-smell. He flared his nostrils and squinted again. There were schools of striped bass toiling beyond the pounding surf. This was his land, and he smelt money fish out there. The market was paying $3 a pound for 'stripers', ten times the price of bluefish. There were bills to pay. Today was going to be payday.

Heavy slicks of current rose beyond the breakers when Jake suddenly tugged his long-billed cap and yelled at his crew. He'd caught a quick run of slatches. With astonishing speed and agility, Harvey Dealer and Eddie Silver leapt into the trailered dory. Harvey crouched in the stern, his thigh-high waders up around his chin. Beside him the coils of seine net were ready. Eddie took his position.

He pulled on the cord of the Johnson 25hp outboard. It fired up first time.

"Go! Go! Goddammit! Go!" hollered Jake.

Nate Freeman had been revving the flatbed Ford in neutral, and on Jake's command, he urgently shunted the truck into reverse. Jamming his left foot hard on the brake pedal, Nate red-lined the engine without mercy. The fat, semi-deflated tyres threw out a rooster tail of wet sand as they bit down hard. Harvey and Eddie held on tightly to the dory's smooth sides. Slatch or no slatch, this was going to be one of the roughest launches ever. Nate, driving backwards, hard and fast, rammed the dory's trailer into the breaking surf. Then he jumped on the brakes. Over his shoulder he watched the dory catapult off the trailer straight into a wall of foaming green water. Nate's heart pounded. He'd certainly never launched a dory into breakers like this before. He caught Harvey's big grin. Jake was right. There were stripers out beyond the breaking surf. Salt water drenched Harvey and Eddie, and Harvey got off a quick salute to his younger brother as the dory crested the first breaker.

Then it happened.

A fusillade of freak waves came out of nowhere. The faithful dory weathered the first rogue, just, but the outboard sputtered and died. It was the second rogue that took them out. Like a juggler throwing a baton, the ocean picked up the dory and pitch-poled it through the air. Eddie was thrown clear but Harvey, clinging to the sides, went under with the boat and 500 fathoms of seine net.

Maybe Harvey found a footing on a false bar of sand and was dragged down by the quicksand that was always on its inside slope, or maybe he was simply knocked unconscious under the crashing dory. Either way, when the second wave hit, Jake's brother was gone. Drowned. In all probability, the sand-roil had filled Harvey's waders and he had been sucked away into the Atlantic's dark, swirling currents.

Harvey's body, or rather what dismembered pieces remained after the sand crabs had had their fill, washed up the next day on the beach of the Maidstone Club in East Hampton. Harvey would have liked that. "Upset. Uptight. Up-Streeters. That's all we got in the Hamptons now. They wanna eat fish but they don't wanna see fishermen no more?" That was his refrain.

What of Jake? The crew captain and the man who lost his brother? What did he say? Two things. Both telling of the man.

The first, well, Jake grinned with real pride when he learned that Danny King's crew had hauled nearly nine thousand pounds of 'stripers' from the ocean, just two miles west of where Harvey had gone under that morning. Like the other baymen, Danny had needed a good catch, and it was the biggest for over a year. Second, and Jake told me this without a hint of irony in his voice – Harvey had never learned to swim. Harvey was a bayman who couldn't swim.

"It takes longer to drown than you'd think, Pete, takes all the time in the world. After you're done strugglin' to carry on livin', knowin' that all the while you're drownin'." He paused. "Shit, it made no difference that Harvey couldn't swim. Me and him was brought up to know who's the boss. Always the ocean."

Jake rolled an imaginary grain of sand between his scarred thumb and forefinger as he spoke.

"Fishermen are self-reliant, independent. On the water everything has an order, nature's order, it makes you who you are out there." Jake raised his head as if in a salute. "Everything makes sense, it's here on land that it doesn't. Harvey died like a bayman, Pete, with water in his lungs. Doubt I'll be lucky enough to go that way; most of us die of plain hard work. We grind it. Then we grind it some more. Know many people nowadays who die the way they should? Do you, Pete?"

I've known Jake Dealer since he was a young boy, working with his father on the ocean and inlets of Long Island. It was the first time I didn't have an answer for him.

* * *

M y name is Peter Duxbury. I wrote that article for *The East Hampton Star* in 1981, eleven years ago. To me, it reads like it was only last week. I'm sixty-one years old and time seems to have accelerated lately. I've lived and worked in Sag Harbour, on the South Fork of Long Island, all my life. I grew up in these parts, and except for being in the US Army during the Korean War, I've been a writer with *The East Hampton Star* since I graduated high school here in Suffolk County. Over the years I've chronicled, even championed, the cause of the Long Island baymen. In so doing, I've written about a disappearing America – a dying way of life that I have sadly, yet with privilege, observed.

Still, I'm one of the world's optimists. I've had to be, what with the Great Depression and three wars. I survived and got to return to a place and a job I love. When that happens, you can't help but think your glass is always going to be half full. Until, that is, something changes – a sort of deus ex machina in reverse. When you least expect it. Like what happened to Jake.

Looking back on it now, as I write the prologue to this book on a cold and squally winter Saturday, I'm convinced that this story began with Harvey's death.

Jake didn't seem to mourn Harvey for too long, perhaps on account of his son Dougie's birth five months before, in December 1980. I don't know, but I imagine the symmetry would have comforted him. For the rest of us in this dwindling Long Island community, Harvey's death really hit home. It wasn't that Harvey had been a pillar within Suffolk County – he wasn't – but his passing drew attention to the plight of the baymen, the last of the hunter-gatherers on the eastern seaboard of America. These men had stood sentry over the ocean for generations. Their ancestors had learnt their skills from Native Americans when the Atlantic coast was but a frontier. Nowadays, there are less than 100 baymen working the Long Island waters. Even the Native Americans can't understand it.

Jake seemed to sense, first with Dougie's birth and then with Harvey's death, that all the traditions – and independence – were coming to an end. They say fate likes multiple acts. Trouble is, you just don't expect there to be nearly a decade between the first and the last.

* * *

At the end of May 1990, I received a letter from Eric Tull, manager of the East Hampton branch of the Suffolk County National Bank. He was an acquaintance of Jake's and mine.

For some reason I recall the unseasonable weather on the day the letter arrived. It was a friendless Monday morning. The light was pale, sickly even; the wind blustery. There wasn't a hint of early spring warmth. The sky was raw, as if it had been cast in alloy. A brown and white osprey circled above the chop, its talons poised for fish. The hungry osprey and the angry sea licking across Gardiners Bay were all I registered from my Sag Harbour apartment that morning.

Usually, my mail is the uninteresting fodder of junk and bills. Sure, I get the occasional postcard from my sister in Canada, and letters from a friend who's a foreign correspondent with *The New York Times*, but never handwritten envelopes marked '*Private and Confidential*'. It was Jake's handwriting on the envelope, and it had been forwarded to me by Eric Tull. My subsequent telephone conversation with the banker is a tape that just won't erase.

"Where did you get the letter, Eric?" I asked.

"I was expecting your call, Pete."

"OK. So, how'd you come upon it?"

I was in no mood to fence. Jake was a friend – couldn't say a good friend, he wasn't the sort to have good friends, but when someone I know vanishes completely, as if they've evaporated, I sit up and take notice. Even at my age.

"Beginning of the year, Jake walked into the bank dressed in his working clothes. He stank rougher than roadkill. Haven't seen or heard from him since, until an envelope arrived. Inside was another envelope addressed to you. Jake had written me a note on scrap paper asking me to forward the envelope addressed to you if he didn't come into the bank to cash a cheque for a couple of weeks. I put the letter in my drawer. So, that's why you got his letter now Pete. I thought it was kind of strange at the time, but you know Jake. Always a mystery."

"Didn't you think it was a peculiar thing to do so soon after . . . well . . . you know . . ." I was going to fill in the blanks, he was a banker after all, then thought better of it.

"Frankly, Pete, I must have been busy. Last time he was in my bank, the staff almost ran out the door. Heck, he'd already emptied the place of customers that day."

"As Harvey used to say, '*Folks wanna eat fish, but they don't wanna see fishermen.*'"

Eric Tull was holding something back. I was convinced of it. My line of work teaches you to detect lies of any colour. Even from well-versed practitioners such as bankers.

"Jake's disappearance seems more your line of work, Pete. I thought journalists snooped and investigated. Look, when you've figured it all out, or you've found Jake, just let me know."

He chuckled. I could hear his fat, pink jowls wobble.

"Jake can't owe you any money, Eric, you sound too darned relaxed." I was angry now.

"Too right. You know that family, been the same for generations. Bankers never made money out of them fishermen or their business. Too darned eager to pay off a loan. They're careful people Pete." He paused before adding, "I'll be hearing from you, I expect."

The line clicked dead.

* * *

Jake Dealer was a loner. A man caught between two lines, both of which were, for him, the enemy. Out there in no man's land. I suppose he thought that if he stayed between those lines, maybe, just maybe, he'd be able to provide for his family.

But a 300-year-old way of life had begun its death throes. Jake saw it coming before Harvey's death on that chill dawn in May 1981. In August 1983 Governor Cuomo wouldn't veto New York State's 'Bass bill', which banned striped bass haul-seining from the beaches; then a mysterious pollution – we called it 'the Brown Tide' – killed off the scallops and there were no money fish. And the baymen's crime? Well, it was being visible from the beachfront properties of the newly affluent; their catches were infinitesimal compared to the trawlers far out at sea – and far out-of-sight. With no bass from spring to fall, no scallops in winter, it was the end for the baymen. Some of them went off to be janitors or make motel beds. Or worse.

Not Jake.

He had only ever understood the ocean, for it was his home. His territory. His land. He wasn't about to be defeated. That's the sort of man he was, like a handsome man who knows he's handsome, but never acts it. So, he bought an old down'easter, rebuilt her from the keel up and named her *Sweet Amy* after his daughter, Dougie's older sister. He fixed a short harpooning pulpit and a watchtower, and eked out the seasons as best he could. By the spring of 1986 he had decided to go into the chartering business out of Montauk, not far from where he lived in Poseyville, Amagansett.

I last saw Jake and Dougie in Montauk, just shy of three years ago. Early January 1990. Dougie was nine years old. Jake was born on V-J Day, and I recall he once said, *"That was the day their war ended and mine began."* In 1945, 'bebop' was sweeping the US. He'd remarked that afternoon that he was dreading his forty-fifth birthday. *"You know Pete, JFK died when he was just forty-six."* Jake wasn't being morose, he never was around Dougie, but he'd always had a thing about numbers. And premonitions.

The three of us were sitting on the dock in Montauk Harbour gazing out across the ocean. Jake and Dougie had just returned from an easy-going day on the water – Jake used to say that November to January were 'sometimes' months for fishermen: sometimes bad, sometimes terrible. *"You gotta tough it out with the sea, but it's always a one-way fight, Pete."* The afternoon was gold 'n blue, and mild for that time of year. Jake was hunkered down over a large scrap of paper, his massive, calloused hands working a stubby pencil furiously with spider-like numbers. He was sweating. His ashen forehead contrasted with his wind and sun-scarred cheeks; another 'tell' of the men who work the waters. He put his arm around his son, squeezed him close. Then he looked up at me with eyes kindlier, rounder and browner than a roe deer.

"I never do the state lottery and now I ain't never goin' into the city again!" His toothy smile flashed like a cresting wave.

"What are you talking about Jake?"

"Go figure this out Pete," he said glancing down at all his notes. "You got roughly a 1-in-26 million chance of winning the New York State Lottery, and a 1-in-3,763 chance of being shot while in New York City nowadays? So, that means you got 6,910 more chances of being shot than you ever have gettin' rich!"

Jake laughed and laughed. I just grinned. Again, he wiped his furrowed brow. Of late he had begun to look older than forty-four.

"I was never taught to be rich. I was brought up to fish. Fishermen ain't ever rich. Good thing too – if they were you'd have no fish and no fishermen."

He sighed and balled the paper with all his longhand math on it. He hooped it straight into the yonder garbage bin like an NBA pro and smiled. What a smile!

"Pete, all I ever wanted was to be a sword-fisherman with my harpoon. Guess I was just too late, the swordfish are gone. Now, what with the bass and the new laws, I don't know."

That was the last time I saw Jake and Dougie together. I keep thinking of that handsome little boy and that big powerful man standing on the dock in Montauk Harbour.

And those infernal odds. Jake's odds.

PART ONE

FRIDAY, 12TH JANUARY 1990

CHAPTER 1

**Poseyville, Amagansett, Long Island, New York.
Friday, 12th January 1990. Early morning.**

"Up and at 'em, Dougie!"

"Don't shout, Jake," hushed Lindy, his wife of twenty-three years. She flipped egg-soaked bread in a heavy iron pan, watching it sizzle.

"You taking me to school today, Dad, or should I take the bus?" Amy asked.

"The bus, Amy, sorry. I know it's cold, but I'm real busy mendin' on nets, OK sweetheart?"

She smiled a 'sure, it's OK' at her father. She was twelve years old, almost three years older than Dougie. Jake hauled himself out of his worn tartan chair. Dougie's black Labrador, Blondie, rolled out of his way.

"Blondie, outside! Wait for Dougie in the yard. Go on." Jake opened the screen door and shooed the dog out. "Never understood that dog," he continued. "Only person she ever listens to is Dougie."

"If you don't get in here right now, Dougie, Amy's going to do your paper round and keep the paycheck."

Jake reminded himself how he used to get up before daybreak to help his father's crew on the beach with their first 'set' during the bass season. Then he'd cycle to school with sand in his shoes, sore hands, and a quarter in each pocket. Before he could recite his math tables, his father had taught him where north, south, east and west were by using only the sun and a wristwatch. Who needed 12 x 9 tables? And for some reason Jake could never fathom, the sun had always shone.

Or maybe it was just his memory playing tricks?

Lindy swung her head around the corner.

"Dougie, breakfast is ready," she called out quietly before turning to Jake. "Just you wait and see, he'll be here in a second."

Lindy understood her son and loved him more than life itself. A fact she only dared face on Sundays, when she went to church alone to utter prayers of forgiveness for her sterile love of Amy, her tall and feisty blonde-haired daughter.

Sure enough, within thirty seconds Dougie crashed into the small, warm kitchen. Jake shook his head, grabbed a mug of coffee and peered through the thin net curtains. He tapped the barometer beside the screen door; the needle dropped off it and he squinted at the pewter sky.

"Mornin', Dougie." Jake's eyes creased with pride.

"Mm-mmm-mornin' Dad. Goin' down to the wa-wa-water today?"

Dougie's stutter only improved after he had played the piano.

"Not sure, son. Glass is falling again. Darned weather. What water isn't frozen out there is going to be toilin'. Damn!"

Jake couldn't keep the frustration out of his voice. Lindy turned around, ready to chastise him for swearing, but stopped herself.

Ever since the New York State ban on haul-seining, Jake had tried to make sense of his fishing tradition. More than 300 years ago his ancestors had learned from the Montaukett Indians how to launch a small boat through the Atlantic surf, set seine nets, and haul the catch ashore with horses. All his father's generation had done was substitute a flatbed Ford for horses. Nothing else had changed: the beach, the surf, the cold, the restive sky, the wind, the punishing hours, the danger, the adventure. They'd worked with the independence of having no master other than the relentless ocean. Until politics had intervened.

Jake hadn't left the ocean after the ban, when some of the other baymen had. It wasn't that he was stubborn; he just didn't know anything else. What was he supposed to do? Follow an ant trail to work every morning? Cut grass? Clean toilets? Fold sweaters in an apparel store? Calloused, broken and scarred hands like his were made for harpooning, hauling and gutting, not folding.

"I got nets to mend, sweetheart." Jake grinned at his wife. "They ain't stopped me working the beach in the spring and summer for blues or weaks. Not yet anyways . . ."

The screen door clattered behind him. Lindy looked at her two children and shrugged her shoulders despondently. The life of a bayman, this life, was too hard for anyone. She loved her husband dearly, but she wanted more for Dougie than a whetstone in his hands. She was 'from away' and knew about a life other than working the ocean.

"Dougie, eat up or you'll be late."

"Yeah, Mom, I know." He munched greedily, "I'm going to be back late from sch-sch-school to-to-today . . . re-remember the piano lessons my teacher said she was going to see if she could fix, well she has . . ." Dougie ruffled Amy's hair affectionately. "Don't tell Dad, OK sis . . .?" He chomped his final piece of toast like a boa-constrictor eating a rodent. With cheeks bulging, he grabbed his scruffy rucksack and, scooted over the floor to where his mother stood.

"Love you, Mom! Great breakfast!" He kissed her on the cheek.

She touched her face where her son had kissed her. And before she could say anything, her nine-year-old whirlwind had shot out of the door, shouting, "Blondie, you're gotta keep up. COME ON BLONDIE! You lazy girl!" Then his voice thinned out and she looked through the kitchen window as he ran across the yard to where his bicycle lay propped against Blondie's tumbledown kennel.

* * *

Jake stood beside his dory, its old outboard engine seemingly held together by layers of army surplus paint. He ran his hand along the boat's rounded gunwale. The dory hadn't seen the water since last September, when he and a makeshift crew had worked the beach at Two Mile Hollow for weakfish. The catch had been small and the price of weaks was just that – weak. In the good days, the late 1960's, when the bass were strong, they'd 'set' four or maybe even five times a day. Now, taking holidaymakers fishing during the summer months on *Sweet Amy*, was not what he called work. The pay and the tips were OK, but the next stop would be clipping tickets at the Aquarium.

"D-d-d . . . Da-Dad . . . I was wondering . . ." Dougie hoofed damp earth while Blondie panted obediently at his side, "Ca-ca-can we go out on the water at the weekend if it ain't too snotty?"

Startled, Jake turned and smiled at his son.

"Sure, Dougie, great idea. Maybe we'll luck out, like when we saw Pete in Montauk ten days ago. That was a good day, huh?" The coffee had softened the early morning gruffness in his voice. "Let's hope the catch will be better."

That day hadn't been about fish, it had been about being on the water with his son. Long ago, on the evening of Monday, 8th December 1980, the day Dougie was born, Jake had sworn to himself that he, Jake Dealer, would be the last of the Dealers who sweated on the ocean.

"Gr-r-reat Dad. I'm late for my r-rr-rrround. See you after school."

Dougie hesitated as he gazed up at his father. Jake's wide brown eyes beamed as he admired his handsome, dark-haired son. In that split-second Dougie wanted to tell his father about the piano lessons.

But Dougie didn't tell his father.

In that same split-second Jake wanted to tell his musically gifted son that he'd asked Marty Drew, the famous Long Island singer and friend of the bayman, to help out, and how he'd gotten short with Jake. Anger was a stranger to Marty Drew, but he'd been annoyed that Jake hadn't asked the favour earlier. Everyone knew that Dougie could work the ivories like his father worked the waters.

But Jake didn't tell his son.

"So long, see ya' la-la-later." Dougie hopped onto his old bicycle. "You're gonna have to keep up, Blondie," he laughed, "you lazy girl!"

Blondie followed her master, skidding out of the yard as she jumped over the immense 200-year-old anchor, one that had come from an old whaler a Dealer had captained out of Sag Harbour way back when.

* * *

Jake Dealer was not a man given to brooding, but he was a man who cherished his solitude. He liked being alone with alone. Despite his Mojave-dry sense of humour and welcoming smile, he was regarded as a lone wolf. Even his haul-seine crew had marvelled at how involved – yet detached – he could be. Some people, especially the other baymen's families, put it down to his marrying Lindy Stone, a girl 'from away'. Jake had been the first Dealer to have married someone who wasn't a part of their community. Lindy Stone wasn't even from up state, she was from out of state.

Jake was the most respected fisherman on the South Fork of Long Island, and his fellow fishermen knew his ocean lore went ocean-deep.

"You can't know or predict the unpredictable, and I've never known anything more unpredictable than the ocean." Ever cautious, he often repeated that mantra. Only a handful of families could legitimately claim that they too had worked the ocean as long as the Dealers. Some, like the Edwardses, were more commercially successful, while others like the Bennetts, Havens, Kings and Lesters were more prolific. But no one had the Dealers' 'nose'. Not even Jake's father, Captain Edward 'Tosh' Dealer had Jake's sixth sense for the fish. And it didn't matter what sort of fish – from mackerel, to bass, to seining for whitebait, to where to set eel traps in Georgica Pond. He could have sensed where the last of the swordfish might be. His father used to tease him that he would've made the grade as a skipper of a whaler, if he'd been born in the early 19th Century, when Sag Harbour was the whale capital of America.

Jake sat down hard on a dwarf stool beneath a faded, wind-flogged Stars and Stripes. He looked about the desolate yard as the winter dust from Dougie's bike finally settled. Only his timber-framed shed, from which hung dozens of brightly painted wooden lobster-pot markers, added any colour, any life.

Nets at his feet, Jake's attention was momentarily caught by three rusty, vicious-looking ice saws. He shook his head. It had been a hard winter, and it wasn't over yet. His tackle was battered: oyster tongs, basket rakes, scallop dredges, all of it worn-out. In December, on Dougie's ninth birthday, and against Lindy's wishes, he'd shown Dougie how, when the ponds were frozen and the seas too rough, you could scratch out a living. Someone somewhere always wanted the ocean's bounty, however bizarre. Wrapped up against the arctic nor'easters, together they had sawed through the thick ice on Napeague Pond and caught mudded eels. For a good eel, Koreans paid $10-$12, providing you managed to keep them alive. Dead, the eels were just lobster bait. Jake had never asked the wholesaler what they wanted them for. He just smiled gratefully and banked the money. Live mudded eels! Koreans!

Jake shifted his weight on the stool and grabbed two handfuls of the net that needed the most attention; and they all needed attention. What was really troubling him, on this grey morning of restless clouds, was what he had to do to ensure that Dougie didn't end up holding two handfuls of old net, in a potholed yard, under a bleak sky. Politicians, sports fishermen, licences, pollution – they all had it in for the traditional way of life. So, it would be for Dougie to start a new tradition, he thought. The ocean was no place for a young man anymore.

* * *

"Mor-mor-mornin', Mrs Lewis. Dad says the weather's going to get worse before it gets better. Sorry," added Dougie cheerfully.

"It's not that bad, Dougie. It's winter with a strong nor'east wind, that's all. Least it's dry. Hate the rain. I'm like my cats." She paused to see where Blondie was. "Looky, it can't be that cold, ol' Mr Fontaine is sitting in his rocking chair and it's gone eight o'clock!"

Mrs Lewis pointed to her neighbour, some fifty yards away on the same side of the street.

"Sh-sh-shouldn't say this about your neighbour, Mrs Lewis, but Mr Fontaine gives me the cr-cre-creeps."

Dougie grimaced the way he did when he bit into an anchovy on his pizza by mistake. Together, they both looked to where Mr Fontaine sat, slowly rocking in his wicker and wood chair.

"Teddy Fontaine has been on his own too long now, is all. More than ten years since his wife passed. All he does is read all manner of newspapers on his porch."

"Don't re-re-remind me, Mrs Lewis, he's my heaviest customer!" Dougie chuckled pointing at his laden bicycle. "So long, Mrs Lewis, and see you tomorrow. Come on Blondie, we're off to Mr Fontaine's."

The Long Island railway line had been built to link the fishermen in Montauk with the fish markets in New York City. The houses bordering it were widely spaced and handsome in a suburban sort of way: single-storey, grey roofed with white clapboards and picket fences. Each was like Mrs Lewis' and Mr Fontaine's, with a covered porch where you could sit and be neighbourly. Trim lawns and neat, short driveways with flowerbeds. Fields of potatoes and other soft produce still backed up to the old railway tracks. Theirs was a clean, safe neighbourhood, one Norman Rockwell had forgotten to paint and land speculators had yet to discover. The people who lived there were about as likely to journey to New York City as they were to Paris, France, which is to say it was a neighbourhood where everyone knew, or thought they did, everyone else's secrets.

"Rough morning, Dougie. If your father is out on the water today, there'll be a hard chop out there," Mr Fontaine called out.

Dougie heaved copies of *Newsday*, *The New York Times* and the *Morning News* from his bike and looked perplexed as he did so. Mr Fontaine hardly ever said a word to him.

"Sit, Blondie. Be a good girl." Dougie patted her and she sat obediently.

"Mo-mor-mornin', Mr Fontaine. Windy, huh? Dad's not going out today."

"Did you read the newspapers you brought me yesterday, Dougie?"

"Can't say I did Mr Fontaine. I re-re-read the funnies on Sunday if I get the time."

"Terrible news yesterday. A bunch of kids, not much older than you, burgled an old lady's apartment in the city. They attacked her, stole what little cash she had and sat around laughing as she died of a heart attack from the strain of it all. Terrible. Terrible. Terrible . . ."

Dougie was too disorientated by the fact Mr Fontaine was speaking to have noticed Mr Fontaine's right hand slip down into a brown paper bag beside his chair. Dougie would certainly not have registered the blue-black steel of the .38 revolver, the one Mr Fontaine aimed at him as he approached the bottom step that led up to the porch. And Dougie would not have felt, much less heard, the first of the four bullets that cleaved his chest apart, any more than Blondie would have seen the solitary bullet strike her head between her eyes after she'd bounded off her hind legs to rescue Dougie's crumpling body.

All Mrs Lewis could tell the first officer on the scene was that she'd heard five loud shots before she saw Dougie and Blondie lying dead in pools of blood on her neighbour's lawn, while Mr Fontaine sat calmly rocking himself holding the revolver on his lap.

Mr Fontaine would say later that day: "I'd had enough of bad news. Ain't going to read no more bad news . . . Had enough of bad news . . . Dougie was bringing me more bad news . . . This way, you see, I don't get to read bad news no more . . . No more deliveries so no more bad news . . . No more bad news ever again now the child won't be comin' 'round no more . . ."

CHAPTER 2

**Poseyville, Amagansett, Long Island, New York.
Friday, 12th January 1990. Morning.**

"So long, Pete. We'll catch up at the weekend. The weather might let up somewhat. Sorry to hear it's nasty in Sag too."

Jake, not waiting for Peter Duxbury to reply, replaced the handset and paced the kitchen. Dougie had cycled off nearly an hour ago and the nets weren't going to mend themselves. He went to the stove and poured another mug of strong, black coffee. He took a large gulp and set it down beside the sink.

Lindy had left in a hurry for the Amagansett Farmers' Market, where she worked shifts at the checkout. The breakfast pans and plates were soaking. Jake put his hands in the cold water and began to scrub the egg off the blackened iron pan when the telephone rang.

"Jake Dealer here." Soap suds and cold water ran down his right wrist.

"Are you Mr Jake Dealer?"

"That's just what I said," replied Jake irritably.

"Sorry to trouble you Mr Dealer but it's the East Hampton Police . . ." The policeman's voice trailed off momentarily. Like everyone else in East Hampton he knew the Dealer family. "There's been a . . ."

"Been a what?" Jake prompted. There were certain things you just never wanted to hear, and telephone calls from cops was right up there with doctor's pauses.

"It's your son, Mr Dealer . . ." The police officer hesitated, his voice now almost inaudible. "There's been a shooting." Again, he paused. "I'm afraid he's been mortally wounded."

"What are you saying, Officer?" There was a strange calm in Jake's voice.

"Your son's been shot. He's dead, sir . . . We'll have a car round at your house right away, we need you at . . ."

The young cop couldn't finish the sentence.

Jake dropped the handset on the floor and slumped against the wall. He gripped his stomach, retched, and began to fight for breath.

Finally, he caught a lung full of oxygen. His thoughts didn't run to Dougie, or to 'the who', 'the why', 'the how'; they went straight to Lindy. Dougie's death would kill her. She'd never gotten over the fact that Dougie had been born just one hour after John Lennon had been shot: the night of Monday, 8th December 1980. She'd said on that fateful day that it was the worst of omens. Jake's chest heaved with pain as her words, spoken softly as she'd cradled her newborn son, sprang back into his mind. They were words he thought he'd been able to exile.

"Dougie is a beautiful flame, Jake, and beautiful flames never burn for long. Promise me you'll take care of him. He's been put on this earth to change things, like the way the Dealers have lived for so many generations. 300 years, Jake."

Lindy was right. Beautiful flames never burn for long, and when they fade away their golden luminescence dies away too. All that remains is a hollow spiral of drifting, sad grey smoke reaching for the heavens.

It is said that when the angels play for God, they play Bach, but when the angels play for themselves, they play Mozart. The music of Dougie's piano lessons – and now Dougie – was going to be with angels. Forever.

CHAPTER 3

18 Louisburg Square, Beacon Hill, Boston, Massachusetts. Friday, 12th January 1990. Morning.

Zephaniah Swire yawned, scratched his left ear and swept his hands through his raven-black hair. The winter sun filtered through the heavy brocade curtains; the day ahead was going to be crisp and clear. He loved Boston on days like this. Neither the mansion's dark red bricks, nor the square's elm trees could dull the sky on bright January days. Almost twenty years of waking up in 18 Louisburg Square had taught him as much. He glanced at his antique Breguet. 08:06. He was fascinated with mechanical watches, as Napoleon Bonaparte had been, and Abraham-Louis Breguet had been the diminutive Corsican's watchmaker too. Either Hector was late with his coffee, or his watch was slow. The money was on his valet being tardy.

A midnight-blue cashmere dressing gown, more midnight than blue, lay at the foot of his bed. He pulled it on, tugging the belt tight. The cards DNA had dealt him across the baize were 'pocket aces': he was broad-shouldered, athletic and tall – 6' 2" – with an engaging smile set above a square jaw of the kind cartoonists might draw. Wide-set intelligent slate-grey eyes saw everything and nothing, depending on the target; and they were quick, vigilant and shrewd. Every aspect of his physique had been kitted out for purpose. Handsome? Not especially. Attractive? Very.

Zephaniah flexed out his limbs and muscles as he strode across the rug-strewn floor to open the curtains. He had a distinctive military swagger: straight-backed, right shoulder angled forward and down, as if in preparation for a charge. He drew the curtains back and focused on the iron serpents welded to the Juliet balcony.

The serpents' forked tongues were long and cruelly extended to hold two flagpoles, from which the Stars and Stripes and the Massachusetts state flag drifted in the breeze. It had always amused him that the tongues of serpents should hold the ensigns of country and state. Again, he checked the time. It was now 08:09. Perhaps Hector had died in the night and none of the surviving staff had yet plucked up the courage to inform Zephaniah of his valet's demise? Either way, he wasn't fussed. He just wanted his coffee. His gaze lingered on the statue of Christopher Columbus at the north end of the square's private gardens, before his inquisitive eyes flicked south, to the statue of Aristides the Just.

Zephaniah opened the balcony doors for fresh air. His brow tightened as he concentrated. Breathing deeply, he grazed his hand over the blackened serpents. Where had these treasures come from? He'd forgotten. There had been so many disparate fancies over the years. With the serpent's penitent focus, his thoughts drifted back, almost inevitably, to the font of all his knowledge and ideas: his grandfather, Ollie Swire. And to that morning in 1971, nineteen years ago, when as a twenty-three-year-old First Lieutenant in the US Marine Corps, he had returned home to Boston intact – mentally and physically – from a broken, desolate and scarred Vietnam.

CHAPTER 4

**10 Crick Hill Road, Menemsha,
Martha's Vineyard, Massachusetts.
Friday, 12th January 1990. Morning.**

Ollie Swire, now in his eighty-fifth year, was still refining a talent he'd discovered by chance. In reality, he'd tripped over it by accidental necessity.

Not long after he had founded Swire's, his eponymous Boston company, in 1933, he'd received a wounded oil painting on consignment, against which cash had been advanced prior to its sale at auction later that year. Keen to secure not only the loan, but also to make extra profit, Ollie had begun – tentatively and painstakingly – to restore the modest 18th-Century landscape himself. After his restoration work had been completed, the landscape sold for double its estimate, thereby securing a larger fee for Swire's and the loyalty of the grateful art dealer.

Ollie, a very private man, had only ever shared what had become a secret passion with his beloved grandson Zephaniah. The once-hobbyist was now, in his ninth decade, one of the finest (and forever anonymous) experts in the restoration of Old Masters.

Always punctilious, Ollie adhered to a strict routine when restoring a painting. At 08:00 sharp he would enter his climate-controlled studio, adjacent to his home overlooking Menemsha Harbour, with a pot of fresh mint tea. An actor of sorts in a previous life, he had adapted a 'method acting' approach to his restoration work. The first order was to immerse himself into the life and the times of both the artist and artwork he was dutifully returning to its former glory.

This morning was no different from any other working morning, apart from the fact he was acutely aware he'd set himself a tight deadline: the end of April. He wanted to surprise his grandson with this particular restoration.

The artwork was an early Titian, *Rest on the Flight into Egypt*. Modest in size – 18 in x 25 in – and painted in oils on a wood-mounted canvas in about 1509, when Titian was twenty or so years old. The painting was exquisite: depicting Mary, Joseph and the infant Jesus resting beneath a tree during their escape from Jerusalem and the wrath of King Herod.

The painting had been acquired at Christie's in 1878 by the 4th Marquess of Bath and had hung in Longleat's drawing room ever since. More than 100 years of candles, smuts, tobacco and soot had taken their toll. And it had never before been restored. The current Lord Bath, the 7th Marquess, had consigned it for appraisal, not to Christie's but to Swire's, and Ollie had, of course, ambushed it when it reached Boston. He knew the 7th Marquess to be not only truly eccentric – as mad as a sack of polecats in truth – but Lord Bath was also sharp. And Ollie liked the kooky English aristocrat.

Swire's had long been retained by Baron Heinrich von Thyssen to use its peerless guile to try to purchase the Titian; Ollie had imparted this conflicting fact to Lord Bath. The mission had, so far, been doomed to failure. His Lordship wasn't just preoccupied, he simply had no interest in parting with the Venetian's masterpiece. And yet.

Ollie had schemed that if suitably restored (at no cost) Zephaniah *might* be able to extract a substantially higher offer from Baron Thyssen. The English aristocracy had always had pressing financial demands. In the 7th Marquess's case, it was two varieties of apex predator: the wants of multiple polygamous 'wifelets' dotted around the estate's cottages, and the needs of two prides of hungry lions, both of whom roamed around his 9,000-acre Longleat estate in Wiltshire.

Antics such as restoring a bravura Titian to obtain – perhaps – a fortified bid from the Swiss-Hungarian industrialist was merely another example of what defined the harmonious – and at times symbiotic – relationship between grandfather and grandson.

CHAPTER 5

**18 Louisburg Square, Beacon Hill, Boston, Massachusetts.
Friday, 12th January 1990. Morning.**

Clarence Darrow said that the first half of one's life is ruined by one's parents, the second half by one's children. Zephaniah Swire empathised with Darrow, but only to a degree,

As a bachelor he had jurisdiction over the latter. Accordingly, he was unmarried and childless. But in the former lay an emotional lacuna: he had never loved his mother. This had ensured his inability to offer up so much as one particle of himself, but, most important of all, it had guaranteed his heart against ever being broken. With hindsight, Zephaniah considered these measures to have been entirely positive.

That was not to say he was a misogynist. The exact opposite was true. To Zephaniah, women were to be amused, cherished, admired, even adored at times; and on occasion – but never with malice aforethought – to discard. Ladies *'smelled the way the Taj Mahal looks by moonlight'*, as Raymond Chandler had so fluently phrased it. Zephaniah enjoyed the way they lavished time on themselves. Yet, there wasn't a woman whom he'd permitted to 'know' him in truth. This aspect of his emotional makeup stemmed solely from his mother's gene pool. For her Greatest-Grandmother had chosen the Tree of Knowledge, and not the Tree of Life.

Hephzibah Swire, Zephaniah's mother, had entered young adulthood as a childlike yet passionate woman who'd determined that God had made women weak to make men tender. Or, to paraphrase one of her new young idols, Marilyn Monroe: she loved living in a man's world, so long as she was a woman in it. Allied to her beliefs was her appearance: she was of average height with a voluptuous figure, one flattered by long straight hair the colour of crushed, white almonds. There was a magnetic personality too, fizzing with humour and wit. On her animated face she sported a fulsome smile, and her red-lipped expressions – sad, happy, teasing – were in symmetry with what would become her principal calling card: wide, emerald, slow-dance eyes that sparkled with a thrilling and volatile mix of self-doubt, giddy innocence and promise. Of arguable virtue however, her actions – and her inactions – were all governed by her own inimitable sexual semaphore. If Gil Elvgren had ever met her, he would've asked her to pose for him. And, she'd have agreed with alacrity.

Her core self-belief, together with her knock-out looks, would be more than sufficient for what would become, unknowingly, her tragic purpose. Until, that is, three almost simultaneous events overtook her: first, she found out, aged seventeen, that she could achieve far more by manipulation, emotional and sexual, than by any other means. This discovery, aided and abetted by her extraordinary talent for mendacity – usually calculated, sometimes capricious – led her to believe, erroneously, that she possessed real power. At the same time as this self-revelation, she met, seduced, and miscalculated. Math had never been her strong suit. Pregnant. The father? A handsome young buck named York Swire. The third event in her life was having Ollie Swire as her father-in-law the following year, 1948. There were to be no fourth or fifth events.

Her son's birth – she named him Zephaniah – in that same year, when both she and York were just eighteen, became a mere passing inconvenience to her. And nine years later the donor of the seed that fertilised the egg that became her second son, Jedediah, was a mystery, even to her.

So it was that on a fine spring day in 1967, with a flourish worthy of P.T. Barnum, Hephzibah fired off two .41 rimfire bullets. The first into her lover's left temple. The second into her right temple. All in fit of jealous rage. In the back of a Boston taxi cab. Zephaniah was nineteen; Jedediah was ten.

York Swire was seemingly unaffected, possibly even relieved. His wife's continuous adultery (for which she was forever unapologetic and regarded as little more than a life enhancing whim) had been profoundly soul shattering to him. With her death – 'suicide' was not a word the family ever used – York, at thirty-seven, hoped his broken life might be remade. Naturally, it wasn't. Soon after her funeral, York Swire filed for divorce against the living and thenceforth adopted a Howard Hughesian existence. Eschewing all visitors, his hoary face prematurely baggy from drink, he rarely stepped over the threshold of 6 Acorn Street, an elegant Beacon Hill house secreted in a cobbled alley, a three-minute walk away from his son's grander affair in Louisburg Square.

It was left to Ollie, who had long despised Hephzibah (not for the treatment she had meted out to his only child, but for her cunning) to remark to his sanguine grandson that her automotive death wasn't as glamorous as Isadora Duncan's. Although Ollie did concede, and he offered up the statement as if it were a consolation prize, that the pearl-handled two-shot .41 rimfire Remington derringer she'd used to splatter the insides of the taxi cab with two sets of skulled brain matter, had demonstrated a certain elan. Ollie had always had a begrudging respect for flair.

Ollie, however, had been economical with the story.

He had omitted to tell his grandson that the Remington derringer he'd presented to his mother had once belonged to the family of John Wilkes Booth. One of a matched pair he'd secured at great expense, and in what he perceived to be entirely appropriate taste, as a suitable wedding present for his pregnant daughter-in-law.

Promptly after Hephzibah's funeral, Ollie instructed Zephaniah to go, not run, to war. Since the beginning of time, war had been mankind's natural order. Peace was but an intermission – a time to plan, to ready, to prepare – for the next, inevitable, conflict. War was inextricably part of manhood, and had a place in a man's life, even if this war was a politician's war, not a businessman's war. Ollie had counselled Zephaniah that if he could survive war, then perhaps he stood a chance of surviving the rest of his life. And if he didn't live through war, well, so be it.

The United States Marine Corps took the nineteen-year-old volunteer and promptly turned him into officer material. As a Second Lieutenant with the 1st Marine Division, Zephaniah Swire arrived in Saigon just before the Tet Offensive rumbled on 30th January 1968, with all the might of the Division's history in World War II and Korea behind them. Soon after the Tet Offensive began, he was promoted to First Lieutenant, and on 11th February 1968 he was awarded the first of two Bronze Stars. Even at his young age, he recognised that the Vietnam War was a catastrophe without parallel in American history. There was not one moral absolute that did, or could, govern this conflict of horrors. 'We *hold these truths to be self-evident, that all men are created equal, that they are endowed by their Creator with certain unalienable Rights, that among these are Life, Liberty and the pursuit of Happiness . . .'*

Ollie had been right, of course; truth was always the first casualty of war. Vietnam was a politician's war, and Zephaniah's job was to prosecute the atrocities ordered by his generals. In France's stillborn Southeast Asian ambitions, he bore witness to America's dying ideals. Not true was General Patton's cuff-remark: *'I am a soldier, I fight where I'm told and I win where I fight.'* The truth was, there was no God, any more than there weren't any atheists in foxholes. And if there happened to be a God, well, he was just a sick old comedian who'd given baboons scarlet asses and forgotten to kit out ostriches with wings.

A life lesson Zephaniah's grandfather had ingrained in him as a boy was that the *execution* of a plan was the all-important factor: better to execute a second-rate plan perfectly, than to execute a first-rate plan badly. And the US General Staff's plans – together with their executions – were all fourth-rate. At best.

First Lieutenant Swire witnessed his men struggle, with an ebbing futility, to hold on to the crumbs of a life they had known before. It was as if by doing so, they could convince themselves that the stoop, the mutt, the white-picket fence of their humanity still existed. Somewhere. Early on he'd grasped how not to bestow the brazen immorality of this war with any vestige of humanity. Accept the outrage for what it was. Make it bearable if you could – and he could – and you made the war survivable.

Zephaniah wasn't an officer who washed sins away in the tears of his men. He was a survivor who'd blink grit out of his own eyes. Soon though, he realised that if you went further down that road, you saw another sign, but this one was flagged 'Learn to Love the Inhumanity' and if you took that fork, you'd be enveloped in an impenetrable armour. This was the road the young officer took.

As a ruthless warrior, ruthlessly committed to his men, he had earned their respect and loyalty. Long after the green thrill of killing had soured, he began to understand the harsh codes that would govern their justice. After all, it was President Lyndon B. Johnson who had ignored the First Rule of War: **'Geography'**. Wars had been won and lost on geography alone. And the Vietcong had mastered their terrain centuries ago. But worse: Johnson then ignored the First Rule of Law: **'NEVER** *pick a fight on the wrong side of the tracks.'*

So, with the triage of assassinating North Vietnam's leaders – Ho Chi Minh and Le Duan – off the table, he studied his commanding officer's methods in order to teach his NCOs his job. During two tours of combat, he kept what he wanted, erased what he didn't and nurtured what he needed. And he did survive. Solely because of his discipline and dedication to one cause: his continued existence.

In Vietnam, 'mercy' had long ceased to exist; it was but a word nobody ever uttered. Victory was defined by the number of dead, be they mothers, children or Vietcong. Yet, a persistent respect for his enemy informed him that over 500,000 American soldiers were only going to lose this one. Both sides were in the orphan-making business. So, fuck the notion that the deadliest weapon on earth was a US Marine and his rifle. Fuck *semper fidelis*. Fuck victory. Fuck 'God Bless America'. But, oh yes, God Bless the Dow Chemical Company's napalm, with its inescapable stench of petroleum and murderous hellscape of flames.

From the pleas of surrender to the screams of the wounded and dying, Zephaniah never saw any mythology in this struggle. There was no quest for justice, for reason, even for a rationale. There was only endurance this side of eternity. Then, there was the hypocrisy armed with more politics and lies; and it was Ollie who'd taught him that the napalmed fires of hell burn hottest for hypocrites. No, the Vietnam War was not how John Wayne, or Ollie Swire for that matter, would have had it. It was dirty, cruel, exhausting, and above all, gratuitously corrupt. He was done trying to keep Johnson's promise. In addition, he hated pot, heroin, Jimi Hendrix and pox-ridden oriental whores. The Band's anthemic 1969 anti-war song, 'The Night They Drove Old Dixie Down', looped in his subconscious every day:

*'You take what you need and leave the rest,
but they should never have taken the very best.'*

They already had.

* * *

Unlike other veterans, Zephaniah's memories would forever remain unalloyed; Logan Airport had never looked so good as on that bright Boston spring morning in 1971. As he deplaned with his fellow soldiers, all dead beat and wearing combat-stained fatigues, he marched, right shoulder down and forward, across the tarmac until he glimpsed in the distance familiar silhouettes: his father York, drawn and hunched from the burden of existing, standing next to his slothful teenage half-brother, Jedediah.

And what could have been a country mile away – two feet, in reality – stood his grandfather, Oliver Swire: trim, proud and smiling. This man had been the nexus of his world for longer than he dared recall. It had been his grandfather who'd moulded, educated, taught, loved, beseeched, scolded and valued him. This man was his sun and moon.

Zephaniah caught sight of the deep diagonal scar – a half-inch above the right eyebrow and a half-inch below it – from a distance. It appeared angry in the sunlight. Was it luck or skill, knife or shank, attack or defence, that had spared his eye? Nobody knew – and no one dared ask – its brutal legend. To Zephaniah it was an insignia – Purple Heart perhaps? – from one of his grandfather's unknown wars. More importantly, Zephaniah had long ago understood that its history was none of his damned business.

Once again, there was one rule for Bostonians and one for the Swire family, for no other family had been allowed inside the airport perimeter. Alone, and like a dismal island in a sea of concrete and tarmac, what remained of his bloodstock waited beside a black Lincoln sedan that shone brighter than any sun he'd seen in the jungles of Vietnam.

In that split second, Zephaniah saw his entire future reflected in the car's sheen. It was as if the corruption of valour-unto-death, together with all the telegrams he'd sent which had begun: '*The United States Army regrets . . .*' had created this black hole in time. No smirking at death now; he was like a man drowning, except in reverse. Every action he *was* still to commit was there. Every ballgame he was to endure. Every Swire's board meeting he was to chair. Together they all flashed in front of his eyes. Like a 3-D kaleidoscope, facets of his preordained future evolved in front of him. He'd grasped the unwritten expectations; his grandfather had positively trailblazed for him. And, as he took vigorous strides towards the Lincoln, the prophetic images served to unlock the manacles of being possessed of the name Swire, of being part of the family who owned Swire's, the single-most influential – and private – auction house in the Americas, if not the world. The company his grandfather had founded in 1933.

Stopping just short of the car, Zephaniah shook his father's hand and instinctively looked at the empty space beside him. It hadn't always been empty. Now, as the heat rose up from the gritty tarmac, the space his mother had occupied seemed greater than the total space occupied by his father and half-brother. Hephzibah Swire had always stood, just there, just to his father's right. Always half a step in front. Or had his father always been half a step behind? Good question. And now, he didn't care. All he understood was that his mother's suicide had been an act of immense selfishness. And he knew a thing or three about death. And life.

Ignoring Jed's limp, outstretched hand, Zephaniah stood to attention. Crisply, he presented a US Marine officer's salute to his grandfather. Then, in silence they all climbed into the Lincoln.

"So, you quit while you were ahead, Zeph," said Ollie, breaking the quiet.

"No. My second tour was over. I'm a decorated US Marine. I beat the jungles. It was time." Zephaniah took a deep breath. "I got out from in front of the guns, and I rogued the snipers." Sitting beside their chauffeur, he faced forward as he spoke. He waited a beat before adding. "I didn't quit Ollie. I chose to survive."

The only sound to be heard was rubber over tarmac. Even the sound of breathing ceased.

"I'll buy that." His grandfather leaned forward and tapped his grandson on the shoulder. "Do you remember when you were a young boy on the Vineyard, I taught you how to snag the wins at the hermit crab races on the beaches?"

"Course I do."

"I told you then that winners never quit, and quitters never win."

Zephaniah understood that all wars were fought twice: the first time on battlefields, the second time in memories.

And knowing this, he turned around and shot his grandfather a sphinx-like smile.

CHAPTER 6

**Poseyville, Amagansett, Long Island, New York.
Friday, 12th January 1990. Late morning.**

All throughout the morning after the news of Dougie's murder had spread, well-wishers, friends and strangers came from all points of the compass rose to the baymen's enclave known as Poseyville in Amagansett. They followed each other in silence to the home of Jake, Lindy and Amy Dealer. It was as if the South Fork of Long Island had lost its chosen son. And perhaps it had.

Nature's delicate equilibrium had been the governing force for the Dealer family for generations, and in its poise, there was a long-standing decree that avowed: *'A child shall not predecease a parent.'* This decree had been written in hope on the day the oceans took their shape. Nature had now decreed otherwise for Jake and Lindy, and their days would no longer have a pattern. Their nights would never ever have an end.

As the morning unsealed itself, the Atlantic Ocean grew fierce, with a cruel, vindictive run as the unwanted dawn crept deeper into the Dealers' lives. No longer did Jake's old quip, *'Any day above ground is a good day'*, hold true. No. If the ocean had a religion today, it was Catholic, it was Old Testament: without mercy, unforgiving and vengeful. It wanted its eye. It wanted its tooth. And then some. Dougie was *our* child too, hissed its angry, bitterly cold spume.

The wild surf grew higher, and a curious salted wind, straight out of the south, carried in from the dunes and sand banks all the aromas Dougie had ever known. With it, the wind's grey-green mist filtered in like a spectral hand, and gently, ever so gently, haunted the trees, the scrub, the wildflowers and all that surrounded the Dealers' once-proud yard.

Beside the 200-year-old anchor, the one Blondie had leapt over, the one that had belonged to a Sag Harbour whaler captained by a Dealer, lay flowers, wreaths, notes, mementos, expressions. A respectful calm had descended as the mourners came, bowed their heads and departed in bonded silence.

Lindy, or so Jake and Amy had thought, had collapsed on her bed after having been sedated by a doctor. Jake shrank his body into a foetal-like clench, paralysed by grief. Amy hid alone with sob-wrenching dry tears in her room. Jake, inanimate on the stone-cold kitchen floor, lived a deep and vivid dream, the kind of predawn dream that's not quite tactile. But close.

He drifted in his own unconscious darkness of monochrome imaginings. In one such vision Lindy had deserted him and Amy, too lost in her own anguish to know what she was really doing. One minute she was there, the next her footfall echoed like a bass drum around the yard. Yet no car had started and there were no footprints in the dirt. There was just frosted quiet, as there would be forever.

He startled awake. His heart raced and the pit in his stomach opened wide. Jake tore upstairs, his brow sweating, and found their bed empty. His girl from away had gone away. She had always had his true heart. It was as if it had always belonged to her and had only been on loan to him. All that produced in him was guilt. Survivor's guilt. He needed to find her. Not for himself. Not for Amy. But for Lindy. Survivors had a duty, and his family's 300 years on the ocean had taught Jake Dealer all about duty.

Panicked, he rubbed his eyes and tear-pickled cheeks, the ones that had only ever known the ocean's salt. What mattered now was the living. The fact that he could not count himself amongst them didn't mean he couldn't help them. He crashed through the screen door, fell down the porch steps and landed hard.

He looked about the yard. His flatbed Ford was there, as was Lindy's rusty-tan compact. His heart beat a retreat. He picked himself up and brushed the dirt from his denim. His eyes searched throughout his kingdom for his Queen. Where was she? Lindy was nowhere to be found. Terror-stricken, he tore back into the house, hoping beyond peradventure that she was lying with Amy, sharing her grief and halving her own. With an unexpectedly light touch, Jake opened the door to Amy's small bedroom. A fully clothed and sound asleep Princess, but no Queen.

Again, he ran downstairs and across the yard. Oblivious to all that lay about the mighty anchor, his eyes searched the road and then the potato fields. She had vanished. With tears now coursing down his face, he knelt on the ground. He no longer knew what he wept for: the sheer brutality of his son's death? Lindy's heart crumbling inside her chest until it too would cease to beat? The terror of loss for Amy?

His knees could no longer support him, and like the dead man he so nearly was he toppled forward into the dirt and gravel with the force of a crashing oak. His saliva and sobbing warmed the winter mud in his mouth like a paste, and his body heaved involuntarily with the rock-solid rhythm of Dougie's metronome.

Once a month the full moon exerts its powerful force on the earth. The waters ebb to new lows, and rise, like the moon, to new heights. While far away in the western night sky, an ethereal Venus shimmers as stars shine unsteadily in her grace.

Jake's moon would work its magic many times before he understood that he was stranded in no man's land. Deaf, blind and frozen voiced as if screaming into infinity. But the tar-black void of a polar night promised nothing in return, save for a forever-dark darkness.

CHAPTER 7

18 Louisburg Square, Beacon Hill, Boston, Massachusetts. Friday, 12th January 1990. Midday.

Hector's knock on the bedroom's mahogany door brought Zephaniah back to the present. Again, he glanced at his watch. It was now almost Twelve noon.

"Where've you been, Hector?" Zephaniah asked in his crisp New England voice.

"I was making coffee for Mr Jedediah, sir. He's waiting for you in the hall. Shall I show him into the drawing room or the dining room?"

Hector knew better than to announce him as 'your brother'. It was an expression his employer disliked. Guilt by association. The randomness of gene pools. There ought to be a law against it.

"Neither. Have him wait in the hall."

What on earth was Jed doing at his home, uninvited, unexpected, unwanted, and before lunch?

He winced at the thought of having to greet his habitually lymphatic and impassive half-sibling. On an empty stomach. And *that* handshake: cold spaghetti squelches as it sought to avoid contact, but when caught, it's as robust, as, well, cold spaghetti. Lips that weren't so much thin as non-existent – more like a crease in a permanently sour expression – meshed with insipid close-set pale eyes; a face as vacant as any Edvard Munch had ever painted. And as for the torso, he'd seen bigger shoulders on a banana. Altogether, aesthetically very displeasing.

He tugged at his dressing gown and went out onto the landing, Hector a shadow. He'd long suspected that his valet had had an affair with his effete half-brother, who his sources had informed him, had the temperament of a Kmart light bulb: guaranteed to blow on day one.

"How's your sock drawer today, Jed? Tidy?" he asked in greeting as he ambled down the stairs.

"What?" His half-brother's eyes were red-rimmed and squinting. He looked terrible.

"Oh nothing, just commenting on your obsessive need to rearrange," said Zephaniah. "Are you alright? You look like hell. Have you been up for a couple of nights? What do you want?"

Any semblance of politeness had long ago sailed.

"Some of your best advice," Jedediah replied.

"Full marks for your directness. What sort of advice?"

Zephaniah was perplexed. With no thirst for relevance on any subject other than his own vanity, his half-brother's thought process generally exuded the sublime joy of the condemned.

"Advice on an oil."

"From the ground, from a tree, from a brush? Please God, tell me you've not taken up painting?"

"I've found a painting I'd like to buy, and I think it's not what it seems. I think it's a genuine Dalí," Jedediah stated with finality.

"Listen up Jed. Dalí is the most forged of all the 20th-Century painters! At last count, and I don't know who even bothers to do that anymore, there were more than 200 Dalí's listed as forged or stolen. Don't go near it is my advice." Zephaniah breathed in deeply, trying to locate some patience. "Have a guess who's second in the 'most forged' league?"

"I don't know," his half-brother replied meekly.

"Picasso, of course. Any idea how many works of art are forged or stolen? Of course you don't. It's my business to know these details, not yours." Zephaniah coughed before continuing. "There's an axiom that states if Corot painted 500 works, then 900 of them are for sale in America alone. At present Jed there are about 300 Picassos and fifty Rembrandts listed as stolen. Yes stolen." He heaved a sigh. "I haven't even mentioned Renoir, Miró, Chagall, Dürer, Warhol, Hockney, Monet, Manet. The list is endless. For God's sake, there are more than forty stolen Henry Moore sculptures out there somewhere, and you need a damned truck with a crane for most of those. Of all the artworks for sale at any given time 40% are fake. Leave this Dalí alone."

As always, Jedediah was defeated by Zephaniah's authority. His inert china-doll-like eyes turned on his elder half-brother. Zephaniah shuddered. He disliked being appraised by this flâneur not because he despised him, as truth to tell he didn't care enough to, but because Zephaniah knew Jed was waiting for him to fail in any endeavour. Usually, Jed's close-set gaze only ever sought out the inconsequential: the nap of a suede shoe that had been brushed in the wrong direction, the length of a shirt sleeve, an errant cuticle . . . Zephaniah had long ago concluded that his half-brother was no more than an inchoate biomass that breathed. There was also an insufferable birthright arrogance he'd awarded himself: one that stated *'stubbornness = strength'*, together with a resentment for all Zephaniah and Ollie stood for, despite being afforded (only out of respect for York) a substantial allowance – one large enough to be privileged, but seemingly not happy. However, in Jed's defence, his emerald-envy had evolved out of self-knowledge; he *knew* he truly was second-rate. Even worse, he knew that Zephaniah knew it too.

"The Dalí is being *sold* as a forgery, and I don't think it is. That's the help I need, that and your eye."

"Did you listen to anything I said?" Zephaniah's mind was elsewhere now. "Ask someone in my research department."

"I don't want anyone taking this from under my nose."

Little chance of that happening, thought Zephaniah meanly. "You've heard of our Head of Research, Cory Mount?"

"Yes," he replied.

"Good. He's seriously competent and I'll call him later. You speak with him this afternoon and let me know what's involved." As an aside, he added, "you've enough money of your own for this kind of purchase, whether it's forged, stolen or genuine. Why bother me?"

Ignoring Zephaniah's question, Jedediah turned to the front door and said, "I'll call you at the office this afternoon."

"One of the hassles with you Jed is that when you're not drunk, you're sober. You've lost a day. It's Friday. I'm headed out to the Vineyard later this afternoon to see Ollie." Without so much as a parting murmur, Zephaniah walked into the dining room and left Hector to open the front door.

The truth was he wasn't going to see Ollie until next Wednesday and had postponed today's meeting. He intended to spend a quiet weekend alone in his basement study reading. He had to inspect an important collection of 18th-Century Russian icons on Monday and pronounce on them that evening. Zephaniah wasn't sure he appreciated the deadlines set by this squadron of freshly minted Russians, but it was the lure of the untold – and surely soon-to-be plundered – riches from the vaults of the Kremlin and Hermitage that checked his riled mood.

Whatever hare-brained scheme his clueless half-brother was up to with a Dalí – stolen or forged or, knowing him, both – could wait awhile. Like a decade.

CHAPTER 8

**Poseyville, Amagansett, Long Island, New York.
Friday, 12th January 1990. Early afternoon.**

"*Jake, do you think we'll ever have a life that doesn't smell of fish and damp, and rotting wood?*"

Lindy had never liked their lean-to shed. She never went near it, and inside, the lights never seemed to work. Another fixer job. Jake wouldn't have wanted anyone, least of all Lindy, to see him like this. Mud had crusted onto his cheeks, his eyes, his mouth and his matted hair.

He looked up and then closed his eyes and felt for his whalebone jack-knife. He unsheathed and opened it. The polished steel of its large blade gave a flicker of life to the chiaroscuro shadows. He went to touch the whetstone in his pocket, hesitated, and ran his middle finger down the blade's cutting edge until blood flowed freely. Razor sharp.

It didn't take him long to cut through the seine net. Christ, he'd spent his entire life cutting nets. He sliced through the net hanging from the rotting oak beam and gently took her limp, dead body in his arms. Her face blue, her eyes staring, he laid her down ever so tenderly on the chill earth floor. What would take time was removing the meshed twine from where it had sliced deep into her neck and behind her ears and her hairline. Cautiously, Jake used the jack-knife's tip to prise free each thread of the net, knowing that he wouldn't be able to live with himself if he so much as scratched Lindy's ice-cold skin.

All Jake knew was that he was too late. Again.

CHAPTER 9

18 Louisburg Square, Beacon Hill, Boston, Massachusetts. Friday, 12th January 1990. Early afternoon.

"Hector!"

Zephaniah glanced at his watch. It was now 13:52 and Jimmy Snale was many things. Punctual to an irritating fault was just one of them.

"Yes, sir." Hector appeared from behind the staff's door.

"Who's on duty today?"

"Only me. Cook is off and you gave Juanita and Eli the afternoon off too. You said you didn't need driving this weekend."

Zephaniah knew exactly who was, and was not, on duty. Snale was due in eight minutes. Time to hustle Hector out of the door.

"Please go and buy me the English newspapers. *The Times, The Daily Telegraph* and the *Financial Times*. Thursday editions will do." He smiled disarmingly. "You won't find them at the 7-Eleven on Charles Street. Try the Ritz-Carlton or another hotel."

"Of course, sir."

Zephaniah returned to the financial pages of *The Boston Globe* and continued to sip his black, unsweetened, Blue Mountain coffee.

At precisely 14:00 the doorbell sounded, and Zephaniah opened the front door.

"Thanks for coming over on a Friday afternoon. Trust I'm not spoiling any weekend plans?"

"You know me Mr Swire, you call and I'm here. Thanks for asking."

"I do know that Jimmy, and your presence is never taken for granted. Wait for me in my study while I fetch some papers from upstairs." He let a beat slide. "You know the way, take yourself down to the basement."

Jimmy Snale, half Montaukett Indian, was short and military-fit at 5' 10" and looked much younger than his forty-three years of age. He was dressed in a blue button-down shirt, plain navy vest, tan chinos and black lace-up shoes so mirror-polished you could shave in their sheen. He sucked in his dark, hollowed-out, pock-marked cheeks and began to fidget with his wire-rimmed spectacles. His employer's basement made him anxious, made his heart race and his body sweat. He *hated* that study with a passion – one that went far beyond his loathing of all things federal. And that was saying something.

"If it's OK with you, Mr Swire, I'll wait here."

"Please head on down Jimmy. Wouldn't want anyone disturbing us."

With that request (Zephaniah no longer ordered Sergeant James 'Sly' Snale to do anything) he descended the stairs.

What was it with Jimmy and his study, Zephaniah wondered – was it the basement, or was it the jellyfish? Twenty-one years had passed since First Lieutenant Swire had found – and rescued – his senior NCO, caged and buried underground by the Vietcong in a bamboo prison smaller than a car's trunk. Perhaps those horrors were still with him, Zephaniah concluded as he gathered up his papers.

During the war, Snale, had been a 'Lerp', who served in the Long-Range Reconnaissance Patrol or LRRP on secondment from the 75th Infantry US Army Rangers to First Lieutenant Swire's platoon. Like the Navajo, Montaukett Indians understood that tribe was above self, an ethic the Rangers only reinforced. And Sergeant 'Sly' Snale was dedicated to his new tribal leader, his CO. Along with three other heavily camouflaged Ranger scouts, he would penetrate deep behind enemy lines for two weeks or more, subsisting on rainwater and grubs, surviving only by their tracking skills. They were to 'out-guerrilla the guerrillas'. Gather intel, spy, and, in Snale's case, return with Vietcong scalps. Physical scalps. The man was a stone-cold killer. Knives were his silent weapon of choice. It was simply in his Indian DNA, he'd explained after a long mission deep into the mountainous jungles of the A Shau Valley, hard on the border with Laos.

Following a far shorter mission, a solo mission, Sergeant Snale had failed to return. First Lieutenant Swire had straight away 'volunteered' two grunts and set out into the jungle – in breach of orders – to track his NCO and return with him, dead or alive. The rest (with his second Bronze Star) soon became US Marine lore. But at least this morning Jimmy had the jellyfish to keep him company.

Ten minutes later, Zephaniah opened his study door and walked past his 1820 ivory chess set – Napoleon a soft white, Wellington a blood red – and deep into the grey-lit basement. Window-less, it was a place where light played hide-and-seek with shadows and corners. A peculiar suspense swelled through its cherry-wood panelling, due in part to an immense flush-walled glass tank of seawater which ran seamlessly behind his modernist David Linley desk. This was no ordinary fish tank. The aquarium was deep, wide, and full of vibrant rainbow-coloured Scyphozoan jellyfish, free swimming medusae, with long trailing tentacles.

Scyphozoan medusae consist of almost 99% water, feed on what they catch in their tentacles, have a remarkable ability for self-defence, and are neither male nor female frequently changing sex. They have no sense of right or wrong, exhibit no cephalisation, have no brain, a radial symmetry, locomote by contracting and relaxing their bell muscles, and have no codas or laws that govern their existence. Therefore, they appealed to Zephaniah as ideal household pets. Best of all, they looked simply stunning when lit by the high-intensity lights – above and underneath – in the tank's body of seawater. Theirs was a sort of translucent balletic art as they moved constantly, randomly, and when a specimen died, he/she/it was replaced by the kind folks at the Boston Aquarium. His pet jellyfish had long motivated his imagination in the hours he spent alone in his study: Einstein had been right when he'd said that imagination was far, far more important than knowledge.

"Jimmy, sorry to have kept you waiting."

"No problem, Mr Swire," replied Snale with obvious relief. He stood to attention from out of a wing chair. "What can I do to help?"

"Firstly, sit down," Zephaniah said pouring himself a glass of water. "Full details later. For the moment, all you need to know is we need one capable, strong Caucasian man, and two complete Boston Police uniforms. I don't mean go find a costume-hire shop. I want them from the BPD depot, understand?"

"Who's the second uniform for?"

"You."

"Where are you headed with this Mr Swire?"

NO MAN'S LAND

Ignoring the question, Zephaniah continued with his instructions. "In addition, you'll need an ordinary car, a dark colour, local plates, make it look like an unmarked BPD vehicle. Now, back to your prospective partner, and this is important – I'd suggest you track him from mercenary sources. I want a professional and someone who lives and works outside America – say, in Asia, Europe, Africa. My first choice would be a Brit, an ex-Royal Marine type working freelance. Ensure he's no one we've used before. You'll need a man who's aware of how to take his pay, and how *not* to spend it. Understand?"

"Loud and clear, sir. What is the pay?"

"A solid payday Jimmy, and it'll come in three stages: 50% now, 50% on completion. In addition, a bonus of a further 50% will be paid in five years. Assuming he's still alive."

"OK, Mr Swire."

"You know me, I don't pay good wages because I have a lot of money." Zephaniah narrowed his eyes. "I have a lot of money because I pay good wages."

"I still need a number, sir," Snale said cutting to the chase.

Zephaniah had anticipated this perfectly reasonable request. As always, he allowed his actions to do the talking. He pulled a hefty leather folio from his desk and slid it across the table.

"That's his first half. Your pay will be exactly double, and I'll have it in your Cayman account on Monday." Zephaniah dropped a fat manila envelope on the desk. "Expenses."

Sergeant James Snale knew his former CO too well to ask how much was in the folio, let alone open it. He merely nodded in assent. His boss was many things, but mean wasn't one of them. Besides, the calf skin folio looked fully loaded.

"Listen up. This is important. Whoever you choose must have no record at all, and both standard-issue BPD weapons you'll carry are to be loaded with blanks. You *must* check that yourself. We're not in the blood-spilling business, nor are we undertakers."

"I've carried loaded weapons on previous assignments before, so what business are we in?"

Zephaniah treated the question with the contempt he felt it deserved. He ignored it completely.

"There are to be no concealed weapons either. Any part of what I'm saying that you don't understand?" He drew in a deep breath. "The time frame is about seven weeks. You'll only get final details six hours before, no sooner. Understood?"

"I hear you Mr Swire." Snale hesitated. "Can you give me an idea of what we are to do?"

"I want a bit of law-breaking done."

"Well, it wouldn't be the first time Mr Swire."

"No, and I doubt it'll be the last either Jimmy," he grinned momentarily. "But this time it'll be a little different."

Jimmy Snale had undertaken far too many jobs for the Swire family to know that no two jobs were ever the same. A valuable piece of art would have to be transported, either out of state or to a foreign land, without any authorities knowing what the hell was going on. Situation Normal. This was Swire's after all. Don't let the right hand know what the Jesus H. Christ was even being entertained by the left hand. The trouble with Lieutenant Swire was that he never flew straight and level. It simply wasn't in his nature to abide by any rule that either he, or his rattlesnake-mad grandfather, hadn't dreamt up themselves. However, Snale had always known where he stood. And that was more important. Zephaniah Swire, as both civilian and soldier, was not a man given to fickle and arbitrary moods and every detail would have been thought through to ten decimal places.

Sergeant James Snale, twenty-one years later, still could not escape the fact that he would always owe Lieutenant Swire his life. So, why not tell Jimmy what was needed, up front? What was ol' Sly gonna do? Grass out the man, who with two grunts, had crept into a Vietcong camp in the dead of night and ripped open the carotid arteries of five Commies and saved him from certain death? No. He worshipped the man.

It would be a cold day in an Indian hell before ever forgot that truth.

PART TWO

WEDNESDAY, 17TH JANUARY 1990

CHAPTER 10

**Oak Grove Cemetery, Amagansett, Long Island, New York.
Wednesday, 17th January 1990. Early afternoon.**

If ever there was a requiem to the end of the Long Island baymen it took the form of Douglas L. Dealer's white coffin. Jake Dealer had never known that children's coffins were white. It figured though. But he had never known that fact. Like so much else.

Oak Grove Cemetery in Amagansett was a fine place for a Dealer to be laid to rest. The cemetery was true to itself, honouring its name and independence of spirit. There appeared to be no order to the random lie of oak and birch trees, graves, and small, proud Stars and Stripes that stood, sentinel, beside most headstones. But as with everything else in the life of a bayman's family, there was order. Families were buried with families, and that was that.

Ten generations of Dealers were buried hereabouts, men and women in a land where there was no king other than conscience. Fisher-folk all. Jake and Amy had come to bury the last Dealer these fine oaks would ever see. The end of the line had been reached. There would be no more Dealers interred here. Jake had decided that. No, he and Amy would leave to try to find their peace, and if they succeeded, they could then seek their own resting places far away from here. To stay here would be to die.

Jake, Peter Duxbury, Nathan Freeman and Eddie Silver stood beside the mahogany coffin of Linda M. Dealer, née Stone. Amy, her generous smile absent, had borne Dougie's small coffin with Marty Drew, and now stood side by side. Proud and forthright, Jake raised his square jaw and took Amy's soft hand. He held onto her as a shipwrecked man would driftwood. She smiled up at him and he smiled at her. They owned their own secrets.

There was an old saying hereabouts that nobody should be invited to a funeral, but everybody should come. And Jake looked about him at the sheer number of people who had travelled from near and far to pay their respects. To what and to whom, he was not entirely sure. Dougie and his mother, certainly, but also for generations of kinsfolk and a life everyone knew was dying.

The winter sky had turned a flinty shade of white, and it hung low as if it too were in mourning. Calmly, Jake and Amy stepped towards the newly dug graves to shake the hand of each of their pallbearers. Not one word passed between any of them. In their collective silence was the rage of God. Neither Jake nor Amy, nor any of the gathered souls had the stomach for the Lord's Prayer. In its stead, Marty chose to recite in a slow tempo, and in his crisp voice, Dylan Thomas's poem: 'Do Not Go Gentle Into That Good Night' as the mourners gathered around the two graves.

> *And you, my father, there on the sad height,*
> *Curse, bless, me now with your fierce tears,*
> *I pray,*
> *Do not go gentle into that good night.*
> *Rage, rage against the dying of the light.*

With his grandfather's old black fishing cap pulled down hard, and the last verse echoing in the empty chamber that was his soul, Jake turned on his heel and led Amy silently away from this place. Father and daughter had already said what needed to be said when they had buried Blondie in the woods behind their house that morning.

For all that was good in the world lay dead beneath their feet.

CHAPTER 11

**10 Crick Hill Road, Menemsha,
Martha's Vineyard, Massachusetts.
Wednesday, 17th January 1990. Early afternoon.**

Ollie Swire, the eponymous founder of Swire's, had been an artist his entire life, albeit one who'd begun his illustrious career as a con artist.

He had been born with no name, no history, no known parentage – nothing, in truth – in June 1905 (no precise date was ever specified). These commonplace facts of life were only disclosed to him upon his mandatory departure, aged sixteen, from St Joseph's Home for Boys, a Catholic orphanage in St Louis, Missouri.

In June 1905 he'd been abandoned at the gates as a 'door-step' summer newborn; winter 'door-steps' (as the Sisters referred to them) invariably perished as the St Louis' temperatures fell below freezing. Luck, fate, destiny, good fortune, providence, the alignment of the stars – call it what you will – would all come to hallmark the foundling's life. The Sisters, having plucked names at random from a Missouri telephone book, chose Oliver Swire.

Like all the boys, he was an 'only' child, and the little boy grew to regard the other thirty or so orphans as brothers. With no yardstick to compare, he made the very best of his lot, and proudly regarded the orphanage as his home. The Sisters were, for the most part, caring educators, and there was only ever calm discipline at St Joseph's.

With a birthright instinct, he grasped early on to take his own bearings – daily – from others, be they the Sisters who taught them, or the boys themselves. He absorbed all that surrounded him. Interested curiosity sparked not just his imagination, but subliminally began to fuel his life. Like the proverbial sponge he soaked up all he could.

Lessons were long, and were held throughout the entire year, save for Easter and Christmas holidays. Broad schooling in all manner of topics, with vigour and diligence being first and foremost. The gentle mannered, intelligent, intuitive Ollie (as he became known) excelled in all his classes as he matured. History, English, math, reading, and the composition of stories, were his fortes. He liked his orphanage home, a sentiment that was reciprocated, for everyone liked Ollie. He appreciated his good fortune in being at St Joseph's, a compassionate environment despite the fierce depravations of the austere times.

The Sisters encouraged outdoor pursuits, and whilst Ollie didn't excel at sports, he devoted fall and winter to reading voraciously in the library, and during spring and summer he spent time outdoors in the kitchen gardens cultivating foodstuffs. In later life he declined to share (even with his grandson) that the genesis of his love of simple food and cooking had been seeded in the orphanage's vegetable plots.

In June 1921, Ollie Swire left St Joseph's, and as he walked out of the gates for the very last time, he awarded himself one indulgence. He elected to choose his own birth date. Or rather birth day: *'Saturday's child works hard for a living'*. Saturday, 10th June 1905 became his birthday that morning.

Distance from St Louis, he had decided, would keep him on his toes. So, the tall, lean, blue-eyed sixteen-year-old autodidact, with an unruly mop of auburn hair, headed east to Chicago, where he'd heard work was to be found *and* rewarded.

St Joseph's had taught him a rudimentary 'right from wrong', yet he rose (he never regarded it as falling) into grifting in the Windy City, for the true grifter was not a thief. A grift requires the telling of a tale with wit, a light touch and flair. All of which the young Ollie Swire had in abundance. Violence is never exercised in separating marks from their money; of all the grifters, the *true* confidence man is the nobleman. Unlike pickpockets and gangsters, there is no larceny involved when removing money from trusting – and wholewheat – greedy individuals.

Conmen were not crooks in common parlance: they are highly intelligent, believable, suave, slick and – much like politicians – skilled in the dark arts of deception. A conman succeeds, primarily, due to the inherent dishonesty of his chosen mark. It is only ever the overly trusting man who willingly parts with his bank roll – a man fed by his *own* greed. Humans are essentially cooperative beings. For the talented conman discovering the marriage of self-deception and wilful blindness requires no ju-jitsu, however it demands narrative. And having unearthed it, seduction, wit, humour, ingenuity, audacity and strategic patience all lie at the heart and soul of the con, and in that very truth lies its artform. And Ollie excelled at his chosen artform.

By 1928, now twenty-three, and more bored than tired of playing the short cons, Ollie figured it was in the big and long cons where his talents, and his future, lay. So, he decided to step up. He was sharp, skilled, knowledgeable and possessed of a gentle manner. There was no abracadabra to him, no magical wizardry to ward off misfortune: planning and execution were his two monarchs.

Swiftly, he became the youngest, and some say, most remarkable, insideman ever to play the big cons. It was Ollie's instinctive understanding of human nature that enabled him to keep a mark under perfect control, throughout the days and weeks in which the mark's greed led him unwittingly to part with all that he owned. And, oftentimes, all he could borrow too. In the fall of 1928, together with much older pros he'd brought on board, Ollie led the $275,000 take from a Cleveland mark in Buffalo in a 'Big Store' con. The takedown cemented his reputation and much more besides.

Afterwards, Ollie rented a cold-water one-room apartment in Kansas City. There he stuffed his share of the take – $55,000 – into the horsehair mattress. He continued grifting in the Midwest for a while, but only ever played the insideman in a big con once more: New York, the end of summer of 1929, when the stock market was insane. Ollie was working the inside with three older pros, all with improbable monikers: Plunk Drucker, Limehouse Chappie and Nibs Callahan (who was the roper) in his elegant frock coat and sporting a Van Dyke beard. They were the finest and most daring of conmen – artists too. They were men of dynamism, resourcefulness, verve and energy, and were all at the top of their game. This time, their long con was 'The Rag'. Their chosen mark was a Canadian gambler: avarice and other people's money was always a mark's trigger, the tell, the scar. Like a lemming at a cliff's edge, a mark's appetite for quick, easy money would lead him onto the rocks below. Their sting from the Canadian gambler? $325,000. In cash.

Without delay, Ollie boarded a train back to Kansas City and padded his mattress with a further $75,000. He paid the rent on his seedy one-room apartment a year in advance and went to ground in California. 'Rest and sun' were the reasons he gave his disappointed fellow artists. In truth, he wished to fulfil one prosaic dream he'd long harboured: to swim in the Pacific Ocean. Living (and working) close to the Great Lakes of Michigan, Huron and Superior had ignited inside him something he couldn't yet fathom. He'd never seen such vast expanses of water growing up. A fascination with the sea and oceans became almost an obsession, one that would also hallmark his later life. Besides, in that summer of 1929, he'd sensed the tide was turning, and it was time to furrow new plains. His extraordinary premonitory instincts, and his ability to see around corners, were, of course, pitch-perfect.

When 'Black Tuesday' hit Wall Street on 29th October 1929, Ollie was already in the parched heat of New Mexico, where he'd intended, literally, to sit out the crash he'd seen coming. But not even he had envisaged how long and deep the Great Depression would be. He'd never trusted banks or stocks. He'd figured out early in his career that if you bought a stock – or even deposited money in a bank – you had a partner. What did he know from partners? Nothing. All he knew was the 'inside'. He collected one item: money. To him it was abstract. An abacus, by which he measured himself. A yardstick. It really was as simple as that to Ollie Swire.

In the first winter of what became the Great Depression, he found a job as a ranch hand a few miles outside El Paso for the room and board, more than the pay. But as this new way of life stretched out in front of him, he immersed himself in the workings of the ranch. He taught himself new skills, ones that complemented his tenacious and independent discipline. He learned to ride a horse well and helped to round up cattle. He drove tractors, repaired fences, and even fixed the old, dying windmills.

It was on the ranch, so it has been said, that the handsome, wiry, hard-muscled young Ollie met a lady, striking, with raven hair and tall in an almost masculine manner. Her name was Hannah McGovern. She was a parlour maid for another old money El Paso family.

Emotional intimacy, let alone love, was an alien concept to a Midwestern orphan and loner like Ollie. Yet his feelings for Hannah grew to be near to that state of topsy-turvy emotions often called 'love'. As time passed, these emotions fused into a profound love, and it would be the only time he would ever feel that way towards a woman.

So, when Hannah died in October 1930 giving birth to their son, York, Ollie soundly rejected the screaming infant that had killed the one person he had ever cared about. Her passing gnawed away at his core as a bubonic rat would a fleshless corpse. At night he delved back into history and brooded over counterfactuals – change one element of history and you change everything – before sleep would confiscate his shattered heart for a handful of hours.

Each and every night a different tectonic shift of history took place in his head and heart. From the absurd, like the notion that Mark Antony's obsession with Cleopatra's proboscis had determined the fate of the Roman Empire, to the plausible, such as what might have occurred if Germany hadn't dispatched Lenin to Petrograd in 1917 to foment a revolution and hinder the Tsar's allegiance to his World War I allies. It was as if Ollie was playing a different 78 on his phonograph, whilst striving to rewrite history's biggest sin: Hannah's death. He didn't care that history wasn't there for the changing, try as he might, but his iron will drove him on like he was a shark moving to survive. Until one moonless night, the phonograph's needle, worn blunt from overuse, played no more. Hannah *was* dead. And buried. Deep in her New Mexican earth. She was as dead as the Chinese butterfly that had flapped its wings furiously, yet still failed to cause a tsunami in California.

The next morning, Ollie and York moved from the ranch to the mansion where Hannah had lived and worked, to be close to her spirit if nothing else. Her employers offered him a handyman's job and allowed him and his son an apartment over the garage. There Ollie and York lived, not so much as father and son, more as uncle and nephew. But not for long.

By the early spring of 1933, Ollie now almost twenty-eight, had tired of reading greedily and living frugally in New Mexico. So, he and York took their leave of Hannah's employers and went on the road. Together they headed northeast to Boston – via his Kansas mattress – with the $130,000 intact.

He had selected Boston because it was a city of wealth, not because it was the capitol of that curious state of mind that is 'New England'.

It was a city of Brahmins who relished indulging those it one day intended to humble. Comfortable with his iron-willed humility, Ollie never sought to be indulged – or humbled – least of all by a Brahmin state of mind.

And as if to celebrate Franklin D. Roosevelt's change of address to 1600 Pennsylvania Avenue in March of that year, he opened a discreet, brass-plaque, pawnbroking business in Beacon Hill, within sight of the Massachusetts State House. He named it Swire's as a compliment to his new President. It was his New Deal. If his President could have one, so could he.

In Boston, Ollie Swire's antennae told him the days of the big cons were over, especially for young, ambitious men. Those with whom he'd worked since his teens – who knew no other life – continued grifting. However, the Great Depression had run almost four years, and the federal government was beginning to flex its considerable muscles. Hard time, federal style, was not worth it.

Free enterprise made Ollie's world go around, and grifting, well, now that was just something you got caught at. So, he reinvented himself in New England. It was time to try his hand at business. Pawnbroking was a game at first, for Ollie secretly hankered for the bygone days of the big cons. Until the day he advanced $350, against his better judgement, to a gentleman who proffered a disquieting lead and charcoal drawing titled *Portrait of Max Jacob*. It was the work of a Spaniard, one Pablo Ruiz y Picasso. Some months later when the gentleman failed to redeem the pledge, causing title in the drawing to revert to Swire's, Ollie cursed himself daily. Six months passed before he sold it to a Parisian dealer for $1,500, who positively beamed as he'd counted out the cash. Apart from a forgery he would knowingly acquire when in his mid-eighties, *Portrait of Max Jacob* was to be the first and last painting Ollie Swire would ever own, as a principal, in his entire life.

Gone forever were any thoughts of working the inside again. The money lay in the middle. That was where the big scores were now to be had. Not long after he'd sold the drawing in the spring of 1937, Andrew Mellon pledged Raphael's *Alba Madonna*, together with twenty-three Rembrandts and six Vermeers to the US Government.

With Mellon's donation, Ollie's mind became truly focused. They – and he had begun to study the way families such as the Morgans, Rockefellers,

Huntingdons, Mellons, Gardners, Fricks, Kresses and Hearsts collected – could all do precisely what they wanted with their art, subject to one proviso: Swire's would get a percentage, on both the artworks' inbound, and outbound journeys. And Ollie didn't care if the train stopped at their vainglorious museums, the trusts of idle offspring or the coffers of wasteful governments.

As if by an osmotic process, Swire's metamorphosed into a quasi-dealing and auctioning enterprise. One where seller and buyer were matched with the utmost discretion. Two years later, fortune again smiled on Ollie's new venture, when the famous British art dealer Sir Joseph Duveen died. Ollie had recognised that together with Bernard Berenson, Duveen had assembled the great art for the barons of American industry. Under a mid-Atlantic fog of their own creation, they sold the idea that buying important art could confer an upper-class status.

Duveen's death, not long before the outbreak of World War II, left the field wide open for Swire's to exploit. Who would care if the exceedingly rich derived a bizarre, and profound, gratification in outspending each other? So it was that Ollie began to view Swire's as a *chemin de fer* for fine art. One that connected wealthy collectors, in the manner of a banker connecting a new railroad to a new enterprise.

As with any skilled banker, Swire's did not withdraw once the transaction was complete. It continued to monitor the investment. In effect, Swire's became the guardian of the piece, and then, instigator of where and when it should move on down the line to another collection. It was as if the owner or museum had little say in the matter. It might have been whispered that it was sleight of hand. But it never was. Swire's were just *too* good.

In a society without an aristocracy, 'collecting' became an aristocracy. And Ollie understood that there's nothing the rich like better than a *perceived* bargain. It took him very little time to figure out that all collections were, and needed to be, fluid. And like many aristocrats, constant attention and re-invention were essential. Furthermore, he recognised that serious collectors were – and this was without exception – solitary, obsessive, single minded and neurotic human beings. 'Collecting' as such was a quest, and a primal one that had at its core the pursuit of immortality. Consequently, to a man of Ollie's concealed talents, a collector's behavioural patterns were easier to keep in check than any unknown (and soon-to-be-ruined) mark he had ever taken down. This *modus operandi* became Swire's individual method of business: a hybrid of selling, buying, curating, auctioning and advising.

While living and working in New England, Ollie promptly formed the opinion that behind every great fortune lay a great crime; *vide* Joseph Kennedy, who he'd witnessed shoeing-in FDR. All that had cost the bootlegging, stock-manipulating crook was a miserable $200,000. Ollie reasoned that if the presidency was for sale, then, so too was America. A land full of wealthy people with pasts to obfuscate and futures to crystallise. Ollie just wanted his share. And, ever the patriot, he hadn't even begun to dream the American Dream.

In the clandestine world of fine art Swire's soon came to approximate white-shoe firms such as Sotheby's and Christie's – but only in the way that Balik salmon approximates fishfingers. Swire's distinctive methodology, together with their client list, was matched by their skill at harmonising buyer with seller, museum with benefactor, in silence, with prudence, and above all, without cutting their fees.

Headlines, noise, discounts, bartering and price fixing or guaranteeing were common enough words in the art world, but they belonged on the tongues of Sotheby's and Christie's staff. By 1990, Swire's had effectively assumed the very pinnacle of placing all manner of fine art and sculpture: other items such as jewellery or silver were deemed merely collectibles, and as such, belonged in malls and arcades. Or in the needlessly show-off catalogues of Sotheby's or Christie's.

All the while Swire's remained a highly profitable private company. One hundred per cent of its stock was owned by a wealthy, yet curiously humble, octogenarian gentleman who treasured his privacy, whilst despising self-aggrandisement in others. With close-cropped white hair, he was fit and trim in both height and build. His demeanour was neither fissured with happiness nor unhappiness, but his Husky-blue eyes were, perhaps, well versed in scepticism.

Never known to have raised his baritone voice, he was a mild-mannered man whose disposition was sometimes referred to as 'taciturn'. In fact, it was rarely that. Ollie Swire was a man who had long ago learned to appreciate the true value of reticence and understood that silence was an underrated virtue. His principal hobby was restoring – anonymously – oil paintings, almost as an ironic jolt to his other 'artistic' skills, and he collected, in a casual manner, ancient Chinese funerary objects. He dressed minimally, usually in dark blue or black, and wore proprietary white Brooks Brothers shirts with their penny loafers.

In short, he was a self-sufficient man with vanilla tastes and needs who wasn't given, even at his age, to thoughts of mortality. For Ollie, such thoughts were for tomorrow. And wasn't tomorrow something that kept happening in Australia? He was also, among other things, a teetotaller, a non-smoker and an excellent cook. A good listener too, who possessed neither a television nor a home telephone. When he spoke, his voice was soft and mellifluent; not unlike Sinatra singing a Nelson Riddle arrangement, but Ollie's intonation was always one step ahead of the beat.

For nearly forty years Mr Oliver Swire had had been a 'cricker'; that is to say he had resided at 10 Crick Hill Road, a blink of a cul-de-sac, above the fishing harbour of Menemsha, Martha's Vineyard. There were but a handful of cottages on the gentle green slope, and Ollie loved his modest three-roomed cottage and studio, with its small boat house and dock below, at the water's edge.

From his home he could overlook the fishing boats, Poole's and Larsen's fish markets, the ever-changing harbour and the coarse sand of Menemsha Beach beyond, whilst being nourished by the sea air. And when the winds gnarled the waves, he'd walk the beach so the spindrift could cleanse his soul. As an inordinately rich man, amidst the men who worked New England's unforgiving Atlantic waters, he was able to go about his affairs in quiet anonymity, something he cherished far more than his wealth.

It was in this reflective mood that Ollie Swire awaited the arrival of his grandson. Since birth, he had truly loved Zephaniah. Amongst the myriad reasons, and Ollie guarded this secret, was the fact that Zephaniah was the living and breathing likeness of Hannah – without her kindness and her tenderness, which he'd long held was a good thing in a man.

Whatever was on his grandson's persistently alert mind this chill January afternoon, it was always good to gaze upon a vision of Hannah. Especially as the sun sought to escape this foreboding sky – spectral, white-hued and menacing – before it lost itself in the angry ocean that lay, like so much else, beneath his feet.

CHAPTER 12

**Logan Airport, Boston,
to Martha's Vineyard Airport, Massachusetts.
Wednesday, 17th January 1990. Early afternoon.**

"Talk to ATC when we're clear of Logan please Jeff. I'd like to approach from the south today, over No Man's Land, then track northeast to Chappaquiddick before we land. When we're over No Man's Land, keep it low and slow please."

"Will do Mr Swire. I'll give Vineyard's tower a heads up when we approach Buzzard's Bay and Vineyard Sound."

"You're in charge Jeff, not me," Zephaniah said buckling himself into the seat of his King Air 300.

Jeff Hindle, another Vietnam veteran, had been Zephaniah Swire's pilot for ten or more years, and knew not to question an unconventional request. This was a regular trip for Mr Swire, but he also knew that his mood shifted – always for the better – during the forty-minute flight south from Boston to Martha's Vineyard. He'd long ago ceased speculating on the why, or the wherefore. Any attempt to fathom any of Mr Swire's reasonings was as futile as chess-by-post was quick.

Shortly after take-off, Hindle turned around and gave a thumbs-up signal; they were clear of the dense clouds and chop. Zephaniah unbuckled his belt, went to the refreshment cabinet and opened a half-bottle of 1982 Château Gruaud-Larose. He enjoyed his wines in the manner that he admired his art, and Californian wines, like Californian art, belonged on the taste buds of Californians. And only then in California. He slipped off his suede loafers, settled into the tan leather seat and gazed out of the oval window into a far horizon. The soothing hum of the King Air 300's twin turboprop engines was all he heard, all he listened to. He enjoyed time on his aircraft, and there was currency in the distinction that the King Air belonged to him and not to Swire's. Sipping wine, above the dense clouds, he found he could relax in solitude, with nothing other than his own thoughts for company, for Martha's Vineyard held the archaeology of his past.

* * *

If ever there was an acorn, it was surely planted during the summer of 1955, deep in the calm northeastern beaches of Martha's Vineyard: East, State, Lighthouse and Katama, none of them far from 'Teddy's Car-Wash', as his grandfather had later renamed Chappaquiddick. Zephaniah knew, flying south high above the mysterious and ominous thick blanket of clouds, that if he ever had had a 'favourite' age it was being seven. Yes, the summer of 1955.

His childhood summers had always seemed longer, when time was a concept yet to be understood. He had so adored being alone with his grandfather: April to September with the sailing regattas in July. Just the two of them. His grandfather had been his school, his mentor, his parents.

"Tell me Zeph, do you think that when a magician does a trick, that he's pulling a hoax? Is it deceitful, cheating? He's not telling a lie, remember, he's performing his act, he's a magician after all. Deception is also an appearance. When the rabbit comes out of the hat, you ask yourself, perhaps, what was the rabbit doing in the hat in the first place? Sitting in there all snug and waiting to be yanked out by the ears? I don't think so! The rabbit is happy to be free of the old smelly top hat. The audience applauds. The magician bows in thanks knowing he'll be paid his wages. Everybody wins. You see, if you win, you win, and winning is all. Second is nowhere. Anything you do to win, cannot therefore be considered dishonest, unless of course you're a rabbit!" His grandfather had laughed heartily. *"Understand now Zeph?"*

Zephaniah had had no idea what his grandfather had been talking about on that hazy July afternoon. But before the sun would set over Menemsha's harbour that evening, he would understand fully.

"Come along Zeph, let's go and do some winning. Allow me to teach you how. Follow me."

With that fateful remark, Zephaniah trailed behind his spry grandfather. And together they walked in the direction of a group of men, who were talking as they sat on the sand beside their wicker picnic hamper and drinks cooler. They were all young looking, tanned, athletic; they'd been racing in the July regattas.

"*Gentlemen,*" Ollie announced as he walked up to the group of six strangers, "*my young grandson here would like to challenge you all to a 'Hermit Crab' race. He's only seven years old, and a tad shy. What do you say?*"

Perhaps it was the man's unblinking ice-blue eyes that brought them out of their easy conversation. Ollie was good at the disarming intrusion. Once the insideman always the insideman. First as an orphan, then as a grifter, he had known that most individuals (and *all* marks) have an internal schism that differentiates what people *say*, from what they *hear*.

"*Excuse me, sir?*" replied one of the men politely.

"*You know, 'Hermit Crab' racing. We'll draw a large circle in the sand and place our crabs in the middle of the circle and give them all names too! Then, whichever crab escapes across the circle line first wins the race. It's very simple and a lot of fun. Zephaniah here will go into the rock pools to find the crabs while you enjoy your drinks. So, what do you say?*"

Who would, or could, refuse an invitation like that, especially one that had been delivered by Ollie Swire? It took Zephaniah only a few minutes to find seven nearly equal sized crabs and less than one minute to etch out the large circle in the sand.

"*So, gentlemen, shall we begin? Zephaniah, place all the crabs on the sand and let the gentlemen choose their own. Whichever one is left will be ours. We wouldn't want them to think we had a pet racing crab, now, would we!*"

Zephaniah looked up at his grandfather; he knew he was being deadly serious. His grandfather's tone was now his 'business' voice. He hadn't laughed and his eyes had grown wide. Most telling of all, his grandfather had stopped calling him Zeph. Only Zephaniah.

Each of the six men chose their crabs, named them improbably, and the game began. Zephaniah and Ollie's brown hermit crab, which they called *Invincible*, kept losing, sometimes last, but never first. After half a dozen races, the competitive juices in the yachtsmen began to flow. Ollie caught this and declared: "*Gentlemen, now let's have some fun! How about a big-stakes game? Say, each of us put $5 a race into a pot,* *and let's say, four more races? The winner of the very last race wins the entire pot. How about it?"*

Ollie bargained on two men who appeared to have winning crabs bringing the other four to the party. One in particular – a brash Ivy Leaguer – stood out. Ollie was right. He had caught the man's 'tell', the one all marks had, imperceptible to all but an insideman. A devoutly avaricious eye-glint. Hastily, the man tossed a $20 bill on the sand.

"Good, here's Zephaniah's stake." Ollie bent down and placed his $20 next to the other. By the time Zephaniah had gathered up all the errant crabs, there was $140 wedged under a stone on the coarse Massachusetts sand.

Ollie had his hands deep in his pocket at the end of the third race as *Invincible* snailed towards the line, last again. Ollie paid no attention to the race; his eyes were tracking the competitive greed that had crept onto the brows of the wealthy yachtsmen. Straight away he clapped his hands loudly and scooped up *Invincible*. He placed him plum centre of the circle with the other crabs.

"OK! Final and winner-takes-all race. They're off!"

Invincible proved to be just that. Zephaniah's crab screamed across the sand and over the line. First by a country mile. And *Invincible* just carried on and on, hurtling as fast as a crab could in the direction of the cool rock-pools. Ollie picked up the $140 and handed the money to Zephaniah, who stuffed the cash in his shorts. They both thanked the men with wide smiles and took their leave with their winnings. A little perplexed, the yachtsmen's eyes stared as the fifty-year-old gentleman, who held the small boy's hand, calmly strolled away across the sand towards the parking lot.

Ollie drove the Alvis westwards in silence, allowing the taste of victory to distil in his grandson. With the hood down, the wind in their hair, the car swept them down-island towards Menemsha, until Ollie pulled off to the side of the road and got out of the car. He wanted to explain just how *Invincible* had won, when it had counted most. With a magician's flair he produced a very small phial of red paste from his pocket. He opened the phial, touched his finger to it and told Zephaniah to stick out his tongue: wow, it burnt, it stung, and it made him sweat a little.

Ollie assured his grandson that the burning sensation he was feeling was far, far less painful than it would have been to *Invincible*. He demonstrated how he'd dabbed a smidge of the home-made chilli paste into the mollusc's insides, seconds before he'd placed *Invincible* down for the final, and winning, race.

Zephaniah would always remember what his grandfather had said that afternoon as the Alvis glided effortlessly back out onto the road.

"I'd rather win than be right Zeph." PAUSE. "Who knows from what's right, who knows from what's wrong? But I do know two people who know about winning. Ollie and Zephaniah Swire."

His grandfather then turned obliquely to look at his grandson, his crystal-blue eyes narrowing. They had the patina of freshly cut slate, and all of its warmth.

That silent stare, etched into his young psyche, became Zephaniah's touchstone from that day on.

CHAPTER 13

**10 Crick Hill Road, Menemsha,
Martha's Vineyard, Massachusetts.
Wednesday, 17th January 1990. Late afternoon.**

"I spotted your plane in my binoculars, Zeph. You came in low over No Man's Land. Jeff usually flies you straight into the airport. Bad weather aloft?"

"You don't miss a beat do you, Ollie?" said Zephaniah. "It was a flight down memory lane. Remember those crab-racing stunts you used to pull?"

"I only pulled the first one! It was all you afterwards. You kept working and winning those beaches, year after year, you never quit . . ." Ollie laughed, his bright eyes coming alive. He loved his grandson. "Listen, Zeph, the best lesson I ever learnt is that you never learn any lessons. All this Buddhist nonsense that we're destined to repeat our mistakes until we learn from them is just that – nonsense. Every action, every reaction you confront is new. Whatever wisdom you think you've acquired along the way won't fit. Won't play. No two dawns are ever the same."

Ollie understood his grandson better than Zephaniah knew himself, and not because he'd taught him everything. Ollie couldn't help but notice any out-of-character act. Like a trip down memory lane. Lessons? No, not you, Zeph.

"Are you staying the night? Your room is made up."

"Yes, I'd like to. Nothing to rush back to Boston for."

"No one expecting you, Zeph?"

"My mind is elsewhere." He caught himself before continuing. "Ollie, tell me about No Man's Land, its history?"

"Pull up a chair and I'll fill you in on that strange, deserted little island. The Crane family bought the place in 1914 to keep cattle, hogs, even pheasants. They had family live there to look after it all. When Prohibition came along in 1920 – people forget that lasted until 1933 – the rum runners played cat 'n mouse with the Coast Guard for years. Always outran them as they headed to Oak Bluffs. During World War II Crane leased it to the US Navy for target practice, and they carried on during Korea and Vietnam too. As the 'gull flies, it's three miles from here. Nobody lives there now, or is even allowed to set foot there, it's a real no man's land. There are shipwrecks, but local fishermen still work the waters illegally, despite unexploded ordinance around the island. The Navy built a runway, but nowadays it's a lonesome deserted island is all."

Ideal, thought Zephaniah. His mind began to relax, safe in the comfort of his grandfather's company. He had long ago reconciled himself to the fact that Ollie had written his prologue – and probably his epilogue too – and he was OK with that. Out of the corner of his eye he caught the sun drift below, and out of the unsettled, ghostly white sky. He'd never seen a sky quite like it.

What's this about? thought Ollie. Perhaps a tedious history about a barren island, told only the way a grandfather could tell a story would flush out the truth.

He wasn't a gambling man, and he certainly wouldn't bet the ranch on any play, but now, he'd almost bet the ranch that his grandson was up to something. But what?

He suspected he'd have to wait. He gave good 'wait', did Ollie. He'd had a PhD in patience since 1905.

PART THREE

SATURDAY, 17TH AND SUNDAY, 18TH MARCH 1990

St Patrick's Day Weekend

CHAPTER 14

**Shiner's Diner, 86 Van Ness Street,
Fenway Park, Boston, Massachusetts.
Saturday, 17th March 1990. 20:10.
St Patrick's Day Weekend.**

People lived. People died. And the only people who *really* gave a damn were those caught in the wake of raging grief. It had been nearly two months since Jake and Amy Dealer had buried a son, a brother, a wife, a mother and their dog. Two hearts dead. Two hearts torn apart. And out of the anarchy of unknowable anguish, Jake had resolved to protect what remained of the survivors' hearts. During the days and nights that were full of endless pain following Lindy and Dougie's funerals, he'd been able to form the bare bones of a plan.

He would work the Long Island spring and summer from Montauk on *Sweet Amy*, doing anything and everything – from fishing to chartering – to raise money until Labor Day, Monday 3rd September. Then, he and Amy would leave Poseyville. Probably forever. Shadows had closed in on what remained of the Dealers and their traditions. With them came a dusk that would continue to encroach ever closer, ever darker. Jake understood this, like he understood the ocean, and that Amagansett would always remain haunted.

Marty Drew had offered to rent their house from Labor Day: *"Jake, you never know, Amy might want to return and here's how she can. Trust me on this."* Jake had appreciated Marty's generous offer – and agreed to it, as Marty had said, for Amy's sake. So, after Labor Day weekend, they would climb aboard the *Sweet Amy*, together with whatever they could carry in a couple of duffle bags, haul the stern lines aboard and head northeast: Martha's Vineyard, Nantucket, Cape Cod, Boston, Cape Ann, any port in Massachusetts. He'd considered heading further north into the wilderness to Maine, Nova Scotia and even Newfoundland. His mind wasn't yet made up. They weren't just names on a fisherman's chart, and all were as good as each other. The safe bet, however, was Gloucester, some forty miles northeast of Boston. It was America's oldest seaport, a solid working fishing town and community. It was a safe harbour in *any* storm. Even their storm. Almost 400 years of Atlantic fishing lore was embedded in the Cape Ann Peninsula: Essex, Gloucester, Rockport, Manchester-by-the-Sea. He could spend a season or two there. Besides, he'd heard the schools were good. That was going to be important. And a man with his credentials was sure to find work in the waters off Gloucester.

Amy was his sole priority, and when the East Hampton High School got out, he'd have an overnight holdall ready and collect her in his old flatbed Ford. Poseyville was haunted at the weekends, schooldays were already hard enough. Each weekend, they'd drive north into the night for hours as shadowless beings who had only each other.

* * *

On arriving in Boston late the night before, they'd spotted a small diner – Shiner's Diner – not far from the Freedom Trail Motel they'd checked into. Shiner's Diner was behind the famous baseball ground, Fenway Park. Warm and clean with thick aromas of coffee, home-fries, fresh eggs, pancakes and crisp bacon. All the customers, regulars by the look and sound, beamed with a homecoming relief as they walked in; it was that sort of place. The booths were nooks of upholstered red vinyl, the counter and stools a gleam of steel and red again. A 1950's Pepsi-Cola clock ticked away the time, and the walls were decorated with long-faded photos of Babe Ruth, Ted Williams, Carlton Fisk, Bobby Doerr and other Red Sox legends.

It was a slack Saturday evening; the beer 'n whiskey-fuelled revelries of St Patrick's Day were for other establishments. Jake stood inside the door holding Amy's hand and looked around for somewhere snug and safe.

A kindly lady (who Amy instantly took to be Mrs Shiner) spotted them as out-of-towners and hurried over to greet them.

"I've got just the booth for you two," she announced, and led them to a windowed corner with Fenway Park in view. "Shannon will be your server. I'll send her right over. Enjoy."

Almost immediately, a younger woman arrived with calm efficiency. Mid-thirties Jake guessed, tall and striking with red tousled hair, olive-green eyes, freckles and milk-white skin. The name badge on her gingham uniform read '*SHANNON*'. She had high cheekbones that hinted at an easy blush.

"Just arrived in town?" she asked as she handed over two menus.

"Yes, matter of fact," replied Jake, "but it's not our first time in Boston."

"Coffee while you decide?"

"Thank you, and a vanilla milkshake for my daughter please."

Amy looked around the diner and caught Mrs Shiner's eye as she bussed the counter customers. They swapped smiles, as she issued short orders to the cook working the ranges. Jake began to relax and take in the warmth of the diner and its mood. He soon became aware of a sense of security in Shiner's Diner, perhaps because like his own traditions, diners such as this were also becoming a footnote in a disappearing America.

Jake and Amy sat in silence – there had been many of late – but this one felt awkward, being in public, and all. Unsuccessfully, Jake tried to catch Shannon's attention. Not comfortable with the silence, he began to roll his sleeve up as Amy sipped her vanilla shake.

"Did I ever tell you the story Amy?"

"No," she answered with a feint and a tilt of her head. A smile creased her freckled cheeks. She slid her puzzle book aside. "But tell me again please."

Jake grinned at his twelve-year-old daughter, her long blonde hair falling around her face. He hooked his shirtsleeve over his muscled forearm and bicep. The tattoo on his right arm, the arm he threw his harpoon with, was large, six or more inches long, its blue ink had seeped deep into his skin, and it depicted in detail a man 'ironing' – harpooning – a mighty swordfish. The legend – '*Lindy*' – was scripted beneath. He'd had his only tattoo inked seven short days after meeting her. Twenty-three years ago. He'd been twenty-two. Lindy was twenty. The summer of 1967. Frankie Valli was singing 'Can't Take My Eyes Off You'. It was on every radio. All the time. Just for her. Just for Lindy.

"You're just too good to be true,
Can't take my eyes off you,
You'd be like heaven to touch,
I wanna hold you so much,
At long last love has arrived,
And I thank God I'm alive,
You're just too good to be true,
Can't take my eyes off you."

Jake poured milk into his coffee and spooned in sugar.

"Daddy, whadd'ya doin'? You're thinking about Dougie and Mom, aren't you?"

"Why do you say that?"

"You take your coffee black with no sugar . . ."

A heavy lump formed in Jake's throat, and he fought it back with a frown. Eyes averted, he fidgeted with his long-billed cap.

"Yep, I was thinking about your mother."

Amy began to blink back tears. And at that moment, the cavalry arrived.

"What do you think of Boston then?" asked Shannon, making eye contact with Amy.

"It's fun, I really like the Aquarium, but it's weird seeing people everywhere with green hair and green flowers."

"Well, it's St Patrick's Day weekend, and the Irish like to celebrate. Even I've got some dye in my hair today," said Shannon as she swished the green flecks in her unruly mane.

"Oh yeah! So, who's St Patrick?"

"He's the patron saint of Ireland," Shannon replied as she took her shamrock badge from her blouse and pinned it onto Amy's red woollen cardigan. "The flower's a shamrock, Ireland's emblem and St Patrick's flower. It's three leaves on one stalk, the Holy Trinity from One God." Shannon grimaced. "Well, that's what they say sweetheart." She caught a look in Jake's eye, as he lowered his head to look down at the tabletop.

With a tremor in his voice, he whispered, "We're not church-going folk. But thank you kindly for the shamrock."

Shannon asked in a soft lilt, "Now, what can I be getting you folks?" She took their food order and a silence once again descended on the booth. Jake gazed out of the window lost in the darkness. Amy made sure not to slurp her milkshake. Speedily, Shannon returned with their orders. Having set them down, she fixed her eyes on Jake's tattoo and his weather-beaten cap. She topped up his heavy white mug with fresh coffee.

"Forgive me for asking, sir, but are you a fisherman?"

"I was a fisherman. Not sure now," replied Jake.

"Then you still are. If there's salt water in your blood, there ain't nothing you can do about it. I'm from Gloucester, my family are fishing folk too."

"That's where my dad and me are headed in September. We're moving and I'm going to school there." Amy announced before adding, "my name's Amy Dealer and this is my dad. His name's Jake. Pleased to meet you."

"Likewise, Amy, Jake. My name's Shannon O'Leary. Well, Gloucester, that sounds exciting, so where's home now?"

"We're from Amagansett," Amy replied.

"Whereabouts is that?"

Good question, thought Jake, who continued to stare out of the booth's window. He'd seen enough ghosts for one night. "It's on the South Fork of Long Island, near East Hampton," he muttered.

Then he looked up.

Never in her life had Shannon O'Leary seen an expression like the one she received then. It wasn't discourteous or blunt. It was just as if she'd gazed deep into a chasm of abandonment, of aching loss. She had never seen a death-mask, but the shiver in the fisherman's gentle, dark brown eyes was one of unfathomable sadness. It held a mien that would remain with her for the rest of her life.

Jake caught the visible shock in her wide eyes and turned his head away.

Shannon wrote out their check while Jake continued to peer outside, his thoughts disturbed only by the aggressive Boston streetlights and the headlamps of passing cars. Rain was in the air and there was no one on the sidewalks to add dimension to the darkness. Instinctively,

Jake searched for the North Star, but the sky was cloaked in a pall of ominous clouds.

That was the one thing he'd observed about city-dwellers: no one ever looked up into the sky. Men of the sea always did. Day or night. Storm or shine. The Back Bay Fens beyond were as foreboding as the Atlantic's titanic swells that were a hurricane's postscript. Jake shuddered as if someone had walked over his grave.

He didn't look at the check but slid $20 under his coffee mug. Without acknowledging Shannon, he dipped his head, took Amy's hand and led her away from Shiner's Diner.

CHAPTER 15

**Corner of Palace Road and Tetlow Street,
Back Bay Fens, Boston, Massachusetts.
Sunday, 18th March 1990. 00:36.
St Patrick's Day Weekend.**

Zephaniah Swire poured a beaker of black coffee from his aluminium thermos and sipped on its dull warmth. Feline-like, he eased himself deeper into the leather seat of his dark blue Mercedes saloon. Coffee in hand, he drew the collar of his black cashmere overcoat up around his neck, partly for comfort, mostly for cover. Rain fell lazily onto the windshield from the dense foliage of the oak tree he'd chosen to park under.

He'd pulled up south of the Palace and Tetlow intersection, hidden from the streetlights on Palace Road. His military training had taught him to stake out vantage points. This was one of them. Sipping the coffee, he wasn't entirely sure why he'd wanted to view this part of his soon-to-unfold-production.

Snale had his full confidence, and the British mercenary who'd been recruited (Zephaniah had not, nor would he ever, meet him) had a flawless jacket. As always, Snale had followed his orders. Maybe, Zephaniah mused, he was merely curious to watch the actual curtain rise? That was it. Yes. The theatre's 'Safety Curtain' had already risen, when a few hours ago in Zephaniah's basement study, Snale had been fully briefed with all the essential details to ensure a rousing end to Act One.

All Snale had said was "Holy shit!" In fact, he had repeated it no less than three times. But Jimmy had known his employer far too long, and seen him work in too many different theatres to have stated the obvious: *"You* cannot *be serious Mr Swire?"*

If Snale had been in any doubt as to his employer's intentions, then the glimpse he'd caught of Lieutenant Swire's disquieting smile, made even more chilling by the backdrop of those frickin' jellyfish, enlightened him as to just how frickin' serious his employer was.

CHAPTER 16

**Freedom Trail Motel, Back Bay Fens, Boston, Massachusetts.
Sunday, 18th March 1990. 00:36.
St Patrick's Day Weekend.**

A sleep-sniper had relentlessly hunted Jake since the funeral. A highly skilled marksman, he squeezed the trigger to drill off a 7.62 mm round the instant Jake's eyes even fluttered. The sniper hit the bull's eye each time, leaving Jake pug-dog-eyed awake to study whichever ceiling he was lying under. And they were all the same. Jake had tried many tricks, from doing complex math problems, to reciting the alphabet backwards, all to no avail, unless being able to say ZYXWVUT . . . had become a marketable skill.

In turn, he shot a fleeting look at the night clock 00:36. Another bullet had just struck home. His eyes went to the other bed where, foetus-like, Amy lay in an uneasy sleep. Suddenly she kicked her legs from under the thin blanket. In the glow of the streetlights, he could make out small beads of sweat on her brow matting her soft blonde hair. Her breathing grew heavier – noises and incoherent words were forming deep inside her. For one so young the sounds were remote, other-worldly. Jake sat up to be ready for the inevitable; he'd waited at this dock many, many times in the last two months. His daughter was trapped in an infinite nightmare, yet he knew not to awaken her.

Amy's body began to thrash. Depending on how deep her sleep – and how overwhelming her terrors – he had to steady his hand. From bitter experience, she would wake soon. Her body would then be chilled by cold fear and sweat. It was always the same. Amy would literally scream herself awake, as if her frail body and her raw horrors couldn't co-exist. She would then lurch bolt upright, a primal yell hanging over her vocal cords. Overflowing, body-racking sobs would follow the screams that emanated from her pretty mouth and deep inside her soul. Then, when history repeated itself as it surely would, Jake would hold his daughter, would rock her, stroke her hair and wipe her brow until she drifted back into a another deep, but gentler sleep, only to awake in the morning having not remembered anything whatsoever.

"What nightmare, Daddy?"

This time though, Jake vowed, would be different. He would keep her awake. Go for a night-walk, to try to exorcise the demons from out of her soul. And then, like a dragon-slayer of old, he would slay these demons. Like he knew the sun would rise in a handful of hours, Jake would protect Amy until the oceans ceased to hold water, or his lungs ceased to hold air. Whichever came last.

CHAPTER 17

**Palace Road, Back Bay Fens, Boston, Massachusetts.
Sunday, 18th March 1990. 00:36.
St Patrick's Day Weekend.**

"When cops sit in a car doing fuck-all, do they have their caps on or off?"

"Why ask me? How'd I know, I'm a bloody Brit," hmm'd the mercenary. "My guess would be if the car was marked, yes, unmarked like ours, no."

"Well, take your cap off then."

"Snale, you concentrate on driving. My bloody cap hasn't been on since you picked me up."

"Don't get smart, OK?"

Snale headed slowly north on Palace Road towards The Fenway. Spotting a space, he parked the car in a gap next to Simmons University. He inched slowly forward, leaving the front wheels turned out should a fast getaway be needed. Only then did he cut the engine. Directly opposite was 2 Palace Road, and the side door he and his mercenary were to enter. Perfect. And in front of them lay the India-ink darkness of Boston's Back Bay Fens.

Snale cussed under his breath. Since returning from Vietnam, he'd undertaken many different jobs for the Swire family, but this one would be a first. He glanced at the crisp A5 piece of paper in his hands – it looked like a shopping list – which he knew had been typed earlier by Lieutenant Swire on his portable Olivetti Lettera 32 typewriter, the very same one he'd taken to war. As with the lieutenant's footprints: never a track to follow, never a carbon. One original *only*. A Swire tic. One of many. Even the letters he'd typed out late into the night in the officer's mess – alone, and over and above his duty – to the families Stateside who'd lost sons, grandsons and nephews; no copy was ever taken. Snale flipped the sheet over to study a pencilled sketch of a floor plan; it resembled a route map of a store's aisles marked with numbered X's.

Of course, there'd been 'legal undertakings' before (he'd long grasped that to his employer 'legal' had as broad a definition as Texas and Rhode Island were analogous, size-wise) but this was a first. Outright theft of someone else's property had not been on any agenda. Until now, that is. The returning of goods to their rightful owner, in the aftermath of an unwanted or commissioned theft – unwanted *only* by Swire's that is – by a money laundering South American drug baron or a philistine Japanese *Yakuza*, yes. That was all OK by him, after all, they had obtained the artworks by larceny in the first place. But theft on 'our' own book? No. But with Lieutenant Swire there would be an endgame, of this Snale was sure. What the hell it would play out to be – well, that was anybody's wildcat guess. And it certainly would be wildcat, and certainly beyond his comprehension and paygrade.

Snale's continued daily existence meant that he'd forever owe Lieutenant Swire his unswerving devotion. He was a Native American. It was tribal. It had been their way for centuries. He owed a debt of life. His. So, it was his duty to obey without question. Yet even he'd grasped earlier that afternoon that if it all went according to the immaculately researched plan he'd been briefed on (and there was no reason it shouldn't), this 'undertaking' would be the greatest theft of artworks in this century.

Frickin' Nazis excluded, of course.

CHAPTER 18

**West Fens area, Boston, Massachusetts.
Sunday, 18th March 1990. 00:52.
St Patrick's Day Weekend.**

Jake was well and truly lost.
He had dressed hastily and crept away from the motel, holding a reluctant Amy's hand. He had kept her pyjamas on and just pulled her sweater and jeans over them; it was cold outside. Then he'd swaddled her in a windcheater. He yanked his long-billed cap down, tugged at his own windcheater and together they'd crossed Boylston Street to head south towards the Back Bay Fens.

It was a raw, wet and friendless night. And the Fens, despite the oaks, willows and wild reeds sure wasn't Amagansett. Even the Canada geese ignored them. The earthen paths had turned to patties of cloying mud. Two large garbage bins had been upended. Trash and detritus were on the wind, not the ground. Despite it all, Jake sensed that it was crucial that Amy stay awake tonight. The nightmare from which she had just awoken had been the worst he'd ever witnessed. He had to try to bump her back into life. Her skin had had a mortuary-chill; her brow ran with the sweat of the condemned. Jake had been afraid, very afraid, yet he knew from storms past that fear was only a wish that something would end. And he had *needed* Amy's nightmares to end. Her anguish was beginning to cloud her eyes like the anvils of a *cumulonimbus*; and all those clouds ever did was shut out light, create violent storms, generate thunder and lightning, hailstones the size of golf balls and induce terror before taking flight and leaving behind havoc, as if it were a mere comma in its passing. If the nightmares continued like this, they could haunt her forever.

Lost and tired, he tried in vain to retrace his steps back to their motel. It was difficult here on land, especially under a low, mean cloud base with no celestial sky to guide him. On the ocean there would be no problem. *Terra firma* was hostile. Seawater was a trusted ally. Ever hopeful, he stared up into the murk of the night sky. In vain he sought out the Polestar but found only pewter as chill rain ran off the peak of his cap onto his cheeks.

When he was Dougie's age, his father had taught him how to locate the Polestar: *"At night Jake there are about 2,000 stars visible to the naked eye, so, first you'll have to find the Plough, and when you're locked onto it, look to its right, and there will be Cassiopeia. It's a large constellation shaped like a 'W', and it'll be right at the very end of the Milky Way. Now, trace an imaginary line from the Plough's handle,"* – his father had swept an arc in the heavens – *"and there, Jake, plum in the middle of your imaginary line, you'll find the Polestar, and with it, your way home."*

Tonight, when Jake pleaded with the night sky, it failed an honest ally.

CHAPTER 19

**Palace Road, Back Bay Fens, Boston, Massachusetts.
Sunday, 18th March 1990. 01:17.
St Patrick's Day Weekend.**

Snale pressed the LED button on his Casio watch. Its green-hued light blinked 01:17. He slid the list and floorplan into the top pocket of his dark blue Boston Police Department uniform. Looking at his reflection in rear-view mirror, he dabbed at his false black moustache and touched the cold steel of his pistol; only he knew that both his and the mercenary's weapons were loaded with blanks.

"Check yourself and your moustache too," he ordered, angling the mirror to the right. Then, pushing his spectacles onto the bridge of his nose, he slapped the mercenary's muscled thigh. "Come on let's go."

Peering through the rain-splattered windshield, all he registered were eerie silhouettes thrown towards the Back Bay Fens by the lights of the faux Venetian *palazzo* that was the Isabella Stewart Gardner Museum.

Nothing could stop them now, save for a direct order from Lieutenant Swire. But he was not here to issue an order to retreat, let alone sound the Last Post. No sir, his employer would be tucked up in his bed sleeping the sleep of the innocent. That was for shit sure.

CHAPTER 20

**Palace Road, Back Bay Fens, Boston, Massachusetts.
Sunday, 18th March 1990. 01:20.
St Patrick's Day Weekend.**

Whether it was the nightmare that had exhausted her, or just the cold, wet night Jake no longer cared. He wanted her back in their motel. In bed. Exorcising her demons would just have to wait. He opened his windcheater and hauled her up into his chest. His strong arms held her tight as her head flopped in final surrender onto his damp shoulder. Amy once again found sleep.

Rounding a path in between a thicket of willows and weather-beaten bull-rushes, Jake caught sight of a large well-lit building that loomed like an iceberg. Speedily, he scrambled up a small incline from the muddy path towards it and the main road that was The Fenway.

There in the middle-distance he spotted two uniformed police officers walking towards him up the side road that ran beside the strange looking building. A compact car, like Lindy's, slowed to a crawl and halted his progress across The Fenway.

Its driver, a lone woman, glared at this man in his forties who held a young girl with long wet blonde hair to his chest on a night such as this; the girl's face was hidden by a yellow windcheater. Oddly, she noticed, the tall man who carried the girl wore his windcheater's sleeves rolled up above his elbows; she caught sight of a tattoo.

The driver wound her window down – eager to record what she saw – as if she one day might have to scrutinise an I.D. parade. Jake's frantic eyes locked onto hers: his look was one of desperation, hers was one of hostile suspicion.

Hurrying on over The Fenway towards Palace Road, Jake shouted into dead air, "Officers, officers . . . Hold up! Please, please . . ."

The compact picked up speed, leaving behind a halo of crimson tail lights in an accusatory blur.

CHAPTER 21

**Corner of Palace Road and Tetlow Street,
Back Bay Fens, Boston, Massachusetts.
Sunday, 18th March 1990. 01:20.
St Patrick's Day Weekend.**

Zephaniah Swire understood only too well, from lessons learned from both Ollie and Vietnam – that there was no such thing as the 'perfect operation'. If that was a given – and it was – then it followed that there could never be the 'perfect crime'. You *would* get caught. There were just too many imponderables: the lists of details, would never actually be complete, and all the bases could never be covered. Forget human nature at your peril. No. Never. Ever.

It was as if all man-made actions were disasters waiting to happen. A cluster-fuck of minor incidents, which when taken singularly, meant nothing whatsoever. But deus ex machina, when all the minor incidents were gathered by chance, by coincidence, by whomever had made the pips in avocados too big – who knew, who cared – whoever 'they' were – when 'they' FUBAR'd the minor shit, that *would* beget a catastrophe. Life was all in the minor details. For when He, the one who'd goofed up baboon's asses, grounded ostriches, and messed with squishy green fruits, loused up on the 'small stuff', imagine what He would do when the 'big stuff' blew into His Universe.

But not tonight.

For Zephaniah Swire knew precisely why the pips in avocados had been made far too big. That's where the vinaigrette went. He *had* thought of everything.

* * *

So the dispatcher of Trans Florida Flight 733 from Tampa to New Orleans had a fight with his girlfriend. So the Captain broke the 'eight-hour-between-bottle-and-throttle' rule by just one hour – blame that on the foxy brunette stewardess from Minneapolis. So the co-pilot had only a few hours on type. So Trans Florida's forecaster hadn't logged United Airlines' prior wind-shear alert. So the McDonald Douglas MD-80 rolled on runway 18L fourteen seconds early, and the co-pilot called V1 six knots before he should have, on account of the dispatcher overlooking the last minute cargo-addition – revenue was revenue and there was talk of layoffs. So the Captain's reactions were one step behind the beat . . . but what actually 'turned' a routine flight was when they took off behind a 'Heavy' – a Boeing 747. If it had been a 737 or a 727 none of the individual incidents would have added up to anything more than . . . an uneventful flight from Florida to Louisiana. But, the MD-80 had been doomed long before it was flipped inside the 747's wake-turbulence. And the future of the 108 souls aboard Trans Florida 733 was to be a welcome surprise breakfast for the Everglades' alligators.

* * *

Deus ex machina and the small stuff.

Zephaniah had read that story in the *Miami Herald* a few years ago and committed each detail to memory as an example of how anonymous minutiae govern lives. There was no perfect operation. Ergo there could be no perfect crime. To believe you could have planned such an event was to commit an act of monumental hubris. You'd be scalped for even thinking it. All this and more, he fully understood as he watched a tall man, who clutched a child to his chest, bear down on Jimmy Snale and the mercenary.

CHAPTER 22

**Corner of Palace Road and Tetlow Street,
Back Bay Fens, Boston, Massachusetts.
Sunday, 18th March 1990. 01:21.
St Patrick's Day Weekend.**

An instinctive reflex for self-preservation made Zephaniah slink lower into the foxhole that was the seat of his Mercedes.

'Jimmy, you're a Boston cop on patrol. Behave like one. Calmly, Jimmy, you're a Boston Blue remember. The enemy is approaching at haste. The girl may *not be what she seems. Caution, Jimmy, caution.'* Lieutenant Swire whispered his orders to Sergeant Snale just as he'd done so many times.

The predicament tonight was that Jimmy wasn't in the same foxhole. They were in different parts of the jungle; and this jungle wasn't verdant and steaming with rotting vegetation. It was concrete and wet and even more hostile.

And Lieutenant Swire hadn't noticed the approaching compact car. Why should he have? He had never taken his eyes off his men. Not once.

CHAPTER 23

**Palace Road, Back Bay Fens, Boston, Massachusetts.
Sunday, 18th March 1990. 01:21.
St Patrick's Day Weekend.**

"Excuse me Officer, I'm lost. I need to get back to the Freedom Trail Motel. It's near Fenway Park, you know, the baseball ground."

Jake, slightly out of breath tried to steady himself so that Amy could keep on sleeping.

"Look, sorry, we're on an emergency call! Can't stop!" Pausing in his tracks the police officer pointed north, "Fenway Park is over there."

"I know Officer, but I need better directions." Jake's voice held a plea.

"We're on our way to a brutal domestic, a crime scene."

"But . . ."

Jake's immediate reflex was to free his right arm. He went to grab one of the officers, who recoiled instantly.

"Whoa! Not advisable, sir!"

One of the officer's lurched back onto his left foot. The other's right hand fell to his side.

"Sorry Officer. My mistake. Sorry."

Jake, now steady and with the benefit of a streetlight, looked at both men in same way he would scan his instruments on *Sweet Amy*: with skill, with speed, with precision, with piercing eyes. And the police officer caught the hard stare.

The more senior looking of the two officers appeared to be in his late thirties, early forties, Jake's age maybe. He was shorter though, perhaps 5' 10', and wore gold rimless John Lennon type glasses. The face was narrow, and even under the streetlight he registered a darker, pock-marked complexion. He sported a heavy black moustache that was out of sync with the short hair that came out from under his cap. The other cop was an altogether different fish: over 6', heavy set in a robust and military way, younger too, early thirties, longer thicker hair, in need of a cut. Jake noticed that it hung over his collar. But he was powerful, 200 pounds at least, the sort of man you'd want on the deck of your dragger in a Gale Force 8. He had a rounder face, with an almost identical black moustache. And he hadn't uttered one word. It was as if he hadn't grasped where he was. Added to which, Jake thought it was odd that neither of the radios hanging from their heavy belts had so much as crackled. Weren't they heading to a crime? Why was the larger, younger man fidgeting with the grip of his police-issue pistol?

"Please Officers, where will I find a cab at this time of night?"

In the way the Dealers had always lived by their intuitions, Jake sensed that perhaps, just perhaps – and that was good enough for him – he and Amy were in danger; were better off on their own. Away from this place. Away from these police officers.

"Head back across The Fenway towards the Boston Art Museum, it's not even two blocks away, the large building over there. Cut behind it, and you might find a cruiser. Good luck fella."

The officer then turned on his heel to head back down Palace Road, from whence he and the other cop had come. Momentarily, Jake anchored himself under the streetlight as the two officers seemed to hurry *away* from the crime scene, they'd said they were going to.

"Strange," he murmured to himself as he turned towards The Fenway and Back Bay Fens. He squeezed Amy reassuringly. She was all that mattered now.

"Dammit," whispered Zephaniah coolly to an audience of none, as he observed Snale and the mercenary head to the museum and the scene of the yet-to-be-committed-crime. Concealed in the seat's dark leather, he pondered with a cynical smile on the absolute inevitability of 'small details'.

Fortunately, his own brutal survival instincts had placed him precisely where he now was. Observing a small detail.

CHAPTER 24

**Isabella Stewart Gardner Museum, Employee Entrance,
2 Palace Road, Boston, Massachusetts.
Sunday, 18th March 1990.
St Patrick's Day Weekend.**

01:22

Richard 'Rick' Abath, one of only two nightwatchmen, had worked the museum's 'graveyard shift' – midnight to 08:00 – for almost a year. The part-time job paid $6.85 per hour, but it suited the long-haired, twenty-three-year-old full-time *Grateful Dead* fan's free-wheeling lifestyle. A music-school dropout, his shifts sometimes included a bottle of wine in an empty gallery, some shut-eye on one of Mrs Jack's pieces of furniture that littered – literally – her museum, or a 'toothpick' spliff of Jamaica's finest in its courtyard gardens, with only the night's bats for company.

Despite the antedeluvian security system, something he griped about, it was an OK gig. A pitstop between his real gig of being a guitarist with *Ukiah*, his so-very-not-so-grunge band. Unarmed, save for a flashlight and walkie-talkie – and wearing a tie-dyed shirt and sporting his black Stetson – he sat behind the security desk with its four black and white TVs, monitoring the outside perimeter.

But now, Abath studied the inside of his eyelids instead, content that the panic button was within arm's reach. This solitary red panic button inside the pokey security office was the *only* in-place alarm in the entire, sprawling faux-Venetian *palazzo*. Strapped for cash, the Isabella Stewart Gardner Museum's board of seven Harvard-educated trustees had, in their infinite wisdom, deemed this *solitary* button to be a sufficient 'system' to alert the *outside* world should any problem arise *inside* the museum.

Meanwhile, the *only* other security guard, Randy Hestand, twenty-five, and on his first graveyard shift as a relief for the regular nightwatchman, was taking his own ponderous time ambling around the creaking, empty wooden stairs, corridors and galleries of Mrs Isabella Stewart Gardner's expansive mansion.

CHAPTER 25

**Isabella Stewart Gardner Museum, Employee Entrance,
2 Palace Road, Boston, Massachusetts.
Sunday, 18th March 1990.
St Patrick's Day Weekend.**

01:24 – 01:48

Rick Abath shook himself out of a nap. He grazed his eyes over the four screens and saw two Boston policemen approaching the heavy oak door of the museum's employee entrance. The door's overhead camera showed the shorter of the two men reach for the entry-buzzer.

"Police! We're here about the disturbance. Open up!"

What disturbance, thought Abath. OK, it was St Patrick's Day weekend and some drunk fool had climbed over a fence, or pranked a 911 call, or the clowns on duty at Simmons University had called the police. This was all he needed right now.

He groaned, opened a black lever arch file and scanned the standing protocol: *'In the event of a member of the Boston Police, or other US Government Agency, requiring entry, first call Boston Police with the badge numbers to obtain verification. Time log your call and name and the rank and badge number of the officer answering the call. Under NO circumstances allow entry without said verification.'* Clear enough.

He studied the monitor. They looked like BPD. Proper uniforms. Patches on their shoulders. Full-lapel insignias. And the one who'd buzzed was even wearing rimless glasses. All seemed A-OK. Ignoring protocol, Abath buzzed them into the 'man trap', a small space between the street entrance door, and the second – locked – door to the museum proper. There was a glass observation screen into the 'man trap' from the desk; all the better to see their credentials before calling BPD for verification.

Once off the street and inside the 'man trap' Snale barked. "You alone? Anyone else here with you?"

"Just one other guy, he's on his rounds."

"Well get him down here now!" Snale snarled the command, as only a US Ranger sergeant could.

Abath grabbed his walkie-talkie, hit the PTT button and instructed Hestand to return to the security office ASAP.

"I think I recognise you. You look kinda familiar," Snale narrowed his eyes through his fake spectacles. He got right in the goofy-looking nightwatchman's face through the glass screen that separated them. All he had to do was get him on the back foot. "I think we've a warrant for your arrest. Come out from behind the desk and show us some ID. Right now!" Snale wanted him far away from the desk's 'panic button'. The one Lieutenant Swire had briefed him on earlier.

Abath had no warrants, but he knew the BPD to be aggressive. If he didn't comply, he could be arrested, tossed in a holding cell and would miss the *Grateful Dead* playing in Hartford later that Sunday night. Compounding his first mistake of allowing the two men into the 'man trap', Abath stepped out from behind the desk. Outmanned, he now faced two armed men. And up close, they each were sporting identical fake black moustaches. These two *were* hoods. Fuck! They're *not* police officers, Abath figured. And I let them in . . .

Within seconds, Snale hauled Abath's head against the wall, kicked his legs apart and slapped handcuffs on him; he didn't even frisk him. Then, Randy Hestand unlocked the museum door and walked into the 'man trap'. The mercenary abruptly spun him around, spread-eagled his legs and snapped handcuffs on him.

"Am I being arrested?" Hestand demanded incredulously.

Snale and the mercenary ignored the perfectly reasonable question. A few moments later, the mercenary responded politely, in an accent that wasn't Bostonian. "Gentlemen." Pause. "This is a robbery." Pause. "Please don't give us any trouble, and you won't get hurt," he added matter-of-factly.

"Don't worry. They don't pay me enough to get hurt," sneered Rick Abath.

* * *

Snale and the mercenary pulled a couple of rolls of grey duct tape from their coat pockets. Methodically, they 'mummified' the heads of both handcuffed nightwatchmen – vertically and horizontally – blacking out their vision and covering their mouths, leaving only breathing holes. Then they carefully proceeded to frogmarch them down the stairs into the murky basement. They had no need to ask how to get there; Snale's earlier briefing from his CO had been as clear as a sea-eagle's eye.

And they took their time. Why rush? The Isabella Stewart Gardner Museum had long ago been abandoned by its own appalling security. There were no trip wires, no video cameras secreted in the panelling, no beams of Hollywood infrared wizardry, no alarms. Mindboggling though it seemed to both Snale and the mercenary, there were just two hapless nightwatchmen in their twenties – one of whom was a stoner – to safeguard more than 7,500 paintings, sculptures, furniture, silverware and ceramics, 1,500 rare books and over 7,000 archival objects collected from far and wide: from Rome to Asia and all across Europe and the Americas. Artefacts worth literally hundreds of millions of dollars.

Until the next shift change at 08:00, Mrs Gardner's mausoleum would be as defenceless as true guilt. It was theirs to do with as they saw fit. And they owned it.

Once in the basement, Randy Hestand was handcuffed with a second pair of cuffs to an old sink, while Rick Abath was seated on a chair and cuffed to a standpipe beside a workbench. More duct tape was wound around their hands and feet. Snale rummaged through Abath's pockets in search of his wallet; the mercenary did likewise with Hestand.

"OK, we know where you both live," announced the mercenary reading their driver's licences aloud. His voice was calm and polite, relaxed even. "Continue to do as we say, and no harm will come to you. If you don't tell them anything later, you'll get a reward from us in about a year." (Other than a large bag of marijuana Rick Abath found outside his house a year or so later, there would be no rewards.)

Snale checked his Casio. Twenty-four minutes was all it had taken to 'overpower' and secure the Isabella Stewart Gardner Museum. So, like the dutiful NCO he was, he fished out his CO's shopping list from his top pocket.

CHAPTER 26

**Isabella Stewart Gardner Museum, Employee Entrance,
2 Palace Road, Boston, Massachusetts.
Sunday night, 18th March 1990.
St Patrick's Day Weekend.**

01:48 – 02:45: The Dutch Room, and the Short Gallery and the Blue Room.

The extensive catalogue of the museum's atrocious security deficiencies was further evidenced by a typed Aerotech motion detector message sent three minutes after Snale and the mercenary had walked up the marble stairs and entered the Dutch Room for the first time. At 01:51 it typed out: *'Someone is in the Dutch Room. Investigate immediately.'*

It was the first of many messages, from over sixty Aerotech motion detectors, that were delivered that night. However, they were *only* delivered to the *only* museum security office. The one without any guards. Nowhere else. Not to a central alarm company. Not to the BPD. Just to the junky little office with its four old black and white TV monitors, and a steel garbage bin full of polystyrene coffee cups.

And it was in the pale green silk-walled Dutch Room that many of the museum's greatest treasures – in total, four Rembrandts, a Vermeer and a Flinck – were to be found.

Snale would later comment (still in disbelief) to Lieutenant Swire: *"Take candy from a baby. It cries out. It raises an alarm. You were on the money sir when you said we'd only have Mrs Gardner's ghost to watch us."*

#1 on Snale's list hung on the south wall of the Dutch Room. Rembrandt's *Christ in the Storm on the Sea of Galilee*. Finished in 1633, when he was twenty-seven, it was the only seascape the seafaring Dutchman ever painted. The magnificent oil tableau (63 in x 50 3/8 in) depicts Christ calming not only the sea, but his apostles during a terrifying thunderstorm. Next to it was #2, Rembrandt's *A Lady and Gentleman in Black*, a double portrait also painted in 1633 (51 13/16 in x 42 15/16 in). Mrs Gardner had purchased both paintings in London in 1898. A few weeks later, her husband dropped dead of 'apoplexy' in his Boston club, aged sixty-one.

Snale re-scanned his list. "'#3. Rembrandt. Self-portrait. Etching.' Any ideas?" he asked brusquely. Both men looked around the Dutch Room. All they saw was a large oil painting of a young man, in an immense gilt frame, whom they presumed was a youthful Rembrandt staring down at their plundering disapprovingly. Anchored to the wall, they struggled with it – unlike *Galilee* and *Lady and Gentleman*, which were painted on canvas, – they soon discovered that the self-portrait had been painted on a heavy, solid wooden panel. Straight away, they discarded it as being too unwieldly. Moreover, it wasn't #3. As if it were an afterthought, and hanging just below the dado, Snale's gimlet eye caught sight of a small frame nailed to a cabinet, which held a tiny etching: *Portrait of the Artist as a Young Man* circa 1633. The miniature self-portrait mystified Snale – it was the size of large postage stamp (1 3/4 in x 1 15/16 in) – but it certainly wasn't his place to question. #3 was in the bag.

Snale's life wasn't one where art had ever featured, any more than his life had been one where rights amended wrongs. However, #4 on his CO's list, held him as flesh holds bone. Perhaps it was the streetlight's flavescent serenade, one that washed through the window and across Vermeer's *The Concert* that captivated him. Beside the window, a comfortable chair had been placed in front of the easel, the better to admire the painting. He sat down and studied the small oil-on-canvas (28 9/16 in x 25 1/2 in) before lifting it from its easel. Having done so, he removed it from the frame, which he then discarded. Little did he appreciate that for those few frozen moments in time, he alone 'owned' one of the, if not *the*, single most valuable artworks in the entire world.

Long believed to have been painted by Rembrandt (and it had been purchased as such) was #5, *Landscape with an Obelisk* (21 7/16 in x 27 15/16 in). In the 1980s it was attributed to one of his followers, Govaert Flinck, who'd painted it in oil – on an oak panel – in 1638. Being a landscape, it had pride of place beside a sunlit window overlooking the museum courtyard. Snale removed the painting from its tabletop stand and added the work to the growing swag.

Standing in front of the south wall and to the right of the now empty space where *Christ in the Storm on the Sea of Galilee* had hung, was a low wooden table covered in fabric. Above which hung Francisco de Zurbarán's giant portrait, *A Doctor of Law*. The painting was as tall as a New England Patriots quarterback and at the 1635 law professor's feet #6 was to be found. Hushed by the immense painting above, the bronze beaker, a *Gu*, resembled a medium-sized 'waisted' vase (10 7/16 in x 6 1/8 in). It was of Chinese origin and had probably served as a vessel in ancient rituals to hold liquids. It dated from 1200 BC – the Shang Dynasty – and it was one of the oldest pieces in Mrs Jack's emporium; she'd purchased it in Boston in 1922. Snale double-checked his list. There it was. Halfway down his CO's inventory. So, he tucked it under his arm. And that was the haul from the Dutch Room.

As if the *Gu* and the Rembrandt stamp-sized etching weren't idiosyncratic enough, there was more to come. They passed through the Early Italian Room, the Raphael Room and into the Short Gallery. One of the smallest rooms in the museum, it housed all manner of personal artworks, books, sketches and even bric-a-brac, as well as portraits of Mr and Mrs Jack Gardner. Inside the cluttered space, Snale and the mercenary busied themselves with what appeared to be a mixed bag of further idiosyncrasies. A selection of five Degas sketches in different media. Pencil, charcoal, chalk, watercolour and washes, their themes were horse racing, dance and music: *Three Mounted Jockeys, Leaving the Paddock, Procession on a Road Near Florence, Studies (2) for the programme de la soirée artistique du 15 Juin 1884*. Five artworks in total were secreted away with the plunder from the Dutch Room. In a corner, somewhat neglected, languished a Napoleonic battle flag. Atop the *tricolore* was a gilded bronze eagle finial, with the figure '1' beneath its talons. It was the insignia of the *First Regiment of Grenadiers of Foot of Napoleon's Imperial Guard*. The heavy finial – ten inches tall – was #12, and the final piece to be taken from the Short Gallery.

At approximately 02:28, Snale and the mercenary decided to check the two hog-tied guards in the basement. Again, Snale was following orders. Making no pretence at stealth, they clumped down the stairs – no buck-skinned tiptoeing for these foot soldiers. Abarth, with deft humour – gallows or otherwise – was humming Bob Dylan's 'I Shall Be Released' as best he could through a taped mouth, as Hestand pondered upon his fate in silence.

The mercenary asked, in a considerate tone, if each guard was OK? If the handcuffs were too tight? The tone was coarse – British perhaps? – and he finished with a statement: *"You'll be hearing from us."* He was following Snale's orders, who in turn was following his CO's script. What was that about thought Snale, knowing that his CO would've had a reason.

Finally, they returned to the ground floor to find #13 and complete the list. *Chez Tortoni* (10 1/4 in x 13 3/8 in) had been painted in 1875 by Édouard Manet and it hung in the Blue Room, next to the main, public entrance. It was the only painting appropriated from the ground floor. Snale took it down from its very unsecure 'secure wall bolts', and removed it from the frame which he leant against a table leg; unbeknownst to the mercenary, he was far from finished with it.

"You stay here, I've one last errand," Snale informed the mercenary as he gathered up *Chez Tortoni's* gilt frame. He left the Blue Room, checked his layout map and headed off down the corridor to Lyle Grindle's small office. Grindle was (at this moment in time at least) the Isabella Stewart Gardner Museum's Security Director. Snale hefted a boot at the hasp and the locked door flew open; why was Grindle's office locked? Nothing else was. Again, he shook his head in amazement. For no other reason than 'proof' – if it were indeed needed – he snatched up the motion detectors' dot-matrix printouts of all their movements that night. Lieutenant Swire would skim over them, shake his head too, and enjoy using them as kindling in the drawing room's hearth. Snale left the computer's hard-drive backup in place; removing paintings was one thing, footling around with geek-tech was something else altogether. Following orders to the letter was a way of life for him, and Lieutenant Swire had instructed him to leave the *Chez Tortoni* frame on the Security Director's office chair.

Zephaniah Swire had mulled over whether the frame was to be an anonymous 'calling card' or a 'thank you card'. By the time he'd given Snale his earlier orders, he'd decided the frame was a rare beast. It was to be a two-fer.

***

02:41 – 02:45

Security Director Lyle Grindle's store-bought desktop registered the employee entrance door opening at 02:41 and closing – for the last time – at 02:45.

***

02:47

Sergeant Snale and the mercenary took three minutes to load their plunder into their modest, unmarked 'police' car on Palace Road. He looked at the Casio's stopwatch. It informed him they'd been 'on property' for eighty-one minutes. The CO was correct. Again. He'd said the mission would take less than ninety minutes.

Together with the disparate collection of thirteen works of priceless art, they simply vanished into the night's shadows, never to be heard of again.

Like the echo of a sigh fading away. Soon gone. And forevermore . . .

CHAPTER 27

Palace Road, Boston, Massachusetts.
Sunday, 18th March 1990. 02:49.
St Patrick's Day Weekend.

All Snale had to do now was drive to South Station, no more than fifteen minutes at this time of night, to drop off the mercenary. Then he had a ten-minute drive to Louisburg Square to deliver the full shopping basket to his employer before heading home. He looked up and down Palace Road and eased out into the deserted street. The mercenary unobtrusively removed his Boston Police uniform and yanked off his false moustache, balling them up into the foot-well. He then grabbed a bag from the back seat. He pulled on a heavy black sweater, black track-pants and a snug baseball cap. No labels. No logos. Snale took the bag from him and slid a hefty, padded envelope inside it. All this was performed in absolute silence. Words were not their currency of choice. Actions, even silent ones, were. As was money, of course.

"In there is the rest of your fee. Taped to the envelope you'll find $200 in small bills for incidentals at South Station and Logan, the airport's only ten minutes from South. Taped to the other side of the envelope is your airline ticket to London. After I drop you, wait until three hours before your departure before you take a cab to Logan. Understood?"

The mercenary merely nodded as if to say *nothing less or nothing more was expected*. Both the mercenary and Jimmy Snale had been professional soldiers for long enough to know that you spent more hours planning your escape than you did planning your attack. If you wanted to stay alive, that is.

"Snale, why did you have me say before we left, *'You'll be hearing from us?'*"

"Because my employer told me you had to say those exact words. That's his business, not ours. You did it well too, you sounded like that actor of yours, what's his name? He was in that movie where they heisted all the gold?"

"Michael Caine," the mercenary smiled. "I can't believe we're having this bloody conversation."

"Fair enough. But stay alive for the next five years. My boss likes to pay his bonuses. That's the way he wants things."

"It's been a very unusual assignment," he added quietly as an afterthought. "Thanks for the job, Snale." The mercenary continued to look ahead, scanning the road as they turned right onto The Fenway, as if his very life might depend on it. Which, in fact, it did.

* * *

Zephaniah Swire held the Zeiss night-vision monocular to his right eye. He kept his unblinking scrutiny on the hired help before training it on Jimmy. He creased a grin. He could read his Sergeant's expressions like the proverbial book. This one barked: *All clear Lieutenant. Mission Accomplished.*

Solid work, Jimmy.

PART FOUR

SUNDAY, 18TH AND MONDAY, 19TH MARCH 1990

CHAPTER 28

**Poseyville, Amagansett, Long Island, New York.
Sunday, 18th March 1990. Early morning.**

After Amy's harrowing nightmare, and his run-in with the shifty BPD patrolmen, Jake decided to flee Boston without any further delay. He bundled Amy up inside a blanket he'd torn off the bed and paid the motel bill in cash. He laid her exhausted body down to sleep on the bench seat, and then raced out of the city in the dead of night to head south to Amagansett and its ghosts.

Each dawn used to bring an understanding to Jake. With the rising sun – to Jake it was nature's true rainbow – came the promise that all would be well with the world. As the sun climbed higher it imbued him with a purpose, at the same time as reaffirming the Dealers' place in the world. Then, with Lindy's first smile, the frown of sleep would disappear. And all *was* well with the world. But that was another life. Another dream.

Jake hoofed the yard's fog-slicked earth 'n gravel like an impatient bull. His broad shoulders were stiff, and he tried to loosen them; they used to ache from hard work, now it was from no sleep and long drives. During the journey home last night from Boston, he'd taken another decision.

All that he needed, as he watched the sun try – and fail – to burn off the grey-bearded fog that had crept in before dawn, was the 'when' and the 'how'. The cold and the fog were seeping into his bones and the dry paste of ashes clammed up his mouth. He shivered as if someone had trodden on his grave. He yanked up his collar. For Jake, fog at sea made his senses taut and deepened the isolation between ocean and man. He didn't fear fog, he greatly respected it. Usually, within thirty minutes of being at sea, all the conventional norms of right, wrong, blame and responsibility would disappear. It was him, the fish, and the glacial ocean, with its suspiciously warm lips eager to embrace you if you so much as put one foot wrong. And in the far distance, the smudge on the horizon that had been land, that had been chaos, would soon disappear from sight. The weather, well, like this morning, it was rarely anybody's true friend.

After the horror of Amy's nightmare, he was going to leave her to sleep. He fidgeted in his breast pocket for what felt like a small pebble but was in fact a solitary pearl. It had been Lindy's pearl. He'd had given it to her within days of meeting her. *"You know something Lindy, Greek fishermen believed that pearls were made when lightning struck the water, and the Polynesians said that pearls were their god's teardrops. I read that someplace, kinda makes sense too . . ."*

Ever since he had found her hanging from the rafters, her neck broken by his seine net, he'd kept her pearl next to his heart. And at sunrise he would hold it tightly in his fist and ask for her forgiveness. A lightning bolt of forgiveness. A teardrop of forgiveness. Just forgiveness. Please . . .

Over by Blondie's now forsaken kennel, the sun had swept away a layer of mist, leaving the skinny, bare birch trees looking weary from winters gone and fierce nor'easters blown. Absently Jake kicked a wooden crate full of ropes, greasy with algae: their time was past too. Discarded in the crate he caught sight of an old flag. It had once been bright scarlet, with a black square in the centre, now it was just a sun-bleached and wind-flogged *'Storm Front Approaching'* flag.

"'Approaching', shit, the hurricane has been through." Jake shook his head as he spoke.

He pulled up his long-sleeved tee from under his blue and red plaid shirt. Then he picked out what remained of the tattered flag and wound it tightly around his scarred right fist, as if to form a makeshift boxing glove. The ends hung loose, it was spent, much like his heart. This morning there wasn't even a void in the pit of his stomach, much less a stomach. His fish-stained dungarees hung loosely over his legs as he ambled back towards the shed. He closed his watery eyes and smacked his forehead onto its old, grey wood. Then, as if by reflex, he swung his fist like a desperate, bout-losing southpaw. He could take it no more. Slowly, he dragged his hand back through the hole of splintered and rotten timbers and unwound the flag. With it he wiped away yet more tears and rubbed at his knuckles; his hand had been through much worse than rotting wood.

"Daddy, come inside now please." Amy was staring hard, and without flinching, she spoke in her sturdy young voice. She took her father completely by surprise; he believed she was sound asleep. "It's not a day to be outside, let alone on the water," she continued. "I've made a pot of fresh coffee and eggs, just the way Mom used to. We'll have breakfast together and rest up. And tomorrow you can drive me to school."

Framed in their doorway, dressed neatly, her green eyes fresh, her blonde hair brushed into a tight ponytail, stood Jake and Lindy Dealer's twelve-year-old daughter. Older than her years, and without a trace of pre-teenage disdain, she set her firm gaze steadfastly on her father. She was not asking her father to come inside. She was telling him. If ever the daughter was the parent of the father, it was now.

And Jake saw this. And Jake went inside.

CHAPTER 29

**Woods Hole – Vineyard Haven ferry,
Vineyard Sound, Massachusetts.
Monday, 19th March 1990. Early morning.**

It seemed as if the buoy's bells had clanked and rung throughout the entire trip across Vineyard Sound. That's what Zephaniah's headache informed him anyway. New England's dawn fog sat heavy in his lungs like unwanted cigar smoke. His eyes ached from peering into the murk in the futile hope of catching a nascent sunrise.

And this morning he wanted to see the sun. Like he wanted to see Ollie. In addition, he'd always liked sun-up, especially by the ocean. Even after he'd purchased his King Air, he often chose to drive to Woods Hole to take the car ferry to Martha's Vineyard. When he drove, come rain or shine, in summer and winter, he would leave Boston before sunrise, drive for ninety minutes to catch the ferry, knowing he'd be sitting on Ollie's stoop, or in the snug kitchen, in time for breakfast.

Always on a Monday too. Against the weekend trippers and commuters. It was their twice monthly 'board' meeting, and whether Zephaniah drove himself, or had Jeff Hindle fly him, he brought fresh flowers for Ollie every time. The reason – and there would have been one – was long forgotten.

Zephaniah secretly admired that in this modern age his grandfather, a prodigious letter writer, continued to eschew telephones and communicated solely via his Underwood typewriter; one that scuttlebutt stated had once belonged to Jack Kerouac. There was a time, as a child, when Zephaniah had been asked what his grandfather did. By reflex he had answered, giving Ollie a profession: *"He's a typist."* His third-grade teacher's smirk had taught him two things: first that he was wrong, and second, that if you don't know the right answer, then shut up.

Over time, Ollie and Zephaniah's fortnightly meetings had, inevitably, taken and held a shape. They would discuss, without any formal agenda, all manner of subjects: from the so-called 'competition', to theatre, ladies, film, art, with only politics off their menu. They would break for an early lunch of grilled fish and would wrap up any loose ends – they'd even gossip at times – before 4 p.m., when Zephaniah would return to Boston.

Moreover, Zephaniah had always suspected that his grandfather was aware of all matters regarding Swire's before he imparted them. And it was true. Ollie's forever chameleon-like expressions would change – disbelief to incredulity to respect – never letting on that his grandson wasn't conveying anything *nouvelle*. Yet, this was no game of shadow boxing. Both men needed this symbiotic workout: Ollie to reassure himself that all was well in his grandson's world and with Swire's; Zephaniah to reassure himself that all was well in his grandfather's world and with Swire's. For Ollie had long decided that nepotism – with the chosen scion – was not only an enlightened way to run his business, it was extraordinarily efficient.

Zephaniah sucked in damp sea air as the ferry slowed at the mouth of Vineyard Haven harbour. He'd wrapped up warmly: heavy denim jeans, Timberland boots, blue and red plaid shirt, blue cashmere sweater, and a murderously expensive Italian shearling coat. Tied around his neck like a cravat was a yellow cashmere scarf. He tugged on it firmly; soon it would be time to go below and rejoin his cold Mercedes. Clenching his teeth, he squatted down on his haunches. Then he lowered his head and stretched back his arms in a taut isometric exercise. He held himself still as all his muscles fought against each other and blood rushed into his clean-shaven cheeks. Slowly, he unbound himself and the pressure against his temples eased somewhat. Only when the dock was in sight did he allow himself a wry smile as he recalled Jimmy Snale's telephone call of yesterday.

"You always say, Mr Swire that time spent on reconnaissance is seldom wasted. Well, in Mass this morning, just before the sermon, I was sat one row behind Edward M. Quinn. I'd long ago checked out his credentials. He's the head of the FBI's Reactive Squad here in Boston. I kinda knew where to be sitting if you know what I mean, and I figured, like, he's *going to be the first to know. Sure enough, his pager goes off just as Father Dicking is clearing his throat. Quinn cussed and was out of the church quicker than iron to a magnet. Just thought you should know Mr Swire. Enjoy the rest of your Sunday."*

And Zephaniah did enjoy the rest of his Sunday. He'd instructed Hector to tell any callers that he was out of town. He'd read the newspapers in peace, completing *The New York Times* crossword in record time; decanted a bottle of decent Burgundy; went for a brief walk; rang his father's doorbell as he did every Sunday, waiting the obligatory five, long, minutes for it to go unanswered; returned home and ate a hearty lunch during which he drank most of the Romanée Conti. Then, he dozed contentedly while an old film starring Cary Grant and Grace Kelly played on CBS, his 1973 Delamain going untouched on the coffee table. As untouched as the nine-figure-dollar cache of stolen art in the trunk of his Mercedes. The one that was now parked safely in the underground garage at the Ritz-Carlton, while above ground the Boston Blues scorched around the city burning rubber.

He had decided during his solitary lunch that the telephone call of condolence – was that the right word? Or was 'comfort' or 'support' or 'sorrow' better? – to Anne Hawley, the newly installed Director of the Isabella Stewart Gardner Museum, could wait until Monday. There was a payphone at the Black Dog Bakery Café on State Road from Vineyard Haven to Menemsha.

An aptly named establishment from which to make this particular call.

CHAPTER 30

**Poseyville, Amagansett, Long Island, New York.
Monday, 19th March 1990. Morning.**

After Amy had cooked another hearty breakfast, Jake had driven her to school, and hadn't let on to her his plans for the working day ahead. He was going to finish the job he'd started the day before. He parked across the street and then strode towards the yard.

Jake kept shifting his stance as he began to rip the slats of wood from the shed. Christ, it was easier to punch the darned thing down than it was to demolish it. At his feet lay, to any other bayman, the tools of destruction: an axe, a ball-peen hammer, 'Dirty Rigger' work-gloves and a regular nail-hammer. The last thing he needed was tetanus from a rust-sick nail that held together this place of death.

Today, these were his tools of construction. With Amy's strength, a force seemingly far beyond his own, his decision made during the drive back from Boston had got easier. He had long thought that parents were there to protect their children from the world as they saw it. Only now, as he tore down the structures of the past and renounced thoughts of self, did he realise that it was in fact the children who protected the parents.

Throughout the time he pulled apart Blondie's kennel and the shed he reminded himself, in slow motion and pain-addled detail, a story his father had once told him. It was a true story of hardship and a will to live that had befallen a distant Nova Scotian cousin, Howard Blackburn, over 100 years ago.

"Howard Blackburn and Tom Welch were Gloucestermen out trawling for halibut on a wintry January night in 1883. It was 'sometime' weather and soon they were swamped in snow flurries and freezing fog. This was not just a fog-haunted night. It had been a bad summer, they had 'em in those days too. Anyway, the weather became so rough that they lost

all bearings. No stars. No lights. Just cold, snow and certain death. Soon they'd be as frozen and as dead as the few halibut in their dory. During the second night at sea, Tom Welch died, and Howard knew if he was to survive, he had to act. He thought hard and fast as he secured Tom's body in the bilge. Howard's extremities were frozen and his ability to row was ebbing like the tide. So, he took the decision to cement his hands to his oars. He had to do it if he had any chance of survival."

Jake recalled his father fixing him with a fierce stare before continuing . . .

"Terrified, Howard plunged his hands into the black, icy Atlantic waters. With salt and ice dripping off his hands he wrapped them around the unvarnished wood of his oars. When he had formed them into a cylindrical shape, he removed his hands and held them aloft. There, in the biting wind and snow, his hands froze. Solid. Carefully, he threaded his brittle hands over the oars again. And then he began to row. And row. And row. There would be no other way of being able to reach shore if he let the currents and weather do their worst. Five days later, he beached the dory in Newfoundland and carried Tom's body ashore. Later, Howard told your grandfather that it was better to watch his frozen hands crumble from the inside, than his very life from the outside. Howard Blackburn went onto to live, and fish, and sail, without fingers or thumbs until he was seventy-three. The story says he even sold his catch, frozen good by now, and gave the meagre amount to Tom's widow. That's the mould we come from Jake."

With his task finished Jake stood beside the huge pile of old timber that'd mountained up in the corner of the yard. The mutilated remnants of a kennel and a shed. The shed where his wife had hanged herself as she'd drowned in guilt and remorse. Where she'd died, not from asphyxiation, but from a broken heart. Jake now understood that people could, and did, die from a broken heart.

All he had to do now was burn it all: ashes-to-ashes and dust-to-dust. But there was a problem: one he could hear Lindy laughing aloud at. The pesky old wood wouldn't burn! Even with his oxyacetylene torch blazing, it wouldn't ignite. The wood was too darned sodden!

How Lindy would have enjoyed the sight of it all. God, I wish you were here beside me right now, he thought as he wiped laughter-tears from his unshaven face. He looked around the yard. She was here. He could feel her, sense her, smell her. His face opened into a wide grin as he knelt in the ground and fired up his blowtorch again.

"Jake, do you think we will ever have a life that doesn't smell of fish and damp and rotting wood . . .?"

CHAPTER 31

**Black Dog Bakery Café, State Road,
Martha's Vineyard, Massachusetts.
Monday, 19th March 1990. Morning.**

Zephaniah squeezed out one too many eye drops. His eyelids batted involuntarily as the residue ran freely down his face. Blinking and re-focusing, he climbed out of the Mercedes outside the Black Dog Bakery Café. He didn't need a fruity muffin or a T-shirt with their ubiquitous black Labrador dog on it. A strong coffee, a pocket full of quarters and a payphone were on his dance card.

The call to Anne Hawley had to be dealt with before he reached Menemsha. He was going to have his hands full with Ollie. This was not going to be an ordinary twice-monthly meeting.

"A black coffee and as many quarters as you can spare, please," said Zephaniah, sliding a $10 bill across the counter.

"The payphone is over there by the newspapers." The girl pointed towards a deserted corner of the bakery, lit only by shafts of light from the low, dreary sky. Handing him $5 worth of quarters, she added, "I'll bring the coffee over sir."

He thanked her, rattling the coins in the palm of his hand. His eyes caught sight of the newspapers, and, odd that it seemed, the idea of the media intruding on *his* theft irritated him. He disliked in equal measure intrusions and inaccuracies – unless, of course, they were of his own making – and the media were distinguished in their ability to be both intrusive and inaccurate.

So, here it was. A-List art thefts would forever receive marquee-sized billing the world over . . .

$200m Gardner Museum Art Theft

... trumpeted the front-page of *The Boston Globe,* in a typeface reserved for cataclysmic earthquakes and the like. The paper's three subsidiary headlines, only marginally less bold, were: *'Two men posing as police tie up night guards'.* Accurate, no problem with that. *'Vermeer painting, one of 32 in world, called greatest loss.'* Wrong, there were more than thirty-two attributed Vermeers, none in private hands, unless you counted the Queen of England's hands as private: her magnificent Vermeer, *The Music Lesson,* was often referred to as *The Concert's* twin. What did irritate was the third subsidiary headline: *'Secret collector's passion or ransom seen as motive.'* It won't be long before the 'ransom theory' is consigned to the shredder where it belongs, thought Zephaniah. The Isabella Stewart Gardner Museum, with its solitary wisdom legated to it by its founder Mrs Gardner, did not hold so much as $1 worth of theft insurance. Ergo, there was no insurance company to ransom the stolen artworks back to, even for ten cents on the dollar. Ergo, the only *credible* theory would be a commissioned theft. He tasted the black, stewed liquid masquerading as coffee, winced, and flipped to *The New York Times'* front page. Above the fold. Top billing. And a tour de force of slack journalism – the *Times'* persistent use of capital letters further irritated him. *'Boston Thieves Loot a Museum of Masterpieces.'* The by-line was Fox Butterfield. What an obtuse name, reflected Zephaniah, son of Hephzibah and York Swire. A mental picture emerged as a droll smile crept up on him: a marble font, a priest, two proud parents, a regiment of relatives . . . *"and I baptise you in the name of the Lord"* – the priest would surely have coughed here – *"Fox."* And couldn't Mr Butterfield have found in his thesaurus a more appropriate verb than 'loot' to announce to Sulzberger's readers what had transpired in Boston? Loot . . . looting . . . That was the province of rioters, of thugs, of envy, of greed, of pillaging soldiers. If Zephaniah had wanted to 'loot' the Isabella Stewart Gardner Museum, he most certainly could – and would – have done so. The museum had been his and his alone for many hours.

He deposited the vile coffee on top of the heap of newsprint and turned to the payphone. From memory, he punched in a Massachusetts phone number and deposited the relevant coins. The line crackled, went silent, then rang.

"Isabella Stewart Gardner Museum, how may I direct your call."

"Anne Hawley please."

"Sorry sir, but Ms Hawley cannot be disturbed."

"I'll wait while you go and inform her that Zephaniah Swire is holding. You'll find that she'll take my call. Thank you."

His intonation was polite but firm, and the receptionist wisely chose not to doubt him. He heard the scuffing of a chair as her footsteps disappeared. He didn't have to wait long.

"Anne, it's Zephaniah, I'm not going to say I'm sorry, I'm going to ask what I may do to help."

"Thank you for calling Zephaniah." Her voice trailed off. Like every museum director in the world, she had her own unique relationship with Swire's; you could like the firm, loathe the firm, but you could only ignore Swire's at your peril. Anne Hawley was barely six months into her new post at the museum, but even she knew this. She continued. "I've got calls into Sotheby's and Christie's, so far, both have gone unreturned."

"I'll call them. Tell me what you want me to say."

All either party could hear was the silent, persistent hum of the telephone line.

Zephaniah wasn't going to interrupt Anne Hawley's thought process. Napoleon had once remarked: *'Never interrupt your enemy while they are making a mistake',* and whatever she was going to say – was going to do – was going to be a mistake.

Finally, she said, in what could only be described as a stage whisper, "Did you know the museum is not insured against theft? You understand the constrictions and problems with Mrs Gardner's Will, and now the museum's trustees think if we posted a reward . . ."

Zephaniah closed his eyes.

"The museum held no theft insurance at all Anne . . .?" ran his spoken voice. *Of course, I know you had no theft insurance Anne . . .* ran his inner voice.

CHAPTER 32

**Poseyville, Amagansett, Long Island, New York.
Monday, 19th March 1990. Morning.**

Amidst the lazy and reluctant flames that rose skywards from the Dealer family's yard, was hope. The smoke offered up by the remains of the shed and kennel was thick and grey and heavy with oil, paint and the sea's moisture. It clawed at Jake's throat, yet he stood, as close as he physically could to the flames, as he knew he must. Arched and sad, Jake saw that from out of this pyre of damp lumber – built on an altar of earth and gravel – something was rising phoenix-like, and with it came the promise of a future for Amy.

This was no ritual pyre. The phoenix's brilliant plumage was absent, as were myrrh, aromatic spices and scented wood. Were these rising flames a resurrection of life after death, or another myth, like ghost ships, white whales and the ocean's black holes?

He breathed in the flames' smoke. He didn't even care to know if it were truth or fable, for he'd found a truth: he would fight for their newborn future as if he were Ra. He'd taken Dougie to see the sun-god's two obelisks in Central Park, the only time he'd ever taken him to the city . . . Yeah, that was a truth for sure.

It all seemed like another life, not just a lifetime ago . . . But then it was.

CHAPTER 33

**10 Crick Hill Road, Menemsha,
Martha's Vineyard, Massachusetts.
Monday, 19th March 1990. Morning.**

Ollie Swire had heard the familiar scrunching of rubber on gravel. Buttoning up his blue woollen cardigan, he opened the front door and stepped out to greet his grandson, who, contrary to his usual practice had reversed his car up the short driveway; details, even trivial ones, never escaped Ollie. But it was Monday, and he was looking forward to starting the week with his grandson's arrival. The last two weeks had him laid low with a chill and a grating cough. Set in routine only, he hadn't even put a temporary halt to his daily constitutional along Menemsha Beach or beside the cliffs at Gay Head. His lip-service concession to the weight on his chest was to put an extra turn in his black silk scarf.

"Zeph, how good to see you," Ollie opened his grandson's car door, and Zephaniah embraced his grandfather as he always did in private: three kisses starting and ending with his left cheek.

"How are you, Ollie? You look tired, a tad drawn."

Ollie frowned playfully then coughed. "Zeph, why don't you drive away and arrive again, and then you can tell an old man what he wants to hear. The truth can be unwelcome when you are going to be eighty-five in a few minutes."

"More like three months! I'm sorry you've been under the weather." Zephaniah was ever mindful of his grandfather, and he was annoyed with himself. "Let me give you some flowers, I hope you like them. You know me and anything green, if I had a window box, I'd pave it."

Zephaniah went to the trunk of the Mercedes, opened it and concealing himself behind it, removed twelve short-stemmed yellow roses from their tissue-paper. Simultaneously, he unwrapped a dark brown vase from a piece of green baize. It was small and heavy – ten inches high – and its rim was wide and generous. Ideal for roses in fact.

As Zephaniah presented him with the roses, the years appeared to ebb like a tide from Ollie's taut and fatigued face. His crystal-blue eyes smiled. Roses had been Hannah's favourite flower, and yellow her favourite colour; the colour of happiness and optimism. Had he once told his grandson? Surely not? These were Ollie's secrets, and secrets were curious things; he'd spent a lifetime exhuming the secrets of others, whilst never revealing any his own. Even he was allowed a secret or three. Like how Hannah had looked, in her daisy and white dress, the first time he'd met her. Her raven-black hair had truly shone under the crisp New Mexican sky, her smile white against tanned, clear skin.

It all seemed like another life, not just a lifetime ago . . . But then it was.

"What beautiful flowers. They're wonderful, thank you, Zeph."

Ollie held them up to the daylight, as if to use their diaphanous yellow petals to induce colour, some New Mexican sun perhaps, into the gloom overhead.

Only that wasn't what he was doing.

This was a *Gu* he was holding, an ancient Chinese bronze vase, with heft too, between two and three pounds, guessed Ollie. Rare and extremely valuable. He recalled there was an almost identical one at the Isabella Stewart Gardner Museum. It stood on a small table beside their Vermeer. Recently, on a rain-swept afternoon, he'd popped into the museum to study *The Concert* and left aghast at its shocking condition, it was as if Vermeer's treasure had been allowed to petrify. And this *Gu* his grandson had given him was very similar, right down to the motifs engraved on its surface, and its green coating appeared to have been removed. Strange? Knowledgeable Oriental collectors prized their bronzes in their original condition, the way they had been cast, as they had lain buried for centuries in the soil of the North China Plains.

"Look Zeph, look, look just here. There's a hint of life coming through the petals. Can you see how they brighten the horizon?"

Ollie raised up the flowers into his grandson's line of sight. All Ollie wanted to do was study the base of the *Gu* without being noticed; a task he accomplished with a minimum of guile. Even in his eighty-fifth year his hands were as nimble as his eyes were cunning. He kept his counsel as he realised that the vessel he was holding aloft *was* from the Shang Dynasty. The very first Chinese Dynasty. From his pin-sharp memory, he dated the Shang to 1600–1200 BC. Slowly he lowered the *Gu* and headed indoors.

Their normal practice would be to walk to the Menemsha Market, a bold name for the ramshackle grey-wooden outbuilding, a few hundred yards from his home on Crick Hill Road. The store stocked a meagre selection of essentials, as well as hosting a dog-eared noticeboard for all manner of services that no one who lived thereabouts needed or cared to use: the fishermen Ollie knew – and he knew them all – supposed yoga to be a cartoon bear or a famous Yankees baseball player, and t'ai chi was where countless US Marines were killed in '69. The store did perform a service for Ollie, however. They ordered his multiple daily newspapers. And the actual purchase of his newspapers, together with the stroll there and back, was always the first of Ollie and Zeph's fortnightly rituals. But today would be different. Ollie decided to delay their walk until he had prepared a pot of his grandson's favourite Blue Mountain coffee: Zeph's would be as black and bitter as a moonless winter night; his, as warm and sweet and golden as a New Mexico sunrise.

CHAPTER 34

**Poseyville, Amagansett, Long Island, New York.
Monday, 19th March 1990. Mid-morning.**

The telephone rang. And rang. And Jake let it ring itself out. It was the third time he'd let it do that this morning. He'd never much liked telephones, besides his fire was really cookin' now. Earlier, the smoke had been thick and heavy when the damp wood had smouldered like a sulking neighbour. For a reason he couldn't fathom, the smoke now tasted sweet in his throat as if the gold and red and orange flames had been soaked in soft brown sugar.

And as the flames licked greedily into the clearing sky, Jake couldn't help but feel proud of just who he was. And what a fire it was! It was the kind of fire you could toast marshmallows on while warming your cold bones from the inside out, as someone set off rockets on 4th July. Heck, it was the sort of fire that could unite families and douse feuds. Not many fires could do that. But then this was no ordinary fire. This was Lindy and Dougie's fire. Besides, it would be embers and ashes soon. The phone can wait, this moment is too damn good, thought Jake.

The phone began to ring for a fourth time.

Jake felt his stomach constrict and a vacuum form. And he ran into the house faster than a swordfish dove to the ocean's depths.

CHAPTER 35

**10 Crick Hill Road, Menemsha,
Martha's Vineyard, Massachusetts.
Friday, 30th March 1990. Mid-morning.**

"Do you like it?"

"You know I do." Ollie raised his eyes. "However, I prefer your flowers."

"I thought you might say that."

The *Gu* stood between them like an outsize chess piece, its unknowable history, together with the depth of its handsome verdigris colour held both men's attention. Between them was also the tingle of excitement that was as compelling as the aroma of fresh Jamaican coffee was sweet.

Ollie salvoed with an uncharacteristic bluff. "So, how did you get the Gardner Museum to part with it? You know them, never bought or sold one item since Mrs Gardner died in . . ."

". . . 1924 . . ." interjected Zephaniah, before asking, "was that auto-suggestion, knowledge or Five-card stud?"

Without even dropping his gaze by so much as one millimetre – down and to the left would have been anyone else's reflex – Ollie, a man with zero 'tells', ignored the question and carried on speaking.

"Yes, that's right, 1924. Nine years before I started Swire's. You do know the precise terms of Mrs Gardner's Will Zeph?"

"I believe so."

"I'm sure you do, and her testamentary conditions are as crystal clear as they are perpetual. Not one painting, artefact, piece of furniture, sculpture, book or for that matter any one exhibit, is allowed to be sold. Not one item is to be bought or even added, even by way of a third-party bequest to her collection. Not one solitary item is allowed to be moved permanently to another location within the museum, which quite frankly I regard as a cross between an overly decorated mausoleum and the Grand Bazaar." He took a beat. "In the event of her Board of Trustees, Harvard-educated Brahmins all of them, doing any of those things, the entire contents of her museum are bequeathed to the President of Harvard, with the *caveat* that he sell every single artefact, from the chairs to the Rembrandts. He must then dissolve the museum proper and pass the entire cash proceeds to Harvard University." Ollie poured himself a splash more coffee. "Powerful stuff. So where do you think the Gardner's trustees get their self-perpetuating and damned moral certainty from?"

"Why are you telling me all this?" Zephaniah asked in a low voice, for it was obvious that Ollie was amusing himself at his expense.

"I'll tell you how you get moral certainty in this world of ours, and it's in one of two ways. Having a poor memory or Alzheimer's, or both." Ollie chuckled mischievously. "My dear Zeph, all I'm attempting to figure out is how you overcame this cabal of New Englanders and their damned moral certainty to achieve the impossible. You persuaded them to part with this exquisite *Gu*. I can only assume the President of Harvard is in our pocket?"

Ollie was only half joking. He tapped the three-and-half-millennia-old bronze *Gu* and shot Zephaniah a piercing look.

"Don't misunderstand me my dear grandson, I love that you've succeeded where countless others have failed. Amuse my base curiosity please. Fascinating stuff. What were the mechanics of how you achieved all this?"

The statement – and the question – were loaded. Both Swires knew that. It would not have escaped Ollie's attention if Swire's had been in secret negotiations (and they would have to have been that) with the myriad of interested parties if the Gardner, and the 'unbreakable' covenants of the Will that governed it, were ever to be 'broken'.

Zephaniah said nothing.

Ollie said nothing.

They quietly sipped their coffee.

Ollie frowned and thought fleetingly that maybe at almost eighty-five his touch was slipping. Doubtful.

Across the table, Zephaniah wore an implacable expression, one that reminded him of Nibs Callahan, his 'roper', when he'd played the 'inside' for the last time. Nibs had been the best: a face of granite throughout their last great con back in 1929. The trouble was Ollie's grandson now wore the same granite expression.

Finally, it was Zephaniah who spoke.

"Ollie, let me ask you a question." The mug's rim hid a creased smile. "Can you name me one principal museum or any serious collector, anywhere in the world, who we've failed to do business with? By that I mean sell, acquire, advise or even simply broker a transaction."

What was he up to? Ollie pondered, as he searched his memory.

"There's going to be an institution or a collector somewhere. Japan, Russia, Korea."

"Wrong. Try Boston. It's called the Isabella Stewart Gardner Museum. It's the only one. The only one, Ollie."

"I may be alone in this Zeph," said Ollie, "but I don't rate the Gardner as a museum. They bill themselves as such, and yes it houses more than 7,500 paintings over 1,500 rare books and Lord knows how many thousands of archival pieces, nearly all of which are now in terrible condition. Museums curate. Museums preserve. Museums evolve. Their art, some of it fine, stands, sits and hangs, sure, and the public visit, but it's all rotting, and all in memory of Isabella Gardner's vanity. A paean to her egotism." Ollie spoke with passion. "A museum is a living entity and it's supposed to add to the world, not subtract from it. It shouldn't hoard treasures like a love-sick pirate. The Gardner is impotent, unable to perform, and we all must perform. To exist is just not acceptable, even in a museum. Zeph, there's value in inertia, yes, but this is . . ."

"Never knew you felt so strongly about the place."

"I don't. I've never concerned myself with them. I understand Swire's keeps a line open, but I've personally never bothered, principally because they're flat broke. They don't even have any money for restoration, advice, climate-control systems, nothing. They've only recently installed a second-rate alarm. What's more, I hear there's no money in the kitty even for theft insurance. Can you believe that? The reason being if ever there *was* a robbery, they're forbidden to spend the insurance money on any new art . . ."

Zephaniah Swire, ever Ollie Swire's chosen scion, held firm his facial muscles.

"... and all because of her monstrous Will. They can't even sell one item to save the other ten thousand or so. It's a ridiculous state of affairs. Never do business with stupid people." Ollie paused to cough. "Zeph, do you know what other gems there are in that document of hers? Try this, every year on the anniversary of her death there must be memorial requiem mass held in the faux-Venetian *palazzo* in her memory. For God's sake, prayers in perpetuity are accorded to saints, martyrs and royalty, not conceited magpies!"

Ollie sighed, something he rarely did. Zephaniah knew not to speak. This was just another of his grandfather's signals; and he could read them as if they were his own. He didn't have to wait long.

"Thinking about it, what do they have of value to Swire's apart from the Rembrandts? There's the Vermeer of course. She bought *The Concert* at auction in Paris for about $6,000 in the 1890s. Her agent had an eye. Vermeer was relatively unappreciated then, and he died broke when he was about your age. He was just forty-three. The painting hasn't been cared for since the day she bought it by the look of it. Even un-restored, we could place it today with any number of collectors for what, $30 million?"

"Nearer to $50 million," Zephaniah spoke assuredly. "Not one Vermeer has come on the open market for decades, and its twin, *The Music Lesson* was bought by King George III in about 1760, and it has remained with the British royal family ever since. King George may have lost his American colonies at the same time, but he did gain a Vermeer."

"Well, I am out of touch," lied Ollie, ignoring the wisecrack and instead fixing his grandson with a hard look before continuing, "and I don't understand all the fuss about their Titian, the *Rape of Europa*. Kings begged for Titian's work during his lifetime, personally I don't like it. I do however like both their Rubens', the *Earl of Arundel* especially. John Singer Sargent's *El Jaleo* is magnificent, despite its size. The small Matisse *Saint Tropez* and Manet's *Chez Tortoni* are good. I like them, they're jaunty, fun paintings."

"Ollie what are you restoring at the moment?"

Rarely taken aback, Ollie found himself simply answering the question.

"A small Titian, *Rest on the Flight into Egypt*. Now, that is an exquisite painting. It belongs to Lord Bath. He consigned it to us for a general appraisal, and I ambushed it when it reached Boston."

"I know the piece well. It's been in their family for over 100 years, they bought it from Christie's. I've been trying, and failing, to acquire it for Thyssen, a saga that's been going on and on," Zephaniah cocked his head to one side. "Are you telling me Ollie that the Titian is in your studio?"

Ollie nodded. "Knowing that His Lordship wasn't interested in parting with it, I thought if it was restored, then we might be able to extract a substantially higher bid from Heini Thyssen . . . and well, you never know, the English aristocracy always have pressing financial demands . . ." Ollie knew his thought didn't need completing.

"You amaze me sometimes Ollie!"

Ollie raised an eyebrow. "Then that's your mistake."

Zephaniah stood up from the kitchen table and walked to the large, solitary window that unlocked the simple beauty of Menemsha Harbour and the Atlantic Ocean beyond. His broad back was probably all Ollie could see now.

"Is *The Concert* in such bad condition that it's beyond restoration?" asked Zephaniah.

"Very few paintings are beyond restora—"

In the split second that he failed to complete the word, the sentence, the thought, he got it.

Ollie got it.

* * *

It was a much longer second – a drowning second – before Zephaniah realised that his grandfather had got it. Like his voice, Ollie was always one step ahead of the beat.

Zephaniah, a man unburdened by self-doubt, carried on looking out of the window. In complete silence. He thought he could hear his blood coursing through his veins. The next move could never be his. He knew that.

Then Ollie coughed. This one thin and reedy. Not one from his chest. Now Zephaniah could move.

"I stole the *Gu* in the early hours of Sunday morning, with the Flinck, Manet's *Chez Tortoni* and, of course, the Vermeer, the Napoleonic finial and some unimportant Degas sketches. With no TV, no phone and no newspapers this morning, I knew I'd be the first to tell you."

Zephaniah continued to gaze out at the ocean in front of him. Hadn't Christ delayed his reveal until the Last Supper? Time to deliver his.

"I also stole *Christ in the Storm on the Sea of Galilee* knowing it to be your favourite painting. In fact, I took all the Rembrandts, except the grandiose self-portrait."

Deeply absorbed, he didn't hear Ollie get up from the table and put his arm around his grandson. Together, they took in the frail fishing boats and the all-powerful ocean.

"How did you know *Christ in the Storm on the Sea of Galilee* is my favourite Rembrandt? It's not considered one of his masterpieces, but it's the only seascape he ever painted. I think it's magnificent."

Zephaniah nodded silently. Of course he knew his grandfather had always prized the work. That was, after all, one of the principal reasons he had stolen it.

Ollie continued speaking in a low voice, one clotted with history and memory. He knew it would take his grandson back to his childhood: the Martha's Vineyard, grandson and grandfather childhood.

"It may sound strange, but whenever I see that painting, or even a photograph of it, I always think of the fishermen who work the waters hereabouts – Nantucket, Montauk, Block Island. In the dead of winter, in the middle of storms, in any conditions, and all to put food on their families' plates and clothes on their backs. When I see the waters boiling over out there, I think, Zeph, well, there must be a way of providing for those you love without risking your life every day. Then I get to realising, that they wouldn't have a life at all if they didn't risk it all. Because that's just the way these men are made. Fishermen aren't just brave hunters, they're instinctive hunters. And that makes them the best. They're hardened gamblers too, with their lives on the line for the chance of one big haul, the catch that'll settle the bills . . ." Ollie let his arm fall from Zephaniah's shoulder and he continued to look straight ahead . . . "When I see Rembrandt's painting in my mind's-eye, with the spume flying off those huge waves, the sails shredded, halyards flying, the small boat is floundering. The heavens are being ripped open and the sky is green with hatred. Christ is calm. He's trying to keep order on board, while the disciples secretly believe that death, drowning, cannot be far away. There's a loss of faith in their faces. The sea can do that to a man Zeph. It can confiscate faith, even a disciple's. There is no power like it on earth."

Ollie turned and looked up at his tall grandson. "It must be terrifying being in the eye of a raging storm at sea, even if you are Jesus Christ." He then nodded respectfully in the direction of the fishermen in the harbour below.

"You know why these men put to sea Zeph? It's because nothing else on this earth makes them feel *alive*."

CHAPTER 36

**Poseyville, Amagansett, Long Island, New York.
Monday, 19th March 1990. Mid-morning.**

"Shit, Marty . . ."
"Whoa Jake! Get your breath back! Listen, you OK?"
"Sure, why shouldn't I be?" Jake was still breathing hard.
"You know how it is man . . . This is the fourth time I've called . . ."
"What's up Marty? Don't follow you."

Jake held the phone less tightly than he had the second after he'd answered it.

It was Marty Drew. No police. No doctor. No teacher from Amy's school . . . just Marty.

"Well, like I said you know how it is, like . . ."

Marty was struggling for words. They wouldn't form, and he was the wordsmith, dammit. But his whole morning had been like that. The melodies were playing hide 'n seek under the Steinway's lid, whilst the lyrics skulked inside his green roller-ball pen. No one would come out to play. The pad was still yellow. Still legal. Still lined. Still blank.

"Lookit' Jake, I got a call from Danny King, he's kinda worried. Says he saw clouds of smoke coming from your area. He's over in Albert's Landing. Must be some monster fire you got going there."

"Yeah, it is. Mighty fine fire, Marty. Real big. Be just piles of hot ashes soon . . ."

Jake was rattled. So, all about him thought he was going to burn his house down while Amy was at school, huh? *Thanks guys, but we're doing OK, me and Amy.* But in truth Jake hadn't realised that since the funerals he hadn't once seen his crew, shared a beer, shot the breeze with anyone other than Amy. He *should've* added *'just'* after . . . *we're doing OK* . . .

Everybody in Amagansett and East Hampton who knew Jake recognised that he was a loner, but they also saw that he'd developed skills to rival Blondin; he was on a tightrope over the Niagara Gorge, and a fall could occur at any second. Or not at all. It was anybody's guess. But nobody dared guess. He'd dropped off the radar completely. If Peter Duxbury, Marty Drew and his old crew were to be the safety net for Jake and Amy, well, they couldn't let him know that they were that net: aside from Amy's life, his own pride was just about all Jake had left.

"These ashes of yours, they wouldn't be the house I've rented from you guys in, er, October, would they?"

Marty Drew, somehow, could get away with saying clumsy stuff at just the wrong time. It was another of his God-given knacks, and when he did so, which was often, his friends laughed it off as a just another component of his charm.

"Marty, you know something, you're the best . . ." Jake began to laugh. "I'm answering the house phone, aren't I? So, I'm not burning MY house down, I'm clearing out the yard, something I should have done years ago. And yeah, Blondie's kennel and the old shed are smokin' right now. You good with that?"

"Sure Jake, good thing too." Marty realised that he'd unintentionally stepped over the clumsy line. Again. "Did you keep all the old lobster markers, the ones your father collected? They're great."

"I sure did, I kept all those. Tosh started saving them with his father after the first war, like you did in those days. All I did was carry on."

It was ever thus with those Dealers, thought Marty.

"Listen, Jake." He had given up digging himself out of the Australian hole, just as he was about to give up writing songs for the day too. "When was the last time you had swordfish, an ironed one?"

"Hell, probably the last time I harpooned one myself. That would be a long time ago. Why?"

"I'm at my studio in Montauk, and the juices just ain't flowing today." He sighed. "You remember Mikey Vanderpool, works out of Menemsha. Well, he ironed himself a mighty sword yesterday. And guess who's got part of it now?"

"You inviting me to lunch, Marty? It's too early."

"Yeah, too right I'm asking you to lunch. And it's never too early for ironed sword. So, do me a favour. Fill an aluminium pail with some of those ashes and get your sorry ass to Montauk."

"Be with you in an hour Marty." Jake hesitated. "Hey, er, sorry for not answering the phone sooner. Thanks, yeah, thanks . . ."

* * *

Marty Drew ambled over to the immense sheet of glass that gave onto a panorama of Montauk Harbour and its activity, its life. He pivoted it open to suck in the briny sea air. He liked his studio here. It was away from his Amagansett estate, his Central Park South apartment, away from people. It was just away. And he was through with work for today, all he had to do now was go and secure a quiet table and settle down to a lunch of ironed swordfish. The very best. None of that tough, adrenaline-poisoned sword-meat caught on the long-line just clean-killed with a harpoon. He was proud to call Jake Dealer his friend, for he could iron a fish like nobody else.

Easing the huge window shut, Marty reckoned he'd earned some down-time, even if Columbia was on his case for a new album. He edged over to the Steinway grand dominating the vaulted studio. Before he closed it, his hands began to run across the keys with a bridge of chords. He hooked the piano stool out with his foot. He had heard a something. A whisper. Not sure what. He sat down. He played the bridge again and again. And again. Then he shut his eyes. He concentrated on the dark in front of his eyes. He saw melodies. He caught words. He smelt water. They all took on a shape. They formed a picture. A palette. A coloured one.

That was how it had always worked for Marty. In dreams.

And Jake was an hour out.

Sounds good.

CHAPTER 37

**10 Crick Hill Road, Menemsha,
Martha's Vineyard, Massachusetts.
Monday, 19th March 1990. Late morning.**

Ollie's kitchen and dining area were one, and furnished as if he might have been, perhaps, an ascetic. The chairs, the dining table and the sideboard were all precious woods: dark and plain and solid: black persimmon, Congolese wenge, ebony and mahogany, with fillets of pale cedar and iroko teak to lift the daylight. Each piece had been skilfully crafted by hands that were part of a soon-to-be-forgotten Midwest. Not one item was out of place, any more than any one object might have been deemed superfluous. Everything followed its function; every item had its use. Even his one flash of giddiness – an exquisite pair of 1833 Paul Storr silver candlesticks – fulfilled a purpose.

Everything had to have a use, had to work. The curtains were of a simple muslin, and on the walls were a remarkable series of twelve black and white photographs by Doug Kuntz. It was Kuntz, who in the early 1980s had documented the lives of the fishermen and baymen who worked at the eastern end of Long Island: that ninety-plus miles of treacherous, open ocean that separated Menemsha from Montauk. Kuntz's photographs spoke of a disappearing America, a freer America, one with fewer judges, one where politicians and lawyers didn't rule. And Ollie liked to bear witness to that America as he worked in his kitchen and looked out of his window, alone each morning, sipping strong coffee, or piping hot chocolate, as the sun lipped into his day over the faraway horizon.

This morning, Ollie stared single-mindedly at the only true colour in the room – Hannah's yellow roses nesting in an ancient and stolen Chinese vase.

"Let's go down to the harbour and see what fresh fish we can find. We'll check out Poole's and Larsen's too. I'm starving. All this talk of

Vermeer and Rembrandt has got my appetite up. Besides, wasn't it Churchill who said that everything looks better after lunch?"

"Yes, it was, but he also believed in the divine right of kings." Zephaniah caught an off-key in his grandfather's voice. "Why the frown, Ollie?"

"Nothing really, other than I'm dying for you to open the trunk of your car and show me the paintings."

Ollie smiled his smile. It was Zephaniah's turn to be caught off guard.

"Why else would you reverse your car up the drive? What do you take me for, an old man?"

He unhooked his astrakhan coat from the cherry-wood stand, criss-crossed the black silk scarf across his chest and walked out of the front door. Slow steps at first, he sniffed at the air as a Black Mouth Cur would, and without waiting for his grandson, trotted off nimbly down the sloping lawn. Peppering his tone he called out, "Just pull the door, Zeph. Don't bother to lock up. No thieves hereabouts."

There was motive behind his attempt at lightening the mood. He was, like the Cur, wary. For as he paced on towards the harbour, he realised just how much he loved his life here. And just how much he missed Hannah, and what might have happened if life had hummed a different melody. Would she have exchanged the warmth of New Mexico for the cold of New England? Honestly, he didn't know, and he was not a man to speculate on something as precious as his contentment. After all, the only certainty in life was that it was uncertain. But if he was ever sure of a person, it would be Hannah. And this was not an old man's dream flattering a young man's memory or desire.

Maybe now, in his eighty-fifth year, Ollie had grasped that – conceivably – crime wasn't just something you got caught at?

* * *

"Mikey! Long-time no see. How are you? Family well?"

"Likewise, Mr Swire. Yeah, family's fine. Thanks for asking." Mikey Vanderpool raised his right hand in a respectful salute.

"Mighty fine-looking swordfish you got there."

"Too right Mr Swire. Ironed it yesterday. Pure luck it was too!"

"We all need luck Mikey, makes us look more skilful."

"I had the harpoon right here; old habits die hard." He pointed to a run of stainless-steel brackets bolted inside the port quarter of his boat. He touched the bronzed tip of the harpoon. "I wasn't even looking for any big 'uns, and suddenly I came upon her. She moved slow like, off the port-side she was, half a boat away, you know, say twenty-five feet. Tryin' to sun herself, brilliantly blue eyes as swords have. She wasn't skittish, or lazy, just unawares, I guess. Before you could say a word Mr Swire, I had the harpoon right behind the head. Clean too, an' it was a big throw."

"You wouldn't be selling me and my grandson here a couple of steaks, would you Mikey?"

"Nah, sorry, Mr Swire, not today."

Mikey Vanderpool looked down at the magnificent 400-plus-pound swordfish in the belly of his boat; the dorsal fin and flat-edged 'sword' were proud even in death. Her body was covered by shards of crushed ice that shimmered in the light. And, as if in a nest, the ice packed around it ran to pink and then deep crimson where some of the flesh had already been carved away.

"What I'll gladly do, Mr Swire is *give* you and your grandson a pair o' steaks before I go take her ashore." He nodded at its filleted back. "I gave the guys in Montauk a few steaks earlier this morning."

"Let Poole's and Larsen's have a few pounds too please Mikey, then everyone's happy. No one has seen an ironed swordfish in a while," Ollie beamed as he spoke. "There was a fisherman who worked out of Montauk. Same age as my grandson, I guess. Had a dark green down'easter, he'd bring an ironed sword in sometimes. Those days are gone now, eh Mikey?"

Mikey Vanderpool had worked these waters all his life, and he understood that Mr Swire didn't need an answer. This catch was luck, and yes, those days were gone. He'd had the privilege of working with Jake Dealer, the fisherman ol' man Swire was referring to. But these were questions you never ever asked, unless you were one of them. People like Jake you knew by sight, by reputation. They guarded their privacy in the manner in which they worked. Fiercely.

Taking a whetstone from his oil-skin pocket, he sharpened his jack-knife. Then, he deftly sliced two of the largest swordfish steaks Ollie Swire had ever seen.

"Be safe Mikey, and thanks again," said Ollie as he took the newspaper-wrapped steaks, in his left hand. Nodding a salute, he leaned over the boat's gunwale to shake the hand of a great hunter who could harpoon a magnificent fish such as this. Hands like Mickey Vanderpool's Ollie cared to shake. Another of his superstitions. If you were gifted at something, then, usually, you were *very* gifted. He'd witnessed it often. That was more than enough for him. Losers were just that. Worse, in fact – losers were to be avoided. Contagious. Yet another superstition. Turning to Zephaniah, the newspaper dripping iced-water and blood, Ollie announced: "We're done here Zeph. Let's go eat. Then we'll talk."

With purpose and pride, he marched back up the gentle incline from Menemsha Harbour to 10 Crick Hill Road. Any, and all, melancholic thoughts that had burrowed into the forefront of his mind dissolved with each step.

CHAPTER 38

**Poseyville, Amagansett, Long Island, New York.
Monday, 19th March 1990. Late morning.**

Jake spread the smouldering remains of the fire about his feet. The embers would die quicker that way. This was what it had all been about. Death. And life too, of course. An aluminium pail stood off to one side and a shovel lay in the dirt. Wisps of smoke rose in eerily vertical spirals from isolated pockets, like they were being teased ever upwards. The flames had all but died. Briskly he chopped up an area of embers with the shovel and scooped them into the pail. When it was full, he strapped the pail into the corner of his flatbed Ford, the one that had replaced the Montaukett Indians' horses.

Over by a rusted ice-saw his eye latched on what looked like a steel frisbee. He went to check it out and discovered that it was a piece of aluminium from the dory they'd used the day Harvey had drowned. In the years since his brother's death, Jake had cannibalised the old dory for parts and repairs. Harvey would have liked that.

Jake glanced over at the dory's replacement – painted the same colour, it could have been the same one. On land and on its trailer, the dory looked helpless, out of place. Working boats belonged in the water, working for a living. Everything and everybody had to work. The 300 years of striving on the water, in the bays and on the treacherous winter ice, had taught him that. That and the simple truth that every boat had its own story: who had loved her, what she had caught, what storms she had weathered, who had drowned in her . . .

Picking up the piece of aluminium, he secured it onto the rim of the pail of ashes before climbing into his flatbed's cab. He shot the dory another glance. Marty will find a solid use for the dory, thought Jake as he turned the ignition key. The Ford's engine fired up. Yeah, Marty will put the dory back to work, somehow.

Jake knew he couldn't anymore. He was good, but he was also done.

CHAPTER 39

**10 Crick Hill Road, Menemsha,
Martha's Vineyard, Massachusetts.
Monday, 19th March 1990. Lunchtime.**

Ollie stood behind the wood counter which doubled as both work surface and side table in his kitchen. With the swordfish steaks to one side, he prepared a salad dressing with dark brown balsamic vinegar from Modena and pungent green oil from Sicily. A neat, black apron was tied around his waist.

He always cooked in silence; a fact Zephaniah had grown up with. The discipline of preparation, timing, organisation, cleanliness, simple order. It suited his mentality. And, of course, it relaxed him and taught him patience. He had always known how to play it long – one of his greatest talents – but patience was altogether a different authority. It mattered not one whit – or so he had convinced himself – that it was Hannah who had taught him to cook well, and how to develop his taste buds as if they were sensual organs.

He sparked up the gas on the large stainless-steel hob, the kind they had in restaurants. The flame turned blue, and the heat intensified. With a steady hand he placed a heavy skillet on the stove. He allowed the heat to sear into the guts of the solid piece of iron.

Ollie stepped away to open a temperature-controlled cupboard, in which were to be found more than 100 half-bottles of wine. Despite being a teetotaller, he was an oenophile who enjoyed keeping superb wines for the privileged few he elected to break bread with in his modest Menemsha home. Returning to the stove, he finally spoke.

"Zeph, please help yourself to a bottle. I know how you enjoy wine with your food. Take the Montrachet again, you enjoyed it so much last time. You said it was excellent, and this fish will need something robust, perhaps a red even? You choose."

The iron skillet smoked faintly black, whilst the heat it retained scorched white. He turned off the gas and counted down from thirty. At zero, he placed the two swordfish steaks onto the skillet and watched them cook themselves – ninety seconds each side – as the juices petrified inside the meaty flesh. Blackened stripes from the iron – the paradox never went ignored – told the story. He then served each steak on a plate of fine white bone china. In a bowl carved from solid ebony, he heaped salad leaves, now wilting ever so slightly under the heavy Sicilian oil and Italian vinegar.

Lunch was served. Conversation would be the only dessert.

CHAPTER 40

**Gosman's Restaurant, Montauk Harbour,
Long Island, New York.
Monday, 19th March 1990. Lunchtime.**

Jake Dealer wiped the corners of his mouth and grinned. Across the rough-hewn wood table – carved with names and dates of dreams; cherished, broken, mended and lost – sat Marty Drew sporting an equally big grin. Between them stood a pitcher of iced water. At their feet, in a tin pail of yet more ice, was a bottle of fine Chablis. Marty had scooped it from the wine rack in his studio after he'd transcribed what would later become one of the most popular songs he would write in a long and storied career. A song about water and dreams. Marty had known it the minute he'd gotten it down. It's one of those things he was able to recognise – felt it in the quarry of his stomach – much like Jake with the ocean, Marty thought as he'd grabbed a-hold of the bottle and jogged out of the studio with the melody and lyrics still bouncing in his head.

Over lunch Marty had a glass or two and Jake had toyed with his out of politeness, not being a wine kind of man. But it didn't show in his friend's eyes. Something else did. Jake sensed, for a reason he'd yet to fathom, that Marty was angling to head out to sea. Sure, the sky was bright, and Mare's tails were absent. But – and it was a 'but' born generations ago – the sky and the winds were conspiring. They were telling lies, flattering to deceive, as they did oftentimes. This weather could, and probably would, turn. Jake knew of old that the ocean and alcohol didn't mix. Unless, of course, sucking on a gutful of chilled salt water was your cocktail of choice.

Both of their chipped, oval plates had been swept clean, juices 'n all. They'd eaten Mikey Vanderpool's swordfish seared, with a half lemon for Jake, and a smattering of herb-butter on the side for Marty. The swordfish devoured, they ate salad and baked potatoes like men who'd been on a forced march for two days.

"It's enough to make a man head back out to sea with his harpoon and nothing else. Thanks, Marty. That was terrific."

"I can't remember when I feasted like that. All those fancy restaurants we get to visit on the road. Hell, give me ironed fish here in Montauk any day."

"Did Mikey say where he got her?" Jake asked.

"Nah. Somewhere between here and the Vineyard. My guess is well east of the Vineyard. He wasn't saying, so I figure he was too far offshore for comfort."

"If you want the big fish that's where you got to go now. As far as Atlantis. Giants are out there in those canyons."

Marty looked away momentarily. "You ready Jake?"

"Ready? For what?"

"I know you are. Been sipping on the wine. Not one Bud, only iced water. We're heading out to sea, you and me."

"Sorry Marty no can do. I'll be pushed to get back in time to meet Amy off the school bus."

"I took care of that."

"What do you mean?"

"Danny King is picking Amy up. She's going stay with his family for a few hours, and he'll have her home by dusk." Marty removed the toothpick from the corner of his mouth, poured himself a large glass of water and took a deep swig before continuing. "We'd better leave."

"Marty, I don't trust the look of the sea out there. Sure, there's been a weather bounce in the last couple of hours, but it can get snotty out there real quick."

Marty leaned across the table, the toothpick back dancing between his teeth. His tongue hadn't been thickened by the wine, and he spoke with clarity, buoyed by the voices of those who had willed him to do this: Peter Duxbury, Nathan Freeman, Eddie Silver, Danny King, Jake's crew, the members of the East Hampton Baymen's Association, in fact all those who knew Jake and Amy Dealer. And all those who had ever known Lindy and Dougie Dealer.

"We all buried their bodies two months ago Jake. Now, we're gonna head out with your pail of ashes to bury their souls in the ocean." Marty didn't blink as tears rose like a gentle tide into the corners of his friend's kind brown eyes. "Jake, they lived with the ocean and its ways too, and now it's time for a part of them to go back there. More important Jake, it's now time for the living to live, while the dead continue to live on in all, and I do mean all, of our hearts. No one is asking for that to stop Jake. Just the grieving. For Amy's sake."

"One day it'll be weeks, months, years ago. But you know something Marty, to me it'll always be yesterday."

Marty got up from the table.

"I can't say I know how that feels Jake, but now you go collect your ashes."

Marty, short in stature and broad in build, nodded a respectful thanks to the owner as he walked off the terrace. Not once did he turn his head as he headed down the quay to where *Sweet Amy* was docked. He didn't need to look back. It wasn't something Marty ever did. Besides, Jake's heavy but surprisingly eager footfall told him that his friend wouldn't be too far behind.

Snotty weather or not.

CHAPTER 41

**10 Crick Hill Road, Menemsha,
Martha's Vineyard, Massachusetts.
Monday, 19th March 1990. Early afternoon.**

Ollie Swire switched off the Zenith radio and shook his head in slow disbelief. "Where *do* they get these numbers from? Thin air? How can you value something that the market hasn't tested for a hundred years, and won't be able to for another hundred? Money got cheap in the '80s, along with some of the people."

"What do you want me to say?"

"I'm not sure what I want to hear." Ollie narrowed his eyes. "We could talk about mundane issues if you want, like what's going on in Boston. Are you seeing anyone? Have you seen your father? How is he? Is he planning anything for his sixtieth birthday? Hang on, I know the answer to that one, no, of course he isn't."

"Enough. Please Ollie . . ."

Rarely, unless they were in the heat of a pro/con debate about a transaction, did Zephaniah address his grandfather in an abrupt manner.

"I'm half afraid of the answer I'll hear to the question I have yet to pose."

"That'd be a first."

"What?"

"You, being afraid of anything? Ask what you want. Besides, you know the answer as much as I know the question."

Zephaniah's come-back removed the stern mask of indignation – albeit false – from his grandfather's brow.

"OK, so go on . . ."

"Yes, I do have a good plan."

"You better have Zeph. Carl von Clausewitz, a wily Prussian general said: *'The enemy of a good plan is the dream of a perfect plan.'*"

"It is a good plan."

"Allow me to be the judge of that. Meanwhile, that's what I wanted to hear from the man who bears my name and who has just orchestrated, *behind my back, Zeph*," Ollie's tone dialled up one notch, "the theft of thirteen artworks from the Gardner Museum. My trusty old radio informs me the value exceeds $200 million and that it's the biggest ever 'heist' – awful word that – in the world."

* * *

Despite what had transpired, his grandson was not a man who had ever neglected Swire's. Ollie, 100% owner of its stock, knew this better than anyone. His grandson was a highly resourceful businessman. Not a conformist in his personal life, and certainly not a conformist in business, Zephaniah was nonetheless both conscientious and reliable. Ollie had learned during his days working the inside that you could never con – or cheat – an honest man, for honest men had the luxury of objectivity. To this end he had directed Zephaniah years ago by saying: *"Zeph, we're in the money-making business, not the money-stealing business."* Ollie had told him this without irony; he'd never regarded separating incurably greedy, dishonest marks from their money, as theft, per se.

An early lesson Zephaniah had grasped – much to his grandfather's pleasure – was the conundrum that any business comprising conformists is doomed, and a company whose management does not conform is equally doomed. In squaring that circle, Zephaniah had grasped how to run a complex business such as Swire's, which was, after all, a people business, one where the principal assets went home every evening via Swire's elevators.

"Zeph, I'm not critical of what you've done. Demand will always lead supply in what we do, and frankly, theft *could* be viewed as just another form of supply."

"Are you assuming that was the motive?"

"Of course, I am. Maybe not on your own account, but of another collector perhaps? Did someone commission you? Us?"

"Let's not speculate."

"Why ever not!" Ollie kept his pitch in check. "You're speculating with my company. You're more of a gambler than I am. I'd never bet the ranch, but you just have. And it's *my* ranch you've bet. I don't trust people who gamble Zeph, it's a mug's game, and if placing a bet isn't gambling what is?"

"It was you who taught me that if you toss a coin three times, and it comes up tails three times, the odds on it coming up tails a fourth time are the same."

"I hope you realise what you're doing?"

"I know precisely what I'm doing. No scorpion and frog punchline here."

Ollie glowered. "Fine. The strong take from the weak. The clever from the strong. We're all animals and we'll compete ferociously for each other's possessions. The vulture steals the antelope's eyes while the lion that killed it feasts on its flesh. Life is about acquisition and defence." Ollie picked up a soft cloth and began polishing a Baccarat tumbler. "To basics, Zeph. You're sure of *your* man Snale?"

Zephaniah didn't miss the emphasis. "Categorically. 101%."

"Your hired hand?"

"Never met him. Only Snale did. A Brit mercenary, ex-Royal Marine."

"What about any witnesses?"

A shimmer. "Only the guards."

Ollie caught it.

Zephaniah's left eyelid had feathered. A whip too long. Anyone but him would've missed it. Something was off. Not quite right. His grandson wasn't lying to him. He was lying to himself. I'll deal with it later, thought Ollie as he put the tumbler on the sideboard.

* * *

"People assume art thefts are targeted where there is the most art. That's not true. Targets are chosen because of their ease and accessibility," said Zephaniah.

"That's as maybe . . ."

"Wait a minute please," continued Zephaniah. "The authorities aren't interested in the recovery of artworks; they're only interested in arresting bodies, guilty or innocent. Recovery is the job of a financially motivated insurance investigator, and there isn't going to be one here. Besides, 90% of stolen artworks are never recovered."

"I know. What about a reward?"

"Using what for money? Shirt buttons? The Gardner has no money and no insurance." Zephaniah edged his elbows across the kitchen table. "However, I called Anne Hawley this morning."

"Busy man, with time on your hands too," cracked Ollie.

Zephaniah ignored the jibe. "She told me she's made calls to Sotheby's and Christie's."

"What's she calling them for do you suppose?" asked Ollie, knowing the answer.

"I suspect to help raise money for a reward or to pay a ransom. Rewards are usually 10%. That would be $20 million. The Gardner's own kitty is empty, and the Gardner's trustees won't pony up, that's for sure. With no insurance to put up a reward they're in bad shape as far as recovery is concerned. Ransom is out as well, due to zero cash, and frankly it's harder to ransom stolen art than it is to steal art."

"Don't be so sure on the ransom aspect Zeph. Whatever I may think of it, the Gardner enjoys a place in the heart of most Bostonians."

"I'm aware of that. But this was more than just a robbery."

Zephaniah spoke of his theft in the abstract; as if he were merely an observer, not the conductor and principal player. Being able to stand outside and look dispassionately at all that had so far transpired in his life, had ensured his survival in Vietnam. He hadn't apologised then, and he wasn't going to start now. Even to his beloved grandfather.

"Do you know if anyone from Christie's or Sotheby's has spoken to the museum?"

"Neither of them, so far."

"Good. You get to them first and suggest a sufficiently demotivating, but still generous, reward, $1 million will get it done. Don't forget people are fixated on round number psychology. That number will keep the bounty hunters at home too. Taubman will give Dede anything she wants after that ten-day Warhol auction she staged, when she sold his cookie jars and other tat for $25 million!"

"Do you want to make those calls Ollie?"

"No. This is your deal Zeph. It may be my ranch you've bet, but this is your hand to play out."

Zephaniah caught the chill in his grandfather's voice.

"That old cynic Mark Twain remarked, *'How easy it is to steal a white elephant, but how hard to get rid of it.'*"

"You fishing again, Ollie? All in good time."

Ollie straight-up ignored the comment.

"Indulge me for a few minutes. Let's discuss past art thefts. Perhaps we can both learn something from history, I doubt it though."

"Sure Ollie."

"The details of the theft of the *Mona Lisa* in 1911 are too well documented to bear further scrutiny. But on that hot August day in 1911, the same day President Taft was signing the bill making New Mexico the 47th State of the Union, one Vincenzo Peruggia, a casual worker at the Louvre, coolly removed the *Mona Lisa* from its four fixings in broad daylight. Then, while hiding in a broom cupboard, he carefully discarded its bulky frame. He concealed Leonardo's 400-year-old wood panel in his white Louvre-uniform smock and walked out of the museum into the morning sunshine and crowds on the Rue de Rivoli. All fine so far?"

"I know the story, Ollie."

"As we all do, but here's my point. Interest in the Louvre, and the Florentine lady herself, soared in the two and half years that Peruggia kept the painting hidden away in his Paris garret and later in his studio in Florence. In no time at all, the *Mona Lisa's* absence made the not-so-faint Parisian heart grow extraordinarily fond of what the nation had lost when it was stolen. Objects, like people, often take on an undeserved lustre of interest after they've gone. Take something for granted and then have it disappear, and well . . ."

"Your point, Ollie?" prompted Zephaniah.

"Please tell me you didn't orchestrate this theft to promote the Gardner?"

"Nothing could have been further from my mind. The opposite in fact."

"Well, that's what you will have accomplished Zeph. You'll have made this museum a cause célèbre. People will flock to the Gardner from now on, in droves. Even the postcards in their shop will sell out. Such is human nature." Ollie paused. "My understanding of Gardner's Will is that it states the Trustees will have to leave the spaces where the stolen paintings used to hang. So, visitors will be treated to gaping and empty frames that read: *The Concert, Christ in the Storm on the Sea of Galilee* and so on. Tell me that isn't totally absurd?"

"It is."

"The perfect crime of the Modernist era, no? The public will congregate at the Gardner to gawp at empty frames and bare spaces, just as they did in Paris. For God's sake Zeph, even Franz Kafka lined up at the Louvre to stare at the blank wall where the *Mona Lisa* once hung!"

Zephaniah toyed with what remained of his wine. He said nothing.

"Let me continue. Another fascinating theft occurred in 1953. A dealer I knew well, Gustav Delbanco, received a telephone call at his London gallery requesting that he leave right away, and head for Room 24 in the Victoria & Albert Museum. In that room, the anonymous caller advised, he would find the small Rodin sculpture, *Psyche*, which had been stolen in broad daylight from Gustav's Cork Street gallery some four months earlier. Do you know this tale, Zeph?"

"No."

"Well, much to Gustav's relief, and surprise, *Psyche*, was in the V&A, where the caller said it would be. When Gustav picked it up, he found an envelope underneath. He tore it open and read the letter which began with a few lines from Yeats. I have a copy in our Boston archives. Gustav was a friend who knew I would appreciate what had happened." Ollie poured himself a glass of water. "Anyway, what became apparent was that the thief was not really a thief, but merely an art lover. In the letter he had written to Gustav, he explained there had been no mercenary intent behind his appropriation, merely that he'd wanted to live with 'her', the exquisite beauty that was Rodin's *Psyche*. Now, at the same time the Tate Gallery was attempting to raise the funds to buy Rodin's *Le Basier*, and the thief, who'd signed the letter *'An Impecunious Art Student'*, had pinned a ten-shilling note to his letter, as his contribution to the funds being sought. End of story. The dealer got his sculpture back. The Tate got their money, and in 1955 the nation got their Rodin for £7,500. And a flat-broke art student had an affair of the heart satiated. Everyone was happy."

Zephaniah took a last sip of wine.

"No Ollie, there was no altruism to what I did. You know me too well to think there ever could have been."

"I'm usually good at figuring out motives, and whilst altruism was never going to be yours, it might have played a small role, no?"

"No," added Zephaniah with finality.

Ollie shrugged. "Alright. So, unlike Gustav's student, how about sheer mercenary intent then?"

"Perhaps . . ."

"Terrible word that, Zeph. Indecisive."

"We both know it's much harder to ransom paintings than to steal them, but find a use for them as collateral . . .?"

"We've been trying to buy the stolen Caravaggio you're alluding to for years now." Ollie shook his head in a silent sigh.

"Ever since *The Nativity* was stolen in 1969 from the Oratorio of San Lorenzo in Palermo, the *Cosa Nostra* has for years passed it around as collateral for various payments. Deals. Drugs. It's just money on the wall to them, not a magnificent painting." Zephaniah drew in a deep breath before continuing. "There are a couple of different leads on its whereabouts. We do know the *Cosa Nostra* stole it as a gift to the speciously corrupt Prime Minister Andreotti. When Andreotti inspected its condition he handed it back to them, in exchange for more favours of course. Last I heard, it was in South Africa having been paid for in blood-diamonds."

"And no one cares now. Even the Italian government seem to have forgotten their own Caravaggio. Do you think it'll ever surface Zeph?" asked Ollie.

"No, not now. As you said, no one cares. In America the notion of art theft has not really hit us. If Philadelphia woke up one morning to find the *Liberty Bell* was on the missing list, and that it might be languishing on the ranch of a corrupt Mexican politician, well, maybe people might sit up, but even then, I doubt it. Art is the preserve of the rich and most people aren't rich."

"OK Zeph, put motive aside, where are you going to hide them?"

"In the absence of a forgotten Austrian salt mine, I'd suggest No Man's Land?"

Ollie just smiled.

So, that was what it had all been about that day? An art theft. People never failed to surprise him. And that was what had given him an edge all these years: the element of surprise, as donor and recipient of the same.

"Altaussee had been a salt mine for over 700 years. Disused when the Nazis discovered it and, in those mines, they stored their plunder and Europe's treasure: 6,500 oils, 1,200 watercolours, countless books, tapestries and armour, all in perfect condition. The salt mines' humidity was never above 65%, in summer the temperature was a constant 40°F, yet in winter the temperature rose to 47°F. An ideal environment for the preservation of art." Ollie sipped his water. "There's nothing so accommodating on No Man's Land I'm afraid."

"Did you know that Vermeer's *Painter in His Studio* was in the Nazi's Altaussee cache?" deflected Zephaniah.

"Hitler was obsessed by Vermeer. *The Astronomer*, was his finest painting to my mind. The Nazi's looted it from Édouard de Rothschild in 1940 when they invaded Paris. We tried to buy it, remember, a few years ago but failed. In 1983 the Rothschild family, outraged at having to pay French inheritance tax, begrudgingly gave it to the Louvre in lieu. Win some lose some, eh Zeph?" Ollie shot his grandson an uncompromising look. "So, is this why you need your grandfather's help? To hide your stolen art?"

"No, but can you come up with a better, more secure place? Somewhere that doesn't make this crime federal. No Man's Land is in Massachusetts. Transporting stolen goods across state lines would make the theft a federal offence."

"I hadn't seen that angle," lied Ollie. "For the time being they're better stored in my studio. Unlike the Gardner, it is temperature controlled and extraordinarily secure. Peruggia kept the *Mona Lisa* stashed amongst the kindling wood in the fire grate for over two years. The idea of hiding these paintings where no one is allowed to set foot is very sound." Again, he waited a beat. "One last time Zeph. Why?"

"In good time, my time. OK?"

"For a while. But *my* sense of a while. Fair?"

A brief silence spun open. Zephaniah nodded in agreement.

"So, off you go down to our branch office and call Sotheby's and Christie's. Take an old man's advice. Fix the ransom at $1million. That's only half a cent on the dollar according to the valuation of $200 million.

Offer to split it three ways, and you transfer our $333,334 into *their* escrow accounts. They'll go for it. Believe me. Your deal-closer will be your promise to remain silent about Swire's involvement. Make it so that Sotheby's and Christie's get all the news coverage for the reward idea tomorrow. You know how much I detest PR. After that's agreed, call Mrs Jack's museum with the good news. Swire's will then bank all the Gardner's gratitude. And with that gratitude will go the kingdom, the power and the glory for ever and ever. Amen."

Zephaniah rose from the table, and without another word, he opened the front door to the porch.

Long before the theft, he had decided on the exact same strategy as Ollie had just suggested. Great minds do think alike. Not 500 yards in front of him stood Swire's branch office: the public payphone in the car park beside the gritty sand of Menemsha Beach, the Texaco station and Poole's and Larsen's fish markets.

The same phone booth that had served Swire's for years, just as it served the men who put to sea each day to earn a living.

PART FIVE

FRIDAY, 30TH MARCH 1990

CHAPTER 42

**The Garden Flat, 4 Bina Gardens,
South Kensington, London, England.
Friday, 30th March 1990. ?**

Dr J. Flack DClinPsy just about made out the shrill ring of her telephone from where she'd been living – deep underneath a mound of bedclothes. The bloody answering machine was failing in its duty; a simple one too. All that was demanded of it was to answer her damned calls and take her messages. The insistent ring continued, as if it would do so forever. There was a hideous air of permanence to it.

Jessie had lived alone, very alone, and for far too long under her duvet (or comforter, as her American friend Cory Mount insisted on calling it), to have recalled that you had to play – then erase – the messages before the machine would pick up calls anew.

Her reflex reaction was to bury her head deeper into the soft folds of the duvet. She was NOT going to leave its safety, or its snug-fug, to answer the phone. Life was almost bearable under her duvet. She liked it here, no, she loved it here. At last, she had found a place where she could cope, somewhere she could call home; this place was her home, tepee, yurt, tent, in fact it was her entire universe, and it had been for, how long was it now? It could be days, weeks, months even . . . Her calendar was no longer diurnal, canonical, sidereal, Babylonian, Islamic, Gregorian or even fucking menstrual. Huh, and that opportune reminder of mood-swings and cramps that retreated into blood, well, that too had ceased God only knew how long ago. No, the effluxion of time was a meagre hypothesis to Dr J. Flack DClinPsy and was as abstract as time can only be to the truly damaged and broken. To Jessie Flack, no, Dr J. Flack, DClinPsy child psychologist and near burnt-out resident of the delightful garden flat at 4 Bina Gardens, South Kensington, London, England.

The telephone continued ringing. Was it inside her head? Or was it ringing outside her head? She was no longer sure. So, like a wary meerkat in a hostile savannah, she popped her head up above her burrow. It was dark. But then it was always dark.

And the telephone was ringing. For real. Damn.

Her intestines and stomach hurt momentarily at their release from the foetal position she had long adopted. Hunger-pangs were the only reminder that a world did exist outside of her Laura Ashley print duvet, (Lordy, how she hated the blue and yellow flower print bedlinen, and not just because it was another one of her mother's mail-order *I-REALLY-do-love-you-but-I-just-don't-have-the-time-to-shop-for-Christmas-presents* offerings). Throwing all the covers off her back, with a combination of anger and desperation, she staggered out of bed. The insistence of whoever this caller was had caused her to lose patience, something she, never, ever did. Truth at volume yes, and then rarely. Anger never.

This call would get answered, and woe betide the poor sod on the other end: hospital colleague, parent of a patient, friend, (were any left? She wondered) or just a wrong number. With her left foot squashing a discarded pizza box, she wiggled her toes through the tissue-thin cardboard into what remained of an ancient *Quattro Stagioni* – and she stood absolutely still, her baggy men's pyjama top hanging unbuttoned and open. Only her toes moved. Suddenly, she felt a chill. Then she grabbed the walkabout handset and extended its chrome aerial. It fizzed and crackled hopelessly. Without cutting the line, Jessie hurled the handset into the pile of dirty laundry occupying her sofa like a family of grubby squatters. Bloody walkabout phones never did work properly.

Her skin goose-bumped. She looked at the safety of her bed as the landline continued to ring on mercilessly in the sitting room, the miserable portable now muted by manky clothes. Damn it, this call I am going to answer, she muttered to what remained of her inner self.

With that very action, that very thought, she became conscious that she might have at long last regained the ability to make a decision. Deep down, she recollected that the ability to form rudimentary decisions often led to the altar of reason. And from there: right from wrong: good from bad: truth from deceit.

Jessie dithered as these random notes flicked REM-like in front of her eyes. The darned phone was still ringing . . . but worse . . . her bed was winking at her as seductively as a lover she had only ever known in dreams might have done.

Good Lord, it had all been too blurred for too long.

Tentatively, she lifted her foot off the pizza and inched towards the sitting room door. She felt her brow and top lip moisten. Her mouth dried up at the possibility that the duvet as opiate might, just might, be coming to an end . . .

Then she shivered as she remembered what had caused it all. It had been a telephone call. One out of thousands had penetrated all her defences. But there had been so, so many calls. Maybe they had all accumulated and struck her down. Semi-naked, she now heard an orchestra of thin, desperate voices in her head and in her heart. And once again Jessie turned back towards her bed.

If there was a good Lord upon high – and she doubted there was – what she'd been allowed to hear, to see, to weep to, and finally succumb to, no one should ever have had to bear witness to. Not even God, let alone a gifted and professional child psychologist of just thirty-six. And certainly not the children. No. There was no God out there. Proof existed: no God – male or female – would have allowed the doctor in her to crash and burn. No, a God would have kept her sane and whole, so she could protect those who could not protect themselves. It would be many months before she grew to accept that if she hadn't had her breakdown when she did, she might have unintentionally let down an innocent child. And that if she couldn't give 110% to those who had suffered at the hands of adults, then she had no use, no value, no worth in this world. None at all.

With an effort that would be minimal to any other human being, but one that was Everestic to her, she lifted her chin and jumped over the detritus of her room and ran to the telephone.

"Who is this?" she whispered in a faint voice, one that trembled as the broken wing of a butterfly might.

There were only background noises and fumbling sounds at the other end.

"Who is this?"

"Jessie, it's me. Cory. I thought you were never going to answer. I've been letting it ring and ring on the speaker," he said softly. "How's it going Jessie?"

"Been better. Been better." So much for giving the caller a lungful of undeserved invective. "Leave me be. OK?" Jessie managed another whisper.

"Well, no, not OK actually."

"What do you mean?"

"I need your help."

"I need my help too. I'm not much use to you or anyone."

"Let me be the judge of that, Jessie. Lookit, it's gone 9 a.m. here in Boston . . ."

Jessie pulled a silent face of embarrassment. That made it after two in the afternoon in grey old London Town. She really had lost track of her life, she thought; then, as if it were a postscript, she added, 'what life?'

Cory was still talking. " . . . you could be here in time for a late dinner if you jumped on a flight. My treat too and not coach. How about it?" He fell silent for a second. "I really do need your help."

"Pass. Thanks anyway."

"You can stay with me. We can play catch up. We've not seen each other in over a year."

"Ordering takeouts is the most I can do. An airplane seat is, just, well . . ."

"I'll do all that, all you have to do is simply turn up at Heathrow." She *heard* his smile. "So, what's your call Jessie? Window or aisle?"

Cory Mount, long-time friend, and oh-so-very-*nearly*-once-upon-a-memory her lover had grasped only the sketchiest of details as to what had occurred. And that was due to the fact that he'd tracked down two other doctors who'd been volunteers with her at ChildLine since its inception in the fall of 1986. No one would give him anything other than a picture painted with broad, ambiguous strokes. No one was talking – apart from hundreds of 'in danger' children who rang ChildLine every day that is. Not even Jessie.

"Cory, I've got to go now."

That said, she replaced the receiver with deliberate precision and sank to the floor as dry, heavy sobs convulsed her entire being. Her body, her mind, her soul, all shook as if they were being rent asunder.

Which they were.

CHAPTER 43

SWIRE'S, 84 Beacon Street,
Beacon Hill, Boston, Massachusetts.
Friday, 30th March 1990. 09:05.

Despondently, Cory laid the handset in its place and looked about his elegant, panelled Boston office before dropping his head in his hands.

"Oh Jessie," he muttered aloud. ". . . Jessie."

His dear friend was that rarest of human beings. She had an intuitive gift, singular and unteachable, for seeing others – adults and children alike – in the shade of their successes and the sunlight of their failures. Yet all she now saw was her own perceived failures in the noonday glare of an equatorial sun. He rubbed his blue eyes to beat back a well of tears until, Bugs Bunny-like, stars illuminated his dusk.

His employer, Zephaniah Swire, had instructed him the day after the theft to undertake additional research on the principal paintings that had been stolen. The media had already dubbed the Isabella Stewart Gardner Museum heist as *The Theft of The Century*. And that was twelve days ago now.

His eyes still blinking, he scanned his Chippendale Partner's desk, its mahogany barely visible. Neat vanilla-coloured folders covered it, and each bore just one word: **SWIRE'S**. Inside were Cory's voluminous notes – all handwritten in purple ink on fine vellum paper. Despite his labours, he was none the wiser. He was nowhere closer to figuring out a 'why' certain paintings had been taken, and 'why' others remained hanging. It was very puzzling, to say the least. He needed a puzzle expert. He needed Jessie.

* * *

Cory picked up an HB pencil from his desk and leaned back in his chair. He had to think his pitch through. It was no office secret that during his tenure as Head of Research he'd grown a CIA-like army of 'agents in the field' around the globe who fed him intel on all manner of subjects: divorces, death and fiscal doom usually topped his billboard chart.

But Jessie was very different from an indiscreet Swiss private banker. She was a doctor of child psychology who was (had been, anyway) a highly respected expert in disciplines such as 'profiling' to solve crimes. Not long before her breakdown, she'd been feted for assisting Scotland Yard in a gruesome case of child abduction involving two six-year-old twins: she'd built a psych profile of the paedophile which had led to a swift arrest and the twins being rescued unharmed. The story had played out in all the news headlines. And Cory knew that Mr Swire read the English newspapers.

Cory began his 'contact juggling' with his HB pencil in between T, T1 space, and 1 of his right hand (a wildly irritating skill he'd mastered in Tokyo during his Brown University days whilst studying Ukiyo-e) but it helped to concentrate his mind on the dilemma.

He had a choice. He could inform Mr Swire – knowing that Jessie's reputation might ruffle his feathers. Or he could elect not to inform him – he had the authority to hire and fire. Or, better still, he could give him a nod as to his intentions. And move on. Then again, he knew his boss had no truck with interlopers, ambushes or unknowns; cautions born in Vietnamese jungles no doubt.

After a solid five minutes of 'pencil 'coptering' at great speed, he pressed the intercom with his left hand.

"Good morning, Mrs Elliott."

"Good morning, Cory. How may I assist?" asked Mrs Elliott, who had trenchantly guarded – Cerberus-like – Mr Swire's outer office since the beginning of time. The woman was formidable.

"Please don't disturb him if he's in a meeting, however I'd like five minutes on the phone as soon as."

"Hold on please."

Only two employees – Cory and Head of Accounting – had been granted by Mrs Elliott *'Mr S. Privileges'*: the ability to interrupt any meeting, any call, any time.

"Good morning, Cory how can I help?"

He'd had been put straight through to Mr Swire.

"After the Gardner theft you asked me to start digging. Well, I'm now empty handed and I'm in Sydney."

"I see," said Zephaniah. *Tell me something I couldn't have guessed*, he thought, but continued by saying. "Now that you and your army of spies have been through the Earth's Inner Core, what's your next move?"

"I'm going to take a different tack Mr Swire, and this call is to give you a heads-up."

"That's good of you. But there's no reason to. Your department has no reporting or budget restraints."

"I've asked someone I met in London when I worked as Christie's to assist. Her background is in psychology, and she consults with Scotland Yard on difficult criminal cases." Cory knew he was skirting the edges of vague.

"I repeat, your hires are your call."

"I know that sir, but I've invited her to come to Boston. She's not 100% confirmed yet. If she accepts the temporary post, she won't be based at our office, and I'll organise her accommodation."

"And her brief would be what precisely?" The hairs on Zephaniah's neck itched. His Head of Research had a global retinue of disparate sources that he gathered all manner of tips from. He viewed Cory as a 'results and solutions' man. A darned good one too.

"In brief, I'd like an outsider's profile of the artworks themselves. As I can't find any trace of any of them, I'd like to know more about why this piece and not that piece was stolen. Frankly, I'm running out of ideas."

Instinctively, Zephaniah didn't like the sound of this. Spying. Hunting. Prying. All skills he'd used in Vietnam when he'd set traps for the enemy. His gut informed him that there was something vaguely threatening in Cory's idea of hiring a Brit profiler. However, this wasn't his move to make. Slamming the brakes on Cory's initiative – and it was a good one, the FBI were using profilers more often now – might arouse suspicions. He'd never before squashed any of Cory's ideas and doing so now was not the smart play. Itching neck and raised hackles or not. So, let Cory be Cory, he thought wryly.

Then he too had a flash of inspiration. Another tactic he'd deployed in Vietnam. A 'False Flag' mission. Distraction. This time, worldwide. Perhaps Cory's smorgasbord of contacts could pin the blame on an organised crime syndicate? Boston's own Whitey Bulger's 'Winter Hill Gang' were always a target for major city crimes. Sicily's *Cosa Nostra* were well known for using stolen art as collateral. The list of possibilities was endless.

"I gave you a task, just complete it however you see fit. Hire who you want. I have faith in you and your resources. Use your wide-reaching international cast of snitches, Cory. Just get the job done."

"Do you require a memo from me? Her name, qualifications, age, etc?"

"Of course not. Have I ever requested the names of Zurich concierges or Brazilian tax inspectors and God knows who else you keep on your 'black box' payroll?" Zephaniah laughed, hoping to wrong foot him.

"Never sir."

"Fine then. We done?"

"Yes. Thank you, Mr Swire."

His neck-hairs stood down. Let's send his Rolodex of spies down dark rabbit holes to hunt and confuse, reflected Zephaniah. All they'll return to the surface with will be rabbit shit in one hand, and the answer to *'What's the square root of zero?'* in the other.

CHAPTER 44

**The Garden Flat, 4 Bina Gardens,
South Kensington, London, England.
Friday, 30th March 1990. 14:07.**

"Gone two o'clock in the afternoon, not bad, not bad at all. Christ Almighty, what kind of state are you in girl?"

She spoke aloud, and with absolute clarity, as she studied herself in the bathroom mirror. The fluorescent light was doing her face no kindness whatsoever, which was a good thing. She saw, as opposed to pretending not to notice, what she looked like: her ever-present smile-creases now resembled fault lines, and her cheeks were puffy and pizza-spotty. Her thick, naturally auburn hair hung in greasy, petrified mats, and like waning moons, patent-black crescents sagged below evergreen eyes. They too were now dull and shot-red, their whites yellowed with terror. What had happened to the little girl from Barbados she wondered, as the full horror of what stared back sunk in. That little girl, the one whose good 'county' British parents had moved to the Caribbean when she was just two years old?

Jessie's father, a calm and mild-mannered GP, long defeated by bleak British winters, vain politicians and a domineering wife had been an impatient emigrant. It was he alone who had filled their crumbling plantation house with warmth. He had delighted in the Bajan sun, its people, the cricket and even grew to respect the tired – and often tiresome – ex-patriot community he was there to serve with his unassuming, wrapped-in-tissue-paper bedside manner.

England, its mores akin to its blanket-grey weather, receded into someone else's history with each sunset green-flash he'd been able to catch. But her mother had remained that bastion of all things British, and worse: colonial, judgemental in private, obsequious in public, ambassadorial in bearing and church-going on Sundays – for the gossip only. Ironically, it was she who'd led the only of child Dr and Mrs Flack into caring for children, and not into the swirl and chatter of the Home Counties with its preordained conclusion. A suitable marriage.

Jessie had grown up in love with their patrician garden, one of dense and tropical foliage: Royal Palms that swayed, fronds of banana trees that mapped shade, old Cannonball trees whose vines hung like verdant Spanish Moss, funny looking bearded fig trees, Casuarina pines that rustled in the sultry breeze and her favourite, a gnarled but handsome Pride of India tree. For as long as she could remember, 'her' tree had been home to a family Green Monkeys. She'd made a triangular nest in carpentry class on her bedroom terrace, to attract her favourite island bird, the Bananaquit. Smaller than a wee sparrow, they sported a vibrant yellow chest plumage, as if they wore tailored Savile Row waistcoats. With piercing red eyes and striped heads, akin to Badger's from her favourite book – *The Wind in the Willows* – they did come, they did settle, and they did breed. And before she left for school each morning, a teaspoon of demerara sugar dissolved in water was placed – just so – for her new family of sugar birds. And it was in this magical garden of butterflies, birds, monkeys, wild orchids and pink ginger lilies that the local children would come to play, and where, as an only child, every visiting child became her brother or her sister.

Even into her teens, she was always surrounded by children of all ages. And as she grew older her voice took on a soft West Indian lilt, which as a young adult had ripened into one with the pace and texture of the sweet sugar from the nearby cane fields. Aside from her seemingly endless patience, it would be her voice, her unique tone as a doctor, that would prove to be her greatest ally when she needed to coax a deep, hidden trauma from a child. That, and Jessie's obsessional need to do what was right, and to live by that, however violent that truth sometimes was.

And as Jessie turned away from the mirror, she saw, at last, what was right, what was wrong, what was, perhaps, even true. The mirror on the wall had told her all that and more. Now it was time to do what was right again.

Dr J. Flack DClinPsy had *really* had enough of doing what was wrong.

CHAPTER 45

18 Louisburg Square, Beacon Hill, Boston, Massachusetts. Friday, 30th March 1990. 09:07.

Zephaniah Swire sat behind his glass-topped Linley desk at 18 Louisburg Square with a straight-backed military bearing, as if he was presiding over a court martial. In fact, all he was doing was sipping his Blue Mountain coffee while he perused an article from below the fold on the front page of *The Boston Globe;* his Scyphozoan medusae were certainly not on trial.

There was one section, towards the middle of the article, that brought a sardonic smile to his face. His eyes lit up momentarily with what might have been delight, but could also have been derision. It could even have been both.

Discarding his coffee, he stroked his shaven cheeks with a light touch, then slowly closed his eyes to shut out the world outside. He gave off the hazy air of a man faintly perturbed, though not, it had to be said, unduly perturbed.

CHAPTER 46

**10 Crick Hill Road, Menemsha,
Martha's Vineyard, Massachusetts.
Friday, 30th March 1990. 09:07.**

Ollie Swire rose to his feet and leaned against the wall beside his kitchen window. In his left hand he held a glass of warm mineral water, into which he had squeezed the juice of a whole lemon. He gripped the crystal tumbler firmly.

Stretched out before him, the Atlantic looked strangely docile; the ocean's appearance can be so deceiving at times he reminded himself. *The Boston Globe* lay discarded – but read – on a cedar footstool next to where he stood. Ollie picked an imaginary wave on the far horizon, where the sky met the sea, and locked his gaze on it as if he were a hypnotist.

Soon, very soon, Ollie was a man so deep in thought that it rendered him almost cataleptic.

CHAPTER 47

**Montauk Harbour, Montauk, Long Island, New York.
Friday, 30th March 1990. 09:07.**

Jake Dealer busied himself about the deck and cabin-house of *Sweet Amy* prepping all manner of details: lines, bait, harpoon, provisions, engine oil, bilges, electronics, nets, windshield seals . . . the list was endless if you were to survive on the ocean.

The weather forecast was in: not great, not bad. Marty was late as he'd been held up in the city the night before on business, so Jake would make the final weather call when he fetched up. After all, Montauk to Martha's Vineyard was a ways away, ninety plus miles into open ocean.

Jake had adapted the plan so as to arrive in the Vineyard before nightfall, moor up, grab an early feed and get a predawn jump the next day. This was a long-planned trip, and they were both eager to hunt for their own swordfish now.

As he organised the boat, he caught sight of his battered thermos full of coffee and a copy of *Newsday*. Plenty of time for that tabloid bullshit later when they were steaming east to the fishing grounds off No Man's Land. Besides, he only ever really used his daily paper to wrap fish in. They never did offer much news of interest.

CHAPTER 48

**SWIRE'S, 84 Beacon Street,
Beacon Hill, Boston, Massachusetts.
Friday, 30th March 1990. 09:07.**

Cory Mount returned from the outer office, where others in his department sat sorting the chaff from the wheat that was the lifeblood of Swire's research department. Somehow, he now found himself, at the age of just thirty-eight, as its head. There never had been, nor ever would be, such a thing as a 'mission statement' at Swire's, but his employer had told him on his first day just what the company's keystone was: *"Mr Mount, there are no such people as art fences, there are just art dealers. Research and provenance are all."*

Cory removed his copy of *The Boston Globe* from a slim, leather briefcase, the one Jessie had given him years ago. A story below the fold caught his attention and he began to read it avidly. Too avidly, in fact.

CHAPTER 49

**Further Lane, Amagansett, Long Island, New York.
Friday, 30th March 1990. 09:07.**

Marty Drew felt a tad groggy; surely red wine had been classified as a 'food group' by now? He'd been flown into East Hampton Airport on Columbia's luxe helicopter late in the evening, and his driver had pit-stopped at The American Hotel in Sag Harbour for a snack. Then, one thing had turned into something else . . . Thank heavens for the permanent suite he kept there.

He really needed to hustle, as Jake would be itching to leave for the Vineyard. He was looking forward to a day or two of zero business, salt water under the keel, fresh ocean air in his lungs, and to watch a master work his magic. Besides, he'd just worked his magic with Columbia; they'd loved his new song.

The immense range in his beachfront Amagansett kitchen was littered with newsprint, but he only ever read *The New York Times*. He glanced at the front page; Christ was he sick of politics! Hurriedly he flicked through the pages, until on page five a small article, on a topic he knew nothing about, slowed him down. He speed-read it, while praying to God that the sea air would clear his woozy head. It usually did. Running late, Marty glanced at his old Rolex, grabbed a cap and windcheater, headed out the door of the sprawling mansion and hopped into his British Racing Green Jaguar.

Hell, nothing wrong with a seawater shower. It was only later, driving east to Montauk, that he realised the cap had BAD HAIR DAY scripted on the brow. Hey, never a truer word. Who cared. He and his good friend were going to iron a sword.

CHAPTER 50

**Shiner's Diner, 86 Van Ness Street,
Fenway Park, Boston, Massachusetts.
Friday, 30th March 1990. 09:07.**

Shannon O'Leary felt full of the joys of early spring, there was a bounce in her step. After a brief rain shower in the night, the day promised to be crisp and dry. She always walked to work when she could, rather than endure the crowded public transport system; open spaces reminded her of her Gloucester childhood. And at 6 a.m. she'd arrived at Shiner's Diner as it was opening. Now, some three hours later, the breakfast crowd had moved on, and she was sneaking a ten-minute break with a Marlboro and a copy of *The Boston Globe* a customer had left behind.

Coffee and cigarette in one hand, she tucked herself away in a corner booth. Mrs Shiner never minded so long as she was discreet, and business was slack. An article below the fold on the front page caught her attention. Blood drained from her candy-apple cheeks. Shannon stubbed out her unfinished cigarette, mussed her curly red hair nervously, cleared the booth and looked about her as she undid her apron.

Just where was Mrs Shiner?

CHAPTER 51

**The Garden Flat, 4 Bina Gardens,
South Kensington, London, England.
Friday, 30th March 1990. 14:10.**

Jessie moved about her apartment with purpose. In her left hand she held a large black garbage bag, in her right hand, she clenched a cigarette. A French cigarette. She'd quit smoking seven years ago and had taken it up again seven minutes ago. She cared not one whit that the black tobacco was stale and came from an assortment of packs she kept for guests. Her head felt light and fuzzy from the nicotine in her bloodstream, and long dormant neurotransmitters began erasing the sleep out of her. She was not only waking up, she was also living again. And not a moment too soon, she thought, suddenly mindful of time being wasted.

Still dressed in her men's pyjama top, perspiration from a mix of exertion and excitement glued its cotton to her lithe body. Wiping her brow, she sat down on a stool at her breakfast bar. Three black bags lay on the floor. A job well done: two for the Oxfam Shop, and one full of junk, rubbish, old cartons. The wreckage of lost weeks. (Although it would be many months before she recognised that they had been anything but 'lost', for she would emerge stronger and a more insightful child psychologist.)

At her side was a packet of cigarettes – a temporary crutch, she reminded herself – her telephone book, and a pad on which to jot down immediate tasks. First, run a bath. Second, call her tubby Greek-Cypriot hairdresser on the corner of Harrington Road and Queensgate. Never in her life had she cropped her auburn hair short – it had always been long and mane-like – and now was the time to change that. If she didn't like it, *tant pis*, it'd grow back. Third, find a cleaning service in the Yellow Pages to spring-clean her apartment. Fourth, where was her handbag with her chequebook and credit cards in? Fifth, call Cory to establish what he needed. And it must be important. He was one of life's givers, not takers, and she was dying to tell him that she'd love to come to Boston, as soon as possible, if the invitation still held. She hoped it did. And in her heart, she suspected it would. The very idea of America at this moment in time was not only healing, but persuasive.

As she drew heavily on another cigarette, she worried about her chequebook and credit cards and where she had 'hidden' them. How was she going to pay for the radical haircut, much-needed manicure and facial and a new pair of Levi's, a white shirt and a dark blue blazer before she fled to Heathrow? Everything else she'd need, toiletries included, she'd buy at the airport. But only if she could find her money.

Decision: switch task 1 with task 2.

"Hi Panos, it's Jessie Flack. I need a big favour please, a cut, a manicure and an emergency facial. Don't mind who, I just need it all." She paused. "Like very soon-ish."

The voice at the end groaned.

"Please Panos, it *is* very important." She dithered as the reluctant hairdresser began to be seduced.

"How soon is soon Jessie dear?"

"Twenty minutes . . . *please*."

"Jessie, you know how busy we get on Friday afternoons! Alright, come right away and I'll do the cut myself? The manicure and the facial we'll sort out somehow . . . Just hurry!"

Her persuasive Bajan lilt was back, alive and well. Only three more tasks to accomplish before she would allow herself to ring Cory. She giggled like a child. There was only one innocent sound in the world, that of a child laughing, Jessie reminded herself.

Yes, it was good to use those facial muscles again.

CHAPTER 52

**SWIRE'S, 84 Beacon Street,
Beacon Hill, Boston, Massachusetts.
Friday, 30th March 1990. 09:10.**

Just how Cory Mount III had found himself to be working for Swire's was still a mystery to him, even after eight years. Unlike any other organisation in the art world, you could not apply to Swire's, whatever your qualifications. Swire's sought you out with – or without – qualifications; Swire's hired people, not diplomas.

In effect, Zephaniah Swire would (or so legend had it) identify a key position – in Cory's case, it had been Deputy Head of Research. From there Swire's would return to first principles: the starting point being 'research'. The company had built their hard-won global reputation on knowing everything about every major work of art in the world. All that mattered to Swire's was the ability of their chosen candidate to perform exemplary work. Both Ollie and Zephaniah Swire had long recognised that true experts, in whatever their chosen fields, were the spine of their business. The keenest buyers and the greediest sellers were by nature attracted to unimpeachable knowledge. And the power that conferred. Travelling previews, PR campaigns and glossy catalogues were the costly gimmicks of others with less foresight.

As the eldest son of an established and well-to-do Connecticut family, Cory's start in life had been, considering his family's cobalt-blue Democratic background, entirely predictable. Aged twenty-two with sun-bleached hair cut unfashionably short, he had graduated *magna cum laude* from Brown University having majored in Art History. Rather than procure an example of Detroit or Turin's finest as a graduation award, his scholarly father had endowed him with, as he had put it, *"The bread and the butter for two years in London. You want jam Cory, well, that's up to you."*

Without havering, Cory had accepted his father's generous offer, which also came with the rent on a charming mews cottage in South Kensington. But more important, the gift came with his family's blessing. If he had been in America, his rite of passage would be waiting tables for his jam, in England however he wore a different apron; a maroon one with the name Christie's emblazoned on it where, part-time, he humped, packed and sped around their South Kensington offices with an emergent pleasure. There was a certain electricity to the warren of peculiar auction rooms that he found compelling. None of the big-ticket art sales for South Kensington, they all took place at the Christie's HQ in St James's. 'Christie's South Ken', as it was affectionately known, was the domain of hundreds of prospectors – as he saw them – digging in their own Klondike: sellers panning for gold with their long-lost trinkets of toys, paintings or furniture, while Argus-eyed buyers sifted through the water and mud until they turned up their own gold.

It was in this warren of corridors that he had first bumped into – literally – Jessie Flack as she'd jostled full pelt in search of the cavern where the annual *'Ski Poster Auction'* was being held. Whilst colliding bodies didn't count as a meet-cute, his wine-coloured Christie's apron must have helped. Knowing a short cut through a private storeroom, Cory sped her into the quirky auction room just as the hammer fell on Lot 1. Subsequently, he learnt over a bottle of Italian plonk in a local basement wine bar, that the lot she'd been after – a 1930's A* poster of the Matterhorn – had been Lot 2. Having had it knocked down to her at its low reserve, she felt she owed the young American a proper 'thank you'. Chuffed with her bargain, she'd sought him out. PDQ. Hence the Pinot Grigio. Painstakingly, she'd explained her symbiotic relationship between surfing on the wild Atlantic Ocean coastline of Barbados, and the beauty she'd later discovered in the mountain peaks of Europe. And so, from the bottom of an empty bottle, they discovered their mutual passion for skiing. A forever friendship had begun.

His two years in London sped past him as if he were on a Swiss express train. He caught sight of this, of that, went to this party, that dinner, but in the final analysis he was never happier than when he was working. Or seeing Jessie.

With his departure from London aged twenty-five, he settled back into

New York where he found a job at *The New Yorker*. Neither columnist nor editor – these were not his skills – but as one of the magazine's celebrated 'fact checkers'. Cory read copy, then checked and double-checked the contributor's statements. He enjoyed the discipline and bookish industry the position required, and soon found his niche working on film and theatre reviews. A particular critic might have observed, for example, that an actor looked *'overly sombre in grey shirt and blue tie at the dinner'*. Cory's job: go see said film/play to ascertain that it was not a blue shirt and grey tie. It was on such trivia that the reputation of many a *New Yorker* writer was secured, and he truly loved his work.

Lapels were narrowing and the dour and pointless 1970s were closing. The Communists had won the Vietnam War. Richard Nixon had been deposed and John Travolta had been crowned. People awaited the 1980s with palpable eagerness. It was going to be a different world they said; it was as if the 1970s had been an almighty belch between the mouthfuls that were the 1960s, and what the 1980s promised to be. Cory included himself in that eager crowd.

The new decade's buzz was still audible when a letter arrived at his Upper West Side apartment. The heavy vellum envelope delivered a typed request to journey to Boston for an interview at Swire's. No mention of position. No mention of expenses. Just a date, a time and a pre-stamped RSVP card. Nothing else. Not even a signature.

At first glance he assumed it might be a hoax from a so-called friend. The hiring practices of Swire's were the stuff of urban myth: 'secretive', 'absolute', 'generous' and 'demanding' were all words spoken in association with the renowned Boston establishment. There was no known newspaper or magazine interview with either the founder Oliver Swire, or his chosen scion, Zephaniah Swire. What did exist in the public domain – even Helen Stark, the fabled Head Librarian at *The New Yorker*, had come up short – was sketchy and could be summed up at best by a quote attributed to Mr O. Swire: *"We are not a secretive family. We are a private family."*

Cory, however hard he tried (and that wasn't very hard, it had to be said) had never been able to shake off his collegiate style of dress: penny loafers, chinos, and a tab-collared shirt with cuffs protruding from an unstructured jacket. The following week he took the shuttle to Boston and checked into a small hotel on Charles Street. The next day at 11 a.m. he was escorted into Mr Zephaniah Swire's office for his interview. Even before he had returned to his modest hotel later that evening, another impressive envelope (this one larger and heavier) awaited him. It contained a surprisingly munificent, and presumably non-negotiable, offer of employment as Deputy Head of Research. Appended to it was an eight-page letter of confidentiality.

What also accompanied the offer was the unmistakable scent of Swire's, its imposing 19th-Century building and all that could possibly happen inside its redbrick walls. Cory had no idea whether that scent was real or illusory, or if the offer had simply lit the touchpaper of his own zeitgeist. All he knew was that it was intoxicating. He aspired to *belong* there. He accepted the position the very next morning before returning to New York.

A position in Swire's research department was the art world's most coveted; the only people who could access their records were senior Swire's employees. Outsiders were truly that, Cory soon came to learn. Amongst the details Mr Zephaniah Swire had informed him of that morning, was that between 5% and 10% of works that pass through the major auction houses had been, or were, stolen. Mr Swire had likened it, in simplistic terms, to a laundry. Swire's, it had been impressed upon him, were not in the money-cleaning business. They were in the money-making business.

At his interview Cory had longed to ask just how his name had appeared on their radar. But he had held himself in check, sensing that if he posed the question the job would be lost. He had to content himself with the fact that it would be another of the secrets sealed within the mahogany panelling of Mr Swire's office.

Instead, Cory had played to his talents. He had enough poise (ill-fitting clothes aside) to know that a sprinkle of East Coast and London stardust had accompanied him. And he sensed that Mr Swire had noted that. In his own way he had taken to Mr Swire's direct approach, but with caution, rather in the manner of someone who has an allergy to lobster: he so wanted to be able to like it, there was something primal about it – it held such promise – but he was in fear of its potential, possibly even lethal, consequences.

Cory wound his watch unhurriedly, a tick he had developed, while waiting. That done, he looked at the notes arranged on his desk and grinned one of his charm-infused smiles; two suggestions forming one thought. Relief. Jessie was coming to Boston for herself, as well as to help him. All he had to do was organise her airline ticket. Then, after a rest, perhaps her nutcracker intuition would be able to assist him with the riddles presented by the research his boss had requested.

She knew nothing of art, and to talk through his suppositions (however fanciful they might be) with someone who knew nothing about his subject would be helpful. Or so he imagined. For Jessie was able to read backwards. That was one of her talents; why she was – or had been, until her breakdown – the very best at what she did. Unlike many, she recognised that there was no algorithm to a child's mind; they had their own inner cultures. Jessie understood behavioural patterns and was able to solve the puzzles they produced. The same ones that weren't obvious to other adults, let alone parents. Cory had seen with his own eyes how she instinctively grasped 'it' (whatever 'it' happened to be) and what 'it' meant to a child. Basically, his friend could read ciphers few others could. And that was what he needed. A code breaker.

Impatiently he buzzed his secretary and asked her to book a first-class ticket on British Airways from London Heathrow to Boston's Logan Airport. The return, open-dated. The passenger, Dr Jessica Flack. There would be a flight leaving around six o'clock. Oh, and please note the reference for accounting is '*Cory Mount/ISGM Theft/Supernumerary Research Assistant*'. Finally, he requested the cost difference between business-class and first-class to be relayed to accounting, and the extra was to be debited from his in-house account at Swire's.

That done, and with the spring of his watch wound tight, Cory frittered away time as if waiting for a lover to return a promised call. Jessie had never been his lover, but it didn't stop him – on rare occasions – thinking of her as such. He was not a man who lived anywhere other than in the present, any more than he ever harboured regrets; a carpe diem man, his mother often remarked. But every so often, his uncomplicated attitude would melt at the memory of what might, just, have been as they'd navigated the 1970s together. And love was in the air somewhere, but it wasn't in London's air. Was it really fifteen years ago?

The intercom flashed on the phone and brought him back into the final decade of the 20th Century.

"Mr Mount, I've booked Dr Flack's flight. The pre-paid ticket will be at the British Airways counter at Heathrow. She can collect it just sixty minutes before departure. I've reserved a window seat, 2A. I hope that's OK?"

"That'll be fine, thanks Sylvie," he said ending the call. He held onto the handset and dialled Jessie's home. It barely rang before she answered.

"Hi Jessie, it's all booked. You leave London at tonight at 6 p.m. and arrive in Boston tonight around 9 p.m. I'll pick you up at Logan."

Silence.

"It has been a long time, Cory . . ."

"Yes, too long. Time does fly. My mother says it just dissolves now."

He heard Jessie draw on a cigarette. "Are you going to tell me how I can help you?"

"It'll keep. I'll give you a hint though."

"Go on . . ."

"Remember you once told me how you use occasionally use a Sherlock Holmes analogy with your patients?"

"Sure, I have many, but I suspect you're referring to *'The Dog That Didn't Bark'*. I employ it with children who clam up on me when they're in danger. Usually that danger comes from a family member."

Cory took a short, sharp intake of breath. "Well, I might need you to use it here in Boston. I've done some research that's clammed up on me. It's not telling me the truth. It's hiding something." He coughed lightly before adding, "Sounds stupid, doesn't it?"

"No, nothing you say sounds stupid. Confusing sometimes, yes, stupid, no. But what possible use can I be to art and history? What's this got to do with buying or selling paintings?"

"Nothing at all," he faltered. "However, it may have something to do with stealing paintings."

"You know I love you, but I don't *love* you love you, dearest Cory, partly because I rarely understand half of things you gas on about!"

"That makes two of us, so go and pack. I'll see you tonight. Safe flight. Oh, and Jessie, if you see a biography of Rembrandt at Heathrow, please grab it. It's as good a place as any to start," he concluded enigmatically.

Cory didn't give her the chance to say anything further, he just replaced the handset. Besides, he wanted the BA ground staff to surprise her with her seating. She would enjoy the treat, thought Cory, and from what he'd understood it was the least he could do.

Jessie shook her head quizzically and lit another cigarette. *'The Dog That Didn't Bark'*? It was a clear-cut strategy, one she'd developed from the Sherlock Holmes story, *Silver Blaze*, which her father had read her years ago: Holmes had solved a mystery by recalling that out of all the suspects in a case that had long baffled him, there was one – just one – who in the final dénouement, the guard dog didn't bark at. At the other suspects, yes, the dog had barked. And the reason the oh-so-curious hound hadn't barked was straightforward. It had recognised the scent of the person who had broken into the house and subsequently committed the crime. The murderer, therefore, was not a stranger and posed no threat, for he had long been accepted by the hound. So why bark at a person who had already patted your head and rubbed your tummy? Rarely do dogs bark at people they recognise and who feed them. Jessie referred to this non-bark as a 'negative fact' or for her purposes, an *expected* fact that was absent from a narrative.

Like most things in life Jessie reminded herself, especially those governing a young life, it was the ostensibly insignificant details that told the story. She trusted the veiled minutiae.

But what all this had to do with art was quite beyond her. She sucked the tarry smoke deep into her lungs once more. For Cory she was willing to try to learn what it was all about. Without his intervention, lone susurrous noises would still be emanating from under her grisly Laura Ashley linen.

Jessie owed Cory her best bark, if nothing else.

CHAPTER 53

**Shiner's Diner, 86 Van Ness Street,
Fenway Park, Boston, Massachusetts.
Friday, 30th March 1990. 09:35.**

Shannon O'Leary took Mrs Shiner at her word when she asked for a further fifteen minutes' break. Promptly, she dashed out of the diner, turned right and ran to the Exxon station near Fenway Park. There, panting for breath, she grabbed two maps: Massachusetts and New York State. Then, she added a late edition of *The Boston Globe* to double-check that she hadn't dreamt it all up over her earlier Marlboro and coffee.

She hadn't.

There it was. Below the fold, and it continued in all its horror on page twenty-one.

It was Friday, and early brunches were often busy as people often snuck off work very early. Some even came to line their stomachs for Friday's Happy Hour. With no liquor licence, Shiner's Diner was the food-haunt of choice for the hard-liquor crowd. *'Feed a Hangover and Prepare for a Hangover'* was the fare Mrs Shiner served.

There was no way out of this other than to ask Mrs Shiner straight up. Tell her what though? She didn't know what to say. In fact, as she reread the newspaper, she realised there was nothing she could say. Nothing at all.

Without paying for the newspaper or the maps – she'd do that when the man behind the register looked up from his magazine – she tore open the maps and spread them across the ice-cream freezer. With fierce concentration she pored over them, trying to make some sense of the blue and red lines that squirmed randomly across both states. To Shannon, not the most practised of drivers, they just looked like Mrs Vanderbilt's varicose veins. Dispelling the grim thought of one of her regular customer's un-hosed and unfortunate legs, she called out. "Hey, what are my options for getting to Long Island?"

It was a slow day but that didn't mean he had to answer questions shouted at him. He ignored her.

"Hey, I'm talking to you!"

He looked up with a pained expression, as if he were a judge about to pass sentence. Then, liking what he saw – no, *really* liking what he saw – he replied, "No need to shout lady, I'm not far away. Come on over."

Shannon ambled up to the register. The man's teeth were stained with neglect.

She winced and looked down at the maps.

"You got three options lady. One: fly the shuttle from Logan to La Guardia and rent a car. Expensive, but quick. Two: take 95 south to New York, turn left onto the Long Island Expressway and stay on it. If you get as far as Montauk Point, you've gone too far, unless you got an amphibian car." He chuckled. "About six hours. Tiring too."

Shannon pretended to smile at the joke.

"What's my third option?"

"Best to head on 95 south as far as New London, take the ferry across the Long Island Sound to Orient Point, it's on the North Fork of Long Island. Ferry runs every hour or so, the ride is about an hour too. From Orient Point head to Shelter Island, then Sag Harbour and you're in the Hamptons. Montauk is twenty miles on from Sag."

"Say thanks, you know your stuff," she said handing over a $20 bill and gathering up the maps and newspaper.

"So, out of $20 bucks, here's your change and have a safe trip whichever route you take."

Her mind was elsewhere now. Shannon crumpled the dollar bills into her pocket. She was far too preoccupied to have paid any further attention to the man behind the register. Shaking her head like an animal that'd been beaten and didn't know why, she tore the relevant column from *The Boston Globe* and folded it into the breast pocket of her denim shirt. Stuffing the two maps into her hip pocket she dumped the newspaper where it belonged. In the garbage.

What the hell to do? There was only one course of action, surely? And God alone knew why she should risk it, Shannon thought as she jogged back to Shiner's Diner.

But she'd made up her mind.

Breakthrough in Gardner Museum Heist

Eyewitness sought

By Dan Conklin
GLOBAL STAFF

IT WAS CONFIRMED late last night that after hundreds of dead-end leads and misinformation in the Isabella Stewart Gardner Museum heist there is, according to a joint statement from the Boston Police and the FBI, a real breakthrough.

At last, it appears the investigation into the mysterious robbery dubbed the 'Art Theft of The Century', that has been baffling Boston Police and FBI alike since the night of March 19th, might have taken its first and crucial step towards being solved. With no leads at all, there is no means of tracing any of the $200 million of missing art, which includes Jan Vermeer's masterpiece, *The Concert* and Rembrandt's *Christ in the Storm on the Sea of Galilee*, his only seascape.

Without a clear motive the enforcement officers have said the case will be hard to crack; and they must do it alone, as all the works in the Gardner Museum are uninsured. So, no Faye Dunaway insurance investigator here to pursue Steve McQueen as she did so successfully in the Hollywood movie *The Thomas Crown Affair*.

Not even the $1 million reward, posted the day after the robbery by international auction houses Sotheby's and Christie's, has brought in one tip-off from the shady underworld of art thefts. (It's rumoured Boston's own house, Swire's, posted a third of the reward, although this has been denied by their spokesman). Anne Hawley, the Gardner Museum's Director, together with art experts around the world have stated the stolen works are unsaleable. This has led to speculation of a commissioned theft, but that motive was dismissed last week by Constance Lowenthal, Executive Director of International Foundation for Art Research, an organisation that documents art thefts worldwide. She said: 'These priceless works of art are virtually worthless. They're unsaleable. There's no place for them in the legitimate market. They're too hot to handle. And as far as a collector who orders a theft, we don't have a documented case of a Dr No type character. You see them in the movies, but we don't know about any of them.'

BREAKTHROUGH, Page 21

BREAKTHROUGH, Cont. Page 1

That was the tragic situation for Boston's favourite museum, until last night's statement when Boston Police and the FBI confirmed their solid lead. The one they'd been working on for eight days had checked out. In their joint press release, they stated that just minutes before the robbery, as Bostonians returned home after celebrating St Patrick's Day, a woman (all that has been revealed is that she is from Boston, a widow and in her fifties) was driving by the Gardner Museum when she spotted a man hurrying across the road, in the direction of the museum's Palace Road entrance and towards the two thieves who were dressed as Boston Police officers.

The yet unidentified man was carrying a young girl – her age has been put at 10-12 years old. The girl appeared to be either asleep or unconscious. Fearing the very worst, that the child had been abducted, raped or might even be dead, the woman slowed, wound down her window and captured all she could in her mind's eye. It was, she confirmed '. . . as if I would need this one day for an I.D. parade.'

According to our Boston Police source, so vigilant was this innocent passer-by that upon her return home, she wrote down all she could recall about his dress and appearance. The FBI artists are working around the clock on a photo-fit of the man they would like to question; they hope to release their composite within 72 hours.

In their initial joint statement, the FBI and the Boston Police described the man as tall, over six foot, well built and muscular, yet lean, about 190–200 pounds. Further characteristics noted were that, despite wearing a long-billed cap, the sort favoured by fishermen, she noticed that he was clean shaven, 'handsome but with a rough appearance, not a down-and-out though'. Despite the inclement weather that night, the unnamed woman noticed his sleeves were rolled up and that he had a large tattoo on his right forearm. Perhaps most telling of all was that she noticed 'the man had a desperate look in his eyes. You see, my eyes fixed his, I'd recognise those eyes of his again any day. He really was a desperate man.'

CHAPTER 54

**Amagansett Farmers' Market, Amagansett,
Montauk Highway, New York.
Friday, 30th March 1990. 15:15.**

Shannon had always been good at learning her lines in high-school drama classes as she glanced, yet again, at *The Boston Globe* cutting, the one that was becoming more and more worn with each, nagging, read.

All each reading did was create more questions: what the hell was a thirty-five-year-old waitress, from hard-working Irish–American Catholic parents, doing parked in the Amagansett Farmers' Market on the Montauk Highway? What if this was just old blarney and she'd just plain gotten it wrong? What business was it of hers if the Dealer man and his daughter had witnessed something the night of the theft? What if he was a part of the break-in gang? What in the Holy Mother of God's name was the Dealer man – if indeed it had been him – doing with Amy in the Back Bay Fens at one in the morning? What was she going to do, play Miss Marple and track them down? Even if she did, then what was she supposed to do? And why in God's name hadn't she gone to the police the minute she'd read the newspaper, and told them what she thought she'd figured out? She had no answers to these questions at all.

The heart of the matter was straightforward really, and it lay in the only response that kept ringing in her head: the unconscious expression of desolation ingrained on the Dealer man's face the only time she'd spoken with him – the night of the theft – just shy of two weeks ago. In his eyes that night had lain a wasteland, a destruction so complete that it wasn't only visible it had gained, somehow, an almost tactile aspect. Shannon had detected in those fleeting moments at Shiner's Diner that the man was dying from within. His eyes had told her all but the 'why': there was innocence and terror, there was love and loss, there was history without future, but there was no rancour or hatred. Thinking about it now made her shiver. Goose bumps appeared on her forearms. His eyes had haunted her ever since. Even the motorist in the car had registered them too, dammit. The man just had to be Amy Dealer's father. It was the answer she didn't want, but it was the answer she kept on getting.

Shannon slammed her car door with more force than was necessary. It didn't thud gratefully, it pinged meanly. She had never thought of herself as either a material or an unappreciative person, but she did sometimes wish her father hadn't bought her a Japanese car for her thirtieth birthday. She was more a Chevy kind of girl, although she would never have let on that was the case. With long, athletic strides she walked into the Farmers' Market.

Spread all about her – a girl from Massachusetts whose ancestors had left Connemara during the famine of 1847 – was an improbable smorgasbord of foods she'd never even heard of, much less seen: baby patty-pan squash, oyster mushrooms, yellow tomatoes the size of walnuts, odd-shaped bottles of dark-green oils, purple salsas, orange and ruby spices, and croissants and buns stuffed with anything and everything . . . except pastry . . . all of the wonderful produce meshed with the aroma of impossibly frothy coffee and cut flowers. Shannon thought she had died and gone to heaven. The sooner she got back down to earth the better. This was no place for a Gloucester fisherman's daughter. Even breathing here was going to cost her a week's tips. Tucked away in a corner she found what she was looking for; the Suffolk County phone book hung limp from a steel cable under the payphone. All she had to go on was DEALER and AMAGANSETT. Well, she appeared to be at the hub of the cosmos of Amagansett, and just how many Dealers could live hereabouts? She flicked through the worn pages and held her breath. She was in luck. Just one. '*DEALER, Jake & Lindy*' were listed. Hastily she scribbled down the address and the telephone number.

"Excuse me, could you direct me to where Jake and Lindy Dealer live? I've got their address here, but I'm from out of town," she asked the smiling cotton-haired elderly lady at the checkout.

Shannon was totally unprepared for the response her polite question elicited. What was it with this man? She thought as she took a step back, as if in self-defence.

CHAPTER 55

41o 10' 27.8" N
71o 15' 30.6" W
Mid-way between Montauk, New York and Menemsha,
Massachusetts, Atlantic Ocean.
Friday, 30th March 1990. 15:25.

"Hey Marty, you gotta feelin' for this?" Jake shouted over the noise of the engine.

Marty shot him an edgy 'what-the-fuck-you-asking-me-for' frown in response. Ignoring him, Jake turned to face forward. He didn't need to check his anemometer to see what had been twenty-five knots blowing east-of-north was building into thirty knots. That put the low-pressure south, south-east of Martha's Vineyard, and worse, it had probably stalled further east, somewhere out over Nantucket. With luck it might keep on heading east, right back into the Atlantic with the same speed that it'd arrived. The barometer had dropped rapidly and was now holding steady at around 1,000 millibars. Good.

The waves, however, told a different story.

They were getting more agitated. That troubled him. He could feel in his feet the heavy percussive thud, like a bass drum, increasing on *Sweet Amy's* hull. And he read waves like Marty read music. What were now low-rising eight footers, could, just might, turn into tens or twelves. If the barometer fell again – and the low deepened – that could happen, then apartment-block waves would be on the cards. His instinct told him that the low had stalled – dammit – and if he was correct, then a high would build rapidly over the northern landmass of Connecticut and Rhode Island, compressing the pressure over Rhode Island Sound and Vineyard Sound ever downwards. Jake didn't trust these micro-systems, like this fast-appearing and fast-paced low-pressure. Just like he didn't trust the politicians who barked that there was nothing to fear from climate change. This had been the Dealers' backyard for 300 years. Washington and Albany were lying to themselves – and to the fishermen – but there was nothing new in that. It was all changing out here; the old lore needed to be re-written by one God Almighty nor'easter storm. But for the moment, all Jake was concerned about was the slamming body punches *Sweet Amy* took from the more frequent rogue waves. So long as the crests were just spitting angrily at him that was half full. What he didn't want to see were the edges beginning to break. That'd be half empty. Keep on spitting, thought Jake, spitting eight footers we can handle.

Holding on tightly, and two paces behind and to the left of Jake, Marty stared forward. This day on the water had been planned after they'd sent the ashes into the deep. He was a musician who liked to be on the water, not a fisherman who liked to play the piano, and he knew when to call it quits. Like now. But quitting to Marty was like having a manager – something best avoided. Unless something named an angry Atlantic Ocean got into the frame. Marty had only ever figured it one way: in any kind of argument with the ocean, work on one basis only – it was goin' to win. It wasn't rocket-science, it was real simple. If you let the ocean, even get to the spat stage, it would fuck you quicker, harder and more ruthlessly than all the managers on the East and West Coasts put together. So, whatever it was Jake wanted to do was fine by him. Jake was no manager and Marty trusted him with his life – which, he reflected wryly, was lucky for him as it was the only choice Marty had right now. Hungering oceans had only enemies; and this trip to the fishing grounds off No Man's Land had ceased to be a solid day on the water with a great friend. All too fast, it was becoming a cold and wet bad dream.

Jake's eyes shuttered like a camera's iris. He scanned his gauges and checked the compass. Heading due east and on course at 085°+/-. Then, he glanced down at the LORAN to confirm what he'd already calculated. At 41o 10'N and 71o 15'W they were past the point-of-no-return. Wiping his salt-stung eyes he rounded on Marty; he released a smile and faced him straight on.

"Lookit Marty, we're aways past the point-of-no-return. We *can* turn back and run west for Block Island and shelter in Great Salt Pond, 'bout twenty plus nautical miles away, or keep pressing on for Menemsha, 'bout sixteen nautical miles on the nose. The tide might give us a leg-up soon, and we should get a lee-break off the Vineyard's north shore when we get to Vineyard Sound. If the visibility drops, which it could, I'll still have a transit from the Block Island Sea Buoy to the Gay Head Lighthouse."

"What's your call Jake?"

"We're better off beating into it and heading for Menemsha. It'll be hard on us though."

Marty knew only too well that boats, even with two on board, were not environments where democracy existed, let alone flourished. There was only one vote, one voice. The Captain's. Jake was only informing him what he planned to do to ensure the safety of the crew and the integrity of the vessel, and to Marty, Jake was a true mariner, and one who wasn't about to become a submariner.

CHAPTER 56

18 Louisburg Square, Beacon Hill, Boston, Massachusetts. Friday, 30th March 1990. 15:25.

The hands of Zephaniah Swire's desk clock told him it was 3.25 p.m. He had long enjoyed the uncomplicated pleasure of admiring the exactitude of execution contained within the Breguet's crystal case. Moving his head slowly, as a diamond-eyed snake might, he marvelled at the overcoil, cogs, wheels, balance springs, triggers and jewels that Abraham-Louis Breguet had fashioned since 1775. Bonaparte had entrusted Breguet's horologic skills with the task of keeping his energetic plans on time. Recommendation enough, thought Zephaniah, as he removed from a nearby drawer his most recent Napoleonic treasure: a bronze finial which had once perched atop his Imperial flag, its eagle's wings stretched a soupçon too wide, much like Napoleon's ambitions.

Zephaniah moved the finial around his desk. It was still new to him, and he'd yet to decide on which side it might serve as a paperweight. The left or the right? He wrote with his left hand yet used his right forefinger to squeeze the trigger of an M16 rifle. The finial would, perhaps, find its own place over time, he thought. For the time being he placed it on top of a brief memo from Cory Mount:

'Dear Mr Swire, you requested I keep you informed on Mr Jedediah's intended Dalí purchase. Despite my February 11th report confirming that in our opinion the painting is a forgery – albeit a good one – I have just learned that Mr Jedediah purchased the painting four days ago. His wish is to trade it, not to keep it. I urge you to deploy one of our amenable New York dealers to acquire the painting as soon as possible, so that Mr Jedediah can realise the profit he believes he can make. It should then be destroyed. From this department's view, we do not see Mr Jedediah's continued involvement as prudent. Sincerely yours, Cory Mount'.

Zephaniah sighed and closed his eyes. He didn't even have the desire to curse. All was very tranquil in the basement study of 18 Louisburg Square. Hector was out running errands, the cook was, presumably, cooking in the kitchen, and unless he was much mistaken Eli and Juanita were fucking in her attic bedroom. With an almost religious fidelity they did that at every given opportunity, as far as he could discern. But he was minded not to mention the matter. Eli was a discreet driver, and if his peccadillo was screwing his employer's housemaid, then, good luck Eli.

Having read the article in *The Boston Globe* a few hours ago, he'd cancelled an unimportant lunch and retreated to formulate his own reaction to the irritant said article had prompted. Just him and his thoughts. By now his grandfather would have read the newspaper too, and that would require a conversation at some point. But it was for Ollie to decide when. The longer his grandfather left it, frankly, the less Zephaniah was looking forward to it.

This was Zephaniah's play, yes, but it was Ollie's ranch as he had so pointedly reminded him in Menemsha eleven days ago. Conceivably, Ollie wouldn't venture down to the payphone beside the dock, preferring instead, to leave any conversation until their next meeting, due Monday.

Getting up from his wing-backed chair he flexed his broad shoulders and sauntered over to the wall of glass. Bubbles, fine bubbles, like those of a good champagne, aerated the water through the coral, stones and lights that made up the tank's floor. The Scyphozoan medusae moved about with a beguiling grace, their diaphanous bodies changing colour as they fanned from one spectrum of light to another, like chameleons slipping noiselessly through a jungle.

Zephaniah's numbing stare locked onto one jellyfish. There was nothing special about it, it was just that he found it more thought-provoking to track the entirely random wanderings of a single creature, one that had no idea from whence it came, or any notion to where it was headed. It was the antithesis of everything Zephaniah had forged himself into. The Scyphozoan medusae were, in effect, his antonym.

Opening his double-breasted vest, its fine wool the colour of anthracite, Zephaniah removed a soft, black leather wallet. And from the wallet itself he slipped out a second, much smaller envelope-like wallet made of the same leather but silk-lined. It had been made to his own design three months ago. It was stiffened by wafers of carbon-fibre, while its corners and buckle were filigreed platinum. His eyes sparkled like a wolf's caught in the glare of moonlight as he watched the meandering jellyfish. Carefully, he withdrew a delicate etching not much larger than a postage stamp: it was a mere 1 3/4 in x 1 15/16 in. He held up Rembrandt's minute self-portrait and placed it half an inch away from the wall of glass.

"Do you like it?" he demanded of the Scyphozoan medusae. He held it steady for a full minute before returning the etching into its protective leather wallet. As he walked back to his desk, he slid it back into his left breast pocket.

Every man should have an original Rembrandt half an inch from their beating heart during their waking hours, thought Zephaniah as he dialled Jimmy Snale's telephone number.

The curious combination of a bloom of Scyphozoan medusae, Rembrandt and Napoleon had helped him finalise his decision as to the next move. Of course, there was no such thing as the perfect crime, so this turn of events was not that unexpected. The solution wouldn't be complex either. It was a matter of timing. But then wasn't everything a matter of timing, reflected Zephaniah as Snale's telephone began to ring.

CHAPTER 57

**Seat 2A, British Airways 747,
Heathrow–Logan, 36,000 ft. Mid Atlantic.
Friday, 30th March 1990. 20:20 GMT.**

Never in her life had Jessie boarded a transatlantic jetliner and turned left. From her window seat, despite craning her neck until it hurt, she still couldn't see even a flicker of the 747's red wing-tip light. As the jumbo jet sped westwards, chasing the forever setting sun, her horizon fringed white, crimson, orange and pink, and all she could make out below were cotton balls of cloud that blushed like rose petals. Even the vastness of the brooding Atlantic Ocean was hiding from her. Above her, the stars appeared so close she thought she could count them all. And in between was a mellow dusk, a warm blue expanse that was now a friend, not an enemy. The engines' hum was muted, constant and comforting. The three other passengers in first class – all men – were dozing, heads at oblique angles, attachés discarded, mouths loosely ajar with cheeks puffy from exhaustion.

Jessie nibbled on a plate of cheese and sipped a small glass of port. A Thames & Hudson biography of Rembrandt lay unopened in the empty aisle seat. She was having far too much fun to bother with another dead Dutch painter. She smiled at a childhood memory: she and her father had played a collective noun word game; his favourite had been *'a misbelief'* of painters. Greedily now, she wolfed down her cheese knowing it might bestow the most vivid of dreams. Then, she placed the plate and glass aside and reclined the seat fully. Taking a long look out of the window at the heavens, she pulled the crisp cotton duvet up to her chin. And no further. She was through with hiding. She closed her eyes and fell – no, *tumbled* – into a deep sleep. A sleep free from tormented demons, but one of kaleidoscopic dreams painted with a soft brush and colours so dazzling that they could only have come from a child's palette.

CHAPTER 58

**Amagansett Farmers' Market, Amagansett,
Montauk Highway, New York.
Friday, 30th March 1990. 15:20.**

"Sorry, did I say something to offend?" asked Shannon, her pale cheeks flushing.

"You don't know do you?"

"Know what? I asked for directions to Jake and Lindy Dealer's house. They live here in Amagansett," she said as she turned on her heel to leave, "I'm sorry, I'll ask elsewhere."

"You don't know, do you?"

The repetition – for a reason she would later understand to have been prescient – made her turn back, and as she did so she witnessed the snowy-haired lady's facial expressions run the gamut from anger-to-protection-to-apology.

"Know what?" Shannon replied as she edged closer to the cash register.

"How long have you known the Dealers?"

Lies, as her father taught her, have very short legs.

"For about ten minutes," she replied, "and only Jake and his daughter Amy. They were in Boston a couple of weeks ago. I wait tables at the diner they ate in. I have some news for him. They told me they lived here in Amagansett." And for no particular reason she added, "I've not met Lindy."

"What's wrong with the telephone? What's so important you had to drive here?"

Only the truth would do.

"Respectfully ma'am, that's between Mr Dealer and me."

"Good answer lady." The lines around the woman's eyes softened. "We're mighty tight around here. We look out for each other. Especially the Dealer family. Now, you go and have a coffee, read a magazine and wait till I get off my shift at four o'clock, I live near them, I'll show you when you drive me home."

And with that curious medley of request, order and invitation, the lady looked at the young couple who'd been flicking through the pages of a L. L. Bean catalogue as they waited in line.

"Next!" she barked.

Shannon took her cue, ordered a coffee and picked up a discarded edition of *Newsday*. Turning the pages without a desire to do anything other than idle away time, she caught sight of a short news item. She wondered if Jake had seen it. If he'd registered it. *Newsday* would be his local newspaper, after all.

By the time 4 p.m. rolled around, she was no longer bemused by her own behaviour or her motive. Having read the story again, in a different newspaper, she understood exactly why she hadn't telephoned. Telephones usually brought bad news, salesmen or politics, or all three at the same time. If what was folded in the breast pocket of her denim shirt was more bad news, she wasn't about to deliver it over the crackle of a lousy phone connection.

Jake Dealer's eyes had told her there was no rooms at the inn for any more bad news.

CHAPTER 59

**18 Louisburg Square, Beacon Hill, Boston, Massachusetts.
Friday, 30th March 1990. 15:25.**

"Do you have a minute?"

Jimmy Snale had been dreading this call. He'd been sitting beside the telephone all day waiting for it. He too had read *The Boston Globe* story.

"Sure, Mr Swire. Been home with bills and stuff," he faltered.

"I'm not angry about what happened or that you failed to tell me there might have been witnesses. You understand me Jimmy, results are the only driver." Zephaniah knew his NCO from tougher battles than this one. And there was a time to use the stick, but now was a time for the carrot. "So, where are we on this?" His tone was breezy, and he sensed the tension easing in Jimmy.

"We're in a far better place than the BPD and the FBI, sir."

"Why so?"

"Because the man asked me for directions that night."

"So . . ." Zephaniah hoisted the carrot far out of reach.

"He asked for directions to his motel. Said he was from out of town, lost he was."

"You remember the name of the motel?"

"Yessir. The Freedom Trail Motel. It's close to Fenway Park. No one will have that intel. All they got is some old kook who saw a man cross a road. That's all they got, sir."

"Not true Jimmy. They'll have a photo-fit of him very soon." Zephaniah held the stick out of sight, but Jimmy knew it was there.

"We can have his name, his address and probably the registration of his car." It was Jimmy's turn to pause. "I take it, Mr Swire that's information we should have?"

"Time spent on reconnaissance is seldom wasted. Think of this as reconnaissance in reverse. Whether I choose to deploy the intelligence you *will* obtain, without breaking so much as one twig or alerting one soul, is entirely my decision. Understood?"

"Yessir."

"I want this intel yesterday, but I'll settle for this afternoon. Track him down Jimmy, as only you can." The tone of Lieutenant Swire's voice made the stick clearly visible. Zephaniah replaced the handset.

Deliberately, he crumpled Cory Mount's memo into a ball and dropped it in the wastebasket. Jedediah's recklessness could wait.

He had a witness to find.

CHAPTER 60

**Further Lane, Amagansett, Long Island, New York.
Friday, 30th March 1990. 16:11.**

It was only a short distance through the back-doubles and lanes from the Farmers' Market to Poseyville, Amagansett.

"Pull over here for a minute", instructed the lady as she pointed to a run-off area in Further Lane. Unsure of so much, Shannon found it easier to obey.

"You already told me whatever business you have with Jake Dealer is between you and him." She looked straight into Shannon's wide green eyes. "Fair enough, but there's something you need to know."

"OK . . ."

"Lady, I'm not trusting you with anything. Nothing I'm gonna say you couldn't find out from anyone who lives in these parts. You got Jake's address. You could've gone to the East Hampton police station. They'd have told you where the Dealer house is. Besides, you'd got a look in your eye that said you were going to do something like that. It seems like that's what you'd set out to do." She hesitated. "What's your name?"

"Shannon O'Leary," she replied abruptly, knowing better than to make a comment or ask the woman's name in return.

"You see, Shannon, the Dealer family have been hereabouts for 300 years or so. They're Long Island folk. The people who come out for the summer and weekends, well, they're just city folk, New Yorkers mostly. The Dealers *live* here. Their kind made this land their home generations ago."

The lady turned away and lowered the window. She stared into the distance. Her eyes were set south, to a point a few hundred yards away, beyond which lay the rolling dunes and the vast expanse of broad Atlantic beaches. Bullet straight, Long Island's southern shores stretched some ninety miles from Montauk Point right into the apocalyptic guts of

Manhattan. The Dealers had worked these Atlantic waters and beaches for generations. This was where Harvey Dealer had died. This was *their* frontier. And no one else's.

"There was a tragedy hereabouts. The sort you don't even read about, and if you *had* read it, you wouldn't have believed it."

She faced Shannon with narrow, rheumy eyes, and Shannon returned her scrutiny with silent respect. Neither blinked. The lady's voice held the bittersweet notes of someone imparting news that shouldn't be imparted to strangers.

"What tragedy?" whispered Shannon, her mouth dry.

"Jake won't talk about it. He doesn't talk about much anyways. Not a man who sees much need for talking." She breathed in deeply. "It started when Dougie, his nine-year-old son, was murdered. Shot four times in the chest whilst on his paper round. That was the first heartbreak. The second came right after, when his wife Lindy hung herself by the neck, using Jake's nets. From a rafter in their shed." The lady didn't draw breath, she just continued. "Some folks say it was grief that made Lindy kill herself. Others, well, they say that being the wife of fisherman, a bayman, added to it. That and Dougie, and then . . ."

Shannon closed her eyes and faced away. Somehow, she was able to shut her ears off. It was as if they had their own, hitherto-undiscovered switch. All she heard was the faint drone of the continuing story. But Shannon had heard all that mattered. She gazed out of the window and felt warm tears begin to collapse down her proud Irish cheekbones. And right away she realised that her tears were not hers alone.

Shannon sensed her tears belonged not only to the fisherman, his wife, his son and his daughter, but to their ancestors and all their history.

CHAPTER 61

**10 Crick Hill Road, Menemsha,
Martha's Vineyard, Massachusetts.
Friday, 30th March 1990. 16:11.**

Ollie Swire had spent most of the day wondering what to do. And at his age conjecture was a new science; one that had never featured in the landscape of his eventful life. His MO – now that *was* a science – had never changed: act swiftly and decisively whilst paying heed to the congruent instincts of gut and head.

This gene was the sole piece of driftwood to have floated his way from the wreckage of an unknown gene pool, and he had clung to it with the iron grip of a shipwrecked mariner surrounded by sharks. Hannah aside, the instrument that was his instinct had meant everything to him. It had been his raft for nigh on eighty-five years.

Ollie had called it correctly: through depressions, booms, wars, crashes . . . Like all hustlers (the mirage of self-deception had never ensnared him), resilience was a core asset. Staying ahead of the game to beat the odds had been 'the game' itself. Wasn't it the house who always won? An honest house – another irony that had never escaped him – had the odds in its favour. The First Rule of Law was *'You CANNOT beat the House'*. Wrong. You can. You just needed his peerless instincts.

'Wondering', in the different costumes it wore – reflection, guesswork, speculation – was a pastime for the undisciplined, the indecisive, the lazy and the perplexed. People who 'wondered' believed in fairy tales and/or the Bible. Looking inwards was an historian's job. And that was just what he had been doing all day long, standing beside the window that gave out onto Menemsha Harbour, the Atlantic Ocean and all that lay beyond. Today, for the first time in his life, Ollie Swire felt like a man who 'wondered'.

What he'd been concerned about all day, was that for the very first time Zephaniah had given the impression that he'd failed to plan both the exit *and* the endgame to this particular play. His spectacular theft.

And if that were indeed the case, nothing less than catastrophe lay on the horizon.

CHAPTER 62

18 Louisburg Square, Beacon Hill, Boston, Massachusetts. Friday, 30th March 1990. 17:46.

"Mr Swire, you got a minute?"
"Sure Jimmy."
"We caught a break."
"We could use some good luck," Zephaniah replied whilst polishing the Napoleonic finial.
"I've got the intel you require."
"So soon?"
"As I said, we caught a break."
"Not a twig broken."
"Not one. An absolute guarantee."
"How so?"
"Right after your call, I went to the motel. It's family run, an old fashioned kinda place. The only thing electric is the light switch. They've got a ledger, the sort that you write in with your name, your address and your car registration. It gets even better," Snale was speaking quickly. "There's a book in the lobby, you know, for comments and stuff. They were changing shift, and I'm trying to register for the night, so I look up the entries from 17th March onwards, memorised a few names. Then I cross-checked them with the comment book. A girl, Amy Dealer, had written in it, she said that her father was a fisherman, even drew a picture of him holding a harpoon. That squares with me. I remember he had one of those long-billed caps, the kind fishermen wear. Anyway, the daughter's comment was the only one around that date. Her family name checked with the register. You want I should repeat the details Mr Swire?"

"No," Zephaniah countered firmly. "Write them down and deliver them here within the hour." Pausing, he asked, "where are they from?"

"Long Island."

"Big place that Jimmy. Where exactly?"

"Amagansett. I've no idea where that is."

"I do. It's near East Hampton. Suffolk County."

"Do you want me to check the town out? Ask around?"

"No. All I need is information. That's all I ever need. Initiative is not what's required. Are we clear, very clear, on that point Jimmy?"

"Yessir."

Zephaniah put the phone down with a wistful smile. He'd always admired the crispness with which Sergeant Snale delivered his salute, and his 'Yessirs'.

CHAPTER 63

**10 Crick Hill Road, Menemsha,
Martha's Vineyard, Massachusetts.
Friday, 30th March 1990. The hour before dusk.**

The late afternoon light had delivered on its earlier omens. As the dusk emerged there was a leaden colour and feel to the sky; this twilight deserved – and had – no friends. The strong nor'east wind stung Ollie's face and made his progress harder than it should have, like walking up a steep hill. There was an ugly storm brewing somewhere out there in the Atlantic, and it had come out of nowhere.

He anchored his feet into the sand, tightened his black scarf and swept a hand across his head of cropped white hair. Then, he tilted into the gale for support and felt the wind rise as fast as the barometer was undoubtedly falling. He took in a deep lungful of sea air – he called it his medicine – and squinted out over the rough ocean. The wind was licking the tops off the waves, as if it were a greedy child attacking a vanilla cone.

Typically, he took pleasure in his stroll beside the harbour and along the beach. But not today. He was through with today and his mind ached. It was a jumble of emotion and business, it was crude oil and seawater, thought Ollie. In the far distance a lone, hardy surfcaster was packing up on the beach. With his back to the wind, the fisherman broke down his rod and gathered his tackle and bait box. No fish to show for his efforts either. Ollie stopped and frowned.

Beyond the fisherman he thought he'd picked out the tell-tale green and red running lights of a boat. He shook his head from side to side in sympathy and said aloud to the wind: "Wouldn't want to be out there in this." With that, he abandoned his evening constitutional and headed for home and a mug of piping hot chocolate. But not before he had accomplished his secondary mission.

Ollie had decided it was necessary to make a pitstop at Swire's branch office. With $200 million worth of stolen art in his studio he figured he'd earned the right to make a call. He jabbed the buttons for his grandson's private home number. He deposited the sum demanded and let it ring and ring. He didn't care if his grandson wasn't at home. The fact that he'd called was message enough. One of his staff would inform him. To wait sixty or so hours until their Monday meeting was not the message he wished to convey. What he had to say couldn't wait that long.

"9862. Good evening," Hector said briskly.

"Good evening, Hector. Is my grandson at home?"

"Yes, Mr Swire, although he did ask not to be disturbed."

"I'm sure he did Hector", grinned Ollie before stating: "Hector, kindly go and inform him I'm holding."

"Of course, sir. I'll tell him right away."

Hector knew better than to ever think of questioning Mr Oliver, as the staff referred to him in private.

Ollie felt the cold winds lash his ankles through the gaps in the booth. Thankfully this was not going to be a long conversation.

"Zephaniah, how are you today?"

The absence of the diminutive was surely noted.

"I've only a handful of quarters, so I'll get to the point. What, if anything, have you learned?"

"Quite a lot."

"Go ahead."

"Are you sure you want this now?"

Was his grandson sniffing out an approval?

Ollie held his breath and let his silence answer.

"OK," Zephaniah continued, "he's a fisherman out of Amagansett, near East Hampton. He and his daughter were visiting Boston for a weekend by the looks of it. God knows what he was doing out at that time of night. I have his name and car registration."

"Well, that might be a stroke of luck," Ollie added sarcastically.

"Come on Ollie, you can do better than that."

"I know I can. But I'm going to save the best till last."

Ollie smiled at the lucky break they'd caught. The one his grandson had not, and probably never would, spot. Both men remained silent.

Each knew that conflict between them had to be avoided. But at what cost? The line hummed as they considered the price.

"How did you find this out?"

"You'll get those details on Monday Ollie." Zephaniah tried to reassert himself; being subordinate, even to his grandfather, was not a position he was ever comfortable with. Ollie permitted him to score the point.

"I know the way your mind works better than you do sometimes. I'm only going to say this once. You will do *exactly* as I say. There will be no ifs, buts or whys now." Ollie did not give his grandson time to agree or disagree before continuing. "You know the who and the where, far more information than the police, no doubt." He drew in a deep breath. "To go looking for him, and then to find him, would make superb Hollywood, but let me ruin your day Zephaniah. It *will* make dreadful real-life."

"What about the reward? One million dollars is a ton of money to a fisherman."

"A million dollars is a lot of money, but money is not the point. We are in the money business. Fishermen are not in the witness business, they're in the fish business. The best break is that he's a fisherman. A Long Island fisherman won't even know or read about this. He'll read *Newsday*, maybe once a week. The story won't even make the local news on his old black and white TV."

"I still say one million dollars is big money."

"You can say what you like, but we're going to play this long, very long." Ollie raised his voice a little, just enough to drive home his point. "We're not going to do anything, apart from plenty of nothing. Is there anything I've said that you do not understand?"

"No. My thoughts on this can wait until Monday."

"I don't use profanities, Zephaniah, and I've never spoken to you like this before, but I don't give a fucking damn for your thoughts on this, now or on Monday." Icily, he then added, "this is scripture Zephaniah. You leave that fisherman alone, not because he's a fisherman, but because I say so. From now on we're going to do this my way and I repeat, we're going to play this long." Ollie's anger, a rare sight or sound, began to cramp his chest. Again, he paused for breath. "Have I ever told you what I did before I started Swire's?"

"No, it's history none of us, not even my father, knows anything about. Why? Why now?"

"All I'll tell you is to trust your grandfather on this." There wasn't even a suggestion of weakness in his voice. Just the opposite. "I learnt all I know, and therefore all you know, by making the long play. Taking the long bet."

"You never gamble," Zephaniah spoke softly, hoping his tone might mute his grandfather's anger.

"That's precisely my point," hissed Ollie before he hung up the phone.

Zephaniah rocked back in his chair. Could have been worse, he thought.

Ollie leant against the cold, damp glass of the phone booth. Not bad for an old man, he thought. Then he grinned, a conman's grin, for he knew that if ever a conman lost his self-confidence, well, then the game was surely up.

And the game was only just beginning.

With that thought, he picked up the telephone again, dialled an out-of-state number from memory. He spoke for under sixty seconds then replaced the handset.

Yes, the game was just beginning.

CHAPTER 64

**Atlantic Ocean, heading northeast to Menemsha, Martha's Vineyard, Massachusetts.
Friday, 30th March 1990. Dusk.**

Marty's grip on the stainless-steel rail eased a fraction. Only after he'd flexed his hands was he aware of just how the sea-spray and cold had numbed his million-dollar fingers, the ones that paid the bills, the ones that Lloyd's of London insured. The lights of Menemsha Harbour were not far off, and he could see them beckoning *Sweet Amy* ever closer.

On the starboard quarter, and in the approaching moonlight, was the low, eerie silhouette of the deserted island that was No Man's Land. Jake had been right – no shit – the sea was being a tad kinder now, even though the waves' troughs were shorter and more aggressive. *Sweet Amy* just kept on slamming into them, still able to take all that the ocean could throw at her. Even Jake's usually immobile expression had relaxed now the harbour lights were in sight, almost striking distance.

"Not long Marty," Jake shouted above the roar of the ocean and motor.

"What about a dock, Jake? I hear the harbourmaster is a real dick."

"What's he going to do? Turn us away? Nah. An' all I care about is getting to a phone to check in on Amy."

Jake looked straight ahead as he hollered. Never once did his razor-sharp eyes leave the horizon. Never once did he stop anticipating the waves and the pattern of the sea. Never once did his stone hands leave the wheel, the wheel he wasn't so much as holding, as *feeling*, as if it were a heart-beating object. Which to Jake, it was. Tied up in port, engine off, lines checked, only then would he turn around to look his friend in the eyes. Until then, Jake only had eyes for the sea. But there was nothing new in that.

Suddenly the VHF screeched. It startled both men. Out there somewhere on the ocean the volume had been turned up full.

"Vessel approaching Menemsha Harbour, state your intentions."

Marty grinned while Jake shrugged. They stole a moment. Both their expressions spoke of relief and 'I told you the guy was an asshole'.

"Menemsha Harbour. You wanna go Channel 72 sir?" Jake called back.

"No sir. We'll stay Channel 16."

"Captain Jake Dealer, out of Montauk, vessel *Sweet Amy*. Intention is real simple sir. To get the hell out of this goddamned blow!"

"You booked a dock?"

"Negative that, sir."

"*Sweet Amy*, stand-by one, this will take a few minutes."

"Roger that, Menemsha. Standing by Channel 16."

The harbourmaster hated this kind of thing. Always at the last minute, always in a storm. It was mighty rough out there, so no way could he send him back out into it, much as he wanted to. The trouble was, as ever, there was only ever one free slip: Mr Oliver Swire's. Nothing else to do but go up Crick Hill and ask his permission. Why couldn't the old coot get a phone like the rest of the world?

* * *

Ollie's hands thawed around a mug of Fortnum & Mason's hot chocolate, and to further warm himself, he stole a glance at the *Gu*. Ever since his grandson had given it to him, he'd kept it on the kitchen table charged with yellow blooms. Smiling at the memory of Hannah, he looked out of the window again. He caught sight of the boat he'd spied from the beach. Only madmen and fishermen would be out there in this kind of weather. Then again most of the fishermen he knew were mad – good mad though – he thought as he sipped his hot chocolate.

Patiently he waited for the inevitable knock on the front door that would only be a couple of minutes away. It would be a meek, subservient knock from the harbourmaster, a man for whom Ollie reserved a special, almost subterranean, level of contempt. Small man, small brain, small harbour, big uniform equalled power-drunk bureaucrat. If Ollie had told the man once, he'd told him a hundred times: *"The only reason I keep my dock empty is for times like these. I elect not to own a boat. The fishermen own 'my boat', if you will. All of them. Do you understand? My dock may be used in any emergency WITHOUT seeking my permission. Is that clear?"* – PAUSE – *"Yes, of course Mr Swire"* had been the idiot's reply, obviously not hearing, much less heeding, a word that had been said. And after an incident at the end of last summer, when he'd turned a down'easter back out into a rough sea, Ollie had had enough. If the harbourmaster thought Menemsha Harbour was small, wait until he saw the miserable inlet in the Elizabeth Islands that Ollie had arranged for him to be transferred to before the summer season started. The man was more than an idiot; he was an unnecessary danger to seafarers. And Ollie was having none it.

"Good evening, Mr Jenkins. You have permission for the boat I can see approaching to use my dock. No charge as always." Ollie announced curtly as he opened and closed the door in the same breath. He had no desire even to hear the question to which he had just delivered the answer.

CHAPTER 65

**Poseyville, Amagansett, Long Island, New York.
Friday, 30th March 1990. After dusk.**

Shannon O'Leary parked her car at the entrance, if that was what it was, to the Dealers' home. To her right and embedded in the soil as if it were a part of the land's topography was a massive, centuries old anchor. She'd seen pictures of ones like it in books that told of the stories and legends of the great whaling vessels. Until now, she'd never seen one up close. It was magnificent. As if to draw courage or borrow a piece of history or both, she hesitated beside it and ran her hand over its rusted and flaking skin. The elements had had their way over the years, but there was life still drumming inside the mighty anchor.

She squared her shoulders, gripped her purse and walked through the yard towards the house, not knowing what to expect. This really was a voyage into the unknown; and after learning what she had, it felt like a ghost ride too. Nervously, as if waiting for a spectre to appear, she looked around inquisitively: the yard had obviously undergone a recent transformation of sorts. Where a shed had once been was a bed of damp ashes – please no – she thought as she grasped that this must be where Lindy had taken her life. A dory sat racked up on a trailer, paint peeling from its gunwales. It had certainly seen service, and loyal service by the looks of it. To an inexperienced eye it would seem fit for the scrap heap, but to Shannon, a Gloucesterman's daughter, she could see it was anything but. The Dealers' dory still had life in her too.

She knocked on the screen door. From inside she heard footsteps running down a staircase, and before she could inhale Amy stood holding the door open.

"Hi. Remember me?" Shannon asked.

"Of course, you're Shannon from Boston. You gave me the four-leaf clover." Amy smiled, and with a beguiling innocence, and an assured maturity, she added, "dad's not home. He's out on the water with Marty. They set out from Montauk this morning for the Vineyard. They're not due back till tomorrow sometime."

"OK. You alright here on your own?"

"Sure. I'm the one that looks after him!"

Amy's eyes betrayed her confidence. She looked away afraid, but not brave enough to share her fear.

"Well, my dad was a fisherman too and I don't ever remember him ever getting home on time. Sort of doesn't go together, fisherman and regular hours, does it?"

"No, I guess not," no longer wary she asked, "wanna come in?"

"That'd be great. Sure, I'm not disturbing you?"

"No, I'm doing homework in my room."

"Then don't let me disturb you, carry right on. Don't pay me any attention, I'll wait in the kitchen till you're done."

"Can I make you a coffee? Dad likes his black and strong. How about I make a fresh pot?" She said seeing the stewed dregs of the morning's brew.

With composure and assurance Amy set about making coffee, while Shannon sat in silence at the worn Formica of the old kitchen table, her legs crossed, her mind racing.

Then the telephone rang.

Startled, Amy almost jumped out of her skin.

"Amy Dealer here who is it please?"

Any premature scars of concern, worry or even fear dissolved as she heard her father's voice. Amy mouthed at Shannon *"It's dad"*. She needn't have done so. Shannon saw the young girl's face light up like a beacon. And for a long minute Amy just listened intently.

"I'm fine dad. I'll call Danny if you insist, OK." She rolled her eyes. "Yeah, of course I can get myself to the school bus in the morning. Daddy please," and as if to take attention away from her father's concern she added, "guess who's here? Shannon from Boston. She wants to talk to you. Can I put her on?"

This was an irony too far thought Shannon: I drive from Boston to Long Island, so I don't have to talk on the phone and here I am being handed one. But Shannon was aware of what was at stake if she fluffed her lines now. Taking the handset she cupped the mouthpiece.

"Amy, please go finish your homework while I talk to your dad." Her tone was one that left no doubt as to what Amy should do, even in her own house.

"Hi, my name is Shannon, Shannon O'Leary. I met you in Boston at Shiner's Diner. I've got something I need to tell you. This is going to sound very strange Mr Dealer, but I'd like you to hear me out please . . ."

She unfolded *The Boston Globe* cutting from her top pocket and spread it out on the Dealers' kitchen table.

CHAPTER 66

Menemsha Harbour, Martha's Vineyard, Massachusetts. Friday, 30th March 1990. After dusk and before nightfall.

Marty was doing comic-book exercises to keep himself warm. The wind was spinning around the deserted parking lot like candy-floss at a Coney Island stall . . . and tooling around outside Poole's and Larsen's sure wasn't his usual 7 p.m. hangout. By now he'd be into his first 'loud-mouth soup'. Yes, this one would be a Gibson; not a fan of onions, but he knew they added a fritz to a Martini. Solving the riddle of what one small white onion brought to the party was one of Marty's more benign quests.

"Shit! You OK Jake? Look like you seen a frickin' ghost!"

"Help me with the lines Marty," Jake shouted above the noise of the wind. "The lines now . . . I'm headin' back . . ."

"Back where?"

"Get the frickin' lines, Marty!" The look in Jake's eyes, and the edge in his voice, could have cut steel.

Realising this, Marty hollered, "you gotta be kidding me?"

"No way I joke about stuff like this. It's my call, and you're stayin' here."

"Too darned right I am. In fact, we're both staying here."

"I'm headed right back to Montauk and home . . ." Jake couldn't finish the sentence.

"What the hell you going on about, Jake? What happened in that booth?"

"Not your business . . ." Words failed Jake, but that was nothing new.

"Like hell it ain't! You call Amy while I jump around like a loon trying to get some circulation back, and figure out who we're gonna stay with tonight, and then you come out and tell me we're going back out into that frickin' storm. What the hell happened in there?"

"Not *we* Marty. I am going back, and it's none of your business . . ."

Marty Drew was an old hand at certitude, hell, hadn't he built his career on it? Shining out of his friend's eyes was pure conviction. There was an ugly, dangerous storm out there, but one look told Marty that his friend was going to do just that. Head right back into it. The man was mad. Or perhaps . . .

"Marty, go and get warm, I'll do the lines. I've really gotta do this. Please trust me. Please, and I'm sorry for shouting."

"You're mad Jake, frickin' mad. Think of Amy."

"That's exactly what I'm doing."

"What the hell does that mean?"

Marty's voice was lost on the wind as Jake ran back to *Sweet Amy's* deck. With natural agility he leapt on board, fired up the engine, checked his gauges – just enough fuel with the reserve tank – and undid the lines. It took less than a minute. Without even waving to Marty, he gunned the engine hard in neutral, spun the wheel, then crashed the gearbox into reverse. He felt the bronze four-blade propeller bite deep into the water. Throttle wide open, he turned her on a dime, headed into the mouth of the harbour and out into the black sweep of the ocean, leaving a bewildered Marty on the quay to witness the phosphorescence dancing in *Sweet Amy's* wake.

Numb from cold and fear, his eyes fixed on Jake's red pilot house night light until they hurt, and the down'easter had disappeared back into the teeth of the storm. Marty shrugged his shoulders as if that was all he could do, unaware of the periscope-like scrutiny both he and Jake had been subjected to from the downstairs window of 10 Crick Hill Road.

Jake, oblivious to all but what lay in front of him, knew that the Atlantic Ocean was his home, even with its rage welded to a coal-faced sky. This ocean robbed souls, yet it could feed his. It would calm the mounting fury inside him, and yes, this storm *would* let him out. It *would* deliver him home to Amy. What was it going to take, seven hours or so with the following sea? After 300 years that was a blink of an eye. This was, and would be forever, Dealer country.

Now, Jake's enemy was time. But time had always been his enemy.

PART SIX

TUESDAY, 15TH MAY 1990

CHAPTER 67

**19 Arlington Street, Back Bay, Boston, Massachusetts.
Tuesday, 15th May 1990. 08:10.**

"Hey Jessie, let's pick up the pace! I'd like to run through what you're going to say this morning."

Cory glanced at his watch and shook his head. Time had this habit of dissolving when she was around. Now in his late thirties, he'd become somewhat prematurely a creature of routine. He liked to be in his office no later than 8.45 to speed-read *The Boston Globe* and fortify himself with strong English tea. Only then would he pore over all the overnight faxes from his network of foreign contacts.

During the years Cory had been employed by Swire's, he'd cultivated disparate – and highly effective – channels of overseas connections with whom he personally maintained regular dealings. The research department at Swire's had been unrivalled in the art world before he'd joined, yet he had wished to improve it markedly. It was the measure of the man that he had succeeded.

He'd accomplished this by digging deeper – with more nous and dynamism – than anyone could have imagined, except perhaps the man who had hired him, Zephaniah Swire. And all with one aim. To ensure that when a Raphael or a Picasso or a Monet threatened to break the surface, for whatever reason – divorce, bankruptcy, prison, tax, or even something as prosaic as boredom – then the network he'd created would hear of it first. It wasn't just art dealers who were kept in his cross hairs: private bankers, journalists, tax inspectors, fences, doctors, shrinks, private investigators, horse trainers, hotel concierges, mistresses, agents, lawyers, select criminals, Freemasons, politicians, accountants, actors . . . The ecosystem Cory had created – and now inhabited – was a shadowy one, where all the finer points of morality had long been squashed by the blunt instrument of personal expediency. From time to time, they each received the perceived largesse of a favour, an introduction, or an unexpected 'gift' from Swire's Head of Research.

In any other arena of employment it could have been said, with validity, that Cory Mount was a man obsessed with his job. He wasn't. Besides being handsomely rewarded, he performed his duties at Swire's because that was what was expected of him. The short-fingered vulgarians at the Getty could (and probably would) end up purchasing the Raphael or the Titian or the Michelangelo drawing, but only after Swire's had surveyed the transaction and secured a fee.

It wasn't just those who lived within his Rolodex who were becoming more than a little bored with an obsession he had developed of late. Where the hell was all the stolen art from the Isabella Stewart Gardner Museum?

Not one person – from London to Tokyo to Bogotá via Zurich – had heard so much as a hushed murmur of where any of the missing art might be. Faced with this unheard-of dilemma, he began to doubt not only himself, but also his previously entrenched opinion that the largest art theft in history had been a commissioned one.

Whatever Constance Lowenthal, of the International Foundation of Art Research in New York, had said publicly after the break-in, he knew only too well that a coterie of intensely private collectors *did* commission art thefts. At Christie's in London, and even more so at Swire's, he'd observed an ego-blaze surface in the eyes of a new owner of a work of art the moment title passed, *however* it had passed. If you had stolen Vermeer's near-priceless masterpiece, and hidden it on your cellar wall, there would be a primal need to show it to someone, or at least tell someone. He understood only too well that the collecting of art and the bragging about it were often entwined; man had been doing the latter ever since he'd etched sabre-toothed tigers on his cave walls. Surely, he reminded himself with metronomic monotony: *'inform three people and you inform the world'*? At the very least, in this case, three people were involved: the two thieves and their commissioner. Yet, thus far, it was as if the Gardner's stolen works had never even existed. They had simply vanished into air thinner than that atop Mount Everest. And that was like defying gravity. Impossible.

* * *

"So, how do I look?" With a theatrical flourish, Jessica Flack, a doctor in child psychology and now an unsalaried assistant researcher at Swire's, appeared from behind her bedroom door. With a ballet dancer's poise, precarious yet sure-footed, she planted a kiss on her host's clean-shaven cheek. She lingered. The citrus in his aftershave was very becoming, she thought.

"You look terrific. Not too serious yet still business-like for Mr Swire. Thank you."

"You chauvinist! What do you mean?" She teased. "That's like saying this is a very flattering outfit."

Cory blushed. She looked the part in dark grey slacks, a white silk blouse that revealed a suggestion of lace from her bra as a vague shadow, and a navy Ralph Lauren blazer – the kind with the faux emblem on its breast pocket – hanging precariously from her manicured forefinger. Yes, you'll do, Cory thought as he smiled. But he wasn't about to go down that rabbit-hole again. That was London – and the Alps – way back when. This was Boston, 1990.

"Be serious, Jessie. Mr Swire wants an update on the Gardner theft, and I told his PA that you'd be coming." Cory looked away momentarily. "We have a regular meeting every two weeks on Tuesday mornings. He returned from the Vineyard last night looking anything but his usual self." He paused. "Something's been troubling him of late. Ambushes I don't need. So, what do you think he's going to say to your ideas?"

"I've no idea Cory. Can't say. I've not met him. All I know is what you've told me, and from that he sounds like a series of contradictions."

"He is, I suppose. Anyway, run me through it please."

Cory led her to the other side of his large and airy Back Bay duplex apartment, situated above Thos. Moser, a storied Maine cabinetmaker. Together with his collection of rare 20th-Century first editions, his home – with its magnificent garden views – was his principal indulgence. Beside the central bay window, and next to the floor-to-ceiling bookshelves, stood an easel supporting a green felt pin-board covered with photographs of the thirteen stolen treasures, each annotated.

This was Jessie's canvas. She'd scribbled notes and pinned and stretched different coloured ribbons in a seemingly haphazard fashion. She'd tacked up cards and jotted down ideas – each appearing to be a *non-sequitur* – and to anyone other than Jessie they were. Scattered across the Native American rug were large cushions – and ashtrays – and more books: some open, some closed, some upside down, but all read and marked up, and all sported *'Do Not Disturb'* notes. Even his Chesterfield looked like it had been colonised by a huddle of penguins; barely a square inch of its claret leather was visible. This area – this project – had been her study, and her obsession, as she had begun the long process of healing under Massachusetts' spring sunlight. Jessie knew only too well that the mind was a jigsaw puzzle. First, you searched out the four corner pieces. Then came the straight-edged pieces. When all those were assembled, there would exist a framework within which one could begin to work *inwards*. That was the way all minds worked. *Inwards*. And it was a *mind* that had conceived the Gardner robbery.

"Each item here is a clue, and each is a missing piece. They inform me about the cogs of the mind which commissioned this theft. What's also important is what was selected to be left behind. These too are triggers." Jessie shot him a disarming look. "You see, even paintings can bark."

Cory listened and tried to concentrate. He failed miserably. Jessie could have been reciting a recipe for homemade peanut butter. Just listening to her speak in those soft tones, yet with authority, only made him wish he was back in London, way back when. It was no wonder she had been at the top of her profession, he mulled over as he wrestled with himself.

Oblivious to her audience, but now in full flight, she continued. "Apart from the Vermeer, I'm hunting down the wee, small items: the Napoleonic finial and the *Gu*. They're almost Turkish bazaar trinkets when you consider . . ."

This time, however, the lilt in her mellifluous voice grabbed his focus by the scruff. Just what was Mr Swire going to make of it all?

"You're not paying attention. I'm not here to exercise my vocal cords. I'm a sketch artist drawing you an image." Jessie drew back her shoulders. "Talking of which, did they ever find the man, you know, the one carrying the child the old lady spotted crossing the road that night? The missing witness?"

"No. A few of the usual cranks came forward hoping to get the $1 million reward, but they forgot that it was for the art, not the witness. As for the witness, there's been neither sight nor sound, despite the BPD composite being everywhere. It is strange no one has come forward, no?"

"Yes, very odd. You'd have thought someone, somewhere would have ventured something. When children are involved, people *always* talk. It's as if they can't help themselves. By protecting the unknown child this witness was holding in the dead of that night, they would be 'protecting' their own children. The reaction to try and help a child is subliminal, inescapable. It's primal."

Dr Jessie Flack's eyebrows furrowed as her own trauma flooded over a breakwater in her mind. Would the nightmares ever leave her? No, probably not. Here in Boston, immersed in something so totally different, she was at least able to view her own 'history' in a positive light. And that could only help in her future work.

Smiling crisply again, she looked up. "Anyway, where was I?"

CHAPTER 68

18 Lindsey Street, Rockland, Maine.
Tuesday, 15th May 1990. 08:09.

Jake Dealer scratched his beard. All it had done since he'd grown it out was itch. He'd been brought up around men with full, dog-like beards – his good friend Danny King had one of those Quaker beards – and wasn't a beard supposed to be the hallmark of a fisherman? Or was that just another crazy idea folks had about people who worked the ocean? Hell with it, Jake thought, this beard is all about necessity, not what others think. Hiding in plain sight.

Sure, in winter he'd gone days without shaving, especially if money was too tight to mention 'razor blades' to Lindy. But this beard was camouflage from the composite pictures of him across all New England. What else could he do until the Boston Police had caught the criminals? Hide, is all. He was a bayman, a fisherman, not a witness man. That was the BPD's or FBI's gig. And the federal government hadn't exactly helped the bayman's cause either. Besides, being a loner meant he minded his own business. Being a witness to anything other than a net full of fish, a pot full of lobsters, or better still, an ironed swordfish, was all the witnessing he was up for.

"Amy, where did all these grey hairs come from?" Jake called out from the bathroom of their two-room efficiency apartment at 18 Lindsey Street.

"Easy one, dad. You're getting older, and men look better with a bit of grey in their hair and beards. Anyways, that's what Shannon says."

"Thanks Amy . . ."

"Well, we both think it suits you fine. I'm late for school, not good to be late when you're at a new school."

"Always the boss, eh, Amy. Just like your mother. Knock on Shannon's door and tell her coffee in ten, OK? I've gotta catch the ferry out to

Matinicus in an hour. You sure you're going to be fine without Ol' Grey Beard around for a couple of weeks?"

"You know I will," replied Amy as she bolted into the bathroom, stood on tiptoe and kissed her father on the cheek. "Eeek! Hedgehog face! Be safe out there on Matinicus. Please call us when you arrive . . ."

"You know I will."

Jake turned away from the mirror and looked at his daughter with more love in his heart and eyes than he could have imagined existed. And for the first time ever, he caught a newborn expression in her eyes. One that suggested she had begun to make peace with her brother's murder and her mother's suicide. Amy's ability to show this now, coupled with his to recognise it, could only mean that their fog of grief might, just might, be lifting.

18 Lindsey Street was a two-floor apartment building, eight apartments in all. It was built of wood and shingle, and even in May its thin walls exhaled Maine's winter chill. However threadbare, though, it was a home of sorts. Until? Where? When? Jake had yet to plot that next move.

The flimsy outer door banged shut, and Jake heard a brisk knock on the next-door apartment followed by Amy's scampering feet as she ran down the landing and off to catch the school bus.

Drained and tired, Jake sat down heavily on the bed and tugged at his boots. What was it about Maine? Cold and bleak, and when the sun shone somehow it never got into your bones. The Maine sun, even on this bright May morning, was something you only saw, never felt.

It wasn't meant to be like this. He was supposed to be further south in Gloucester, Massachusetts working a sword boat while Amy attended school there. Yet, since Shannon had spoken to him on that fateful evening in Menemsha, he had felt like he was running a marathon to nowhere. All he knew was that he had to keep on running, even if the gauge read E. Which it did.

Jake was not a man who complained. He dug in and got on with it. Whatever 'it' was. Seamanship or luck – and luck was just that; a wink from nowhere that flattered to deceive the unwary. But alone during the blacked-out stormy moonless and friendless night, 'something' had joined him as he'd battled the Atlantic's wrath from Menemsha to Montauk. The frenzied gale had not only let him out, the wind and currents had helped him home. So what if it had been the worst all-night roller-coaster ride he'd ever experienced, but nearing Montauk there'd been some visibility. Jake knew from bitter encounters that fog, be it in the head, in the heart, or on the ocean, was the true enemy. Yet how he and Amy – and Shannon – had ended up in Rockland still perplexed him.

At least where they had all fetched up was a working harbour, a place Jake could make sense of, not a prissy Disney-back-lot like Camden. They said: *'Rockland-by-the-Smell'* and *'Camden-by-the-Sea'*. They were right and he was mighty glad of it. Rockland's ground fisheries of cod, flounder and haddock weren't what they'd once been, but they still fished from the same wharves as they'd done for generations.

Back in the day, old schooners had headed way out east to the treacherous, but bountiful, cod-fisheries of the Grand Banks; a good old-age was rare for those seafarers. Jake had thought about those fishermen of bygone days, as he, Shannon and Amy had moored his down'easter at *Journey's End*, as it was named. An all-too-chilling name for a dock. And for Jake's mood.

The Rockland they'd found was tamer now; there was herring and sardine fishing for lobster bait, a fish-cannery and a carrageenan plant which extracted all manner of food additives from the ocean's red and purple seaweeds. Then there was the lobstering. The famed Maine lobster was a thriving fishery from May to November. A good and long season: seven, sometimes eight, months. The lobsters were plentiful; about seven million pounds were caught each year.

And while Jake had fought the ocean and the elements that March night, he'd thought of the Kent family. A handful of years ago they'd surrendered. Nate Kent had waved the white flag on his life as a Long Island bayman. A strong and self-reliant man, Nate had sold his family's home in Amagansett. He'd been able – just – to hold onto their boat, and with it they'd tracked due north, or as they say, Down east to Maine. The Kents had stayed in touch with Jake and Lindy for a time and Nate had ended up getting a licence to go lobstering.

After a good first season, they'd bought a ramshackle house on a bleak island out in the Gulf of Maine. Named Matinicus – meaning 'far out island' in native Abenaki – the isle was the furthest inhabited United States land into the Atlantic Ocean: two miles long and one mile wide, about 720 acres of rocks, coves and a small harbour. Matinicus was a lonely place, more an ocean island than a gulf island, it seemed to belong deep *inside* the Atlantic itself. Isolated and exposed, it was the first rampart the ocean's mighty rollers encountered. The Kents' life was hard on Matinicus, but the erosion came only from the wind, the weather and the sea, not city dwellers. The year-round island settlement constituted about sixty men, women and children – eight or nine families. Lobstermen all. Sure, the politics ran deep, but at least they were local. There was a solitary post office and a school that taught the handful of children. A church built in 1906 doubled as the community hall. Heck, even the Rockland supply and ferry boat only called into harbour once every three or four weeks. Nate had told him that if you wanted running water on Matinicus: *"You gotta fill a bucket and run with it Jake."*

As *Sweet Amy* had thundered across Jake's home stretch of ocean that godforsaken night, he'd figured that Rockland and Matinicus would be the safest of places to go to hide from, or as he preferred to think of it – to wait out – this unexpected storm of events. There he would buy time and hopefully secure what remained of the Dealer posterity. Much like Nate Kent and his family had done. But for different reasons. Nate Kent hadn't been hunted, a man on the lam.

* * *

Exhausted and relieved that bleak March morning, Jake had docked in Montauk before dawn filtered through the mist. Barely pausing to breathe, he'd driven home like a man possessed, grabbed a duffle bag and told Amy to do likewise. Not once – then or since – had she asked 'why'. Amy just 'did' that morning. After all, she was a Dealer, as he'd later reminded himself. She'd mustered her precious keepsakes, photos, favourite clothes and schoolbooks. Then, they had sat down at the kitchen table, and read the letter Shannon had left behind. In the envelope was the newspaper cutting from *The Boston Globe*. Over piping hot coffee and bread, he had read and reread the cutting, and each time the silent need to disappear became more real. Not for good, but until this had all blown over, or the thieves were arrested. He had never quit anything in his life – it wasn't in his blood – but this was survival. This was the only way he knew how to protect Amy. Out there on the ocean, far, far away from strangers with their pale city-faces, lying eyes and trick questions that sought to betray for their own ends.

Not knowing what Jake might do – but guessing that he wouldn't surrender himself to the BPD or FBI as the witness they were tracking – Shannon had provided her parents address in Gloucester, and explained they were like-minded folks who could help him, *should* he ever find himself in Gloucester. She'd said that she was returning to Boston to try to get back on the water. She'd signed off with best wishes to them both and told Jake that his secret was safe with her. And on the third read of the letter, with its neat, upright handwriting, he knew that his secret was indeed safe.

Nerves still jangling from the storm – he'd been at sea for sixteen or more hours – zero sleep and way too much caffeine, there was one more task that remained. He had to write a note to that slick banker in East Hampton, with an instruction to deliver a letter in a couple of weeks to . . . ? Not to Marty. For sure. He didn't need this shit in his life. Besides, he'd just been left stranded in Menemsha. Jake had racked his brain. His crew. No. Danny? Perhaps. But no. The King crew had fish to catch.

Peter Duxbury. Yes. He knew everybody and was one of 'them': a good friend of the baymen and Marty too. Pete was a solid, stand-up man. You could lean on Pete, and he wouldn't bend. Horsing what remained of his tin cup of coffee, he dashed off the letter to Pete, sealed the envelope and knew – with a faint heart – where to find Lindy's stash of postage stamps. This would always be her kitchen.

The sun had barely risen. Nonetheless, its first order that day had been to deploy its supremacy to confiscate the Atlantic's cruel dawn mist. And Jake had used its precious gift to bundle Amy and their meagre belongings into the flatbed Ford. For his plan to work, he had to get away from Long Island. And fast. The truck's flatbed was always loaded with empty jerry-cans; he'd fill them at a sleepy self-service gas station he knew off Montauk Highway. They had a letter box as well. Then, it'd be *Sweet Amy* and the Atlantic. Another homecoming of sorts, as he'd kept on telling himself.

* * *

On that early morning, Jake had parked his truck back in the same spot as he had the day before, when he and Marty had put out to sea. With his boat 'still' gone, folks might figure that the storm hadn't let him out. Perhaps he'd joined Harvey. Marty's office would confirm that he had set off alone from Menemsha into the gale's blackened teeth . . . and with no *Sweet Amy* in Montauk . . . and the flatbed Ford in the same parking spot, perhaps he was home with the ocean?

OK, the deception wouldn't buy him much time, he knew that, because Amy wouldn't be in school. He felt terrible for those who'd be searching high and low. But he'd squared that away with the twenty-four hour jump he'd get. It was enough to put waves under the keel, distance onto the chart. Time enough to disappear. Then, it'd be down to Pete Duxbury to let those who mattered know that he and Amy were still alive.

* * *

They'd slipped out of the harbour under cover of a weather break: an Atlantic squall had brought rain, wind and hailstones the size of marbles. Folks stayed indoors when those fleet-footed wet storms whistled out of the Atlantic across Montauk Point.

Jake had plotted a northeasterly course to the Cape Cod Canal, keeping Block Island abeam on the port side. Then, he'd tracked northeast through Buzzards Bay to the canal. Seven and half miles – toll and inspection free – and back out into the Atlantic. A swing to port, a new course – west of plum north – with Gloucester about seventy nautical miles on the nose. Well inside the twenty-four-hour window he'd planned. With all the boating traffic, *Sweet Amy* shouldn't be noticed. And no one would be looking for her in the waters they were headed to.

* * *

Reaching Gloucester, having run on fumes, coffee, potato chips and little else, he'd moored *Sweet Amy* out of sight. Exhausted to the point of collapse, he and Amy had set about her pretty, varnished stern with some masking tape, two pots of green paint, a small tin of red paint and a stencil.

A nor'easter was blowing, not strong, but a blow, nevertheless. Their task hadn't taken them as long as they'd imagined it might. Amy had held the tins of paint as her father stood on the dock working two brushes at the same time. Together, they transformed the down'easter *Sweet Amy* into the down'easter *Sweet Lindy*. In silence, they stood on the empty jetty and admired their handiwork.

With two clinks, they'd each popped a bottle of beer and emptied them over the stern of their newly christened vessel. They'd already chosen another oath during the trip north. An oath between the two of them like the one they'd sworn when they'd buried Blondie in the woods out back. There were no prayers to a God they knew couldn't exist. And this oath was more a solemn request to the Atlantic Ocean – whose water they floated in – simply to forgive them the bad luck that the ocean had the right to bestow on those who would change a vessel's name.

Finally, they'd huddled into their sleeping bags in the forepeak. As they'd closed their eyes, *Sweet Lindy* appeared to steady herself. Her rocking and shifting in the fresh wind had ceased.

The nor'easter had ebbed into a zephyr. No more than a whisper.

CHAPTER 69

**10 Crick Hill Road, Menemsha,
Martha's Vineyard, Massachusetts.
Tuesday, 15th May 1990. 08:25.**

It had been a long time since Ollie Swire had set an alarm clock. Usually he slept soundly, and for more hours than a man of his age could expect. Of late though he had found an added peace and was eager to rise early and return to that newly encountered state of mind. Forever questioning, what troubled him was the idea that it might just be a trick of self-protection. Or worse, self-deceit. All his life he had been on guard against those bear traps.

Whatever his current, somewhat harsh feelings towards his grandson were, Ollie was not about to allow them to mar the pleasure he was deriving from painstakingly returning, inch by inch, Vermeer's sheer brilliance and gravitas to *The Concert*.

So, armed with a pot of fresh mint tea and a bowl of fruit, Ollie would disappear into his orderly and hermetically sealed studio, with its state-of-the-art air-filtration and lighting systems, to recommence work on his other skill: restoration. With a Chopin piano concerto playing, he would sit in front of the mahogany easel and perform all the necessary tasks with the care, vigour and patience that were required of a master restorer.

Only recently had he accepted the fact that there were so many years, months even, that his hands would remain steady. And his studio was the fullest it had ever been: one Vermeer, two Rembrandts, one Flinck, one Manet. All needed, and were awaiting, his alchemic touch; the five Degas sketches were inked on paper and were in satisfactory condition. Putting his tea to one side, he covered his shoulders with a black shawl and settled into commonplace life in 17th-Century Holland. Vermeer was known to work slowly and meticulously, and it was with that discipline that he studied *The Concert* every day.

The painting's condition was a scandal. At the last restoration (and he had no idea when that could have been, probably before Mrs Gardner had purchased it in the 1890's) it had received poor attention, from slack and lazy hands. The restorer had used wax and resins on the expensive pigments Vermeer had found in Delft, where he'd toiled. When it had been on display at the Gardner it had been behind ordinary – not museum quality – glass, which in turn had accumulated its own ingrained grime and obscured much of the damage.

The Gardner had no air-conditioning nor even an air-handling system. The panes of glass in the roof lights above the central courtyard leaked in winter, and a primitive boiler in the basement blew smuts throughout the building. Whilst in the summer months, the museum's windows were left open to welcome in the city's pollution, fumes and general grime.

If proof were ever needed that the Gardner was not a fit custodian (and that was Ollie Swire's view), it was to be found in what had recently transpired over the one Rembrandt his grandson had elected not to steal: the *Self Portrait* which had been painted on an oak panel. The saga of the *Self Portrait* convicted the museum in his opinion: it had been painted on a seven-foot-square oak panel more than 350 years ago, and with the wood's joins and stress points, the painting needed great attention. The museum's trustees had recently pulled together a paltry $13,000 to have the *Self Portrait* restored, but the much-needed work had never taken place due to the lack of a further $10,000 to insure the painting for the short journey to New York. Just two weeks back, Ollie had visited the Gardner to study the condition of some of their other works; the fact that it was his grandson's crime scene was, he admitted to himself, a contributing factor. There he had seen paint literally flaking off Botticelli's *The Tragedy of Lucretia*, and his estimate for an acceptable restoration for John Singer Sargent's immense *El Jaleo* was at least $250,000.

So, restoring these paintings in his studio (including the challenge of the oak-panelled Flinck, *Landscape with an Obelisk*) appeared to him to be the very least he could do under the circumstances. What would happen to them after he had performed his own masterful talents was, he had decided, not going to concern him. These paintings were, after all, not his. He was merely a custodian, albeit also a gifted restorer.

What might happen to them later wasn't going to cloud any decision he would have to take. Ollie had been a con artist for long enough to recognise that the person who had conceived the con, chosen the mark and assembled his players – as a director would a cast – must be allowed to call, and play out, the endgame. That too was scripture. In this case, that person was Zephaniah. In the final analysis it didn't matter who owned the keys to the ranch.

Besides, he thought rather morbidly as he nibbled on an apple, there was only the mere width of a thread of silk that divided the master thief and the master con artist. And upon that silk thread lay a simple variance: most marks were conmen in their own way, but only *some* owners of fine art were thieves.

So, who was Ollie Swire to preach?

CHAPTER 70

**The American Hotel, Sag Harbour, Long Island, New York.
Tuesday, 15th May 1990. 08:45.**

"Hey Marty! Telephone!" Carlo, the barman announced a tad too loudly.

Marty mouthed, "Who is it?"

"Can't see Mr Drew, sir. Who's calling please?" asked Carlo.

"Peter Duxbury", he replied, knowing full well that the barkeeps at The American Hotel screened for Marty Drew.

"Hi Pete, sorry, I didn't recognise your voice. I'll pass you over," said Carlo cheerily as Marty took the phone without budging.

"How are you doing? All OK? Now you've found me, come join me for a coffee. Too early in the morning for an Irish though."

Ever the barfly, Marty was perched on a stool and dunking a sweet biscuit into the foam of his cappuccino. Rain or shine, breakfast or cocktails, The American Hotel in Sag Harbour had been his home-from-home for years. He liked that it was 150 years old, and that it had been an hotel when Sag was the whaling capital of America. Ever since Marty had hit pay-dirt with his first album, *Fingers Crossed*.

The American had ceased to be an eight-room hotel and had become a seven-room hotel. Not that he often used the small suite he maintained there, but the Long Island boy in him simply liked the idea. A bachelor by vocation, his cosy suite had its uses; ones usually twinned with ladies who cared to shoot the breeze and smoke cigars. Oftentimes they'd stop by, and Marty would catch their eye from his stool at the moody, panelled ground floor bar. And the rest was, as Carlo would have it, *'either history or future'*.

"Thanks for the offer, Marty, but I'm in Montauk. Another time. Got a minute to talk about Jake?"

Kicking the slouch out of his spine, Marty asked. "Sure. Any news?

"I'm cross-checking things. On the drive out to Montauk this morning I called by the Farmers' Market. You know Madge and how she likes to talk, and she gets 'round to telling me about a girl, mid-thirties, tall, redhead, who'd come from Boston looking for Jake. She wanted to know how to find his house, and this happened on the very same day you and he got caught in that bad storm going to the Vineyard. So, Madge sees that I'm interested now, knowing I work for a newspaper an' all, and says her name was Shannon O'Leary . . ."

"She wouldn't have Irish blood would she?" interrupted Marty.

"Hold on Marty, this is where it gets good, she refuses to tell Madge what she wants to see Jake about. She says it's private and it was too important to tell him on the phone. Madge also said this girl didn't even know Lindy was dead."

"She couldn't have known Jake well then. What are you saying, Pete?"

"Me and coincidences don't ever sit on the same park-bench. All I figure is that a few hours after Miss O'Leary comes to Amagansett, our friend, his daughter and his boat all vanish into thin air. Like they never existed. Like that's a coincidence in my book."

"The Dealers have existed alright, for 300 frickin' years". Marty grafted with a tone of protection in his reply. "I see where you're headed now."

"When you and Jake got to Menemsha, did *anything* out of the ordinary happen?"

"Damned right it did. I already told you. Lookit, Jake called Amy from the booth in the parking lot, and then went right back out to sea to smack back into that horrible storm. The man was on a mission. He had that ol' look in his eye. You've seen it before Pete. Jake and that stare of his, shit, it could nail a coffin down."

"OK, so now guess what Marty? I'm asking around this morning, I speak to Mikey, Danny, the guys on the dock, and it turns out that just one week ago a stranger, real out of town type, city-guy, you know, trying too hard, dressing too casually, starts asking anyone who'll listen as to where Jake might have gone. He was tan with a smallpox scarred face, sort of Native looking guy Danny said. Fit, early forties."

Marty coughed and snorted, then said quietly. "Like how this guy even know Jake was gone in the first place?"

"Thank you, Marty."

"Your plot's thickening."

"Can you think of anything that happened when you guys docked? Details, Marty. Details."

"I told you already. Jake went straight back out to sea," Marty shot back.

"Well, what did *you* do?"

"You never asked me that before," he answered sheepishly.

"Just tell me what you did, please."

"I went into the payphone to ring Carly Simon. I said I was stranded, you know, *'long story, I'll tell you later'* kinda stuff, but cutting to the chase it went: *"Carly, can you please pick me up? I need a bed for the night."* I'm frickin' cold an' wet, ain't no hotels nearby and the nearest cab is in Manhattan. So, she tells me, *"Sure Marty, but give me an hour. OK?"* And just as I'm wondering what the hell am I going to do in a parking lot in Menemsha for an hour, it's not exactly Flip City you know, a man appears outside the booth. Looks kind of like a pocket-sized undertaker. Dressed all in black, natty, elderly but trim, white hair. He's like immaculate. At this hour of the night. Like nothing outta place. The wind is blowing like the Devil's ass on Mexican Night, and the stranger asks if I was on the boat that just docked and went back out. I tell him yes, I was. He looks confused, then introduces himself in a slow, deliberate voice. Says his name is Oliver Swire, and he lives just there, so he points up to a cottage on Crick Hill . . ."

"Whoa Marty! THE Oliver Swire?"

"Don't know what you mean?"

"You know, Swire's, Boston. In the art world they got more hitting power than a team of Babe Ruths."

"OK, I heard the name, but, like, I didn't put two and two together then. He seemed real modest and it was a real shitty night. He invites me up the hill and into the warm. That's all I wanted. Warmth. I was freezin' out there. And what with Carly being an hour away I say yes. Thank you, Mr Swire. All he said was: *"Please call me Ollie"* and off we went up to his home."

"What happened next?"

"He sure had some fine old brandy that did the trick. Now you mention art, he had an original set of Doug's pictures, palladium ones an' all, personally signed, hanging on the walls in the kitchen. He seemed to love the ocean. All we talked about for an hour or so was the sea, fishermen. You know, we shot the breeze. Then I see Carly's old wagon pull up in the parking lot, so I thank him and leave. That's it."

"That all?"

"Yeah, sure. He was real kind and helped me out." Marty laughed. "An' he didn't know who I was when he asked what I did. That was a solid bonus too."

"Or so he said, Marty . . ."

CHAPTER 71

**Rockland Ferry Terminal, Rockland, Maine.
Tuesday, 15th May 1990. 09:05.**

"Don't worry about Amy or me, Jake. When I ran into you at my folks in Gloucester, I was looking to get out of Boston. I was done waiting tables." Shannon swept her flame-red hair away from her face, and the sun instantly picked up on her freckles. Rockland's ferry landing was exposed to the northeast, and stiff break-of-day gusts were whipping into Rockland Harbour from Penobscot Bay.

The Maine sky wore its own peculiar hard blue edge. The ocean had a green-grey heaviness about it, a sort of glassy swell. The morning sun gave off its best, but even with the soft glow there was precious little warmth. Across from the landing, and wrapped up against the cold, crews were beginning to prepare the windjammers for the coming tourist season. Gulls circled nearby, incautious and greedy as always. With their outsized wingspan and scavenging beaks they reminded Shannon of her childhood waiting for her father to return home. He would have been at sea for three or four weeks (it had felt like months then), and she recalled that first sign that a sword boat might soon hove into view would be the gulls overhead, all ready to fight each other for fish heads and entrails. Together with her mother and brother, they would say prayers and cross their fingers for a good catch. Then, as now, there always seemed to be bills to pay.

"But Shannon, you're back waiting tables now," said Jake with a smile to bring her back to the moment.

"Sure, I know, and The Trade Winds have cut me good shifts and the tips are OK. Besides, I should get a job as a sternman come the end of June,"

"Do you know how hard it is to get a job lobstering in Maine, even as a sternman?"

"Yeah, I do, but if I told you once I told you a hundred times, I want to get back on the water. My father has retired, his half-share of the sword boat has been sold. My brother wanted nothing to do with the fishin' life."

"Not such a dumb call," Jake said with uncharacteristic insensitivity. The truth was he was nervous about leaving Amy for so long. That, and just what he'd find on the wilderness that was Matinicus, apart from trap-piles, granite, spruce trees, and the constant Atlantic wind.

"Well, maybe, my brother *was* smart. My father didn't want me to go to sea, but it's always been an itch with me. Now's the time to scratch it." And without thinking she added: "You're a long-time dead Jake." Realising what she'd said she looked skywards before facing him again. "You've been kind enough to help me out up here in Maine, and while you're away I'll make sure Amy gets settled, and I'll check on your boat every day. You go lobstering. Get back on the water. You need to Jake." There was a look of real concern in her kind, green eyes.

"I could stay here and 'dig a tide', you know, go clamming again. But I figured if Nate cuts me a break there'll be more money lobstering off Matinicus."

"That's a fact. I'm sure he'll cut you a good deal too."

"All I'm going to be doing for the next three weeks is fighting mosquitoes, flies and feral cats whilst mendin' on a trap-pile 500 deep. I don't even know what Nate is going to be able to pay me, 20% of the catch is usual, but it's work, and I got rent to pay."

"I'm paying my way too, Jake."

"Yeah, I know." He grinned that smile of his. He knew he couldn't be doing this without her help. And she was so good with Amy.

"You're helping me getting back on the water, an' all I'm doing in return is lending a hand with Amy, which is a pleasure anyways. Ain't much nightlife for a single girl in Rockland."

The Matinicus ferry sounded its horns impatiently. Jake picked up his canvas duffel bag and started towards the ramp. He waved at Shannon and walked away angry with himself, cross that he wanted time alone. He thought it selfish, but he knew he needed to be a solitary man for a while. To centre his compass.

"Hey, Jake," Shannon called out. "You take care out there, you hear."

"Sure will. Just look after my girl, eh!"

"Good as done." Then, with a few quick, impromptu steps she was beside him once more. "Like all storms, Jake, it *will* blow over soon. They'll catch the thieves. How can they not? The BPD said they've got an additional twenty FBI agents working on the case."

"I don't want to talk about it, Shannon. I just want to go back to work. That's what I know best." He touched her shoulder. "Thanks again, and kiss Amy goodnight from me."

In front of him the seamless ocean opened up with all the tales it had to tell. Yes, it would be good to be back on the water again, thought Jake as he hoisted the duffel over his shoulder. Without turning back, he strode off towards the ferry that would deliver him to Matinicus in about three hours. Turning back was something he'd never done in his life. Something he wasn't about to start doing now.

CHAPTER 72

SWIRE'S, 84 Beacon Street,
Beacon Hill, Boston, Massachusetts.
Tuesday, 15th May 1990. 10:01.

"Mr Swire is on the telephone Cory, but he said to go on in. He's expecting you," barked Mrs Elliott in her customary guttural tone, one that sounded like she'd been gargling gravel.

Cory disarmed her. "Thank you, Mrs Elliott. We'll do just that." As he turned around, he caught her sideways glance at the smiling lady with auburn hair. Opening the two mahogany doors he heard the unmistakeable voice of his employer.

"Wait a moment, Cory." Zephaniah Swire cupped the mouthpiece, glanced momentarily at the woman accompanying his Head of Research and promptly turned his back on them both. He stood behind his large mahogany desk, in between heavy silk curtains the colour of fine port wine, which flanked him as if they were guards. He spoke in a low voice and gazed down at the street life below. Cory and Jessie remained static in the doorway, mannequins in a shop window.

"Sorry about that. Please do sit down."

He replaced the handset and touched his temple as if deep in thought. With his eyes only, he indicated the two chairs opposite. Cory pulled back a chair for Jessie before seating himself. From the very moment she'd entered the office, Jessie had been aware that she was being scrutinised; she clocked the tell-tale signs, albeit she'd never before experienced them in such grand surroundings. Instinctive human behaviour rarely changes, be it in a slum or a palace. But not once before had she had the feeling that she was being observed by someone with their back to her, as she'd experienced while Zephaniah Swire continued his telephone call. She found this unique sensation disquieting. Instinctively, she began to absorb the sensory information surrounding her.

"All's well, Cory? I'm sorry this is going to have to be brief. When we're done, I'm flying to New York for lunch at Christie's, and then onto Sotheby's. Dede Brooks insists on taking me to dinner at Mortimer's for some reason, I suspect they've cooked up an idea between them." Almost distractedly, he fidgeted with his Breguet. "It'll be about the Gardner. We've all got skin in this game, as well as the reward. So, what updates do you have for me?"

"Firstly, there's the issue of your brother's forged Dalí, but that's waited long enough, so a couple more weeks won't matter." Cory withdrew a sheet of paper and slid it across the desk.

"What's this?" Zephaniah snapped with the voice of someone who disliked surprises. Cory was here for one purpose only, and it didn't involve that craven idiot Jedediah. And he loathed the word 'brother'.

"To save time, Mr Swire, I've listed dealers in New York who owe us a favour."

As Cory began speaking, Jessie shut her mind off to all outside interference. She had long mastered the art of using peripheral vision. With trace eye movements she was able to scan a room, log what she'd need and discard the rest, and at the same time click off mental Polaroids of furniture, layouts, books, pictures, ornaments, anything, all precisely in their positions. So adept had she become at this self-taught discipline that her sketches of bedrooms, playrooms, kitchens, offices, classrooms etc. accompanied her case notes. And in the fleeting moments she appeared to re-arrange herself in her chair, she would have accomplished these tasks.

This done, she then filed it all away . . .

On the wall to her right hung a small but daring Manet oil painting. At first, she thought it had been hung incongruously but quickly changed her mind. The four Picasso drawings that surrounded it – north, south, east, west – were all in perfect harmony. The lighting was flawless, and the five pictures co-existed in an ethereal wash of supple radiance. Genius. What an 'eye' Mr Swire had. On the opposite wall, from dado up, was a library of books. Save for a Morocco-bound set of the works of Guy de Maupassant, each and every one's subject matter was art; all had either worn dust jackets or cracked spines. Here was a man who at least read his reference books. This was no museum show-library. Mr

Swire's was an inner sanctum. A place of toil. There were even trace vestiges of worship. Behind the purposeful chair Mr Swire was now sitting in, she observed – to his right – a bronze bust of Napoleon on a marble pedestal, lit as if Lawrence Olivier were delivering a soliloquy. A crystal clock held stage-left on his desk, which apart from a propriety blotter and a solitary black telephone was barren: no paper or writing instruments. Beneath their feet lay an intricate silk Aubusson rug, thicker than a bear's pelt.

As ever with Jessie, it was what was *not* present, let alone on display, that plucked her Holmesian violin strings. No trophies or diplomas. Not one photograph, nor even a personal memento to jog a memory. Nothing whatsoever. The room was drier than an abandoned oasis. For all its extravagance, size and refined elegance, this office couldn't belong to any other CEO. For they all had living lives. This CEO appeared not to have that simple luxury. Yet she knew that to be false. Mr Swire was a highly successful businessman with a respected career at the pinnacle of the global artworld. He was a decorated US Marine. He had a reclusive grandfather, who he was known to revere. He travelled the world. He owned an airplane. He skied passionately. He had interests in art. He was seen out – although rarely – always in the company of attractive or well-known women. Added to which was the simple fact that Mr Swire's physical existence was smoking-gun proof that there had to have been a mother and father involved at some stage in his genesis.

Yet nothing stirred in this opulent wilderness.

At first, she'd likened it to a desert, but it wasn't. Even deserts speak. Here, nothing whispered, let alone breathed. Was that really the case with a man known to have an incandescent, if brooding, personality? No. Impossible. This was going to be fascinating, thought Jessie as she stood up, tired with both gentlemen's ill manners. She stretched her hand across the expansive desk, interrupting Mr Swire's reply to another of Cory's statements about a forged Dalí.

"Dr Jessica Flack, Mr Swire. Please call me Jessie. It's a pleasure to meet you." She beamed her sun-drenched Bajan smile. Her father had taught her, *'You're never properly dressed unless you wear a smile.'*

Somewhat taken aback, Zephaniah looked at her in silent response. There was a clench-jawed smile however, one she saw was obviously reserved for setting a tone of authority. Without a word he shook her outstretched hand and remained standing until she'd retaken her seat. Here was a man of immense self-confidence, the sort that could – and would – shrink lesser mortals. This notion flashed across her mind, as did an unwanted frisson of physical attraction: he momentarily bit his bottom lip as his pupils dilated, both signs of arousal. Zephaniah Swire was an attractive man, and he knew it, she thought.

"Doctor of what, may I ask Dr Flack?"

"Clinical psychology. Child psychology. I specialise in traumatised children. I'm also an MD."

"Ah yes. Cory mentioned a few weeks back that he might seek your assistance. So, what brings a child psychologist and general practitioner of medicine to my office?" Zephaniah laughed as he spoke; his tone was almost playful. There was no sarcasm or anger in it, and he wasn't being patronising. He was plain curious. That, and he always liked to listen: Ollie had taught him many moons ago that only by listening did one learn.

"I'm taking an extended leave of absence from London, where I live and practise, and Cory asked me to help out on some research he was doing."

Zephaniah switched his slate-grey eyes fleetingly, almost accusingly, to Cory's before fixing on Jessie's again.

Jumping in, Cory said. "That's correct, Mr Swire. We've known each other for quite some years, and I asked Dr Flack to help with the research you assigned to me regarding the Gardner theft." He paused to take stock. His employer's expression was fixed, immobile. "I asked her to compile a profile of the sort of person who might commission a theft like this," and speaking as if she wasn't even present, he added, "Dr Flack has a third eye, a writer's eye. I believe her assessment might've given a head start with my department's contacts. You see, Mr Swire, either the Gardner pictures never existed at all, or they're still hidden in the Gardner's filthy basement. There's not one word from anybody, anywhere. Total silence. And that, sir, is an impossibility," he added with finality.

As a boa constrictor who'd lucked into a plague of rats, Zephaniah Swire digested what his Head of Research had told him. He took his time, enjoying himself, and he wasn't going to be hurried, least of all by his Head of Research and a child psychologist. From behind a mask he stated, "That *is* a maverick approach Cory, but then I'd expect nothing less from you." He considered Jessie, not Cory, as he spoke. His eyes held a mixture of curiosity, suspicion, and grim fascination; almost as if he was now observing a rare and potentially deadly insect amongst rats.

He swung his look away. This stranger in his midst was unsettling him, and his antennae were pricked. What was it? Instinct? Physical? She was easy on the eye. No, not that surely? There was more to her. Uncomfortable looking at Cory, he scanned his bookshelves. Jessie too elected to avert her eyes and for some reason her gaze hunted down the bust of Napoleon first, then the Manet and then the works of de Maupassant. Why? Apart from France, what had formed that triangle in her sub-conscious? And why was Guy de Maupassant the *only* novelist on the library shelves? A French author who'd died before his forty-third birthday, almost the same age as Zephaniah Swire. A writer who'd told eloquent tales of material desires, lust, and sensual appetites where greed and ambition were the driving force. Doom and cruel disappointment starred in all his stories; these and other ideas bounced around her cranium like molecules in an accelerator.

Then one de Maupassant story came forward. *A Coward*. In that short story, the protagonist, the orphan Viscount Gontran-Joseph de Signoles, is sitting in a Parisian café, and in an entirely chivalrous manner, finds himself challenging a man to a duel for staring at one of the two ladies in his party. As the hour of the duel approaches, de Signoles becomes terrified at the prospect of death – or perhaps worse, absolute humiliation. And to resolve this unheard-of dilemma, de Signoles puts the cold steel of his duelling pistol in his mouth and kills himself. End.

Out of the blue, a series of connections presented themselves: de Maupassant and Manet were Parisian contemporaries. Both had died of the same affliction. Syphilis. So what? What kind of answer was that? She had no idea, but at least it was an answer. Yet *A Coward* remained centre stage, not least due to the manner of de Signoles' death. All the squirrelly rumours surrounding the demise of Mr Swire's mother had never truly evaporated either. Guy de Maupassant and Édouard Manet, amongst others in bohemian Paris, had famously frequented the same café in Paris. The Café Tortoni. The same café de Signoles was in with the two ladies when he challenged the man to that fateful duel. *Chez Tortoni*. The Gardner's stolen Manet.

"Tell me Cory, how exactly how does this process work?" Zephaniah feigned interest and tilted his head as if to read a book's title; his tone suggested he could have been asking the price of a pair of shoes.

"I'll answer that question if I may . . ."

Jessie cut across Cory before he could even inhale. She dropped the pitch of her voice, now it was as slow and as deep and as rich as molasses. It was hypnotic. She was back in the game.

". . . in much the same fashion as the FBI's sketch artist drew a composite of the witness, the man no one can find." Jessie leaned forward as she spoke and noticed Zephaniah's *zygomaticus major* flex. But neither his *orbicularis oculi* nor his *pars orbitalis*, had tightened, which is to say the smile he proffered her was entirely bogus. For he was unaware that certain facial muscles would simply not respond to commands. All this and more Jessie observed.

Undaunted, she continued. "My job is to do much the same as the FBI's artist, but I will draw my picture with features of personality. Perhaps not of the face every time, but features none the less. Why this and not that? What might trigger the desire for, say, the Vermeer and a humble finial, and not their Titian and a signed first edition?"

Again, she hesitated, and this time all three groups of Zephaniah's facial muscles responded with a genuine emotion. A true smile. Something she had just said had pleased him. What was it exactly? She'd replay the tape later. Oh, how she *loved* unpacking faces.

"Imagine a game of Blind Man's Bluff, Mr Swire. When my eyes are bound so I can't see, all my other senses are heightened. I can take a hunch and play with it. Toy with it. Give it definition, if you will . . ."

"How so Dr Flack?" interrupted Zephaniah with eyes now colder than a medieval dawn.

"Simply put, Mr Swire, every picture tells a story."

PART SEVEN

WEDNESDAY, 30TH MAY 1990

CHAPTER 73

A few miles north of Matinicus Island, Gulf of Maine, Maine. Wednesday, 30th May 1990. 09:38.

"Jake, you good with this?" Nate spoke over the low hum of the engine.

"Sure, Nate. Why you askin'?"

"You just seem mighty distracted is all."

"You know how it is. I'm grateful for all you're doin' for Amy and me. Gettin' back on the water. Oftentimes bein' out here just takes me places."

Jake yanked hard on the winch lever. He didn't much care for the mix of talk and work. The cogs were hurtin', Jake could tell, as the winch began hauling in a long line of lobster traps. The omens were good. The lobsters were either bountiful or Nate and Jake had hit a lucky streak. Spring lobstering was never usually this good. Come mid-June, with the first of the 'shedders', was when Nate could really expect to start paying the bills. But together they had hauled more pounds of lobster in the last two weeks than Nate had in the whole month of May in any other previous year.

Nate wondered if Jake had brought skill, or good fortune, or both. For sure he'd taken Jake's advice and set a run of smaller '3-footer' traps in a few different areas so maybe Jake's Long Island instinct was working up here in Maine too, thought Nate. Either way, Nate was grateful to have his old friend aboard.

"The isolation, you know, Matinicus, is it getting' to you?"

"I'm missing Amy like hell is the truth." He turned to Nate. "I'm going to head back to Rockland in a few days if that's OK?"

"Sure thing. It'll give me a chance to take a break too. We've been toilin' out here real well, and Nancy has been on my case to fix the truck and the stove."

"Lookit, Nate, if we hit another run of luck then maybe I should stay and fish it out with you. It's the very least I could do. You know how it is?" Sometimes you did just that. You fished till your luck turned, then you headed for home; the ocean was like that at times, and this was Nate's boat and his living. Jake smiled at his friend. His skipper. He understood he was but a journeyman passing through.

"No Jake, you go see Amy. When are you figurin' on coming back out? You're the best sternman I ever worked with. I could use your help for the rest of season in truth."

"I'll be back after the weekend now the ferry is running more frequent. Hope that works for you? We'll talk when I've seen Shannon. I need to figure out what her plans are too. You know I won't let you down, Nate."

"Course I do," Nate paused, taking his hand off the wheel. "You ever miss home Jake?"

"Amy's my home now. The rest is just bricks."

Not wanting to re-open that wound and wanting to leave Amagansett in, well, Amagansett, Jake peered over the gunwale to check the traps' progress up from the depths and through the chop. Hauling up empty traps was no way to secure poundage and until the catch was on board, there was always a moment of dry expectation. And yesterday afternoon had not been so good. Nate had remarked, his eyes downcast: *"All we done is change the water in them empty traps, Jake!"* But now the winch was straining hard. Another good sign. Jake had hunched using larger '4-footers' today and he felt like their luck was still in. When the traps broke the surface, small waves smacked at the boat's side as she rolled on each Atlantic swell.

Far away in the distance lay Matinicus Isle. A trail of smoke took flight from a lone chimney, and drew a spiralling, smudgy grey line against the crisp blue sky, as if a child had painted it. Save for the solitary house on the northern point of the barren island, all around them was deserted, beyond bleak. This was their wilderness. Their frontier. Their ocean. Other, less hardy individuals would perhaps have taken the silence, the desolation and the aloneness as a hostile punishment. Not Jake. To him it was anything but. He revelled in it, and all those elements were coming together and restoring his very lifeblood.

Nate left the helm to join his 'sternman' by the trusty 'n rusty old winch. Jake tapped the end of his long-billed cap in a salute to his Captain. His eyes creased, and he scratched his beard and grinned from ear to ear.

This was going to be another of Jake's bill-paying hauls.

CHAPTER 74

19 Arlington Street, Back Bay, Boston, Massachusetts.
Wednesday, 30th May 1990. 09:38.

Cory had left over an hour ago for the brief walk to his office. The upside was twofold: Jessie had the apartment to herself AND she could now smoke – '*windows open only*'. She slouched deep into the armchair with her lighter, soft pack of *Disque Bleu* and an ashtray. The plan was to relax as she reread all her pages of contemporaneous notes and ideas. At last, and dog-tired after almost two months in Boston of sifting, learning, reading, snooping and drawing schematics she had reached the end of the work Cory had asked of her.

Rashly, she'd announced that fact just as he was heading out of the door. Uncharacteristic timing. Her announcement had stopped him in his tracks, and he pleaded for a quick summary. She steadfastly refused. She was ready, however, to impart the fruits (such as they were) of her labours to him when she was better prepared. They'd struck up a compromise following her suggestion that they meet for lunch in the old dining room of the Ritz-Carlton. Then, and only then, could he read the preliminary draft.

First though, she had to write the damned report, and in longhand. Word processors were just that, contraptions to process words; she'd shunned them. What she did in her professional life was study, learn and observe, then she would draw and design and create. One of the hallmarks of her professional life had been painstaking handwritten file-notes and patient profiles. The discipline of forming her thoughts, with precision and economy, before she committed her fountain pen to paper was vital to her methodology. This case was no different.

The Gardner theft was, obviously, very different. A tabula rasa. This was not an issue of child neglect, or abuse, or even abduction. And yes, she had assisted Scotland Yard in a handful of investigations over the previous five years, and so had an inkling of the workings of the criminal mind. But in the American art world she was adrift on the ocean in a pea-soup fog. Being a clinical psychologist did help, for along with her qualifications and expertise, she'd added her own rigorous and scientific attention to detail and method. From bitter experience she understood that the careful study of the *manner* in which a crime had been committed would, in due course, provide its own clues. So, it had been back to basics, and she had worked on one solid presumption: traces of the perpetrator's character remained not only at the scene of the crime, but, more importantly – like DNA – within each of the stolen artefacts. Pitting herself not only against the theft but the thieves too, she'd devised a route map that would enable her to identify and produce a series of six headings she needed to address.

Jessie gathered up her cigarettes and notes and arranged them neatly on the dining room table. She made herself a large mug of fresh coffee and settled down to work. She had the template of the report in her head: start with an introduction, followed by an index of the topics she intended to write about. Each would be dealt with in turn and summarised in a brief conclusion.

She twiddled her mother's old Sheaffer between her thumb and forefinger and glanced down at a page of outlines. She was skilled enough to have stripped out as much 'intuition' as possible from her notes. Intuition could, on occasions, be a constructive tool if deployed with faultless and objective clarity. If not, it was merely a dangerous extension of the imagination, or worse, a capricious way of cutting corners, of allowing soft ideas to replace hard evidence. Jessie, an old hand at reading and anticipating reactions, knew that intuition did have its place – sometimes she did play hunches – but that place was not here in Boston. Fact, not gut, was going to rule here. With that thought firmly in her head she stubbed out her cigarette, drew in a deep breath, coughed and steadied herself to begin writing in her generous cursive script.

Assessment and analysis of the Isabella Stewart Gardner Museum theft

Dr Jessica Flack

THE FOLLOWING REPORT was requested by Mr Cory Mount, Head of Research at Swire's, Boston. His brief was to learn more about the theft of thirteen works of art from the Isabella Stewart Gardner Museum during the early hours of 18th March this year.

Mr Mount's sole aim was, and remains, to attempt to locate the stolen works of art only. There is no desire to solve a crime. I have therefore subscribed to his view that this theft was a 'commissioned' one.

Investigative psychology is where my efforts have been deployed. To draw a 'photo-fit' profile of the sort of individual(s) who might commit such an offence. I have sought clues of behaviour (in the same manner as a detective seeks clues of physical evidence) that might indicate the identity, or the character, of the person(s) responsible and therefore, hopefully, the stolen art.

This report has six principal headings and one concluding summary. Other than what exists in the public domain, I have neither sought, nor received, assistance from the BPD or FBI. This is a forensic psychological study into the provenance of what was stolen. Additionally, I have examined the minutiae of the execution of the theft itself.

This report is entirely subjective, and the conclusions contained herein are mine alone.

1. **AGE & GENDER.**
2. **POSSIBLE FORMATIVE EXPERIENCES.**
3. **FAMILY BACKGROUND.**
4. **FAMILY STATUS.**
5. **PROFESSION.**
6. **MOTIVE & MEANS.**

Having written the opening statement, together with her list of headings, for a reason she would later understand, but at the time baffled her, Jessie wrote **7. CONCLUSION** on a fresh piece of paper. By reflex, her pen went to the bottom. There, direct from Broca's area (that pesky left hemisphere of her brain's frontal lobe) to her fountain pen, she composed the final sentence of the report's conclusion.

> This report's firm conviction, after analysing all the available information and research, is that the thirteen stolen artworks from the Isabella Stewart Gardner Museum will never be recovered, nor will they ever be seen again. I believe they are forever lost to the world.

Jessie skimmed over what she'd set down and felt her stomach fist into a knot.

She lit a cigarette, inhaled deeply and felt her pulse accelerate. Brief dizziness swamped her nervous system as the dark, powerful Syrian and Turkish tobaccos took hold.

She couldn't take her eyes away from the words and their cruel finality.

CHAPTER 75

**Martha's Vineyard Airport, Vineyard Haven, Massachusetts.
Wednesday, 30th May 1990. 10:45.**

"Don't leave the field Jeff. I'm not sure how long I'm staying."

"Sure thing, Mr Swire. The plane will be refuelled and standing by. If you get the chance before you leave Menemsha please call the tower. I'll file a flight plan for wheels-up at 1400 hours anyways."

Zephaniah was pre-occupied. He'd heard what his pilot had said but chose not to acknowledge it. Jeff Hindle swung down the lever to release the fuselage door and the steps dropped away. Zephaniah left the cool of the King Air's cabin to be greeted by the morning heat rising up from the tarmac. An omen for the day ahead, he surmised. Business was business, however, he had an idea that this was personal. Of only three things worth fearing in the world, his grandfather's blue-steel ire was top of the list: an Atlantic hurricane and a bad oyster ran a distant second and third.

Zephaniah had determined that the standoff between them had gone on long enough. Hence his impromptu decision to fly down to the Vineyard to attempt to bring whatever it was to a conclusion. He'd decided the status quo shouldn't wait until their next meeting, due on the following Monday, 4th June. He'd assumed – wrongly as it would later turn out – that he had the ability to mollify, perhaps even control, whatever it was smouldering within his grandfather. A slow-burn that could ignite. But in making that series of judgements – all scarred by his own hubris – he'd overlooked the basic fact that while his grandfather had taught him, at almost forty-three, everything he knew, Ollie had elected *not* to teach him all that he, just shy of eighty-five, knew. Like his mother had done before he was born, Zephaniah had miscalculated.

The truth of the matter was straightforward. Ollie was, in fact, anything but angry with his grandson. The exact opposite. He was delighted with the fruits of Zephaniah's plan, calmly executed during the revelries of the St Patrick's Day weekend. The sheer audacity! Taking the entire art world by surprise to boot. How could a man shoulder any emotion other than admiration for one who'd conceived of such a scheme? Ollie relished the success of the robbery as someone might appreciate a rare white Piedmont truffle. There was a simple earthiness in the way the robbery had been accomplished. Two soldiers. No weapons. No injuries. No DNA. No fingerprints. No security records to speak of. No witnesses. And if Ollie's instincts were correct, the 'fisherman' witness was in the wind.

It had been superb: the right mark at the right time, on the right day, with the right team with the right planning. Added into the mix, the fact he despised (for multiple reasons) the museum from which the artworks had been stolen, only flavoured the dish. No, the Gardner theft was a brilliant coup.

However, Ollie was damned if he was going to allow those details to become apparent. Praise only dampened resolve. So, even if Zephaniah wished to hold out the exact same olive branch the dove had delivered into Noah's hand, it was going to be inadequate. Conflict would therefore continue. The First Rule of Law was that *CONFLICT* drives people like them. Until he, Oliver Swire, was prepared to permit the discord to cease. That too was scripture. His scripture.

CHAPTER 76

**Portland Jetport to Rockland, I-295 N and US-1 N, Maine.
Wednesday, 30th May 1990. 10:45.**

Jimmy Snale dabbed the Cherokee's brakes. They snatched the 4 x 4 sharply to the left. They'd done that all the way north from Portland. He spat out more obscenities, saving the bluest for Hertz and Swire's. Having landed over an hour ago after a turbulent flight from Boston, his head ached, his stomach was empty, and his usual sense of balance was all shot to hell. He'd had it up to the fishes' rotten gills with this assignment. So far, it'd been one of those *'easy to order, hard to accomplish'* missions. And there had been more than enough of those in Vietnam, even before he'd been rescued by Lieutenant Swire.

Here in the Maine wasteland, Jimmy found even his legendary *semper fidelis* attitude towards his commanding officer was being stretched tighter than catgut. Unlike his Floridian Seminole cousins, all of whom had the work ethic of manatees, Snale was determined to see this mission succeed swiftly. Eight weeks ago, Mr Swire's command had been just two words – *"find him"* – but the reality of implementing those two small words had become a big pain in the ass. He wouldn't have minded if he knew what the next order was going to be, once he found Jake Dealer. But that card Mr Swire was keeping in his breast pocket. Then again, that shouldn't have surprised him. When did Mr Swire ever give anyone fifty-two cards to play with? Like, never . . .

So how did a man with a child and a boat simply vanish? All Jimmy had going for him, he reasoned, was that there should be at least a scent of the man. Like the slugs that slimed across his backyard – before he nuked them with salt – the Dealer man was leaving a trail. Torturous and meandering yes, but a trail, nonetheless. Until, that is, he'd frickin' well vanished from Gloucester. Every time Jimmy seemed to be a few days behind him. Now, as he angled the Jeep into a vacant space in front of The Trade Winds Motel in this godforsaken dump known as Rockland, he muttered a favourite curse: "When God gives the World an enema, the tube's going in at Rockland."

His mother used to say: *"a hungry man is an angry man"* and Jimmy was hungry. She'd been right on a lot of stuff. All he wanted was to be at home. Instead, all he had to look forward to was another cold trail. A damp room, a hard bed, lousy food and warm Coca-Cola. At times like this he almost wished he drank alcohol. To cap it all – and this was boiler-plate certain – the waitress who'd serve him his lunch later would be a Rottweiler with lipstick. Some frickin' assignment this was turning out to be.

Ever the obedient – and cautious – NCO, Jimmy ferreted through the back of his wallet. Sandwiched between two faded photos of his parents he found a Vermont driving licence and a Visa card. He slipped them into the billfold in his jeans. Both were fake and bore the name *Arthur Wellesley*. He still had no idea why Mr Swire insisted he only use this identity for all covert tasks. Once, long ago, he'd decided to ask him what the significance of the alter-ego *Arthur Wellesley* was, but as time had passed Jimmy's will had grown its own moss.

With a mood as cheery as a Pennsylvania coal mine in winter, Jimmy grabbed his sports bag and hoofed the car door shut with his boot. He looked up at the motel. Christ, what a joint. Tucking his head down into his black parka as a wary tortoise would, Jimmy headed for the steps and the dingy reception.

As he ambled forward, hunched, cold and tired, he was completely unaware of a small, muscular Asian gentleman who had shadowed his every action. A man, who, by habit – and often necessity – operated well beneath the sweep of any radar. He stared ahead without blinking. His buzz of jet-black hair matched his obsidian eyes. And those eyes had never left their quarry since the evening of Friday, 30th March 1990.

CHAPTER 77

**The Ritz-Carlton Hotel, 10 Avery Street,
Boston, Massachusetts.
Wednesday, 30th May 1990. 12:15.**

"The unavoidable and clear-cut truth Cory is that we, as a species, are rather disagreeable creatures," Dr Jessie Flack sounded both British and formal, save for the sonorous rhythm in her voice.

"What do you mean?" muttered Cory whilst trying to get a waiter's attention. He'd been digesting the report Jessie had presented him with for ten solid minutes. His iced tea was now anything but that; the outsize beads of condensation on the glass served only to mirror what had formed at his temples, even though the original 1927 dining room of the Ritz-Carlton was air-conditioned. Jessie had sipped her Chablis quietly – her working day was done – as Cory read and reread the full report.

With professional eyes – Jessie couldn't help herself – she caught Cory touch his nose (he was hiding something) and his top lip had begun to moisten (he was anxious about something), probably just the text he was reading. She slowly leaned forward, placing her elbows on the table.

"OK Cory, let me explain," dipping into his attention, "what really motivates *Homo sapiens* is 'self'. We do everything with ourselves, exclusively, in mind. We're survivalists. Out there in the realm of totally 'selfish' in nearly all our actions. Please don't throw out lines like 'offering up seats in lifeboats while ship sinks'. Even those sorts of actions have at their root a selfish motive. It could be guilt. It could be anything. We do what we do because that's precisely what we want to do: be it working for the Peace Corps to murdering innocent people. Our pathology is one of self. As I said, we're not a wholesome species."

Jessie put her wine glass down.

"I thought I was the cynic here."

"I'm not a misanthrope. There's nothing cynical in what I'm saying, any more than there's anything cynical in my report. While we're talking like this, how convinced are you this was a commissioned theft?"

"No doubt at all. It's my business to sense, to know these things." He dabbed his temples and top lip with his napkin. "Trust me, Jessie, this was a commissioned theft," he said draining off the iced tea before adding, "Have you seen *Dr No?*"

"The James Bond film?"

"Yes. There's a scene when James Bond and Honey Ryder, both having been captured by *Dr No*, are being escorted, reluctantly, to dinner at his underwater lair in Jamaica. As 007 goes to climb the stairs, he spies an easel with Goya's glorious portrait of the Duke of Wellington, or Arthur Wellesley as the Duke liked to call himself."

"You'll be telling me he defeated Napoleon at Waterloo next. Forget the history lesson Cory, get to it . . ." Jessie bounced in playfully.

He ignored her and continued. "The film was released in 1962, and in the previous year Goya's painting of the Iron Duke was stolen from the National Portrait Gallery in London, on the 21st of August to be precise. Bizarrely, the exact same date as the *Mona Lisa* was stolen from the Louvre some fifty years earlier. The Goya was the only painting taken in the robbery, and it had the hallmarks of a commissioned theft. No one was hurt. There were no clues. It appeared motiveless. The theft happened after closing time, with the thief leaving through a lavatory window that had been left open the previous day. In the movie, and with gallows' humour, Bond stops to study the painting and raises a sardonic eyebrow. Brilliant!"

"And your point?"

"My point is that real people, not just fictional villains, do commission art thefts," Cory signalled a waiter before continuing, "but the conclusions you've arrived at surprise me. Generalisations aside, you make your case all too well about what sort of person could have organised the Gardner theft."

Ignoring the compliment, Jessie asked, "Do you think my work will help you?"

"I thought it might at first, but now I've read it through, I'm not so sure frankly. It's broad brushstrokes, like a horoscope is general . . ."

Jessie interrupted. "Oh gee. Thanks Cory."

"There are hundreds of people who would fit this profile."

"Don't shoot the messenger. I'm not a detective. I can't pin-point him. Besides, I disagree with you. There are five principal aspects that govern investigative psychology, and one of them is called 'Interpersonal Coherence'."

"Translation please."

"With 'Interpersonal Coherence' you assume that a victim represents something significant in the life of the offender, something outside of the criminal event itself. So, in this case we substitute the Gardner for the victim, while the offender is the commissioner of the theft. Understand?"

"Just about. So, is that why you believe the commissioner of the Gardner theft is someone involved with the art world?"

"Precisely. The Gardner is an anachronism, as is Mrs Gardner's bullet-proof Will, which makes the museum's contents all hostages. It must be beyond frustrating for people in your field. Untouchable, unsaleable, unmoveable treasures controlled by a dead woman's egotistical whimsy. Imagine a physicist with a black hole in space – knowable – yet in practical terms unsolvable."

"True. Isabella Stewart Gardner rules from the grave. There are many people who don't accept that."

"Well, there's also something that's hiding in plain sight."

Cory frowned. "What?"

"Accessibility. Ever heard of an American bank robber named Willie Sutton?" Cory's face was blank. "Thought not. Born in Brooklyn turn of the century. Died in 1980. A forty-year career bank robber who made the FBI's Ten Most Wanted List. Spent half his life in prison. Never hurt a soul. Respected both in and out of jail. He wrote two books on robbing banks. Here's the 'hide in plain sight' part." Jessie knew her audience. Cory was now fully engaged. At a clip, she carried on. "During a newspaper interview from prison Sutton was asked: *'Why do you rob banks?'* He looked at the journalist dumbfounded: *'Because that's where the money is.'* His reply soon became known in medical circles as *'Sutton's Law'*."

Cory's jaw dropped ever so slightly.

"Willie Sutton said that 'banks = money'. Consider first what is obvious. Don't get caught up in details. As a result, medical tests are now done rapidly to obtain a swift analysis. *'Sutton's Law'* is taught in all med. schools. Look for the most likely diagnosis, rather than pondering every different possibility of illness or trauma."

Cory stepped in. "So, let's apply *'Sutton's Law'* to the Gardner theft: the museum was unguarded, uninsured, underfunded, and had zero security to speak of. Essentially neglected. To someone in the shadows of the art world, who's privy to inside information, his law dictates that the Gardner Museum was ripe for plundering."

"Precisely." She paused. "Employ *'Sutton's Law'* and you reaffirm your own diagnosis that this was a commissioned theft, executed by someone on the inside of your universe who knew what they were doing. It was a medical diagnosis writ large in gilded – now empty – frames. My gut informs me that the person who planned this walk-in theft couldn't – and still can't – believe their luck that no one else hadn't looted the Gardner before."

Both Cory and Jessie remained silent. And still.

"Where were we?" She tested, rhetorically. "Your *Dr No* character is a loner. He's self-involved with a deep sense of the historic. With this theft he could do the undoable. Remove items Mrs Gardner had decreed sacrosanct. Sure, the items were cherry-picked, except the Degas drawings which make little sense to me. They're a false flag I'm not going to fall for. However, they do add to the theory that this was about the tangible act of removing the art. Performing the theft was perhaps the ultimate triumph. That's what makes the smaller items, Napoleon's finial and the *Gu,* as fascinating as the Vermeer. They're like small totems. These two pieces are personal items, ornaments you'd find in a study, a dressing room, a coffee table. This whole crime is hallmarked as personal. It's monogrammed."

Jessie had long ago lost her appetite for anything other than the bread roll, the Chablis and her French cigarettes.

"Can you please explain to me the difficulty you have in narrowing it down?"

"Let me try. Usually, I'd take in *all* the visual clues, facial ones and body language. You see, I strive to observe what's *intended* to be hidden. When you see what is *intended* to be hidden, it gives you a new, parabolical way to unlock people and conundrums. Facial expressions are almost impossible to fake. My approach is to try to pick up any discrepancy between what is said, and what is signalled. People believe speech is the primary mode of communication. Forget it, Cory, visual communication is."

"And you look for those contradictions in people."

"Contradictions speak volumes in all human interactions. Sadly, in this instance that's been impossible. All I can observe and interview, so to speak, is the provenance of thirteen inanimate objects. That, and the methodology employed in their theft. I've garnered more from that aspect than I'd anticipated."

"But what about motive? You seem to be quite definite here."

"Not wishing to dilute any of my other points, but I might have got the motive. Stay with me on observations for a while, before I get onto that." Jessie could feel her adrenaline pump. "Can I smoke here?"

"Probably, there's an ashtray on the table."

Jessie lit a *Disque Bleu*, sucked the smoke deeply into her lungs, waited a second or two and exhaled it towards the ceiling through her nose.

"Better now, my little addict?"

"Much, thank you. Where was I?"

"I sense Swire's is about to receive a disclaimer or qualification to your report. You know, the paintings can't talk, and all you know about is interrogating the living, and therefore take all that you've written on this with a truckload of salt etc. etc."

"Nice. Any more cheek from you and . . ."

"Just get on with it," Cory added jokingly.

Jessie took another hit of her cigarette. Again, her facial muscles tensed, her wide, green eyes narrowed, and her mouth assumed a thin but attractive line.

"OK, as much as I try not to use instinct, you can't help it sometimes. Often you look at someone and get a reaction. The longer you do this as a profession the stronger that reaction will be. A person's face is an extraordinarily effective piece of communication equipment. Darwin recognised it over 100 years ago with his work *The Expression of the Emotions in Man and Animals* in which he argued that all mammals display emotion in their faces. Autistic children, abused children, aphasics . . ."

"Aphasics?"

"Aphasia is brain damage, like stroke victims who've lost the ability to speak. All these groups of people have a heightened ability to read and interpret faces. This is especially true of abused children who develop survival strategies based on faces, not words." A hard expression crept into Jessie's gentle eyes. "No, this isn't a disclaimer. I'm explaining the methods I would normally employ, and because I have no faces to scrutinise, I'm like an aphasic here, my other senses and powers of deduction have been accentuated."

"I'm with you now."

"Remember one thing, the face is like a penis. It's got a mind entirely of its own." Jessie smirked at him.

"Thanks for that insight. I'll bear that fact it in mind as I wet shave tomorrow." Cory reddened, more at her mischievous smile than the quip.

"Due to the complexity of the facial muscles, there are forty-three principal movements the face can make. Most of them are involuntary, and that's why I can recognise the masks people try on."

Jessie held herself steady. Because she had the ability to read – to unpack – to 'see' all that people wanted to hide. This meant she had a responsibility to others when she recognised something that was intended to be hidden. Doubly so, with people she knew personally, like Cory. Letting on that she'd 'seen' that Cory was clearly hiding something was a professional red line that she could not cross. Sometimes, she cursed her blessings. Now, was one of those times. Damn you, Cory, she thought.

"So those expressions are the giveaways?" he was determined to keep his mind on the task at hand. Yet Jessie was undeniable when she was at full throttle, as she was now.

"Yes. Remember when I met Mr Swire? He smiled at me three times."

"Can't say that I noticed."

"Take my word for it. The first smile was when he greeted me; it was formal and perfunctory. The second was when I mentioned the missing witness and the FBI, and his oh-so-smooth smile was to deceive, it was entirely false. What I'd said had obviously unnerved him. He was trying to conceal his emotions, and to someone without my training, he would have succeeded. But his third smile was warm, genuine and involuntary, and followed my remarks about the Vermeer and the finial."

"Where are you headed with this, Jessie?"

"Nowhere," she replied cheerily, "I'm just giving you a practical example that you'd witnessed."

"OK, I get the idea now. So, to narrow this profile down, you'd need to interview every person who fits that profile in order to read their faces when you lead them on with questions."

Jessie laughed. Cory had got it in one. Defeated, she lit another cigarette.

"In an ideal world, yes, you're right." Her voice a languorous drawl, smoke drifted out of her nostrils and mouth. Only she could make such a filthy habit look Berlin-sexy in a stuffy New England dining room.

"Well, it's not an ideal world dear Jessie. So, let's move on to motive."

"You told me that approximately 90–95% of all stolen artworks are never recovered, correct?"

"Yes. Absurd, huh?"

"Totally. However, it's a mighty powerful and compelling motive, if you have a 9/10 chance of keeping the swag. Now, add opportunity into the mix, together with useless security, outdated systems and the inside knowledge that these systems might in the future be improved, thereby reducing the odds of the crime succeeding, and you've a menu of motives." She nibbled a piece of bread. "But an exciting motive is the Gardner's *lack* of insurance. Your expert thief would know that without insurance investigators on their trail, the BPD and FBI would lose interest. I've been shocked at how ineffectual law enforcement are when it comes to art thefts, both here and in Europe. It's as if they don't matter. An attitude that says *'so, rich people's hassles are finding what to hang on a blank wall like who really gives a damn'.*"

"Nobody really cares when the rich are robbed, and using *'Sutton's Law'* it *is* incredible the Gardner wasn't stripped bare long ago."

"Correct. The reward was very shrewd too. Who came up with that?" Jessie asked.

"No one knows for certain. I hear it was Oliver Swire himself. The truth is that it was probably Sotheby's. They're publicity hungry."

"It was a very shrewd move. It made it look to the outside world that you fine-art people supervised the policing of your own backyard. What's more it acted as a brake on the BPD and FBI. The reward said: *'Leave it to us art people. We'll take care of our own.'* When in truth, the 'reward' signal was clearly the opposite. The cognoscenti knows that. If the reward had been $5 or $10 million, well, then something *may* have surfaced. Whoever had the idea of setting it at $1 million is as sharp as a tack."

"Again, I heard it was Oliver Swire, but so much is laid on his doormat and little of it is true."

"It's interesting though that the reward was set at a level designed to keep people *away*."

"Keep people away! $1 million! What do you mean?"

Jessie's eyes had taken on an unusually hard edge.

"Simple, you must add in mystery and execution. They too point to motive. As a percentage of the value stolen $1 million is less than 0.5% of total value. What's an insurance company prepared to pay, even under the table?"

"Between 5% and 10% of insured value. On a haul such as this, they'd parlay that down to 3%. So anywhere between $7 and $20 million. Cash. Untraceable."

Jessie took a sip of her wine. "This was, as I've said before, a well-executed planned robbery. If one fact rises to the surface it is that. You and your boss can't see the wood for the trees. To you both this is all about oil paint on old canvases. It's not about that, any more than it ever was, or ever will be."

"How can you be so sure?"

"From time to time I find myself in a place that isn't hunch or instinct. It's hard to explain, it doesn't happen often. I don't know how to describe it other than to say this is what I do." She paused, her voice smoky and hoarse now. "This is what I do Cory. I read and understand hieroglyphics, runes. OK?"

"I'm none the wiser, Jessie."

"My fault. I can't clarify it any better. Anyway, so nothing has been heard of either of the two hired pros. Not a peep. From what I've discovered that's very rare, even for professionals. You tell three people, and you tell the world. Apart from the two guards there was the commissioner of the theft. That's three people. Add in a witness too. And I suspect he's either vanished or been killed. So, ruthlessness is almost certainly a card in your *Dr No's* deck too."

"You sure?"

"Pretty sure. It's another piece of the puzzle that fits. Ruthlessness always brings along its twin – cold ambition. Here's someone who knew what he wanted, for whatever reason, and on the face of it wouldn't stop at anything to achieve it. There can be no other explanation for this witness vanishing into thin air, exactly as the paintings have done."

"I hadn't seen that connection."

"Is he a big shot who's seen and experienced death, perhaps at first hand? Probably a history student. Well read. Why else steal the top of a Napoleonic flagpole for God's sake? There's zero intrinsic value in it. You can buy a finial, but this stolen finial was another signal, one that reads *'Look at me'*. It's like criminals who revisit a crime scene."

"I buy that, but what about the Vermeer?"

"That begs another question. Was this crime about the 'the art' or 'the art of the crime'?"

Cory furrowed his brow. "How about a combination of both?"

"That's the probable answer, but I'm not accepting it just yet. The issue is the Vermeer was *the* headline painting to steal. Let's track back to motive. With motive you have ego. I'm not going down the Freudian rabbit hole of ego, superego and id. Terrific word, ego. Here I'm going back to 'self'. You can liken ego to the moon. It has the power to move oceans, hearts, moods and behaviour. And in this case, it touches not only the art, but the art of the crime. To possess the only Vermeer in private hands, apart from the Queen of England's, is a crushed-velvet ego-massage. Now that *is* something!"

Jessie was in full flow, and he wasn't about to interrupt. He was struggling with where she was headed.

"OK, so, *The Concert* and the Queen's *The Music Lesson* are 'twinned' as well as being the only privately held Vermeers in the world. And one of them is in your thief's hands. That's an ego trip Cory. From that you can deduce that this person is someone who relishes secrecy, privacy. He will probably be single. Very single too. Married people aren't guarded by nature. They think they are, but they're not. Again, it's all to do with survival. In even the most arid marriage the concept of *we* exists. Stealing the Vermeer was about either wanting to own it, or proving something to a third party, or perhaps a bit of both. Either way ego, be it for the art, or for the crime, is an important factor."

"How did you arrive at the age, the fear, the secrecy, the gender?"

"I did what you asked me to do Cory. I built a profile, Lego-like. Brick by brick. I also studied Vermeer's life. There were bound to be similarities and clues. Vermeer died aged forty-three, a broken man, mad and flat-broke. His widow had to settle their two-year-old baker's bill with two paintings."

Jessie broke off momentarily. She frowned. Forty-three, or thereabouts. That age kept reappearing. Guy de Maupassant. Jan Vermeer. Zephaniah Swire. Who else?

"Where did you go?" asked Cory.

"Nowhere." She refocused her attention on her friend. "It's just that people in their forties keep appearing. Forget it. To this day no one knows what Vermeer even looked like. There are no known self-portraits. By all accounts, he was a woman-crazy Dutch Protestant who went on to marry a Catholic. That's odd. His parents and family were all on the fringes of a dissolute life: his father was an innkeeper and sometime picture dealer. His mother sold lottery games. His grandfather Balthazar was the best of all; he was a part-time conman and coin forger. They were hucksters. And what did Vermeer grow up to be? In effect he too was forger. He just chose to forge reality, albeit very beautifully."

"That's harsh Jessie. I've heard Vermeer called many things, but never a forger of reality!"

"It's not harsh, it's factual. Life in 17th-Century Holland wasn't calm and serene, like his paintings depicted. It was all floods, broken dykes, death, pestilence, yet everything in all of Vermeer's paintings is tranquil and measured. Beautiful even. The world is at peace."

"And gender?" Cory asked.

"A hunch. I'm sorry. I'm sure your thief is male. What's more, he's someone who lives with a fear, a past. A man who'll barely know how to trust, hence the secrecy. Secrecy equals safety to this person. Most people buy art to show it off. This time you can't."

"And the Rembrandts, were they any help?"

"Age came up again. Rembrandt lived with his parents until well into his forties and there's that damned age again. *Christ in the Storm on the Sea of Galilee* tells its own story. It's a unique painting. It's the only seascape the Dutchman ever painted, yet Holland in the 17th Century was all about water. The country was an entrepôt that owed its existence to the oceans. The Atlantic was Holland's lifeblood. Literally. The sea brought life and death, as it also brought wealth and poverty."

"What about the etched, miniature self-portrait?"

"Interesting that one. By anyone other than Rembrandt it would be a mere curio, but here it was clearly targeted. I think it's a keepsake of sorts. It's an indication that perhaps your thief is an only child. Singling out the etching is a 'my-my-my' kind of thing." Her eyes grew wide with excitement. "Definitely a hidden secret. It's the sort only children – of only children – would need to possess. The choice of stealing Rembrandt's etching was strictly personal."

"Sometimes, you astonish me Jessie, and it's not just with your conviction," smiled Cory.

Ignoring his remark she continued. "I've said this before, but the conundrum will always be – until the crime is solved – was the motive 'the art' or 'the crime'?"

"You said 'until the crime is solved'. I'm starting to think we should say '*if* the crime is solved'," he added wearily.

"There are very, very few true mysteries in this world, Cory."

Jessie gazed at him with her kind, green eyes and spoke in a comforting voice. She leaned over and touched his forearm.

Something was troubling her dearest friend very much. During her weeks of absorbing work, she'd realised that she'd been ignoring him, taking him for granted. Traits she was ashamed of. She had sat in silence writing the final page of her report, engrossed in the text, and hadn't considered what affect the report might have on him. Yes, she thought, something is troubling him deeply.

The person who commissioned the Gardner theft will be, in all probability, a Caucasian male, single, without siblings or children. In his forties, educated and well read. A shrewd knowledge of art and the way in which museums operate would further indicate that this person has a business connection with the 'art-world': be it as a dealer or a legitimate and successful collector. He will be North American by birth and could well have served in the armed forces, for he understands authority and respects hierarchy. The gravitas of history and fear appears to surround him: family, services, honour, responsibility, duty etc. Yet he will have an ambivalence towards the future. Ruthless and introspective, and an insightful 'chess player', he will have an endgame for his treasures. He will most likely be wealthy, discreet, secretive, cautious and a controlling person who is easily bored. However, he is not greedy. Avarice and riches were **not** motives in the Gardner theft. He will be a man in search of a challenge. Perhaps moving out from underneath a shadow cast by someone close to him will have played a role? A trauma would have occurred at some stage in his early development (abandonment most likely) and the desire to acquire and hoard would have begun to develop then. The precision with which this crime was carried out indicates that it was not opportunistic. Unless he 'requires' other works of art, my assumption is that this crime will be his first and last venture into commissioned thefts. This mastermind set the bar sufficiently high, and having cleared it, his instincts to have committed such a 'perfect crime' will have been sated. Far more overpowering will be his instincts for survival. They will now take over. Above all, this man is a survivor, which is why he would not think twice about destroying all that has been stolen. With no pun intended, his crowning triumph will be the fact that he possesses the only Vermeer in private hands, apart from the Queen of England's.

Cory knew the paragraph almost by heart now. And he wished he didn't.

CHAPTER 78

**The Trade Winds Motel, 2 Park Drive, Rockland, Maine.
Wednesday, 30th May 1990. 12:20.**

"What can I get you?" Shannon enquired breezily.

"How about a coffee and a menu," Snale sniped in response. Consumed by the sports pages of *USA Today*, he didn't even look up. Why bother? He'd seen enough hound-dogs to last him another lifetime.

Great, thought Shannon, I come on a lunch shift and the first diner I get is an out-of-town rude-meister. She sure didn't need this today. The conversation she and Jake had had earlier still shuttled inside her head. It'd been a little awkward. She wasn't sure why, and she knew that he'd thought so as well. The one thing she didn't want him to feel was ill at ease being stuck out on a rock in the Atlantic an' all. She would like his help to get back on the water, and there was Amy to think of. There wasn't a hint of anything between them. Jake had never even given her a sideways look, but that didn't stop her from looking sideways. No, Jake was still, and would be forever, married: to the ocean, to Lindy, to Dougie, to Amy, to the memory of what was . . .

Who can tell really? Shannon had thought. The past haunted some men, blessed others, and yet it was to Jake's credit that if his character was haunted, it was only by his past. She'd long recognised that plain fact; it may have robbed him of his future, but it had given him his present.

For all the history, Jake Dealer was a man possessed of a rare live-for-each-day approach. A man who could set his compass and hold a course – whatever the storm. And Shannon had discovered that truth having momentarily glimpsed a pair of haunted eyes in a Boston diner two and a half months ago. In 1990, and in the hardened America in which they lived, she'd found true honesty and strength in his eyes.

"How about a cold beer, sir?"

"I don't drink. It's a taste thing." Snale replied brusquely, again without looking up from his newspaper.

Shannon's red hair fell over her eyebrow. She cocked her head to one side and placed her right hand on her hip. The ill-fitting burgundy uniform bunched in protest. Dropping the order book into her apron pocket she said. "Sir, do you want me to ask another server to take your order?"

"Can you recommend anything?" Snale asked, finally raising his head from his newspaper. OK, he was wrong. Not a Rottweiler with lipstick, far from it. "So, Shannon," he offered up a bargain-basement smile as he made a point of reading her name tag, "what can you recommend?"

"You're in Maine, so, the lobster," she replied sarcastically.

"OK funny lady. We got off to a bad start. I'm sorry. Been a rough day. Hey, do I look like a lobster kind of man?"

"Not sure what a lobster kind of man looks like."

"Enough of this, how about a menu. Please."

"Coming right up, together with the coffee," Shannon turned away, paused and added, "thanks for the apology, mister."

"No sweat." He retreated into the newsprint.

Now that he was installed in his hotel room, he'd hoped his mood might have eased, the jagged edges come off. Obviously not. Who gives a damn, he thought as he took a notepad and pen from inside his leather flying jacket. For Rockland he decided to use his Gloucester plan. The KISS one. The one that had so nearly worked in Long Island and in Massachusetts. It wasn't exactly complex, and all it really involved was shoe leather. Lots of it. He preferred shoe leather to questions.

In all the years he'd worked for Swire's he'd discovered that discretion really was the better part of valour. Questions brought more questions, especially from the people who you wanted answers from. And all he and his employer wanted were results. Quiet results. Ssssssh results. Zero-decibel results. Ripples of any kind were frowned upon in Beacon Hill where his monthly paycheck came from. So, in his effort to make amends for the Gardner witness fiasco, he'd had to endure places like Rockland. So be it. Up here in cold-ass Maine (why did they call it 'Down East in Maine' he wondered momentarily) people treated 'curious' with the same affection as they did STD's. Maine folks, he'd been warned, kept themselves zipped up. In every way.

The plan for the next few days was simple: walk everywhere – except when he had to go to Camden – check all the docks – there'll be plenty of those up here he assured himself – and see if the darned boat was anywhere to be found. Blend in, observe, hang low in the shadows, leave no footprints or fingerprints. He flipped over his notepad when Shannon arrived with his coffee and a menu.

"Thanks." His mind raced with its own silent apology: good looking, couldn't have been more wrong. "You from Maine?" he asked instead.

"No. Do I look like a Maine kind of girl?"

"Good answer. I've no idea what a Maine girl looks like," he joked.

"Me neither. I'm from Massachusetts. Gloucester, in fact."

"That's strange, I just left there a while back."

"Good, so what can I get you?"

"I'm gonna have the steak with fries, medium rare, and a side of uncooked tomatoes, please."

As Shannon scribbled away, he reassured himself that it'd be safe and more than alright to ask a Massachusetts girl a few questions. Especially this Massachusetts doll.

CHAPTER 79

**Menemsha Harbour, Martha's Vineyard, Massachusetts.
Wednesday, 30th May 1990. 12:20.**

"Wait for me in the parking lot at the beach end. I'm not sure how long I'll be." Zephaniah appeared to address thin air; his mind was focused on what stood behind the wooden blinds of 10 Crick Hill Road.

"Sure thing, Mr Swire," acknowledged the taxi driver.

After he'd deplaned, Zephaniah had spent some alone time in the private lounge before calling the local taxi service; there was to be no Alvis meet-'n-greet today. Now standing not far from Menemsha's beach, he scrutinised the ocean, the fishing boats and all the familiar surroundings of his upbringing. He wondered just what twist of fate – what cards – had been dealt to a man like Ollie Swire that included this small fishing harbour on the southwestern tip of a 96-square-mile island known as The Vineyard. Unorthodox. It always had been, even as child. Thus far, it was just another mystery that would accompany his grandfather to his grave. And the truth of it was, they both wanted it that way.

Zephaniah folded his linen jacket over his forearm and ran his hand, comb-like, through his coal-black hair. The taxi driver's tired old Buick spluttered off; its gearbox clanked in protest as it reversed back down to the main road. Zephaniah rubbed his eyes and strolled to the bottom of Crick Hill. He gazed up at his grandfather's home. He stood very still. Jungle-still. Not because of any primitive emotion, like fear or dread but rather, if akin to any emotion at all, it was one that required he postpone gratification.

He wanted to sear this moment in time inside of him. He looked up at the unassuming cottage with its studio annex that was 10 Crick Hill Road, where more than $200 million worth of plundered art lay neatly arranged within its walls. And in that split second in time, he recognised that he'd spent his entire life in a similar pose. Looking up at – and to – Ollie. Was that what this had been about? Had it all come down to a spat over a witness? Surely not? But they were behaving like a pair of dogs growling over turf.

No, this was about Ollie and Zephaniah Swire, and the shadows people threw. There were very few people like his grandfather. They either cast no shadow at all, or were able to place – with fluid, dextrous movements – their own shadows exactly where they wanted them to be. He knew it was a skill he didn't have. They were illusionists. They worked with sleight of hand, diversion of eye and possessed mercurial minds. For people like them, everyone else was impotent. Ollie Swire, Zephaniah recognised, had a talent that was uniquely his own: he was a man who knew how to camouflage himself in the shadows of others.

Whilst knowing precious little of his grandfather's past, even as a child, he had never had any misconception about him. He'd always accepted the loving, intuitive, powerful – and sometimes elliptical – influence that Ollie had been his entire life. It was a shadow that took, that gave, that protected, that challenged. In truth, and standing here today, Zephaniah could do nothing other than delight in it. Over the years he had appreciated having someone to score with – and to score against.

Wasn't that what Swire's had all been about anyway? Keeping score? There were billionaires and millionaires out there, in all four corners of the world, who collected exclusively through Swire's sui generis ministry: Impressionists, Old Masters and drawings, modern sculptures – anything and everything they could lay their hands on – provided it was the very finest. That was Swire's imprimatur. The finest. People collected like magpies. It was an opiate. And it was sad. Yet, with every falling gavel – and anonymous transaction – Ollie and Zephaniah recognised that all they had ever collected was money. Nothing else. That *was* what it was *all* about, moreover it was exactly how they'd wanted it. And neither were under any illusion. That was their shared secret, that, and being the very best at what they did. That *was* important. The art. The knowledge. The skills – all their skills – they had so painstakingly nurtured were a means to an end. If power, influence and prestige were the by-catch then so much the better. As Ollie had once remarked: *"Zeph, let's see if we alchemists can turn these into gold too."*

That was what it was all about.

Zephaniah had thought that until ten weeks ago: the day he had robbed the Isabella Stewart Gardner Museum. Ollie had sensed it too. With the theft it had all changed for the pair of them. Had Swire's been a huge, dollar-coloured mirage?

Yes.

It was no longer about the money, any more than it was about a witness. It was about the art. The art of removing art from walls. To Zephaniah anyway. The art of restoring neglected and damaged art. To Ollie anyway. Together with religious piety and sex, art and crime were history's long-time lovers. And motives too, apparently. Zephaniah and Ollie's life's work appeared to have led Zephaniah to the door of 2 Palace Road on a rainy St Patrick's Day weekend. If that indeed was the case, then neither of them was so different after all. For all these years they'd both been the artists and the criminals waiting in the wings. It was all so much simpler when it had just been about the money.

Zephaniah put his right foot forward and began to walk up the slope in his inimitable way: straight backed, right shoulder angled forward and down. Only this time he wasn't preparing for a charge; more of a Last Post retreat.

Until halfway up the short drive he stopped dead in his tracks.

Zephaniah's wistful expression evaporated in an instant, and he began to grin, inside and out. His granite-coloured eyes creased with excitement. A large light bulb – a Warner Brothers one – flashed above his head. He stroked his chin while it shone brightly.

He inched his way to the front door. He didn't ring the bell. Instead, he stood motionless, calm, warm in the glow of his idea. He exhaled a sigh of out-and-out pleasure. In that instant he had figured out a flawless endgame: how to drop the final curtain. He realised there and then, that it had never been about the money *or* the crime. It was about something else altogether.

As his grandfather opened the door with his ensorcelling smile, Zephaniah reminded himself of one simple fact: Alexander the Great had cut the Gordian knot. He hadn't even attempted to unravel it.

CHAPTER 80

**The Trade Winds Motel, 2 Park Drive, Rockland, Maine.
Wednesday, 30th May 1990. 13:15.**

"That was a fine steak, Shannon. Thanks."

"I'll be sure to pass it along. More coffee?"

"Nah, I'm going to hit the hard stuff. You got Coca-Cola or Pepsi-Cola?"

"Coke, why?"

"There's a difference you know."

"I'll take your word for it."

Snale released another of his 'I want something' grins. Shannon had long been impervious to smiles like that, but she was savvy enough to know her tips depended on their acknowledgement. Both held each other's eyes fleetingly, neither sensing that at a table, not ten feet away, sat an Asian gentleman of indeterminate age wearing a plaid jacket, rimless reading glasses and a Washington Redskins baseball cap. In his left ear was an ordinary flesh-coloured hearing aid. A seasoned cruciverbalist, the Asian gentleman laboured over *The New York Times* crossword puzzle. Or so it appeared. Crossword puzzles (of which the Asian gentleman was both student and expert) was a favourite cloak when eavesdropping was the sole intent. People tended to pay no attention to the absorbed, or the conscientious, and would leave the tranquil to be just that.

Snale hooked his wallet out of his hip pocket and fished out a grainy newspaper cutting and a photograph.

"You look like the sort of girl who might be able to help me out," he said sliding the two items across the table. "My company is trying to find this man. He's a fisherman, and here's a photo of his boat," he announced cheerfully, without any menace. "You seen either of them around?" Snale gave her a kind of curious, innocent *I've-been-doing-it-for-more-years-than-I-care-to-recall* look.

Shannon froze. However, the professional waitress in her dealt him her $10 grin. She examined the photo-fit drawing of Jake and marvelled as to just how accurate it was; she hadn't seen it before. In the photograph his boat was still *Sweet Amy* and not *Sweet Lindy*. A break of sorts, she figured.

"Do I look like a girl who dates fishermen? I barely know the sharp end of boat from the blunt end." To hide the tremor in her free hand, she ran it through her thick red hair.

"You're a funny lady, but thanks anyway," he replied and put the photograph and the photo-fit back in his jacket pocket.

Shannon leant on the table for support and pretended to whisper. "Tell you what. If he walks in here, or his boat crashes into the dock out front, you'll be the first to know." She shot him another high-end $10 smile. "Should I charge lunch to your room?" She asked nodding to his room key on the table.

"Yes, that'll do fine. Room 1104."

"Number 1104 then," she said handing him a copy.

The answer to the 10-down in the crossword that day was four letters: the clue was *'Blacklisting org. of the 1940s–50s'*. Knowing the answer, the Asian gentleman wrote '1104' in the four boxes instead. Pleased with himself at completing the puzzle in double-quick time, he slid a $5 bill under his coffee cup, and slipped out of the restaurant unnoticed by the side door, sporting his own $10 smile.

PART EIGHT

SATURDAY, 2ND JUNE 1990

CHAPTER 81

**Rockland Ferry Terminal, Rockland, Maine.
Saturday, 2nd June 1990. 11:35.**

The ferry captain slowed as he commenced the docking manoeuvres, ones he could accomplish with his eyes closed after thirty years. The mid-morning sun had burnt off a stubborn Maine mist, and from where Jake stood on the open car-deck at the stern, Rockland had started to look picturesque. At least it was inhabited, he thought as he sloughed off the isolation of Matinicus. The lobstering had been real good, the pay even better, but he'd missed Amy more than he dared to admit. He wasn't one for drinkin' really, but he figured if you woke up and thought about a drink, then you had a problem. And Jake had a problem. An Amy problem. The second he opened his eyes, every single day, her animated, laughing face appeared to him as if it were a vision. Which, to her father, it was.

He knew something was wrong the very second he glimpsed Shannon's expression from afar. He hadn't known her long enough to be able to read her face like he could read the ocean, the sky and the waves, but even from a distance her smile was strained. He hadn't been able to reach her when he'd called the motel from a payphone in Vinalhaven, the ferry's last stop before Rockland. He'd left a message at the motel reception instead, telling her what time he was arriving, and if she could get off work, he wanted to take her to lunch and catch up. So much for that lunch plan. He squinted back at Shannon to confirm his instinct. He was right. Something was off. Immediately, Jake slung his canvas bag over his shoulder, and climbed up onto the rusting gunwale.

"Hey, you, asshole, get off the gunwale! DO IT NOW!" bellowed a deckhand.

Ignoring him, Jake used the height of the gunwale as a springboard to leap the seven or so feet onto the concrete dock. The ferry's two immense bronze propellers churned and boiled the grey water beneath him. He made it – just. Twelve inches shy and he'd have been hog-cleaved into bait. But the bitter taste of adrenaline had been in his mouth.

It was Jake's turn to shout now. He dropped his bag onto the quay and sprinted towards Shannon. His mouth dry and foul, he grabbed her by the shoulders with his impossibly strong, calloused hands.

"Tell me it's not Amy . . . Tell me Shanno—"

"OOOUCH! Jake that hurts!"

"What's happened!" Jake's heart thumped inside a cavity it didn't belong in.

"It's not Amy," she cried out. "She's fine, she's at school. I'd have got a call through if she'd even got a cold." Tears ran like small rivers down her milk-white cheeks.

"So, what the hell is it?"

Shannon looked away, dabbed her face with her sleeve and then sought out the ground with her red-rimmed eyes. Jake's hands curled around her shoulder blades. Slowly she raised her head and fixed him with a hard glare, square on. In silence, and ashamed, Jake let his arms fall to his side.

"It's St Patrick's Day again," she murmured.

Jake needed no translation or explanation. He lowered his head and locked his eyes onto the dirt of the quay's tarmac. Shannon didn't move an inch. She held her breath, afraid, not of Jake, but of tomorrow. And the next day. And the next day . . .

With his eyes scanning the ground as if he were searching for a dropped dime, Jake asked through gritted teeth. "When?"

"Three days ago. Lunchtime," she replied softly. "One man. I served him at the motel. He's staying there. He's got a photo of your boat. A photo-fit of you too. Asking questions, said he's looking for you. He's not police either, Jake."

"Describe him," ordered Jake, the missing dime still eluding him.

"5'10" and 185 pounds of what looks like muscle. I'd say he's Indian from his colouring and the blackness of his hair. Bad skin, and I've seen him wear glasses. He looks fit and tough, Jake. He was still here in Rockland this morning."

"5'10". 185 pounds you say."

"Yeah. I guess that's 'bout right."

Jake slowly brought his head up and looked up at her, just as he had done in Boston all those weeks ago. But this time his eyes weren't hollow voids where all hope had been abandoned. This time, there was no Long Island death-wish mask he was wearing. The wind burns on his face had drained away into a colour more like cigar-ash grey. His eyes were transfixed: wide, staring and beyond alive. Matador-red and Lucifer-black flames licked in the Polar-white of his irises. Molten steel forged by 300 years of love of loyalty, of history, of tradition, of Dealer lore, of Lindy, of Dougie, of Blondie . . . of . . . somehow, they'd all struck a granite slab deep inside of him and detonated into an inferno.

Afraid and scared, Shannon backed away – instinctively – lest she too got burnt. Shivering, she saw that her friend, Jake Dealer, was a man on fire.

CHAPTER 82

**10 Crick Hill Road, Menemsha,
Martha's Vineyard, Massachusetts.
Saturday, 2nd June 1990. 11:45.**

Ollie Swire had never, knowingly, acquired a forgery. Art, with perhaps suspect title or an edgy provenance, yes. His company's blank refusal to become involved with the 'Quedlinburg Hoard' in 1987 had led Ollie offering instead to be *'counsel and broker'* of the medieval treasures looted by a US Army lieutenant in 1945. Such sideshows were not just diversions, they were challenges that burnished his reputation, raised his fee and desire to win. Though never his blood pressure.

But Ollie had not once purchased a forgery. Never. In the fifty or so years since he'd quit the big cons (ahead of his tiptoeing chameleon-like onto a neighbouring tree to recreate himself as Swire's), he'd certainly not committed that particular crime. And now, as he seemed to be regarded (by some) as a Richelieu figure, the fact he had elected to acquire a forged work of art, in his own name, surprised even him.

Then again, Ollie thought, those who regarded him as an *éminence grise*, as someone who manipulated the art world, were simply not as 'proficient' at their own business as he was. It was Alfred Taubman who'd said, *'Auction houses are for fun, not profit'*. Ollie held Taubman in low regard, not for his conceit or hypocrisy, but for his amateur endeavours in criminal practices.

To be an amateur in any game was to sign your own warrant: death, arrest or bankruptcy; often all three. It was a lesson he'd learnt soon after he could cut a deck of cards with one hand, and that was long before the same hand had held a shaving brush and a cut-throat razor. Sotheby's and Christie's day would come, of this fact he was certain; just as he was certain that the sun would set over the Atlantic Ocean later today.

Yet, after he'd sat down at the oak table last Wednesday, armed with only his ever-active mind, he had begun to consider his true motive for the minor crime he had committed. Crime and motive were, after all, subjects he had more than a nodding acquaintance with. However, the motive here was opaque. After much reflection, the conclusion he came to was that nothing really had changed from the days of the big cons. Still that itch to win. Whatever the cost, whoever the adversary. The *éminence grise* bullshit could go to hell in a handcart. That'd been dreamt up by others to salve their own brazen insecurity. His skills as a conman had come not only from solid organisation, but from being able to master – and therefore contain – the random chaos of life. His cool-headed concentration was preternatural; a skill he'd ingrained in himself at St Joseph's.

Survival and winning may have been an elixir, but he was a true disciple devoted to order. That, and knowing where the exits were was key – and there was always more than one – before you even approached a mark. And of late, his grandson appeared to be coming up short on an exit, let alone an endgame.

Menemsha Harbour was virtually empty of work and pleasure boats on this fine June day, and Ollie Swire sat again at the kitchen table. Carefully and without breathing, he drained his glass of warm water and fresh lemon juice. As he did so he made a further judgement call. His eyes positively twinkled as he looked contemptuously at the painting propped up against the wall. Compared to what he was working on in his studio, Ollie concluded that Salvador Dalí was no more than a showman of mediocre talent.

He stood up, rinsed the empty glass and placed it upside down beside the sink. Then, with a cold, enigmatic smile he headed out of the front door.

CHAPTER 83

The Trade Winds Motel, 2 Park Drive, Rockland, Maine. Saturday, 2nd June 1990. 12:40.

"So just what kind of company is it you work for?" Shannon asked as nonchalantly as she could. Acting was not her forte, blushing was.

"Huh?" Jimmy Snale's head snatched up. He lowered his newspaper. Couldn't a man just eat lunch and read in peace? What did she want? All yesterday and this morning had been lousy. He'd struck out again. Jake Dealer had obviously gotten out of Dodge City and headed over the border. The Canadian border. Dammit. To make it worse he'd slept badly after he'd spent the night prowling the gnarled docks of Rockland in vain pursuit of a boat called *Sweet Amy*. Sucking down on the oh-so-sweet stench of rotting fish and diesel was not his idea of 'entertainment'. Small, perfectly formed oriental ladies performing wondrous acts with poles and table-tennis balls were more his bag.

And through his cheap Russian night-vision monocular, all the frickin' fishing boats looked the same, wherever they were moored and whatever they were called. Boy, had he seen some names: *Logan's Pride* (Christ, what was Logan ashamed of?), *Three Sons* (original, huh!), *Perseverance* (you need that for fishing, for shit-sure), *Mirage* (on the money), but the cigar went to the moron who'd dreamt up *Bass Ackwards*. Each and every one looked like they'd disintegrate if a butterfly so much as farted on deck. To Jimmy the only boats that were, well, real boats were the windjammers down by Rockland's ferry dock and the Coast Guard's cutter. Now that was a boat. It not only had attitude, it had spit 'n grit too. To say nothing of the gun on its foredeck. Yeah, he could get more than a damn lobster with that little baby.

Snale creased out a grin from his drawn face. "Say again?"

"Forget it. Sorry to have disturbed you."

"No, say again please." This time he tried a smile. She was at least good-looking.

"I just asked what sort of company you worked for."

"Why?"

"Didn't your mom tell you not to answer a question with a question?" She replied, thinking perhaps she could do this acting stuff after all.

"No. As a matter of fact she didn't. My mother died in childbirth," he lied.

"Oh." Shannon paused. Nervous. "Sorry to hear that. Look, you asked me the other day if I'd seen a boat Sweet Something and I . . ."

"It's called *Sweet Amy*."

"Yeah right, well, I might have heard something."

Trying, and failing, to conceal his now pricked interest, he slid the newspaper away. Shannon's green eyes darted everywhere and nowhere. "I mean, like, are you, er, like a boat repo man? Like is there, like a reward?"

"Yes, that is my line of work. I'm the repo man. Good spot, girl," he added very, very slowly.

"So, you might be tipping a waitress whose name you'd forget if she'd heard something?"

"Sure, you know, Benjamin Franklin's mom had, say, twins." The words almost seeped out of his small mouth as drops of white spittle formed. He was on home turf now.

"I'd heard she had quads, poor lady," Shannon flashed back, quick as lightning.

"Nah. It was triplets. For sure."

"Yeah. Triplets. You're right." She fidgeted with her pad and pen. "I hear he's coming into port tonight. He's renamed the boat *Sweet Lindy*." Shannon almost whispered the last words.

You cunning old sea dog Dealer, thought Snale, wondering if he'd recognise him from the robbery.

"He's been working the local waters, offshore all the time trying to scratch a living."

His eyes probing her every movement, he asked, "How come you heard this all of a sudden?"

But Shannon had a shiny glint in her green eyes. One that could have been misread as 'flirtation', or in a darkened bar, late at night, her eyes could even have had a *come-fuck-me-now* edge. Except they didn't even hint at either. Shannon was a lioness, alone on the savannah with her cubs. And as she fed him her look – which he sucked up – she realised that Jake was a cub too, not just Amy.

"Lissen' up, I'm a waitress and you want a short list of all that we *don't* hear! Jesus!"

"That's my gal!"

Snale relaxed back into his seat, fixated on her eyes, content with her reply. Shannon felt her skin shrivel and tighten around her. His face creased in pleasure – got you now, Mr Slippery Dealer – and the pockmarks folded into his dark skin like waves into rocks. *I'm not your gal, you bastard,* Shannon's inner voice shouted, so she let the silent words turn to bile inside her mouth. By way of release, she stood tall and pulled her shoulders back.

"Know anything else, Shannon?"

"I might do. Depends. Does Ben Franklin have any brothers or sisters?" With growing confidence, she flicked her red hair to shoot him another killer look.

"Smart and greedy too, eh?"

"Nah, just hungry. A girl's gotta eat ya' know."

"Sure, but not lobster." He hesitated whilst considering his choices. But there wasn't even one. "Let's say Franklin had twins, and all of a sudden Benjamin Franklin became William McKinley."

"William McKinley?"

"The 25th President of The United States. Assassinated back in 1901. He's on the back of a $500 bill. Geddit?"

"OK, you win." She feigned a short laugh. "I hear the man you're looking for has grown a beard. Full one too, kind of shaggy looking and grey round the chin. He always wears a plaid shirt and keeps a ratty long-billed cap nailed to his head.

"Sharp look," quipped Snale, who was becoming more pleased with his $500 spend with every passing second.

"You make sure my tip is under the coffee cup. Oh, and this you can have for free. He usually docks the boat at *Journey's End* here in Rockland."

"Thanks for that. Gimme a few minutes to go collect your tip. Don't worry, it'll be here."

Shannon went to walk away, then decided against it. She wasn't through acting. "And if you forget to leave the tip, I know how to warn the fisherman that the repo guy is coming for his livelihood." She drilled out yet another peachy smile.

That trinity of hers: green eyes, moistened pink lips and white teeth. More than good enough to have picked up at least a Tony nomination.

CHAPTER 84

Lindsey Street, Rockland, Maine.
Saturday, 2nd June 1990. 15:40.

Not fifty yards away from 18 Lindsey Street, facing east towards Union Street, an Asian gentleman of indeterminate age sat in a nondescript grey Ford sedan. He no longer wore fake round spectacles or a plaid jacket or a Washington Redskins baseball cap. Due to the clement weather he'd donned sunglasses and changed into a long-sleeved dark blue polo shirt. As if he were nodding in the direction of disguise – which he was not – he sported a New York Yankees baseball cap. The straightforward truth was that he was a Yankees fan.

The New York Times weekend crossword lay completed beside him on the unpleasant brown vinyl passenger seat. A Brahms piano concerto emanated from the tinny speakers, and despite the Ford Motor Company's sonic butchery on the dignity on the late German's work, he was a contented man.

With slow purpose he began to crack each of his twenty-four knuckles in turn. Then he clenched his jaw tight to grind his molars. At times like this, these were rituals he observed monkishly. Aside from immense self-discipline, there was a wadding of hardness to the Asian gentleman. There was a deep, tangible crust to his existence, a second skin covering his powerful body. Such hardness was born out of a chaste dispassion for all things but orders, duty and loyalty. And like the man he had originally been shadowing, he understood how to follow orders.

Abiding by the hypothesis that *'my enemy's enemy is my best friend'*, the Asian gentleman had changed tack. The silent tracker would now observe the not-so-silent tracker's prey.

In the past, such tactics had served him well. Very well in fact, he mused as he pressed his now relaxed fingers together to form a perfect church steeple, as if he were playing a game.

CHAPTER 85

**18 Lindsey Street, Rockland, Maine.
Saturday, 2nd June 1990. 16:35.**

If there was a payoff it was not as insignificant as it at first might seem: Jake would get to shave off his hated beard. A can of Noxzema, Gillette's finest, a pair of scissors and a towel were laid out in the bathroom. In the next room, on the bed's thin mattress, lay a dust-coloured rain slicker, a new black cotton sweater, a black button-down shirt, a used pair of black Levi 501's and a nondescript grey cap that read 'Rockland'. And sprawled out on the floor, absorbed with a 1,000-piece jigsaw puzzle, Amy rummaged in silence for the straight-edged pieces.

Shannon had shopped for these items before she'd set off for her afternoon shift. When she'd returned, she sat Jake on the corner of the bed to cut his straggly hair; aware of Amy noodling with the puzzle, they talked about everything and nothing. Jake asked what was the point of the small buttons on the shirt's collar? Both of them were practical people first and foremost, and this shirt posed additional problems: like two extra buttons to lose – and fiddly as hell too – which had to be undone and done if you wanted to wear a tie . . . And as if to soothe his nerves, more pounded than the desolate coves of Matinicus, he occupied himself with these and other trivial thoughts as he stood very alone in the airless bathroom.

Facing the mirror, Jake rinsed the razor in the basin for the last time. The beard had gone down the drain where it belonged. He dabbed the excess shaving foam from around his ears, then patted dry his cheeks, weathered and scrubbed raw by the Atlantic. His generous brown eyes creased as he looked in the mirror. His brief smile had its roots in history, not his ruggedness. Never a vain man, he permitted himself a fleeting moment though, one that sprang from a sense of pride he felt deep inside himself. Why now? Why here in Rockland? On the run and cornered like a rat in a barn. He recalled what his father had taught him as a child: *"If you corner a rat, be sure to give it one escape route. If you don't, it'll fight harder and longer than a nor'easter 'll blow. Remember that."* He had.

As he stared back at himself, he recognised that whatever had happened to his son, to his wife, to his traditions, and his way of life, he had survived – thus far – in order that he could protect what remained. And that was Amy. He wiped away a nick of blood from his neck. He ran the tap and watched the pinked water circle downwards. Three hundred years of hardships, blights, hunger, politics and whatever the elements had mustered against them had taught him how. Being a wanted man on the run was just another battle in a generational history. These facts he accepted, as he tiptoed into the bedroom to gather his clothes, knowing the Dealers were mighty proficient in the survival business, if nothing else.

Emerging from the bathroom dressed and feeling stiff in his unfamiliar clothes, he called out to Amy. Her head popped up from the puzzle, and she beamed at her father towering over her.

"Phew, looking sharp Dad!"

"Well, thank you!"

He fired off his big, wide smile and knelt as she sat up. He held her close and tightly. Her blonde hair fell about her face, and she looked at him with eyes that wanted, needed, to ask a question, but she saw in her father's face that she could not.

So instead, she whispered softly in his ear. "I love you very much Daddy."

"Me too Amy."

"Me three," she giggled and lay back down on the floor to continue her struggle with the puzzle.

"Shannon will be home soon, and I'll be back after dark. I've got to see a man over in Vinalhaven about the boat, and some offshore work." It was the first deliberate lie Jake had ever told her. He sensed his stomach tighten into knots.

That lie was sure as hell going to be the last, he vowed to himself as he closed the door.

CHAPTER 86

**Lindsey Street, Rockland, Maine.
Saturday, 2nd June 1990. 16:40.**

Was it a matter of training? Was it instinct? Was it a combination of the two? The Asian gentleman had never known for sure. After he'd been plucked from his parents – and school – in Shanghai during World War II and spirited away to Peking, the Party's finest may have trained him, but the instinct/training question was still a circle he'd yet to square.

From the tunnels of Cu Chi and the Iron Triangle to the dank interrogation rooms in Hanoi, he had honed his skills. Obtaining intel was what had been required of him. His masters in Peking had spotted certain skills in him, even as a child, but his methods were – usually – subtle, rarely brutal. His training had taught him to sense a feint – verbal, actual, physical – from even the most hardened of US or South Vietnamese soldiers.

The Asian gentleman saw the man, who he knew only as 'the fisherman', emerge from what appeared to have the jump, just, on a flophouse. However, 'the fisherman' no longer looked like 'the fisherman'. And it wasn't just his attire and the absence of facial hair. It was in his physical deportment. His bearing. He even appeared to be taller. Without turning around, he tracked him as if he were a ghost, to the corner of Union and Lindsey, where he waited, almost indifferently, leaning against a streetlight.

The Asian gentleman studied 'the fisherman' again, who was now barely fifty paces away. And as he did so, the short hairs on the back of his neck fired up . . .

CHAPTER 87

**The corner of Union Street and Lindsey Street, Rockland, Maine.
Saturday, 2nd June 1990. 16:43.**

Shannon had sprinted away from the motel. Breathless and flustered, she bent down to grasp her knees. She'd quit smoking, but still couldn't catch her breath.

"He went for it," she spluttered finally.

"He was always goin' to."

"How do you know?"

"I just do. Like I'd always figured they'd find me someday."

"Jake," she pleaded, "you could sail further north or double-back and head south. There's still time. He thinks you're coming into port at sunset. You could be gone in thirty minutes."

"No, Shannon," Jake stated firmly. "I'm not runnin' anywhere, anymore. I'm through with looking over my shoulder for something I know nothing about." He stared out at the Atlantic, his eyes hard. "Yeah, we could run some more, hell, we could go as far as Lake Melville in Newfoundland. Even Canada has fish Shannon. But you know, we'd all just die tired from all that runnin', because catch us they will. You can run, but you can't hide. Not on the ocean anyways."

"So, what are you going to do?"

Shannon only had to look at him for her answer.

Even if she could have, she wouldn't have attempted to stop him. She was truly powerless; she'd seen that look in his eyes before.

"What am I going to do?" he repeated. "I'm gonna do what I do best. Watch and be patient, just like I used to do on the beach with my crew in the good ol' days. You can learn a lot by doing just that. Watchin' the fish jump beyond the surf line. This way, an' that way. Watchin'. Patiently."

His brow furrowed; his jaw stiffened but his soft brown eyes sort of smiled. He felt calm yet eager, like when his instinct said there were striped bass out there even when he couldn't see them.

"Then what are you going to do after you're done being patient and watching?" she asked in a testy voice. Here she was trying to reach out to a man who was no longer visible, not even a speck on the horizon.

Jake ignored her question. Instead, he muttered. "Does he have a name?"

"Yeah, it's Arthur Wellesley. Expect he calls himself Artie, looks the type."

"I don't have much time. He could be down by the dock already, and I gotta put to sea. Take care of Amy until I return, and don't let anyone, and I mean anyone, in. Whatever the excuse. Clear?"

"I'm saddened you had to say that, Jake."

"I don't have time for this now, OK? I'm grateful, you'll never know how much. Just keep my girl safe."

For no apparent reason Jake felt himself shudder, as if someone had walked over his grave again. He recalled the last time that had happened was at the Boston diner Shannon had worked in. Almost for security – or was it out of fear? – he looked at her square on. Without knowing it, he had the same desperate expression in his eyes she had first seen that day. This time he clasped her shoulders tightly. He held them as if they were the baseballs he'd tossed for Dougie. Quietly, as if he were a lost child, he exhaled a whisper. ". . . Please Shannon, please . . ." before he turned to face the sea.

And with those three simple words, she saw Jake pull himself away from the edge of the flat earth and begin the long voyage back to land. For Jake had looked over the edge of the flat earth, and he'd seen that the vertiginous drop from the horizon into oblivion was too far, too long, and too treacherous for any one man to navigate alone.

CHAPTER 88

**10 Crick Hill Road, Menemsha,
Martha's Vineyard, Massachusetts.
Saturday, 2nd June 1990. 16:50.**

Ollie Swire had never been on a diet in his life. He had too much of a sense of his own identity ever to have needed to. He recalled reading somewhere that Wallis Simpson had ensured that the Duke of Windsor had maintained the exact same weight throughout their entire married life. What a hell that must have been, thought Ollie. Watching and counting were all well and good, but they had to be for the right reasons. Like currency. Calories were not a mercantile commodity anywhere he knew of. And in a peculiar way, his musings on diets this afternoon had started with *The Concert*.

There, finally, as he ran his hand over the buzz of his cropped white hair, and leaned back on his work-stool, his piercing pale blue eyes at last registered a noticeable change in the picture on his easel. In the past, like an obese man who'd amassed pounds after a lifetime of martinis, steaks and a sedentary life, *The Concert* had accumulated its grime and filth. Over time and imperceptibly. To expect the dirt – or the pounds – to come off overnight was nonsense, but after ten weeks of patient work, by skilled hands, the very first glimmer of Vermeer's magic was beginning to return. And what magic!

In *The Concert* and the *The Music Lesson* Vermeer had used similar compositional themes: in the foreground is the same floor, the same *viola da gamba*, the same Turkish carpets draped over tables, and at last they were now discernible as such, especially the *viola da gamba*. Ollie allowed himself a brief self-congratulatory moment. He had no idea how long it would take him to complete the task of restoring all the artworks to their former glory – years probably. This didn't trouble him, for he'd found of late that time had taken on a comforting beat. Being a devout atheist, the notion of time running out was not something he had ever heeded, but now death *would* be an inconvenience. As for Redemption, well, that was a hick-town in Nebraska. No, he was, in a straightforward manner, enjoying the challenge before him, just as he had taken pleasure in many other challenges: from pulling off the 'The Rag' with Nibs Callahan in 1929, to charming the Getty Museum into toeing Swire's line – no mean feat that – to educating his grandson in the ways of the world . . .

While mixing a solution of weak acid, his mind returned to Zephaniah, who was due for a casual dinner in a few hours. He was in two minds whether to show him the progress he was making on the Vermeer. After Zephaniah's bizarre visit last Wednesday, he was keen to get back to business as normal. All his grandson had talked about that afternoon was the trivia of Massachusetts life. No sooner had he crossed the threshold – sporting a cat-like grin of relief – did he return to Boston. Very out of character. Ollie had thought so at the time, and he thought it again now. It was as if he'd flown to the Vineyard for a specific purpose, and then at the last minute changed his mind.

There was no immediate answer, and the Ollie Swire of yesteryear knew only too well that these paintings belonged to his grandson; it was he who had stolen them after all. The *Gu* had been a princely offering, but the ability to restore the Rembrandts and the Vermeer was an even greater one. Maybe they had both miscalculated that aspect of the robbery: Zephaniah in not realising just how bad a condition the paintings were in, and Ollie for not being able to grasp, until he had started work, the gravitas of the task.

He suspected that his grandson wanted the stolen paintings back within his control, at least until this missing witness problem went away. But Ollie wasn't ready to concede – yet – what was not his. He surmised that might have been the issue on his grandson's mind last Wednesday: he wished to stick to his original plan and hide them beneath the ground, deep in the soil of No Man's Land.

The missing witness had also been eating away at him like a piranha stripping flesh from a carcass. Ollie had detected a shift of the tectonic plates that ruled his grandson's core. He should know, for he'd been the one to set the plates' position long before the boy's seventh birthday. The witness *was* consuming his rationale. And that was dangerous.

This old conman, in his eighty-fifth year, chuckled to himself; he had a few moves left before he surrendered the pleasure of his restorations. He'd begun his life working with skilled artists, so to strive now in the esteemed company of Vermeer, Rembrandt, Flinck and Manet was a fitting swansong.

CHAPTER 89

**18 Louisburg Square, Beacon Hill, Boston, Massachusetts.
Saturday, 2nd June 1990. 16:55.**

Zephaniah Swire had spent too much time in his study of late. For company he'd selected his Scyphozoan medusae for his increasingly introspective thoughts. Laid out on top of his David Linley desk were his notepad and two of his most prized treasures: the miniature Rembrandt etching and the Napoleonic finial, which now served, rather prosaically, as his paperweight. Motionless, he watched the jellyfish as they glided, without rhyme or reason, in a hypnotic ballet all their own. The conscious world did not exist for them; their silent, effortless movements were governed by reaction only. Reaction to the currents from the flow of water, or to the lights. Zephaniah decided to interfere with the 'random' process by playing, as a pianist might, on a row of stainless-steel keys at the tank's base. The lighting began to syncopate as his fingers touched each in turn, and the creatures began to move through a differing palette of colours like a box of crayons.

Suddenly, and from nowhere, his peace was shattered. The telephone echoed throughout his study. He turned around and saw that it was his direct private line. Chalk one up to Hector, then.

"Yes," announced Zephaniah, jabbing the loudspeaker button.

"Mr Swire, apologies for disturbing you on Saturday, but I've just heard something that might interest you."

"Go for it, Cory," he answered, relieved it was his Head of Research.

"I'm not sure you're going to like it or believe it," Cory could barely conceal the bewilderment in his voice.

"Try me."

"Mr Oliver has purchased your brother's forged Dalí."

"What!"

"I said you wouldn't like it."

"Tell me the details." Zephaniah's viper-quick brain was instantly alert.

"He acquired it openly, and in his own name, from the New York dealer we'd consigned it to."

"You're joking, no?"

"No, sir."

"How did you come by this?" asked Zephaniah. Now it was his turn to try to suppress an innate need to laugh. This was ridiculous.

"I heard from the dealer himself. He thought it was a hoax at first. Apparently, Mr Oliver telephoned saying he understood that a particular Dalí was in his possession, and he'd like to purchase it, sight unseen, and would he please pack it for shipment direct to Martha's Vineyard, not Swire's. A banker's cheque from Mr Oliver's private bank was duly delivered within the hour. Accordingly, the dealer did as he'd been instructed."

"And he felt no need to tell you or me?"

"Evidently not, sir, and why should he? The request came not only from the firm that consigned the painting but from both of our bosses."

The second Cory uttered those last words he wanted to reach down the telephone line to haul them back. Thankfully for him, his employer was too busy smirking to have cared: he'd figured out what his grandfather was up to. Chalk another one up to Ollie, then.

"Thanks Cory, enjoy the rest of your weekend."

Without another word passing between them, Zephaniah ended the call. OK, so now you've had your little bit of fun, he thought. Then he turned to address the Scyphozoan medusae: "A damned expensive way of reminding me what I already know. Yes, Ollie you *are* the boss, but we're still going to play by my rules."

Returning to his desk, he flexed his shoulders, closed his eyes, breathed in deeply to focus on the emptiness in front of him. He stayed still for a few, long minutes until he felt his heart beat a retreat. Then he picked up his notepad; written in his clear script was a reminder to return Jimmy's earlier call. Hopefully, he'd finally tracked down their witness, under some rock in Rockland.

Dinner with Ollie tonight was going to be enjoyable. With that thought, and wearing an expression a ravening hawk might have had, he punched out the motel's number.

PART NINE

SATURDAY, 2ND JUNE 1990

Sunset

CHAPTER 90

Journey's End **dock, Rockland, Maine.**
Saturday, 2nd June 1990. 19:55.

Could you ever see enough sunsets or sunrises? Jake wondered as twilight began to descend. No. To be tired of sunrises or sunsets meant you were weary of life itself. As brutal as the last months had been, sunrise and sunset had never been sorrowful, except for the day he and Amy had buried Dougie and Lindy and Blondie.

The warming and the cooling of the ocean was but one of its many cycles. From the predatory creatures of the deep, to the scavenging lobsters in the rocks, the migrating bass, the swordfish, the Bluefin tuna and the whales hugging the ocean's currents, there was no sunrise or sunset. There were just times to feed. To survive. To escape from bigger and stronger fish. Like him, he thought. Of late he'd been recalling much of what his father had told him in the years he had guided him in the ways of the Dealer traditions; and when any member of his father's haul-seine crew had arrived at the beach in a crabby mood, his father would bark: *"Lissen' up, any day above ground is a good day."* Captain Tosh Dealer was not a man who tolerated malingerers or grouches. He never added anything else to that. Never needed to really, he'd said it all.

Shannon was probably correct. Perhaps he should've taken the decision to run and hide. Maine's coastline was longer than California's; there were over 4,500 islands. As he'd killed time cruising Penobscot Bay in the afternoon, he'd rechecked his pilot book: Penobscot Bay was 40 miles long, 15 miles wide with 200-plus islands in 600 square miles of Atlantic. And Penobscot Bay was just one inlet in Maine, and there were still more than 200 nautical miles before you even sniffed the Canadian border. You could hide a whale boat out there, let alone his down'easter.

However, in the final reckoning, what it had all come down to was him.

Jake just couldn't run anymore. He wasn't built for it. He was a man who took life straight on, and then heaved it onto his shoulders to be certain he'd done a good job. For sure he carried the world there, but that too was a Dealer trait. And he had heard Lindy telling him to stop running. Not just for Amy's sake, but for his too: *"Turn around Jake, smell the coffee."* Confront whoever it was who was foolish enough to hunt him on his own land. The ocean. But then Lindy had always been the one who had nudged him ever forward. Now she was doing it from the other side as well.

*"You're just too good to be true,
Can't take my eyes off you,
You'd be like heaven to touch,
I wanna hold you so much,"*

For more than an hour now, he'd been sitting crouched behind a chain-link fence not fifty yards from the *Journey's End* dock where *Sweet Lindy* was moored. When he'd come into port earlier, he'd made sure he docked with as much noise and commotion as possible. He didn't want his arrival to go unnoticed. The sun had been lowering itself into the calm, dark waters, and as it did so an evening chill had bitten. Maine would always be Maine, he reminded himself. There were five or more other work boats stern-to, and he'd tied up alongside a small, rusting crane. He'd looked about him and seen nothing move, not a soul in sight. That was exactly what he wanted. This Arthur Wellesley man – if he showed – would probably wait until the sun was below the horizon, by which time Jake would have staked out his vantage point. He'd spent his life trying to surprise fish and now he was trying to surprise a man. An easier catch.

Jake hadn't spotted that amongst the boats on the hard, the trucks and the flatbeds was an ordinary grey Ford sedan. It somehow looked out of place in amongst the working vehicles. But then he wasn't looking for a car, he was looking for male in his forties, who was fit and had dark skin. His new-found adversary.

Snale had been a professional soldier for too long to leave anything to chance. Vietnam was twenty years in the rear-view mirror, but it would never meld into the horizon's dust. The memory was still pin sharp, riding his fender a tad too close, like it always had. Furthermore, working for Swire's had been what he imagined a military academy to be. So, if some dumb fisherman thought he was going to turn Jimmy Snale's retirement benefits of a full refrigerator and a soft mattress with female visitors, into fifty years on a concrete slab with gruel and a tattooed Nazi woodsman for company, then he sure was some dumb fisherman.

There he was, a decorated US Ranger, hiding behind a wreck of a boat as if he were trying to catch a disobedient cat. And he hated cats. Frickin' vermin. Who the hell did this fisherman think he was? Jimmy put away his binoculars and hooked out his shit Russian monocular from his leather jacket. It was too dark to make out any move his man might make and who knows what that might be. The fact was, it was amateur hour and that was needling him. What was it Mr Swire always said? *"Never do business with stupid people."* And here he was in Maine playing hide 'n seek with a dumb-ass fisherman. Stupid or what?

Jake glanced at his watch and rubbed his arms: Maine nights, cotton sweaters and keeping tombstone-still just didn't belong together. He thought of Shannon and Amy laying on the floor with their puzzle. Did he want to be there right about now? He sure did. There was no way he could stay here all night; he was already chilled to the marrow. Sooner or later, he would have to do something. Not yet though. You knew your spot. You'd fished it before. The bait was right. The time of day was good. The lunar cycle was on the money. Yet you still ended up going home with a bucket full o'empty . . . Sometimes it just happened that way. A wrinkle in his spine and a tingle in his neck told him to wait. Big fish *did* get hungry whenever the pickings were slim; that's when the bait would tempt them. It was the law of nature. Dealer law too.

One of the many advantages of being 5' 7" and 140 pounds of unyielding, supple muscle thought the Asian gentleman, was that to origami oneself into the passenger footwell of a car was no hardship. The memory of the Cu Chi tunnels came back to him, and they hadn't been upholstered by Henry Ford. Long before sunset he'd carefully angled the two door mirrors and the rear-view mirror, so that without showing his head above the dash he had a view – not a Panavision one, he had to admit – of where he suspected the fisherman would hide, and where Mr Wellesley might observe his quarry. The Asian gentleman had been correct on both counts. As for his night vision, he'd perfected that more than twenty years ago in Vietnam's jungles. If he could spot a camouflaged Marine sniper at 500 paces – on a moonless night – then tonight was like watching the Yankees play ball under floodlights. All he had to do was wait for someone to make the first move.

Many moons ago he'd discovered the art of moving second or third in any conflict: turn an opponent's force into your force and then back it into them. That and accept the fact that the element of surprise was far, far overrated. These were his mantras. He wasn't a man to wager, but tonight his money was on the fisherman throwing his hand in first. Mr Wellesley, the Asian gentleman had decided over the weeks, had far more skill than he'd credited him with. And it was rare for him to extend a compliment to anyone at all. Especially a real Yankee.

Snale was bored. He had tracked his man, spoken twice with Mr Swire and he wanted to go home. He didn't much care which home. The Trade Winds one would do, he just sought warmth and a TV. Also, he needed this job over with. Again, he asked himself a question he'd asked countless times since the Gardner heist. One he'd never been able to figure out an answer to: if the Dealer man really was the witness everyone was looking for, then why didn't he come forward and at least stick his nose in the trough marked $1 Million Dollars? Some of that cash would surely stick to him like shit to a blanket. Apart from the guards (and he reckoned they were exempted from the reward), the fisherman was the only person who could finger him or the British mercenary. For Christ's sake how many frickin' fish have you gotta pull out of the ocean to make a million bucks? OK, so the snag was to claim the full reward, they had to get the art back, but the fisherman would get his hands on something for shit-sure. What was also shit-sure was that catching him and the mercenary, was *never* going to happen. Like Mr Swire was going to give up $200 million of art, wherever and whoever now had it. And for your next joke . . . So, cold and bored Jimmy knew he would have to wait this one out. Then, he shivered involuntarily. And it wasn't caused by the night air.

"Jimmy", he scolded himself out aloud. "Never say never . . ."

The fish weren't even nibbling. Nothing. It was as if the ocean had become the Dead Sea. Time to move on to new grounds. Oftentimes, that's the way the ocean, the currents and the fish were. So why change the habits of a lifetime? Reinforcing himself with that, Jake jumped to his feet from behind the wooden chocks supporting a weathered old down'easter. He sprinted to the chain-link fence. With a strength and agility that belied his age, he pulled himself to the top of the fence with one short, powerful jerk. Then, in a flowing movement, he vaulted over the top of the fence and landed – feet wide apart – as if he were a cat, quiet and nimble. Twenty yards away lay *Sweet Lindy*. Her lines exaggerated by a shadow cast by a distant ochre streetlight. Jake's heart pounded inside his heaving chest and his temples throbbed. If this has got to end somewhere, he thought, there's no better place than the Dealer family's down'easter. Lindy would approve.

Pleated in the footwell of the grey Ford sedan the Asian gentleman whistled quietly under his breath. Impressive. His survival had been in part due to his clinical obsession with intelligence-gathering, however trivial.

'The fisherman' would be a worthy opponent for anyone. Even him.

It was with a sense of relief that Snale set down the monocular. Let's get this over with, he spat under his breath as he pulled a plastic laundry bag from his pocket. Grabbing the binoculars and monocular he wiped them clean. Then he made sure he had no ID, cash or credit cards in any of his pockets. He found two $10 bills inside his leather jacket and tossed them into the bag. After he'd tightened his belt, he checked his Casio and took in the sea air. Then he set off towards the municipal pier and *Journey's End*, discarding the bag into a nearby dumpster.

"Too frickin' right," he muttered, "Journey's frickin' End."

For a reason he couldn't understand he felt angry. And he didn't want to be angry. He wanted to be his usual professional self and ensure that the man who he owed his sorry Indian hide to was going to be safe. He needed to keep Lieutenant Swire safe. Safe from *every* dumb ass fisherman on the East Coast, if necessary.

In his right door mirror, the Asian gentleman caught sight of Arthur Wellesley loping towards the dock. There was a swagger in his shoulders and upper body he hadn't noticed before. The man was pent-up and raging. It was ominous. And he didn't like what he saw.

* * *

"Say, you the man they call Jake Dealer?" Snale shouted angrily from the dock.

"Who's askin'?" Jake asked calmly.

So, this was it, thought Jake, strangely at ease, for he was on home turf.

"Who the fuck do you think is asking. Me of course. Wise ass."

Now, Snale realised why he was angry.

"You think this is *your* ocean? For centuries my ancestors stood on these shores and hunted these waters before you people even built the fricken' *Mayflower*. You believe this is your history? We're called Native Americans for a reason. These are *our* lands."

"Then come aboard. Let's see what your ancestors taught you about preservation."

Snale leapt over the stern of *Sweet Lindy*. He didn't need a second invite.

Jake edged towards the wheelhouse, purposely putting himself into a corner. Next to his feet was his father's old mahogany fish club. It had heft and power and had despatched worthier catches than this one. But he let it rest. Jake advanced cautiously. Both men began to circle each other in the open space of the aft deck like prize-fighters in a ring. The same worn teak that had seen bigger fish than this one. Warrior fish. Kings of their world. Creatures of beauty and majesty. Their noble blood had seeped over this very deck into the scuppers and back out into the ocean from whence the beasts had come. Beneath his feet his second heart, *Sweet Lindy's* engine, lay idle but ready to beat if asked. His eyes widened and tore into the man.

And with the gravity of ages, Jake saw that the man had come only to slay him, not to warn him off.

"You're Arthur Wellesley, aren't you?" Jake tilted his head as he spoke. He recognised the man from that fateful Boston evening. "You look better outta police uniform and without the moustache."

"You're well informed. God spare us from frickin' smart-ass fishermen," snarled the man who had come to kill him.

"What do you want with me? With my family?"

"You dead. That's all I want. Easy, huh!"

The man could have been a cobra, poised and ready to attack. With his shoulders rounded, not quite crouching, Jake slowed their clumsy ballet. There was a strange hypnotic power that locked his eyes onto the man who wanted to murder him. In those eyes he could see death. A certain death. This man was only here to eliminate Amy's father. With that realisation, Jake instantaneously accepted that this was not self-defence. This was kill or be killed.

Jake's immediate world moved in slow motion. For a reason he couldn't grasp, his instinct told him to attack, not interrogate. He'd seen enough Hamptons' beach fights to know that people never took the cotton wool out of their ears to put in their mouths. Talk about what? Art heists? Boston? Witnesses? No. Death was all they had in common. They were both would-be killers.

Jake stopped momentarily. He stared hard. When landing a large fish, you killed it without hesitation. You strike it fast. Best of all, you ironed it. And that was precisely what Jake decided to do. Iron him with his bare hands. Cut his life off at the throat, starve him of oxygen. There could be no proportional response where Amy was concerned. What was a proportional response to someone who'd make Amy an orphan? Death was too darned lenient according to his understanding of the law. Dealer law. And here on the aft deck of *Sweet Lindy* there was no other law. None that mattered anyway.

All those thoughts played out in the blinking of an eye inside his head, like a slo-mo movie. Then, as if his heart had been syringed with adrenaline, Jake catapulted himself across the deck screeching like a nor'east gale.

The man who would slay him was taken completely by surprise. Jake landed square on his chest. Jake pinned him to the dew-slicked teak. Without thought, much less mercy, he began pounding into his body, his ribs, his chest, his stomach, head, face . . . anywhere and everywhere he could land his brawny fists, he did. Bones were smashed in his ferocious onslaught. On and on he beat him with his bare hands . . . Never in his life had he punched a man, and he hadn't realised the strength within his body, one now powered by primeval fear and desperation. Fear for his daughter. His life was to protect her life. At any cost.

At last, Jake stood up but only to weigh into the man's body with the violent power of his powerful legs and feet, until he could no more. Finally, from his foetus-like position face down on blood-soaked deck did the man stir. In great pain, he rolled over onto his back.

"You wanna talk *now*? I've killed bigger fish here. Get up!"

Jake spat the words out. The man peeled himself up off the deck, leaving blood and teeth behind. He half-stood. Just. His head spun; a native anger welled inside his eyes.

"I'm gonna kill you Dealer!"

With those words, blood leached out of the corners of his mouth. The man coughed out another tooth as gore drooled down his chin. He tried to move his arms but felt only crushed ribs. Shit, the fisherman was frickin' powerful. Without warning, his right eye shut completely, and he cursed Lieutenant Swire under his breath: *"No guns. No knives. You kill him tonight with your bare hands. An ancestor's death. No blood. No mess. Kill him quietly Jimmy. He's a fisherman. A drowned corpse. You're a Ranger."*

"Yessir, Lieutenant Swire."

"If you're gonna kill me on my boat, you're gonna have to do it *after* I've killed you." Jake spoke with an oil-slick calmness, confidence too.

"Asshhssshole . . ." was all Sergeant James Snale could muster as he threw himself at Jake. Despite the beating he'd taken, he was a soldier, and he was in shape. Until this fisherman had used him as a frickin' punch bag. But with a closed right eye, the man caught him with was a glancing right hook, its full force lost, although it stopped Jake momentarily. Regaining his footing, Jake grabbed him by the chest and began to crush him as if he were a spent beer can. The man cried out as broken ribs punctured deep into his lungs. Jake squeezed harder and harder until the cries stopped. Both men, arms clenched around each other, rolled like wrestlers in a lock towards the gunwale. It was Jake who realised where they were headed. With a crashing noise they tripped and fell as one overboard, knocking the air out of three functioning lungs, two of them Jake's. Now, it was the son of Proteus who'd come home. As always – in mariner's lore – the ocean would take as easily as it would provide.

The Atlantic's eternal winter bit into Jake like a shark. The taste of salted water snatched at his throat as darkness enveloped them both. The man tried to struggle as Jake dragged him down as an alligator would drown those who would turn it into luggage. A fierce grimace of power came upon Jake as fat white bubbles of air – of an impending death – drifted upwards. He clenched the man ever tighter, wringing the oxygen from what remained of his one lung.

Jake's ocean wasn't letting this man out.

The man was now static – lifeless – and Jake abandoned him in the silty grey murk to bolt to the surface to feed off the night air. Then, with an arctic anger, he dove back down into the darkness.

This time, Jake grabbed the man's heels and hauled him down, ever deeper, beneath the surface. With two lungs full of Maine air, he held the man there until the very last soda-sized bubble had escaped from his shattered nose. And Jake had oxygen a-plenty for this task. Finally, he let go to tread water . . . and to bear witness as the airless corpse sunk sluggishly into the bitter depths.

The last conscious thought that went through the half-Montaukett Indian, half-Caucasian US Ranger Sergeant James Douglas 'Sly' Snale's mind, as Jake Dealer and the Atlantic Ocean took his life was:

Who's going to look out for Lieutenant Swire?

CHAPTER 91

Journey's End **dock, Rockland, Maine.**
Saturday, 2nd June 1990. 20:24. After Sunset.

Jake scrambled up the stern of *Sweet Lindy* like a giant spider crab and fell panting into what had been their bloodied arena. The iciness of the water had taken his body temperature right down. He was trembling harder than a fall leaf in a September wind. And it wasn't from the murderous act he'd just committed – there had been no self-defence involved, Jake knew that. And remorse? It had never even entered his mind, for he would kill any person who would endanger Amy. He didn't care about: The Who? The Why? The Reason? They were all details, and he supposed they were all to do with stolen paintings. What did he know from stolen paintings? Nothing. Running had been his signal. He knew nothing then, and was going to say nothing now, to anybody. That was the way it was, and the way it was going to stay. Forever. And if there was anyone else out there who needed further proof, well, they could trawl the waters of Rockland Harbour for a corpse.

Jake stood up at last and swung below, into the small forepeak to grab a large rag. He stripped off his clothes, leaving them in a wet pile on the linoleum floor. Naked and shivering, he towelled himself vigorously. The forepeak hummed stale: bread, musty cupboards, a no-air kind of smell. He wanted to get back out into the crisp night and see the stars again. Above all he wanted to get back to Amy. He dressed quickly pulling on an old T-shirt and shorts, and threw on his foul-weather gear and boots. They were the only clothes he had on board.

There was one more job Jake had to do. Going out to the stern, still cold, but with an overwhelming sense that maybe his and Amy's lives were once again theirs. He opened a scupper locker and grabbed his grandfather's spruce harpoon. He'd never used it, and kept it on board as a mascot of the past. Now he removed the leather sheath from its tip.

He pressed the sharp bronze-steel against his thumb until it punctured his skin. He watched a rivulet of blood slowly trickle down its spear. The weapon he held spoke to him of the men who worked the oceans, the rivers, north and south of the equator, east and west of Greenwich: whalers, Inuits, Indians, Africans, Dealers. A harpoon had existed since the birth of mankind. He carefully replaced it and sucked the blood off his thumb. The harpoon was as noble as it was primitive. And it too had survived. Just holding it was talismanic, but he really needed its survival luck right about now.

Jake leaned over the boat's gunwale to scan for the dead body. The man he'd killed. He couldn't see anything; the body had probably been seized by a fearsome undercurrent already. He didn't much care where it was headed. The ocean had been absorbing detritus far worse than Arthur Wellesley since the beginning of time. Another 180 pounds of flesh would go the same way before long. So what if the drowned body washed ashore? There sure weren't any witnesses at the *Journey's End* dock on a Saturday night.

Journey's End for Arthur Wellesley, yes, but not for Jake and Amy Dealer.

Journey's End was their new beginning. Of that, he *was* sure.

The Asian gentleman had observed what had happened with wide-eyed astonishment. Not at the eventuality, but at the velocity with which it had all taken place. It had been years since he had seen fear and adrenaline power a man in such a way. 'The fisherman' had been fuelled by something quite extraordinary. He moistened his lips and snapped his knuckles back. They cracked noisily. So, he had judged 'the fisherman' correctly. He would make a worthy opponent.

Invisible, and slipping silently out from the shadows as if he were wearing a black silk cloak and black silk slippers, he now took up his position, not thirty paces from where Jake stood on the aft deck of *Sweet Lindy*.

He too had orders to follow.

PART TEN

SUNDAY, 3RD JUNE 1990

CHAPTER 92

**10 Crick Hill Road, Menemsha,
Martha's Vineyard, Massachusetts.
Sunday, 3rd June 1990. Morning.**

"You're looking green around the gills this morning Zeph. Drink warm water, fresh lemon juice. It'll clean out your liver."

Ollie busied himself with a pot of Blue Mountain coffee for his grandson and a hot chocolate for himself. As had been his custom of late, he'd risen soon after sunrise. He liked to set out his working materials in the studio, together with his choice of music for the day – Chopin usually – as well as a bowl of fruit and fresh mint tea. Unless an important issue kept them, Zephaniah invariably left shortly after lunch, and Ollie wanted to be hard at work before his grandson was airborne.

"No thanks Ollie, I like to suffer. Good for the soul, and besides, I didn't sleep well. Used to my own bed I suppose." Zephaniah's voice sounded thick and sore.

"You have your own bed here," said Ollie, all too chipper.

"You know what I mean."

"Sure, I do."

For a casual visitor, or anyone who didn't know Ollie Swire, it would have been fair to assume that he was attending a funeral later in the day: his black linen shirt, black cotton pants and black suede loafers all fitted his agile octogenarian frame as if they'd been tailored.

There was, to Zephaniah at least, a vitality in the air – too much for his liking. His grandfather seemed to be moving on the balls of his feet. It was as if nature had overlooked the customary degradations of age. It was all too damned wholesome for his wits this morning.

Dinner had passed off well, full of inconsequential chat and banter. (Ollie had delighted in a tale Zephaniah had recounted after he'd bumped into Larry Gagosian at a Soho gallery opening. His grandson, forever wary, had pitched Gagosian a low-ball question, cocktail party fare: *"Is there anything you'd like to see change in the art market today, Larry?"* Rapier fast, and with a devilish smile, the go-go modern art dealer had replied: *"That's like asking Dante what he'd change about the structure of Hell. The art market suits me just fine how it is right now Zephaniah."*) Ollie didn't yearn for Manhattan, but he sure did miss talent spotting: and Larry Gagosian obviously had it in spades. To a man like Ollie who was often alone – but never lonely – intelligent and informed gossip were always welcome lodgers.

So, in the end, he'd elected not to show the Vermeer to his grandson. If today's meeting ended with their two compasses pointing to the same true north, then he might, perhaps, unveil his progress. Secretly, it was what he would like to do more than anything else. He was proud of his grandson and all that he had achieved, while he, lost in the maze of the restorations, desired a truce.

Even that dreaded word 'compromise' had flown across his line of sight, admittedly with the speed of a swallow, but it had at least been fleetingly visible. Ollie wanted this meeting over and wondered if his usually perspicacious grandson had sensed that fact too. He doubted it. He looked at Zephaniah as he sat at the kitchen table in a towelling robe, unshaven, with his head in his hands as if Central Casting had issued a call for 'Hungover Men'.

"I thought good wine didn't leave souvenirs. I feel very second-hand," he said in a staccato voice, the caffeine barely lubricating his vocal cords.

"I'm informed that is indeed the case. I think you'll find it comes down to quantity Zeph."

"Thanks for that."

"Pleasure. After all, it was my wine you consumed," Ollie paused. "Is there something on your mind? I've not seen you like this in a long while."

Zephaniah looked up at his grandfather as he stood over him. Neat, clean shaven, impeccable. It made him feel even worse. How had he allowed himself to get into this state? Again, he lowered his head back into his hands. The damned fisherman had done it to him. The man was the only wrinkle in his near-perfect crime. But now, thank God, that was all over. Jimmy Snale would've despatched him back into his godforsaken Atlantic Ocean where he belonged. And it was all over now, thanks to Jimmy. Peace at last. For sure the world wasn't going to miss one more fisherman. Zephaniah took another sip of his coffee. He'd call him tonight when he was back in Boston. The debrief could wait until then.

Feeling more robust, but still annoyed with himself, Zephaniah got up. "I'm off for a shower and shave, then let's start our meeting."

"Good idea."

"OK. Thanks, by the way."

"For what Zeph?"

"I don't know . . . how about everything?" His engaging face opened up as he replied.

"Whatever you do, please don't go and get sentimental on me."

"You've got to be kidding. I'm saving that for my next life."

"No Buddhism on my watch either," joked Ollie.

Zephaniah tightened the belt on his gown and headed to the stairs. As he did so, he heard a knock at the front door. It stopped him in his tracks. Apart from the harbour master, no one ever approached his grandfather's house. Everyone knew that Mr Swire liked to be left undisturbed.

With nerves less thorny than his grandson's, Ollie opened the front door.

"Good morning, Mr Swire."

"Come in Brian and meet my grandson, the one you've heard much about." Tentatively, the stranger stepped over the threshold and stood just inside the doorway.

"Zephaniah, meet Brian Rush, he's our new harbour master. It's his first month."

The very last thing Zephaniah needed right now was pleasantries with people who moved boats around. He'd had more than his fill of people who moved boats. From the bottom of the stairs, he waved a 'hello'.

"Pleasure to finally meet you, Mr Swire. Heard a lot about you sir."

"Well, good luck with the new job." Zephaniah went to head upstairs, but something stopped him. Out of the corner of his ever-alert eyes, he spied Rush handing over a folded piece of paper to Ollie and lean in to whisper something.

"Sorry to disturb, Mr Swire." His voice carried; it was almost conspiratorial. "I was asked to pass you this message. The caller said it was important."

Not only did Zephaniah not know about the new harbour master – not one word from Ollie before today – but the only person ever to use the Menemsha harbour master as a messenger boy was him. And only when it was urgent. No one, not even Mrs Elliott at his office, used their system. It was their personal cipher. It was their method of always being able to stay in touch. One that Zephaniah felt territorial over. Evidently, his grandfather not so. That irked him.

Ollie opened the paper, glanced at it and slipped it into his pocket. "Thank you, Brian. Sorry to have troubled you."

"No trouble at all, Mr Swire," he replied with a soapy grin. "I'll be on my way then."

"Hold on Brian, I'll walk back with you." Without even turning around, Ollie called out, "I'm going to the branch office, Zeph. Won't be long."

Before Zephaniah could speak, much less move, his grandfather had closed the front door and set off down the hill with the new harbour master.

* * *

By the time he returned – no more than fifteen minutes later – Zephaniah had regained his composure. Clean shaven, not a hair out of place and his attire was immaculate, studied even. His eyes had regained their clarity and were as confident as his New England voice. Once again, there was poise in all his mannerisms. Relaxed and at ease with his powerful frame, he leant against the breakfast counter as the kettle hissed on the stove behind him.

"Fresh coffee Ollie?" Zephaniah asked as he poured boiling water into the glass *cafetière*.

"Perhaps a small cup. Thanks."

He caught a weariness in his grandfather that hadn't been there a quarter of an hour ago.

"You alright Ollie? You look tired?"

"I'm good Zeph. Tad out of breath is all. Happens sometimes, even to me."

Ollie sat down at the kitchen table, the one they used as their canvas for every meeting. The one upon which they spread out their papers, photographs of paintings or sculptures, catalogues of other houses' forthcoming sales, Swire's figures, ideas, alchemies and schemes . . .

All the decisions they would make around this kitchen table would, inevitably, reverberate around the art world, if not the world. To Ollie and Zephaniah Swire this table was where they brought their oils to paint with. Today, however, for a reason neither could understand, all they were able to bring to the table was themselves. That, and a pot of Blue Mountain coffee to stand beside the ancient *Gu* that was plum centre of the table, pregnant with bright yellow roses.

"Zeph, you've many impressive traits and qualities," Ollie began, "and one of the most admirable is your strike-first personality. The Marines didn't try to curb it, all they did was harness it. But Zeph, it is a dysfunction, one I fostered in you . . ."

Zephaniah went to speak, but Ollie raised his hand to head him off at the pass.

He caught the look in his grandfather's eyes. He'd seen it before. Occasionally, Ollie liked a centre stage soliloquy. This was one of those moments.

". . . a trait like that has its genesis in mistrust and frustration as a child, especially only children, which essentially, you are. A strike-first nature makes friendships or relationships hard, and often brief, but also, and here was my gamble, a strike-first nature can provide you with the tools to survive. To be successful. It can drive people. People like you Zeph. People who strike first need to dominate and control. Losing is like asphyxiating."

Ollie sipped his coffee as Zephaniah leaned back in his chair; all he wanted to do was get down to business. Ollie had been – and Zephaniah was in no doubt about this – *the* mentor in his life. It was a fact he was more than proud of: his mother had killed herself, his father was hiding beneath the earth's crust sheltered by their labours, while his half-brother did God knows what. Accordingly, if his grandfather had played Dr Frankenstein with his psyche during his upbringing the notion neither surprised nor distressed him. In fact, he found it rather flattering. Zephaniah knew precisely who he was. Ollie had been the principal force, more dominating than the Vietnam War.

"Let's get down to work, Ollie. Enough of this kind of talk. If I need a shrink, Boston is full of them."

"Zeph this is work." Ollie lifted his head in mild resignation. There was little humour flickering in his Husky-blue eyes.

"You're losing me here . . ."

And that was a fact. Zephaniah was not only lost, but he was also genuinely perplexed with where this one-sided meeting was going.

"Stay with me awhile, OK?"

Ollie let his head drop to his coffee cup, not to drink but to inhale and awaken something inside himself. "I get up with the sun, and sometimes all I ever notice are grey rooftops heavy with wet fog, and out beyond the harbour wall white caps and swells churn the waters. I see the ocean and sky as one sweep of monochrome, like Doug Kuntz's photos," he said gesturing at the images of the Long Island baymen. "I see a bleakness out there Zeph. It's one that a city man cannot imagine. There's nothing in the elements to add colour or even life on days like that. And then I see men, tired, unshaven. They shuffle sometimes, maybe a child is ill, or their wives have had to skip their breakfasts. But these men are ready to strike out into the Atlantic. These men," Ollie raised his voice a little, "are frontiersmen. These men built this country. Our clients didn't. They just built the railroads and the banks. *These* men did." Ollie turned the volume up again. "Do you really think a large sum of cash motivates them? No, it doesn't Zeph. Sure, they want food, fuel, a well-found vessel, but most of all they want their independence. That was never for sale, and it never will be. You cannot scare these people. If all that the Atlantic can throw at them doesn't frighten them, then trust me on this, threats won't do the trick."

Ollie placed his cup gently on the table. His hard, blue eyes radiated the warmth of pack-ice. He looked at his grandson in a manner he'd never done before. Instinctively Zephaniah inched away. "You cannot intimidate the honest and the courageous, Zeph. It is simply not possible."

"Ollie, look, I'm struggling here," Zephaniah added cheerfully. "First, it's personality disorders, and now it's fishermen . . ."

Zephaniah didn't, couldn't, wouldn't, finish the sentence.

And the word 'fisherman' hung over them like the anvil of a thunder cloud.

At last Ollie spoke, in a low voice.

"You've got it now, eh, Zeph?"

He watched in silence as his grandson's face began to deflate. The colour remained in Zephaniah's flesh, but the cheeks caved inwards, his eyes blinked nervously, and the brows sagged. The truth – as Ollie knew only too well – is always written on every face.

"You got it now, eh, Zeph?" he repeated.

"I'm not sure what I'm supposed to have 'got', so why don't you tell me. You seem to know everything."

"Not a bad comeback, kid. OK, here goes, but it's going to be the *Reader's Digest* version."

Ollie sat upright in his chair, and he too leaned back. It was as if both men now wanted a physical distance between them.

"Your soldier boy is dead. The fisherman killed him. Drowned him like a runt puppy dog. I never did rate Snale. This all happened in Rockland, last night."

"Where the hell is that?"

"Cut it out Zeph. It's Maine, north of Portland. Lobster country. Snale tracked him down to Rockland on your orders."

Zephaniah knew exactly where Jimmy had found him. But questions bought time. Something he needed right now.

"Don't irritate me with questions Zeph. You already know he'd found him in Rockland. You'd sent Snale to kill him." Ollie's voice dropped to an almost inaudible whisper. "And that, my dear grandson was a big, big mistake."

"Why so?"

"Because the fisherman was never a threat to you, me, Swire's or even to your stolen art. *You* were the only threat to us all. You didn't get it did you Zeph? You were blinkered. The man's running was his clarion signal. It was his lighthouse: **'DANGEROUS WATERS AHEAD. NAVIGATE AT YOUR PERIL.'** The most important point you didn't figure out was that I didn't want him dead. Oliver Swire wanted this man alive. Very alive. *My* words *are* scripture Zephaniah."

He weighed what his grandfather had said. He let his mind chew the words searching for any disguised nuances, ones he knew would be in there somewhere. Nothing was ever straightforward with Ollie. They were going to need a corkscrew to bury him. Eventually, drumming his fingers on the table he asked:

"What's more important to you, Ollie? A Vermeer on your wall or a love filled with compassion and desire?"

"Sometimes you impress me very much," said Ollie, "damned fine question. Great delivery. Superb timing. Now give me a moment to muse."

Ollie closed his eyes and felt his mind drift upwards into a clear blue sky, where a jet-stream took him safely all the way across America, to a land he had once known, a land called New Mexico. Ollie had had the answer to the question right away. But he was damned if he was going to share Hannah with a living soul. Even his beloved grandson.

"Here's your answer. The love *and* desire to have a Vermeer on my wall is all that is important."

"Delphic. Exactly what I expected from you but do carry on with your story."

"I've been tidying up your rare messes since you were in diapers. Thankfully you make few errors, but when you do, you really do foul up. Like now." Ollie stroked his chin. "I knew and liked Gerald Ford, knew him way back when, and in those days his motorcade consisted of one car, and he was behind the wheel. People say Ford was a man who never missed the opportunity to miss an opportunity. With you, Zeph, sometimes you never miss the opportunity to really screw things up. It's your scorpion-and-frog tale. You just can't seem to help yourself. Your brother's Dalí could've had very grave implications for Swire's. Whatever the damned cost, you had to prove a point to Jed, to me. It was your cheap three-card monte. Did you seriously think I wouldn't find out about the game you were playing? Cory Mount is good, but I'm better. Remember, hubris is a fate worse than death. The forged Dalí has been destroyed."

"I thought this was the *Reader's Digest* version?" Zephaniah's face had gained a degree of animation.

"It is my boy. I've had the same man follow Snale twenty-four hours a day, seven days a week ever since Saturday, 31st March. That was the day after the *Globe* broke the witness story. I didn't trust you then not to be rash on this, and I didn't believe you'd listen. I told you he was to be left alone. I knew the witness would eat away at you. It was only a matter of time before he turned cancerous inside you."

"So, you had Snale followed for over two months! By whom?"

"A gentleman who has been known to me since long before you went to war. He's been a guardian angel for you, and me, since the mid-1960s I guess. He's protected you against yourself, and me against you, for almost twenty-five years."

"Enigmatic answer, even for you."

"Maybe so, but it's all you're going to get." Ollie hesitated. "But I will tell you how far I was going to go with his. His orders were to safeguard the fisherman, at any cost."

"Are you telling me your man killed Jimmy?"

"No, I'm not."

"Then what?"

"I just told you. The fisherman killed Snale with his own bare hands. No weapons. He acquitted himself very well from what I understand. When you push too hard sometimes people crack. That's what I was saying earlier Zeph. Strike-first personalities are unable to grasp other people's breaking points. You pushed him too far, too hard. He snapped. He killed."

"Any more to all this?"

Zephaniah was losing both patience and interest. If Jimmy was dead, then so be it. He was a soldier; it was a risk that came with the uniform. And at no extra charge. He'd known the rules.

"Yes. Two more points. The first is, and get this, there is never any collateral damage when I act. My man retrieved Snale's corpse from Rockland Harbour that same night. Snale has no family to speak of, and the matter will be closed when he goes to live abroad. Sergeant James Snale has ceased to exist."

"All thought through, isn't it."

Not wishing to be put off his stride, Ollie barely drew breath.

"The second point is, I've had the name and whereabouts of the fisherman since a stormy Friday night, Friday, 30th March."

"How so?" Asked Zephaniah, genuinely perplexed.

"Thought that might get your attention." There was no victory in his tone. "The fisherman in question came into the harbour late that night with a friend of his, a man named Marty Drew."

"Marty Drew, the piano player?"

"We didn't discuss his profession. Anyway, I was looking out at the dock during the storm, when I saw the fisherman's boat arrive. No sooner had he docked in my slip, than he ran to make a phone call. Within two or three minutes, he'd spun his down'easter on a dime and put right back out to sea. Back out into that terrible storm. Alone too. He left Mr Drew behind on the dock. I'm always curious about the extraordinary things people do, so I walked down to the dock. It was bitterly cold, and I invited Mr Drew up here as he was waiting for a ride to a friend's house. We talked and he drank some brandy. You know your grandfather likes to listen. And Mr Drew told me the story of the fisherman."

"What was the story?"

"No, Zephaniah, you have not earned the right to hear the fisherman's history. It's bad enough Snale got you his name so early on. All I will tell you is that I wasn't going to permit you to deal out any more of fate's cards to him." Ollie's eyes were icebergs: they were blue, they were white, and their danger lay beneath the surface. "It's over. Finished. Your pursuit made this fisherman into a killer, when all he was doing was protecting his family, at whatever cost."

* * *

Zephaniah Swire had been educated by a man – and an army – who'd taught him how to survive – to outlast – all-comers. And the secret was to recce *all* escape routes. Confrontation rarely led to survival, any more than cowardice did. Drinking his now cold coffee in silence he mulled over his alternatives. And there were plenty. It all depended on what to pluck from the train-wreck that was this episode. Or so he told himself. Partially fortified, Zephaniah decided there was no real wreckage at all, for he'd always had an endgame. Albeit one he'd refined only last Wednesday, after he'd flown down to see Ollie. No, the play was still his.

This was still his call.

"OK, Ollie, thanks for having my back again." He vacillated. "Are you now going to show me all the work you've being doing on our Vermeer?"

The first-person plural didn't escape Ollie – just as Zephaniah had hoped.

"Not so long ago I asked you if you had a plan, one that didn't involve turning No Man's Land into a $200 million graveyard for Old Dutch Masters."

"The time isn't right. I'm not fencing with you either Ollie. I do have a plan, and one you're going to like. In fact, you'll like it a lot. Let's say the grapes on the vine aren't ready for harvesting quite yet, not for a while anyway."

"How about a clue for an old man?"

"Playing the age card buys you one hint, but no more. Deal?"

"Deal," replied Ollie with a poker-smile.

Zephaniah took a deep breath. He knew the answer would beg more questions, but there was no conceivable way he could inform his grandfather of the entirety of his plan.

"As we both know the warrant on the Gardner theft is for the *Interstate Transport of Stolen Property* and for *Receiving Stolen Property*. This isn't a federal crime, and a theft from a museum isn't federal either. Unless I'm mistaken, Boston, Martha's Vineyard and No Man's Land are all in Massachusetts. Ergo, stolen Gardner property hasn't crossed any state line. What's more, as I orchestrated the theft, there's no '*receiving*' charge."

"We know this."

"Only in the great US of A could this happen. There's a five-year Statute of Limitation on this crime. Five, brief years. Ask me your next question on St Patrick's Day 1995, then?"

Ollie said nothing, for there wasn't anything to add. The Statute of Limitations play was solid. It appeared that Zephaniah did have the beginnings of an endgame. In that instant however, he grasped that his grandson would never tell him what that endgame was. That would ruin the point of it all. He respected that. Even when the Statute of Limitations did expire on the greatest art theft the world had ever witnessed, his grandson would keep schtum.

Ollie didn't mind. He understood that his grandson had to play it out. Like the best of conmen, he'd take it down to the wire. Like only the best of conmen could – and did. Zeph would wait until such time as to make 'the reveal' pitch-perfect: timing and patience were both Swire men's hallmarks, as much as greed and cupidity were those of a mark.

In this case it looked as though the mark was the American legal system with its Department of Justice. Some mark Zeph . . .

Not being able to conceal a dry expression of pride, Ollie moved his chair back to stand up. Zephaniah went around behind his grandfather to hold it for him. Their eyes met. There was a very real history between them that went beyond the mere effluxion of time. Zephaniah's eyes creased into a smile. Was it a smile at his own survival, again? One born in the relief that this was, in fact, 'over'? Or perhaps he was simply pleased that he and his grandfather had their signed armistice.

Ollie had absorbed it all in a split second. Throughout his long and eventful life, he had observed more expressions than anyone. From desperate marks to Hannah's radiance. He had seen and remembered them all, each and every one. With his knowledge and skills, he'd decided that his grandson's smile was the same sphinx-like one he'd received from the front seat of a Lincoln town car, many years ago. The one Zephaniah had shot at him the day he had returned from the Vietnam War.

The day one war had ended for First Lieutenant Zephaniah Swire, and a second one had begun.

A war of legacies. Of birth right.

EPILOGUE

SATURDAY, 12TH DECEMBER 1992

Sag Harbour, Long Island, New York.
Saturday, 12th December 1992. 13:45.

(This article was first published in *The East Hampton Star* in November 1992. It is one in a series by Peter Duxbury who documents the lives of those who work the waters of the Atlantic Ocean).

'ONE OF THE MOST REWARDING aspects of being a journalist is the people, especially those who like to talk, and that's nearly everyone. There are very few 'No Comment' people in the world. I'm not a foot-in-the-door reporter. Those tactics are for the big boys, the big stories, the big cities. As those of you who read our paper know, I rarely write on any topic west of Shinnecock Bay, north of Orient Point, south of Jamaica Bay or east of Montauk Point.

Today is an exception.

Here's why: folks talk, and journalists listen: whispers, bar chat, lonesome ears. As I said, people love to talk. Not being the investigative type, only because the events, the lives, the vanishing history and the very spirit of our community here at the eastern end of Long Island are more thrilling than any shoe-leather assignment could ever be. Be that as it may, I am still a journalist, and when there's a common thread to 'the talk' one hears, you cannot help but pay heed and report it. That is, after all, what I am paid to do.

So, with that caveat, my column this week takes me far away from my usual compass rose. It also takes me into a journalistic land I've hitherto never visited: reporting informed hearsay and scuttlebutt. The reason, I believe, is honourable.

Judging by what I've discovered, this is a story about a true son of the whalers, the baymen and the fisherman who have lived amongst us for 300 years or more. The people who forged our vanishing land with their own lives.

Times change, and with it the oceans and the tastes of man. There was a period when salmon was so plentiful it was against the law to feed it to indentured slaves more than twice in one week. Sag

Harbour was once the whaling capital of America, dispatching ships to the Pacific Ocean via the fury of Cape Horn. Back then, harpooning was not only a New England fishery, it was also a way of life. Now, and thanks to the Japanese and the giant Atlantic bluefin tuna, harpooning is enjoying a renaissance.

The wholesalers at Tokyo's Tsukiji fish auctions demand perfection for their sushi and sashimi – 'maguro' is the reddest, most marbled bluefin tuna – and Tokyo restaurants charge $70 or more for a two-ounce serving. A generation ago, New England and Long Island fishermen described the very same fish-meat as 'horse mackerel, food for cats an' dogs'. A fish that wasn't even fetching a nickel a pound at the docks.

At the turn of this century, a prior generation of our fishermen sold bluefin to the 'oilers', men who'd boil out the meat for lamp oil and the like; Atlantic bluefin tuna, they declared, was poison. Today, the very same fish-meat is the ocean's biggest reward, and this fish is the most prized of all catches. Eager Japanese bidders will pay as much as $40,000 for a grade A, New England giant Atlantic bluefin tuna. That's a money fish alright.

There are forty-eight tuna-like species in the world, (including albacore, yellowfin, skipjack, the bonitos, the southern bluefin (Thunnus maccoyyi), the Pacific bluefin (Thunnus thynnus orientalis) and the Atlantic bluefin, (Thunnus thynnus thynnus). The largest of all fin fish, bluefin tuna present a streamlined ovoid shape that is aerodynamic – imagine a Constellation aircraft stripped of its wings. Giant Atlantic bluefins can weigh over 1,000 pounds and can be 7–10 feet in length. Extraordinarily attuned to hydrospace, bluefin tuna are rheotropic and polarotactic, which is to say they navigate by the ocean's currents and polarised light. With a brain the size of a man's thumb, they read the patterns and shades of light in the water for orientation. Salinity and temperature gradients inform them too, and they follow the oil profiles of their prey.

Like the men who hunt these fish, they too are hunters. Muscular beasts, their crescent-shaped tail is their main engine, oscillating up to thirty cycles per second. Their fin can power their torpedo-like body – water is a medium 800 times denser than air – at speeds in excess of 50 miles per hour. They are a true phenomenon of evolution.

The Atlantic bluefin tuna will spawn in either the Mediterranean and migrate to the Bay of Biscay or north to Scandinavia, or in the Gulf of Mexico and track north, through the Gulf of Maine, towards Newfoundland. This transoceanic beast is unlike most others, in that it is endothermic – warm blooded – essentially a tropical fish, it also thrives in waters as cold as 44°F (7°C). The giant Atlantic bluefin is the ocean's wildest, most majestic creature.

To the fisherman, alone at the end of his long pulpit, his hands rock steady on the harpoon – despite his boat's speed, pitching and yawing in the Atlantic's swells – this charging fish through water, its body gold and blue and silver refracting beneath the ocean's surface as if it were an opal in the shallows, is the Grail.

As a nation of hunters, the Native Americans believe that the ocean held and bestowed power. By killing a great animal – whatever the species – you took a part of its might deep into your soul. Native Americans associate the hunt for bluefin on the ocean to hunting buffalo bareback from an unbroken mustang. They should know. But, enough of the prey, what about its hunter?

Many of the Atlantic bluefin tuna fishermen either know each other, or at least know of each other. It's a small brotherhood, and as such they help each other in times of need. For sure there's a fierce rivalry (name me a fishery where there isn't?) but nothing supersedes their mutual bond of the ocean, the elements and 'There but for the Grace of God . . .' appreciation. Independence is a different emotion, and it plays a big part of the 'why' fishermen go to sea; but true loners on the water are as rare as white whales. Though tell that to Captain Ahab.

Yet out there on the Atlantic Ocean, from Nantucket to Nova Scotia, where the giant bluefin tuna are to be found, I hear there is one such man. A fisherman no one seems to know much, if anything, about. Tall and purposeful rather than muscular, he sometimes wears a full beard and sometimes he's clean shaven. Opinions and stories differ. All that's constant is that he wears low on his head an old salt 'n sweat stained long-billed cap that hides his face. His eyes have been described as brown and 'kindly-looking'. No one can put a name to him. But this nameless man is the one people have been talking of.

Like a ghost ship haunting an Atlantic fog, one day he's there and the next he's nowhere. No one appears to have a fix on where he came from, or where he's headed. Get this, and this is peculiar, no one seems to want to ask either. Even I found myself not asking. He, from what I can gather, just wants to be left alone on the ocean. That's something all fishermen understand, but rarely ever want.

Apart from a sketchy appearance, a few facts have surfaced in the last two years, ones I've slowly been able to cross-check over time. Most of them are meaningless on their own but added together they form a portrait of sorts. Make of them what you will.

He was first seen in September 1990 in the Atlantic waters south of Nova Scotia. He's licensed alright, although no one can confirm his name or even that of his boat. Some say it has no name on the stern at all. If that's the case, then so be it. That's the way this fisherman wants it, and I'm going to respect that wish. Like all fishermen, he will have his reasons. Those reasons may not sit with yours or mine. However, this is a man who wrests his living in an environment you and I would never venture to.

His choice of licence is interesting.

Unlike most men working the bluefin fishery, he's registered under the 'harpoon-category' and not the 'general-category': I found out why. The 'general-category' has a higher quota, allowing the fishermen to use any method to catch the bluefin – from rod and reel to harpooning – and usually 'closes' in mid-September. With luck, those dedicated and skilled enough to earn their living solely with a harpoon won't reach their much smaller annual quota – 52 tons – until the end of October.

And that is when the giant Atlantic bluefins are strong and fat and red, just as the buyers at the Tsukiji market want them. They say the Japanese eat with their eyes: a red circle of raw maguro – on a square white China plate – holds a special significance for the Japanese.

What of his boat? Everyone seems to agree it's dark green in colour. The watchtower is extra high and the pulpit, from where he throws his harpoon, is longer than any other. So long in fact that other fishermen have nicknamed his particular vessel Pinocchio. Those who claim to have seen it up close – and not even his wholesaler would confirm that he has – say that Pinocchio could be a converted down'easter that probably gets used in other local fisheries, like lobstering.

Here are two more interesting facts from which I have drawn one conclusion. I've heard it said this man uses only an old bronze-tipped spruce harpoon, not a twelve-foot aluminium harpoon fitted with an 800-volt electric 'zapper': a 'zapper' is a legal device all other fishermen use to electrocute the fish the moment the harpoon's bronze dart sinks into the bluefin's flesh.

Eschewing the very idea of a modern harpoon makes him the only man to hunt with 100-year-old tackle, yet his strike rate belies that fact.

Secondly, he doesn't use spotter planes. Nearly all the men working the unforgiving stretch from Nantucket to Nova Scotia team up with a spotter pilot. Mostly they're retired Pan Am or TWA guys, keen amateur fisherman too, keeping their skills honed flying single-engine Cessnas and the like. Serving as the boat's overhead eyes, the pilot flies low over the water seeking out bluefins. As he does so, he'll guide the helmsman, the mate and the harpooner – there's usually a crew of three – into the best position to get off the throw; the pilot will share in any of the bounty. It's true to say some of the fishermen want the spotters banned, but the NMFS (National Marine Fisheries Service) aren't about to outlaw the planes.

So, here's a man, who like many others is seeking to return to an era where life was simpler, more straightforward and perhaps more honest. Here's a man who hunts, by all accounts, only the opening and closing edges of the seasons. He's always ahead of – or behind – the big schools of migrating bluefin because of his licence category. In the late spring when the smaller bluefins' are squirrelly and skittish and hard to hunt, it's as if, like Babe Ruth, he's getting his eye in for the fall, dusting away any off-season cobwebs.

Then, come the fall – his 'quota' not fished – he'll catch what he needs to pay the bills and for upcoming winter repairs. By all accounts, his kills are all big, fat and clean. These are the fish Tokyo desires. This man only brings in the best of the best. And then like the ghost ship in the fog that he is, he disappears again.

I hear his summers are spent lobstering from Matinicus Isle, a desolate and all but barren rock off the coast of Maine. His nameless down'easter is stripped of its watchtower and extra-long pulpit. The lobstering will've been good in the summer months.

Some of this article is speculation. The fact is he's a loner who wants to remain that way. He doesn't appear as a blip on any radar-screen, nor any bar for that matter. With fisherman, bars and tales are as much a part of their lives as fog and storms.

After further thought, I'm guessing he's a conservationist too. For sure his ancestors will have witnessed the centuries old Newfoundland cod fishery close. The magnificent three-masted whale ships of Sag Harbour being broken up for firewood. The haddock stocks off the Georges Bank becoming all but depleted. The Baymen of Long Island losing their striped bass and their scallops. And when the sword boat, Andrea Gail, was lost off the Flemish Cap with her six-man crew in the 'No-Name Storm' of October last year, she was too far out, looking for increasingly scarce swordfish.

This fisherman will have borne witness to these communities as they have shrivelled and died. He has been a living partner in a vanishing tradition. He is a man who has heard the fateful echo that 'forever' leaves in its aeonian wake . . .

This man does what he does because he can. Not many men rest up knowing that fact. You have to be born with skills like his. You can't buy or learn them. These are generational gifts. Is this a blessing or a curse? It's in his blood. Yet, he's damned if he's going to be the last in a long line that sees the death of another way of life. For me though, he has become an itch, and being a journalist, I can't help but scratch a little.

Yes, he does have crew on Pinocchio: a tall redheaded lady, only ever seen wearing dark glasses with side shields to keep the sun and sea glare out of her line of sight. She reads the sea for him, spots the bluefin from afar from Pinocchio's watchtower. Another, a much younger girl, no more than a rangy teenager – with freckles and blonde hair – holds the helm steady while he nestles himself into the stainless steel of his pulpit, riding the waves through his knees, using the boat's motion, choosing his fish, calculating the refraction of light and water, the fish's speed in relation to Pinocchio's speed, the sea-state. All this – and more – he knows by instinct. Much like his life, none of his throws are left to chance. His shoulders and stomach muscles are tense, his arms relaxed as he grips the harpoon and readies himself to get off a throw. With that ironed kill – and it will be a clean kill – he is preserving a way of life. Playing his part in keeping these centuries old customs alive.

A part of me would like to shake the hand of the man who can do all that, just to thank him. However, the better part of me never would. His solitary deeds say more than any words of thanks I could ever summon up.'

* * *

I've just got through a call from Europe. I forgot to ask Marty whereabouts in Europe he was calling me from. It's early afternoon here in Sag, an oily grey afternoon. Fast approaching show-time in Europe. I didn't ask what it was like there. It wasn't that sort of conversation. Here it's been cold and squally all day, the wind has dropped, and the clouds are a thick pelt in the sky. If there will be any stars in the heavens tonight, I'm going to have to take that fact on faith. Tonight, will be a night without friends.

The heating in my apartment turned itself off an hour or so ago. I can feel the chill ebbing its way into my bones, through my ever more fragile body. But Marty sounded chipper, and after today – a Sunday of writing and thinking and writing – I hankered for a warm voice. At my age there aren't too many of those out there. Maybe I'm being hard on myself. Today wasn't a day without friends, after all.

Marty left Long Island in mid-October. He and his seven-piece band were going back out on the road. Taking a long, and sold-out, swing through Europe, and even dipping his toes into the old Soviet Union. His new album, the quirkily titled *You Got Nothing Coming*, is a huge hit here in the US, but he told me he was preferring European food. Hence the tour. Creative types, eh? He thought the idea of Christmas away from the US, for a reason I haven't figured out yet, a good one. Again, creative types.

The Maine Man piece (as my editor archly dubbed it) was published two weeks ago. I read it through a couple of times the morning it was in print and wondered what to do. Should I call Marty or not? I always hate bothering people when they're working. I resolved the dilemma by calling his road manager, Nick 'Dingo' Ruggles, a road-hardened Australian. I needed to take a sounding on Marty's mood. And who better to ask than Dingo.

I guessed that when Marty read the article, there might be a barrage of questions. Or there might be none. You never know with him. To be honest I wasn't ready to answer in-depth questions about it. I damned near didn't publish it at all. Dingo told me for sure I should send him the article, hell, the whole paper. Despite all the great food, and sold-out concert halls and stadiums, he said Marty was kind of homesick. As much as he dislikes all things political, I know he enjoys picking over *The East Hampton Star*. The politics are only local, and he truly loves Long Island. I could picture him in some anonymous dressing room, just his regular crew around him (Marty is not one for hangers-on) poring over the boats for sale, motorbikes for sale; the real estate ads too. So, I did just that. I sent two copies of the newspaper by FedEx to a Milan hotel where Dingo said it would catch up with them. I forgot about it, and guessed the phone would ring sometime. I hadn't figured it would be just three days afterwards.

* * *

"Seen any new Ferraris in town Pete?"

'Ferraris' was Marty-speak for great looking girls. Once, from his bar stool in The American Hotel in Sag, he'd explained what he meant. Without irony or chauvinism and with beaming pride he'd said: *"Pete, Ferraris look best in red, especially when they're polished and in the shop window. They ooze trouble and trouble comes as standard with each model. And all other people want to do is steal 'em or scratch 'em! What the hell. It sure does look great to be seen with a Ferrari, but they're VERY high maintenance. A week doesn't seem to go by without them being in the workshop. But, when the sun shines, they just gleam, and when they're tuned correctly, they're the best ride on planet earth. There is simply no sight or sound like a purring Ferrari. They're hard, no, nigh on frickin' impossible to 'trade in', but life is far less beautiful without Ferraris. Trust me on this."*

The Ferrari question was Marty's way of ducking what he really had to say. But I'd known him too darned long to let him off the hook. There was a long pause. Silence was his to give, or to take. At last, I heard him swallow, it drowned out the hiss of the transatlantic connection.

"Is it Jake out there Pete?"

"Your guess is as good as mine," I replied honestly.

"Bullshit it is."

"Marty, listen up, all I did was send you something I wrote." I sensed that perhaps he had an audience. "You on your own, like now?" Before I got deeper into this I needed to know if there were any other lonesome ears open; there usually were around people like Marty.

"I emptied the dressing room to make this call. It's a show night," he replied.

"Yes, I do believe it's Jake out there. Amy too. No idea who the other lady is."

"Could be that one who came snooping around, remember?"

"I thought that too."

"Well, you sure tell it like it's Jake out there. Others will figure the same you know."

"Good luck to them. It's not like Jake's on the lam anymore."

"Then why'd he run, Pete?"

I didn't have an answer. I let it slide. And Marty allowed me that. The line crackled and there was a distant hum – backstage commotion – you could never quite drown it out. I heard the wheels spin inside Marty's head though. The idea that someone didn't *want* to belong, he found unsettling. Jake Dealer was a Long Islander, that's where he belonged. Don't mess with 'the order of life', Jake, the loyal friend in Marty was saying, while the artist in him was willing him to run and run free. I knew Marty was buying time.

"What's to do?" he asked finally.

"Nothing. This is Jake's story to write, not ours. Only he knows the ending."

"Well, I'm just going to keep on paying the rent on that house of his, and maybe one day he or Amy will come home."

"Don't bet your platinum records on that Marty. The waters and the bays and the land hereabouts are haunted for him. Maybe he's found that a life without Lindy and Dougie could work out there. There are way too many ghosts here." I hesitated. "There's nothing we can or should do Marty," I added. "He knows deep down in his heart where to find us you know. He's not forgotten us."

"I buy some of that, but not all of it flies for me," Marty shot back.

"He is our friend. We should respect that."

Marty waited a long heartbeat before answering. "Nah. He was way more than that. He was all that was so good about where we live. He was a history book who breathed."

It was my turn to hang on a thought. "He's not in the past tense. He's still breathing and so is Amy. That's all that matters."

"We'll never know the truth will we Pete?"

"Probably not. Lookit, maybe it's not him out there. Don't forget I just wrote a newspaper article."

"Yeah! Bullshit! It's him all right," Marty laughed, "doing what he always wanted to do. Living his tattoo. Lucky guy in many ways. You know Pete, the truth ain't always what it's cracked up be. Sometimes the truth belongs buried deep in an Atlantic canyon or in the soil. Buried in between what's right an' what's wrong, in between what's good an' what's bad. Buried out there in no man's land. That's where the truth belongs Pete, where no one can get to it. Safe an' sound out of harm's way." He repeated. "In no man's land. You're correct Pete. Leave him be."

Marty Drew was right. The familiar background clamour came between us again. The silence told me that he knew he was right too. Even with Marty's resources – personal and financial – Jake and Amy and whatever their truth was now, were due peace. Marty understood that. They were owed their slice of heaven, if indeed, that was what they'd found at last.

And who were we, a long-in-the tooth local journalist and a respected piano player, to mess with that. Neither of us had been dealt a card allowing us to play God. There was nothing more to add.

"Have a great show Marty," I said quietly.

"Let's bury this, Pete. We owe it to Amy and Jake. Lindy and Dougie too."

Marty didn't say goodbye; unhurriedly he took his sweet time replacing the handset. I know he did it slowly because I heard his opening theme scorch through the PA for far more time than it should have. I recognised it. I don't know, maybe I'm imagining it, but I think I detected real sorrow in my friend's voice as he spoke those last few words.

"Let's bury this, Pete. We owe it to Amy and Jake. Lindy and Dougie too."

CODA

SATURDAY, 2ND AUGUST 2003

Paris, France.
Saturday, 2nd August 2003. Late afternoon.

(The following excerpts are from an article published in *The New Yorker* on Monday 28th July 2003. Written by Cory Mount, a New York art historian and Dr Jessica Flack, a psychologist. Their forthcoming book, titled *St Patrick's Day 1990: The Isabella Stewart Gardner Museum Theft* will be published in Spring 2004).

'... AFTER JESSIE had so dramatically delivered her brief to me in the dining room of Boston's Ritz-Carlton Hotel at the end of May 1990, any further interest we had in discovering the whereabouts of the stolen artefacts suddenly dissolved. Not only in the research department, but throughout Swire's too. It was as if the concise opinions she had put forward crystallised the enormity, not to say the impossibility, of ever finding out what had transpired on that wet New England night in March 1990.

The missing works of art silently became a mere postscript to the conundrum. Whilst the 'profile' ('criminal profiling' was in its infancy) appeared to have merit, it was, like so many aspects of this extraordinary theft, too vague and general to act upon. Like the case itself there was no evidence – hard or soft – circumstantial or actual. Our thieves appeared to have gotten off scot-free.

However, inspired by the Gardner theft, Senator Edward M. Kennedy (D-MA) urged Congress to add the Theft of Major Artwork provision to the 1994 Crime Bill. This new law extended not only the Statute of Limitations from five years to twenty – retrospectively in the Gardner theft – but also made the offence to 'steal, receive or dispose of any cultural object valued at more than $100,000' a federal crime.

Then, as it is today, there are no registers or databanks of 'Known Commissioners of Priceless Art Works', either with US law enforcement agencies or Interpol. In effect the art world was left to police itself, and if we didn't want to admit publicly that such people existed, then why should the authorities? Time is the enemy of crime investigators, and the trail rapidly went cold.

As the long summer of 1990 turned into the fall, and the evenings shortened, the topic arose again. Not often, and usually only in the company of friends. By then, barely six months after the largest art theft in the world, the BPD and the FBI had all but lost interest, as had the media. The $1 million reward (later increased to $5 million in 1997) was treated with disdain. The only unrelated witness to the crime was never found, nor did he ever come forward. So, at Swire's, Christie's and Sotheby's we simply went back to work. Neither the public, nor the authorities cared: wasn't art merely money on walls? We all hoped that somewhere, sometime, someone would see or hear something. You can't hide that amount of art forever. Gravity and greed will conquer all, we thought. History has taught us that.

Ironically, the theft did bestow a blessing that year; its hand in anointing the Gardner Museum, which began to acquire a new lease of life. The museum realised drastic action on all fronts had to be taken if it were to survive at all. It is worth noting that the public flocked principally to see the very same gaps on the walls where the stolen paintings had once hung, in keeping with Mrs Gardner's Will. They came to view empty gilded frames. Needless to say, postcards depicting the forlorn empty frames and the stolen works were usually sold out.

Thirteen years ago, we both held certain thoughts on the theft, ones we shared when specifically asked by friends and associates. In private though we continued to dissect our respective theories into the dead of night. Oftentimes it was the blinding audacity of the theft which prompted the most heated of the discussions. Jessica Flack, as an English woman and a child psychologist, had one viewpoint. Cory Mount, as an American art historian – and at the time of the theft Head of Research at Swire's in Boston – often held a conflicting one.

But those heated, wine-fuelled discussions pale into vaporous mist when compared to those which followed the events that took place but a few weeks ago. The morning of 10th June 2003 to be precise . . .'

* * *

Zephaniah Swire sipped his second *espresso*. The late afternoon sun was shining, it was 30°C in the shade, and with no breeze the café's awning only served to magnify the heat. Nevertheless, it was a glorious day. He had not one care in the world, and heat, of any kind, had never troubled him. Ever. August in Paris was going to be a delight if this afternoon was anything to go by.

A merciful absence of his compatriots (due to the state of Franco-American relations after the invasion of Iraq five months earlier) meant his neighbours at the pavement table he occupied at the *Café Gramont* on the Boulevard des Italiens were all Parisian. He decided to skip a few paragraphs of *The New Yorker* article. It wasn't as if he didn't know 'the reveal'. If his memory served him correctly – and it rarely, if ever, failed him – he had occupied the exact same table when at 08:05 on the morning of Tuesday, 10th June 2003 a regiment of *Gendarmes*, with their frightful sirens blaring, had arrived in full force. Zephaniah had always derived pleasure in watching events unfold from a distance. Even curtain calls.

* * *

'. . . IF THE THEFT OF THIRTEEN, clearly cherry-picked works of art had baffled everyone, the anonymous return of ten of their number took us all to a place beyond astonished.

Headlines around the world have since devoted column yards to the story of the $5 million reward and the Algerian cleaning lady who is (in our opinion, rightly) claiming it and deserving of it. In all the clamour of a human-interest story without parallel, it's worth recapping the salient points of what happened, and in what order:

At approximately 07:30 a.m. on Tuesday, 10th June 2003, a forty-nine-year-old Algerian woman arrived at her place of work. Come rain, sun, snow and the inevitable strikes, she had followed the same routine every single morning – Sundays included – for the previous ten years. She 'opened up', cleaned, and swept a brasserie, La Taverne, a modest establishment specialising in Alsatian food. Panelled and low-lit tables spilled out onto the pavement on fine days. It is to be found at 22–24 Boulevard des Italiens, a Grande Boulevard in Paris' 9th arrondissement. The brasserie is but a brief walk in an easterly direction from L'Opéra and La Madeleine, and is opposite the HQ of the Credit Lyonnais bank, with the Banque Nationale de Paris on the adjacent corner. The brasserie caters for middle management tastes and pockets. Beneath its deep red awnings its principal entrance is at the apex of the corner of Boulevard des Italiens and Rue Taitbout. A massive 1,000-pound clock from a Bordeaux church hangs precariously over the main doors and informs you that you've arrived at your destination. You can hardly miss the place.

There, on that early June morning, beneath the clock and on the immense coir doormat, just to the right of where the restaurant's oysters and crustaceans and lemons would later be displayed for their clientele, and propped up against the green and glass doors, was a very large black leather case. It bore no name and there was no attached note. As would later be discovered, there were no fingerprints or any forensics whatsoever. The case's provenance was a total mystery. Like the person or persons who had deposited it there, the custom-made leather case cast no shadow. It measured 1.75 m x 1.45 m and was not proportionally deep; no more than 50 cms. Heaving and shoving the case to one side (it was too heavy for her to lift on her own), she opened the restaurant's main door and dragged it inside. Curiosity then got the better of her. She opened all six of its stainless-steel buckles, two per side. As the case's hinges fell open onto the tiled floor she gasped. More out of confusion than anything else. Now was certainly the time to call her manager . . . '

* * *

Zephaniah had forgotten just how long and occasionally overindulgent certain articles in *The New Yorker* could be. Yet in this instance, he found himself gripped by the narrative even though he knew the conclusion. Cory and Dr Flack – as the 21st Century progressed he would always think of her as Dr Flack, not Jessie and certainly never Dr Jessie Mount as she now was – had either been on a creative writing course during their honeymoon, or they had a fine editor at Random House, the publishing company behind their forthcoming book.

The same publishing company whose lawyers had been calling not only him, but Swire's lawyers seeking comments about aspects in the manuscript. Their calls, their letters, their faxes, their e-mails, their FedEx deliveries had all gone studiously unanswered, as they would continue to be. To comment would be to dignify the enterprise. Zephaniah had no intention of ever doing so. It was another lesson Ollie had taught him. Sipping the dregs of his *espresso*, he signalled for a third, and with an impish smile delved back into the text.

* * *

'... WHAT FIRST struck both of us, much like all the players – even the bad actors – in a stunned European, American and Asian art world, to say nothing of the various police departments who all vied for precedence and jurisdiction, was what on earth could the motive be?

Why deposit the ten most valuable stolen works of art from the Isabella Stewart Gardner Museum inside a custom-made case on the doorstep of a profoundly average Parisian brasserie? (The only missing items were the Gu, the stamp-sized Rembrandt etching and the Napoleonic finial). If we thought solving the theft was a complex issue, this subsequent turn of events was even more so.

With injudicious haste bordering on greed, the French authorities took all ten works directly to the Louvre for 'identification and safe-keeping'. Within minutes the rumour mill began churning. The most plausible, and the one that stuck for a while, was it was all an elaborate – and grotesque – practical joke.

By nightfall however, the entire state of affairs had become truly bizarre ...'

* * *

Truly bizarre? Not the words Zephaniah would have chosen: interesting, compelling, intriguing, improbable, fantastic, preposterous, yes. Bizarre, no.

Cory, Dr Flack, you can do better than that, surely?

* * *

'... BY 10 P.M. THAT EVENING, the Louvre had pronounced all ten works of art to be genuine. They went further – and here the hand of the Élysée Palace is patently visible – they added a new twist – a typically Louvrian one – whereby they unilaterally declared that full authority over all the artworks was now conferred to France. To a world eager to devour a story that didn't include the words 'Bush' or 'Iraq' or 'WMD' it was a masterstroke.

As only the French can accomplish at times, they had assembled at breakneck speed experts in the Old Dutch Masters and Impressionism. There are few, if any, who will not heed an urgent telephone call from the Louvre's Head Curator ...'

* * *

Point well made, Cory, thought Zephaniah.

***

'... THE FIVE PRINCIPAL PAINTINGS – *The Concert, Christ in the Storm on the Sea of Galilee, A Lady* and *Gentleman in Black, Landscape with an Obelisk* and the jaunty *Chez Tortoni* – had each been magnificently restored by expert hands, the skills of which the Louvre's experts had not seen before. The word was out. Even Vermeer, Rembrandt, Flinck and Manet would be smiling.

Then everyone sat down. The public too. We were all in uncharted waters. And the ocean's fog was galloping in at a lick. Restoration, at any level, but especially at these rarefied altitudes is much like a painting itself. The restorer must be a true and gifted artist. In the same manner, for example, as Rembrandt signed *Christ in the Storm on the Sea of Galilee* on the rudder of the stricken vessel, a world class restorer's touch is known by just that, their touch. He or she has an unseen signature, but to those who know what they are looking for, it would be as clear as Rembrandt's moniker.

Whoever carried out this extraordinarily complex restoration work was not known to any auction house, any museum or any curator. So, who did this? Where did he or she perform these delicate, time consuming and intricate tasks? Where have the paintings been all these years? Why retain three comparatively worthless pieces when the finest Vermeer was yours to behold and enjoy?

The theft had been incarcerated in the history books – as the largest in terms of value at over $350 million and rising – but the also the most baffling. What could the motive be for exhuming it now? Only a handful of years remained as the twenty-year Statute of Limitations would expire on St Patrick's Day, 2010.

We stayed up late that June night, and as the sun was rising in Paris, we in New York decided to start from scratch. Day one. From a trunk we retrieved the original report Swire's had commissioned from Dr Jessie Flack. Having reread it, she confirmed there was no hard evidence per se. In private she had always maintained that the theft was more about the act than the art. That being the case it would be a Three Act Play: The Robbery. The Waiting. The Deliverance. The curtain had fallen. The arc was complete. The play was over. At least that's what we believed...'

***

Zephaniah folded the magazine in two and slipped it into the back pocket of his jeans. He looped his blue cotton sweater over his shoulders and decided he'd finish the article in the comfort of his suite with a

Delamain for company. He toyed with eating at *La Taverne* opposite, but however good Alsatian food and wine were, they were not to his palette; and besides, his business at what had been – once upon a time – *Café Tortoni* was now over. Room service after the twenty-minute walk back to his hotel was more appealing.

Standing beneath the elegant glass canopy of *Le Bristol*, Zephaniah hesitated a while. A thin film of sweat had formed between his shoulder blades and clamped the linen shirt to his skin. The early evening air was soft and warm. He didn't want to leave its embrace just yet.

During the walk back to the Rue de Faubourg Sant-Honoré, he mulled over one salient fact. He had planned it this way ever since that mysterious May afternoon at Ollie's house back in 1990. He would return the paintings his grandfather had been able to restore to what had been *Café Tortoni*, 22 Boulevard des Italiens. He had long ago chosen the date too. It would be on 10th June in the year *following* his grandfather's death.

Ollie would have been a venerable ninety-eight years old on the 10th June 2003. Absent of any senescence, his grandfather had meticulously restored all the art works over the years; always returning however to *The Concert* and *Christ in the Storm on the Sea of Galilee* until they were in a condition both Vermeer and Rembrandt would have been proud of. Ninety-eight years old, Zephaniah reminded himself as he looked up into an azure Parisian sky. Ollie had achieved a fine age. To go to sleep and not to awake had been a fitting and dignified departure.

The very antithesis of sentimental, Zephaniah could think of no finer birthday present to give his grandfather. And throughout the last thirteen years he had never imparted his intentions. Any more than Ollie had ever enquired of them. All Zephaniah had cared about was the pleasure his grandfather had been able to derive from breathing life back into Rembrandt's only seascape. In more ways than one, the ocean's splendour – and its mysteries – had always been Ollie's compass, his touchstone.

As Zephaniah had no interest in retaining the restored paintings – and their cash equivalent held even less appeal – he'd known there would have to come a time when the works had to be returned. Much like the impecunious student who'd made off with Rodin's sculpture *Psyche* in 1953. The world could take this anonymous 'gift' anyway they liked. He cared not. What's more, they could speculate about mysterious characters until all the suns had set. That was their business, and the business of publishers, journalists and their ilk.

This matter was strictly Zeph's and Ollie's business. Their business.

As it always had been. As it always would be.

AFTERWORD

No Man's Land is a novel where fact, fiction and conspiracy theory combine, with each element serving to support the telling of the main story itself: the tragedy that has befallen the Long Island baymen and the fishing communities – north and south of the Cape Ann peninsula – who work the unforgiving waters of the Atlantic Ocean for their livelihoods. The narrative is an elegy to the fishermen of the Eastern seaboard, as well as a requiem to a vanishing America. This is *their* legend, *their* story.

It was in the early 1990s that I became captivated by the history, the clans, the traditions and the punishing lives of the remaining surfmen and baymen of Long Island's South Fork, or as it's known today – rather tamely – 'The Hamptons'.

A dear Long Island friend had sent me Peter Matthiessen's *Men's Lives*. In the paperback that dropped through my London letterbox he'd written an inscription: *'To Simon – These people [baymen] are the disappearing America. Their story needs to be told by a writer with an inspired heart. Good Luck.'* I hope I haven't let them (or him) down.

Jake, like all fishermen, knew that in any argument with the ocean, the ocean will win. They are the *very* best meteorologists. They read the skies, the patterns, the clouds, the currents, the tides and the ocean itself. And when in doubt – which is rare – they might seek out kindred souls who've lost fingers, toes, limbs, to 'read' the weather: an absent limb 'returns' and can be 'felt' when there's a shift in a normal pattern. These men's lives depend on their lore as much as they do their vessels. But the weather *is* a changin' out there.

In the Epilogue, Peter Duxbury writes about the 'No-Name Storm' (28th October–2nd November 1991), a nor'easter that blew 390 miles south of Halifax, Nova Scotia, deep into the Atlantic. This devasting storm caused more than $200 million (1991 money) in damages. There were thirteen fatalities, including all the crew (six) of the *Andrea Gail*, a swordfishing boat out of Gloucester, MA, when she went down. This late-season micro-hurricane later became known as 'The Perfect Storm'.

The research for this book was done the old-fashioned way: travel in person, shoe leather, newspaper reports in hard copy (*The Boston Globe* became a home of sorts), handwritten notebooks grew heavier as lines at numerous airports snaked ever longer. I recall a sub-zero February morning in 2003, and the 40-min. flight from Portland to Matinicus Isle – I had to wear a 'survival suit' – as we flew low across the north Atlantic's ice floes and bergs in an ancient 1973 single-engine Cessna, taking 'research' into perilous territory. I couldn't help but think of the fishermen that bitter, grey morning.

In November 1994, I had sailed from Europe across an angry Atlantic Ocean. The storms, fog and perils I encountered then, and later as I tracked north up New England's seaboard, was like the weather Jake and Marty encountered in Chapter 55. And in Boston, some four years after the Isabella Stewart Gardner Museum (ISGM) robbery, a tragedy of immense consequence, I hit upon a gateway – if you will – to this story.

The ISGM heist was the most extraordinary art theft to have taken place – anywhere – since World War II. It too tells its own story of an America where values have shifted, tectonically, and in many different directions. At this altitude money had become cheap. And art expensive. As for timing, the ISGM theft of thirteen priceless artworks – all have vanished – took place a mere seven years after New York Governor Cuomo signed into law in 1983 the infamous 'Bass Bill', a decree that served notice on the Long Island baymen to begin their own slow – and unforgiving – trek into a vanishing night after 300 years of history and toil from what was their homeland . . .

The ISGM robbery took place during Boston's 1990 St Patrick's Day weekend celebrations. The robbery remains unsolved thirty-five years later. It was a crime – incredibly with modern forensics – where no fingerprints, DNA or clues of any substantiative nature have ever been found.

The fictional story of Ollie and Zephaniah Swire that I weave may seem – at first, perhaps – to be an unlikely foil and backdrop to the principal story. Whilst there is, inevitably, a measure of licence in the fictional elements, the bones of the baymen's and fishermen's lives, and the ISGM theft, are as accurate as possible.

What follows – in a rough chronological order – are explanations of some of the factual aspects of the narrative which deserve their own telling.

Incredible though it may read, the staggering numbers of stolen and forged art Zephaniah rattles off to his uninterested half-brother in Chapter 7 were accurate in the late 1980s and early 1990s. Today, the figures are even more shocking: according to the Art Loss Register, Picasso holds the dubious accolade of world's most stolen artist with 1,147 *missing* works, as of October 2022.

Authorities and organisations the world over are loath to accept the idea that commissioned art thefts do happen. Constance Lowenthal, Executive Director of the International Foundation of Art Research (IFAR is a New York-based repository for information on stolen art) was quoted in *The Boston Globe* the day after the ISGM break-in: *'These priceless works of art are virtually worthless. They're unsaleable. There's no place for them in the legitimate market. They're too hot to handle. And as far as a collector who orders a theft, we don't have a documented case of a Dr No-type character. You see them in the movies, but we don't know about any of them.'* In a 1993 *Los Angeles Times* interview Ms Lowenthal confirmed that IFAR had *more* than 40,000 'unrecovered' (read: stolen) artworks in its database. The London-based Art Loss Register maintains the world's largest private database of stolen art, antiques and collectables; as at end 2024, they have more than 700,000 items listed.

In Chapter 11 Ollie Swire left St Joseph's orphanage and headed to Chicago where he became an accomplished conman. The names of his associates (Nibs Callahan, Plunk Drucker, Limehouse Chappie etc.) and their big cons (The Rag, The Store etc.) are all real people and real cons.

Swire's is, of course, a fictional business, and Ollie often refers to Sotheby's and Christie's. In Chapter 82 he alludes to a possible, future, comeuppance. In the late 1990s, the billionaire owner of Sotheby's A. Alfred Taubman and Sir Anthony Tennant, Christie's Chairman, were accused of price fixing and anti-trust violations along with Dede Brooks, Sotheby's CEO and Christopher M. Davidge, her oppo at Christie's. Together with Tennant, they all proffered evidence against Taubman.

Davidge, first through the Justice Department's revolving door, reaped a full immunity deal *and* an $8 million severance package from Christie's. Dede Brooks – second through the Department's door – copped a plea bargain-deal for her evidence against Taubman – her mentor, boss and friend – that earned her three years in prison (suspended), six months of 'home detention', a $350,000 fine and 1,000 hours of community service. Tennant refused to return to the US, as under English law there was no extradition for the charges levied against him. Humiliated, he retreated from public life, his storied career over. Meanwhile, Taubman, alone in the dock in the 2002 trial, was found guilty and sentenced to one year and one day in prison and fined $7.5 million. Sotheby's and Christie's were *each* ordered to pay $276 million in fines, as well as settling multiple civil suits for a further nine-figure sum. There's a rainforest of books on the saga of these two shamed 18th-Century auction houses, who at the time controlled 90% of the global art market. However, Dominick Dunne, the American writer, was in the Manhattan court for Taubman's sixteen-day trial, and crafted what is feasibly the final word in his 2002 *Vanity Fair* piece: *'What it boiled down to was rich people cheating other rich people, most of whom were so rich they didn't know they were being cheated.'*

Isabella Stewart Gardner's (1840–1924) Will is often referenced in the story. It's a truly astonishing document, gravid with eccentric and idiosyncratic clauses. Mrs Gardner had placed intractable burdens on her Trustees, Harvard alumni all. An executive summary of the most pertinent clause (No. 7) is: the Trustees *cannot* buy or sell any artwork, book, tapestry, bric-a-brac etc., they cannot alter, replace, touch or move *anything* – even the position of a chair – within her Fenway Museum *in perpetuity*. If they do, the *entire* collection is to be sold and all cash proceeds go to Harvard University.

The fateful snag lay in Mrs Jack's endowment: in 1924 her $1.2 million was entry-level substantial (circa $19 million, 2022) and was far from being a Gatesian *'in perpetuity'* amount. So, by 1988 the ISGM's operating deficit was running into six figures. There was no Finance Officer nor fundraising strategies. There was simply no money to pay for insurance, restoration of paintings, alarms, general upkeep, air handling, maintenance and roof repairs etc., and 'security staff' were paid $6.85 per hour, a tad more than the minimum wage. There's scant doubt – and it's an accepted fact – that the woeful lack of proper security systems – and professional guards – contributed to Boston's favourite museum being plundered.

In Chapter 41 Ollie posits his own theories as he discusses with his grandson the future of the ISGM, post the robbery. He echoes the notorious theft of the *Mona Lisa* from the Louvre in 1911, where attendance and interest soared. The Parisians and French public were indignant, as were the Bostonians and Americans. The *Mona Lisa* theft became a national scandal. J. P. Morgan – who'd been on an art buying spree in France – was suspected of commissioning the theft. Picasso also fell under suspicion and was questioned. And Franz Kafka queued obediently with the *demi-monde* to 'view' the now vacant wall space. The two-and-a-half years the *Mona Lisa* was missing were an immense PR coup for the Louvre. And ditto the ISGM stolen treasures ever since.

The ISGM continues to thrive today: over 370,000 visitors crossed Mrs Jack's threshold in 2024. And its success is largely due to Anne Hawley, barely six months in post as Director at the time of the robbery in March 1990; she remained until December 2015. During her twenty-five-year tenure, she oversaw its $180 million capital raise, the construction of a new 70,000-square-foot wing and concert hall, both of which opened in 2012. She created new curatorial positions, increased the board of Trustees and staffing levels, and began charging sensible entry fees – unless of course you are named Isabella, for all 'Isabellas' receive free admission for life!

Before the ISGM robbery, theft of any artwork from a museum was not a federal crime and had a five-year Statute of Limitations. The late Edward M. 'Ted' Kennedy (1932–2009), younger brother of John F. Kennedy (1917–1963) and Robert F. Kennedy (1925–1968), used his not inconsiderable influence as Massachusetts' senior Senator to change that. He added Theft of Major Artwork to the 1994 Crime Bill (after some prodding from Anne Hawley) that was before the Senate, only months before the ISGM Statute of Limitations was due to expire. The new wording of the Crime Bill made art theft from a museum federal and extended the statute to twenty years – retrospectively – thereby pushing out the statute on the stolen ISGM's artworks to St Patrick's Day 2010.

Over lunch at the Ritz-Carlton – Chapter 77 – Cory tells Jessie about the 'James Bond/Honey Ryder/Dr No' scene and its link to the 1961 theft of Goya's glorious portrait of the Duke of Wellington from the National

Gallery in London. This is what happened outside of the 007 storyline: earlier in 1961, Sotheby's had auctioned the original Goya painting (oil on mahogany panel, 25 1/4 in x 20 5/8 in) on behalf of the 11th Duke of Leeds. It was knocked down to an American, Charles Wrightsman, for £140,000 (circa £4 million, 2025). Inevitably, a hue and cry erupted over England's finest warrior being carted off to America. Politely, Wrightsman suggested he leave the *Duke of Wellington* in England, should the Government cover the price he'd paid. Impolitely, the 1st Earl of Stockton (aka Conservative Prime Minister Harold Macmillan) demurred. The Wolfson Foundation put up £100,000 shaming the Government into coughing up the £40,000 balance to match the genial Oklahoma oil baron's price. Amid much fanfare, the Iron Duke was marched off to the National Gallery – Room 39 – where he went on public display on 2nd August 1961. All whilst *Dr No* was in production . . .

A brief nineteen days later however, the Iron Duke was spirited away from the National Gallery – via a lavatory window – by a bespectacled fifty-seven-year-old, 6' tall, 18 stone (252 lbs) gentleman, a retired bus driver from Newcastle Upon Tyne, one Mr Kempton Bunton.

During an unspecified earlier visit, Bunton had gleaned from indiscreet security guards that the museum disabled its entire sophisticated electronic alarms and infrared sensors every morning, so the cleaning ladies could go about their duties unimpeded.

On the morning of the 21st August 1961, Bunton simply unhooked the painting from the wall, stuffed it – frame too – inside his mackintosh, and exited said lavatory window, and down a handily forgotten builder's ladder into the crowds of Trafalgar Square. He, and the Iron Duke, then vanished. It was the first ever theft from the National Gallery. But Bunton was no ordinary chancer or thief, for he had both purpose and motive. He had long campaigned against the £4 yearly TV Licence (£122, 2025) for old-age pensioners.

Safely back in the north of England, amid all manner of consternation rattling through London over the scandal – a reward of £5,000 (£150,000, 2025) was offered – Bunton wrote to *Reuters* offering to return the Iron Duke in exchange for £140,000 to be donated to a charity to pay for TV Licences for pensioners, and amnesty for the thief. His offer was hastily declined.

So, for the next four years the Iron Duke resided behind a sealed wardrobe panel in Bunton's terraced house in Newcastle Upon Tyne. Finally, and doubtless out of frustration, Bunton wrote to the *Daily Mirror* in July 1965 attaching a left-luggage stub to a locker at Birmingham railway station, in which he'd carefully stashed the Iron Duke!

On the 19th July 1965, Bunton surrendered to the police and confessed all. His story was deemed nonsense; Scotland Yard *knew* this had to have been the work of the finest master thief. Following many forensic, fingerprint and handwriting tests, Bunton's fantastical story was proven. Accordingly, he was arrested for *'theft, making demands with menaces and causing a public nuisance'*.

It could have been the phrasing of the last charge that lionised Bunton. The English have an infallible admiration for an underdog, and Bunton, a quasi-hero by now, went on trial at the Old Bailey. Defended, *pro bono,* by one of England's finest barristers (Jeremy Hutchinson QC, later Lord), the jury was persuaded that the only theft – as it had not been returned – was the frame itself, then valued at £100. Reluctantly, the jury were duty bound to find Bunton guilty of stealing the frame. He was sentenced to three months' incarceration in the recently opened (1960) and cushy Ford 'Open' Prison, not far from the Sussex seaside. It wasn't until 2000 that Kempton Bunton (1904–1976) achieved – posthumously – his campaign's ambition. TV Licences for pensioners over 75 were abolished.

To close this story, Sir Ken Adam OBE, the two-time Oscar-winning production designer who dreamed up all the sets for seven James Bond films – including, of course, *Dr No* – had himself painted ('forged', it was that good, apparently) the prop portrait of the Duke of Wellington displayed in Dr No's Jamaican lair. And with an irony only the art world could muster, Adams' masterful 'forgery' film-prop was stolen soon after the production wrapped. It has never been seen or heard of since.

Today, one can visit the National Gallery and greet the Iron Duke and enjoy Goya's *The Duke of Wellington* – back in Room 39 – where it has hung since 1961 – apart from its lengthy pensioner's holiday in Newcastle Upon Tyne.

Sadly, if you were to visit the Dutch Room at the ISGM today, one can view *Christ in the Storm on the Sea of Galilee* but only in one's mind's eye. Its eerily vacant gilt frame is undeniable, and it does whip up the imagination. So, *where* is the magnificent Rembrandt?

At the time of writing, there are still no clues or leads to the whereabouts of the thirteen works of stolen art. It is worth stating that the FBI have come up 'snake eyes': no fingerprint (neither thief wore gloves as confirmed by the two ISGM guards, Abarth and Hestand) nor footprint were found. No DNA samples: not one hair follicle, nor a cloth fibre. Nothing. And the ISGM had no internal closed-circuit security cameras, so, no photos of the thieves exist. The duct tape that gagged the guards was store-bought. The handcuffs used were available from any Boston security outlet or S & M sex shop. Both ISGM thieves that night were seemingly 'off' *all* US and Interpol law enforcement radars worldwide. It was as if they were ghosts.

The haul remains impossible to value. The figure bandied around by the press today is 'in excess of $500 million', the most valuable items being Vermeer's *The Concert* (one of only thirty-six in the world) and Rembrandt's only seascape *Christ in the Storm on the Sea of Galilee*. The ISGM's initial $1 million reward posted after the theft was later increased to $5 million in 1997. In 2018 it was raised to $10 million (with, for an unstated reason, a supplementary amount of $100,000 for the return of Zephaniah's Napoleonic paperweight).

In thirty-five years, nothing has stirred, other than the FBI's hotlines. The FBI have received – literally – multiple thousands of tips that led them to traverse the world: Japan's *Yakuza*, Europe's *Cosa Nostra*, Mexican and South American drug cartels, IRA terrorists, known Swiss and Asian money-launders, organised crime families across North and South America. Yet the supposition that the theft – of *seemingly* random artworks – was commissioned has been discounted by the FBI since March 1990. Yet, in 2005 Robert M. Poole wrote in the *Smithsonian*: '*Were the works taken for love, money, ransom, glory, barter or for some tangled combination of them all?*' Nobody knows. But the artworks have all but vanished.

However, to my mind, the even greater tragedy is the fate that has befallen the fearless baymen of Long Island. The baymen have all but vanished too.

Simon Gaul
June 2025

ACKNOWLEDGEMENTS

Stendhal said, 'A novel is a mirror carried along a main road...'. He is correct. However, *No Man's Land*'s main road was the arrow-straight expanse of Long Island beach at Amagansett. It somehow reaches out as far as the eye can see: east 'n west. To its first settlers – the Montaukett Indians – Amagansett means 'place of good water'.

A dear friend had a house on that beach, one that almost nested in, and amongst, the rolling sand-dunes and the tall grey-green tufts of Marram grass. And after my father passed away in September 1989, I was offered succour and peace there for a time. The empty majesty of that beach, as the sun came up, thirty-six years ago has never left me. And it was then – and there – that *No Man's Land* took root.

Although, I'm not sure I understood that at the time. But, with my feet planted deep in its sands, the raw power of the Atlantic Ocean – one I have sailed across – unfolded in front of me and became a Doug Kuntz-like monochrome image that's been forever nailed to the wall of my consciousness.

I have loved writing this book – for many reasons – one being that I was never alone during its realisation. It gestated over many moons and involved numerous folks from all walks of life. On Long Island – and the entire Eastern seaboard for that matter – you really do meet all sorts. But in the end, Amagansett's beach was my main road. The one I held and carried my mirror up to during this long journey.

* * *

No Man's Land might have remained as 100+ reference books and notepads in a dusty corner of my library were it not for Celia Hayley. Her editorial ruthlessness, tempered with a Mariana Trench-deep understanding of what I was trying to convey – especially with Jake – is the reason you've kindly read this novel; my profound appreciation to her doesn't even scratch the surface.

A salute to the late Captain Danny King (1949–2020), Chairman of the East Hampton Baymen's Association. He, and his wife Marsha, welcomed me into their home, a lighthouse in an Atlantic fog. If you ever visit East Hampton, his iconic – American flag-painted – haul-seining dory sits proudly on display outside the Marine Museum as a reminder of what has been lost forever. Billy Joel's 1989 music-video of the 'Down'easter Alexa' is a 'must' watch (www.billyjoel.com). Other than his band, the cast are all Long Island Baymen; catch Danny sporting his trademark 'chin' beard. Thank you again Bill for allowing me to quote your haunting lyrics for the Epigraph.

I'm fortunate to have had unstinting commitment from my publishers, Whitefox: Julia Koppitz, Publishing Director, supported this book with nerves of steel: 'An art heist and a fisherman. Really Simon?' Chris Wold, Jess King, Hannah Tatem and CEO John Bond didn't blink. Thank you for keeping the faith. Dominic Forbes (who created the artwork of my previous novel, *White Suicide*) stormed in with a masterful cover from a punishing brief. And Nikki Mander, of Mander Barrow PR, was the 'O' to this PR allergic 'H2'.

As always, all errors are on my slate alone. However, I'm privileged to have had critical sustenance from a 'brains trust' traversing all walks of life who've been kind enough to read my words: Philip Thompson, Leonardo Graf von Waldburg-Wolfegg, Michael Bianchi, JSF – the split-infinitive hunter, Eymeric Segard, Michael Mount, Mark Glatman, Albee Yeend, XLP, Daniel Wanger, Yves Ruffeta, Alex Koersvelt, Simon Koe, Nick Edmiston and of course my confidante & PA of 25+ years, Toni Maricic, who knows where all the bodies are buried. Grazie a tutti di cuore.

Another Emmy for Steve Cohen, a gentleman who's nourished my family with love and friendship for decades; words alone don't cut it. René de Freitas brought Jessie Flack's Barbados home – and her Bananaquits – to life, whilst Dr M. Bushnell MBBS cleared her credentials. Hamilton South, and his sister Mary, lent me their igloo-cold house on Matinicus Isle during my quest to find a safe northern wilderness for Jake. The Boo family's chalet in the mountains of the Bernese Oberland was an editing hideaway like no other. Authors with far, far greater skills than mine – Ray Celestin, Charles Glass, Daphne Wright and many others – have given so generously of their words, counsel and time. Thank you. And finally, love to MG who dared to show me that the Sun could also rise in the west.

At its core – its soul – this novel is about the tragic legend of a disappearing world. So, the last word can only go to its future. My five children: Hamilton, India, Orlando, Cameron and Imogen represent all that is the very best in our world today. Trust me on that, if nought else…

Simon Gaul
June 2025

'NO MAN'S LAND'

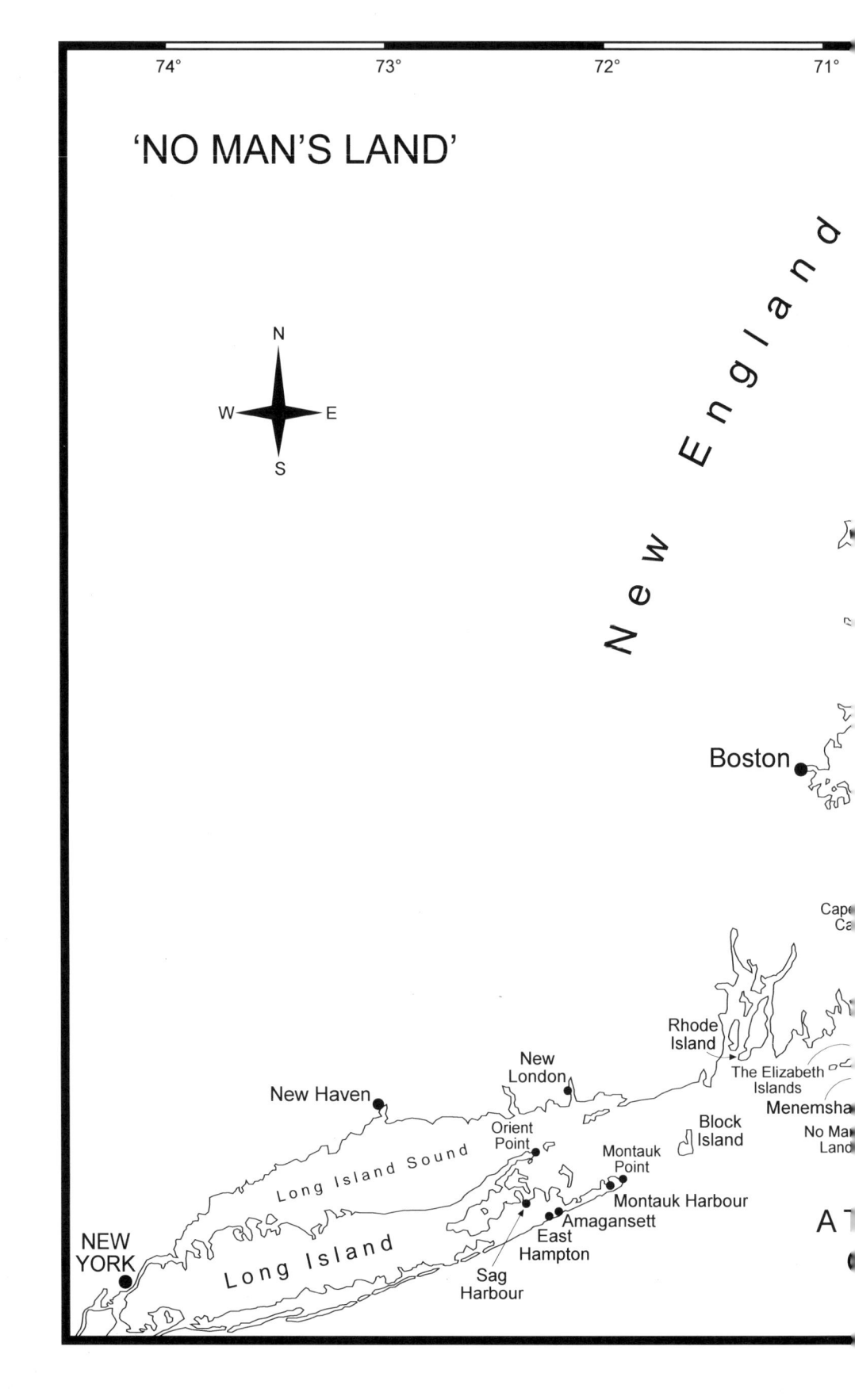

New England

Boston

Cape Cod

Rhode Island

The Elizabeth Islands

New London

Menemsha

New Haven

Block Island

No Man's Land

Orient Point

Montauk Point

Montauk Harbour

Amagansett

East Hampton

Sag Harbour

Long Island Sound

NEW YORK

Long Island

ATL